# LATITUDE 87.7
An Alex Boudreau Adventure

## PAUL H. LANDES

Hunter and Gatherer Publishing Company
Davis, California

# LATITUDE 87.7

**Hunter and Gatherer Publishing Company**

Cover design by Robin Walton

Book formatting by www.thefastfingers.com

ISBN: 978–0–615–85870–8

For more information about this book and other works by the author, visit: www.paulhlandes.com

To Kristen. . . Mycah. . . David

"If you reveal your secrets to the wind, you should not blame the wind for revealing them to the trees."
– *Kahlil Gibran*

"We live in a society exquisitely dependent on science and technology, in which hardly anyone knows anything about science and technology."
– *Carl Sagan*

# PROLOGUE

The room was large, opulent and imposing. Randomly arranged heavy gilt–wood and marquetry furniture stamped a marked contrast to the orderly and soft Rococo palette that blended the walls, ceiling and floor into a unified ensemble. Centuries of history adorned the walls and bookshelves from oiled portraits of the room's past occupants, each ornately trimmed in gold–leaf, to original leather–bound works of literature and jeweled tiaras. To stand amid the aura of this sanctuary had undoubtedly humbled and inspired the most confident of men, yet the room reeked of backdoor alliances and secret handshakes.

Two men stood in the corner in front of a T.V. monitor mounted eye–level on the wall. One man cradled a fluted champagne glass and the other a crystal goblet. They took turns offering up a toast, backslapping and laughing. To any casual observer they would appear to be the best of friends, comrades sharing good times and treasured memories. To those more suspicious in nature, they could be enemies, keeping the other close, within his grasp.

"It's a brilliant discovery, Stephen. Not only can it be used against the masses, but look at this." Alan reached in his coat pocket and pulled out a small needle. A cocky edge trimmed his voice, "I could be standing this close to somebody," his hand moved between them. "Let's pretend it's you. I hide this needle between my fingers, reach out and like that," he tapped Stephen on the neck, "one sharp *prrrick* to the neck and the virus is delivered."

"Let me show you what happens after that." Alan inserted a disc in the media player, hit the 'Play' button and walked back to Stephen. He slapped him on the back. "Let me show you something quite remarkable, Stephen. This is a time–lapsed real demonstration of three men who were used as guinea pigs when this virus was actually tested. You'll want to pay *verrryyy* close attention."

Three men lying cocoon–like on cots, drenched in puddles of sweat, squirmed and their mouths stretched beyond any imaginable limit. "There's no sound to this, Stephen, but you'll get the idea what these guys are going through. Just watch."

Four days of agony and suffering had been reduced to a five minute clip. For the next few minutes, President Stephen Desjardins watched a time–lapsed video of the three men, their skin turned to bruises, then blisters, then blood poured from their eyes, ears and noses. When one man in the video began to vomit and his skin peeled off like wet sand paper, President Desjardins cringed and backed away; his face turned the color of chalk. "Wha. . . what. . . what is this?"

Alan switched the video off. His smug grin was overshadowed by a treasonous stare. "What you just saw, Stephen, were three men experiencing the most gruesome death anyone can imagine. You have to admit the pain they suffered must've been excruciating, don't you think?"

President Desjardins stood stock–still, he ground his teeth and his eyebrows V'd.

"Come on Stephen." Alan threw his hands up and bellowed a ten syllable laugh, "What'd you think? Can you imagine if that was you? Lying on that cot or maybe right here on this floor, with your blood pouring out your eyes?"

The President stepped back from Alan. "What's gotten into you, Alan? What is this? You know very well that this country is a party to biological weapons treaties that forbid this very type of weapon from being developed, let alone someone actually using it. You can't be serious. This is real? You actually have this?"

"Real and available, my friend. Oh yes, it's gruesome. No doubt about that. But what you saw on that video doesn't happen just like that." Alan snapped his fingers—then again. "No, the virus lies dormant. Those who've been infected with it usually have no idea that it's been injected into them. The virus needs to be activated before it starts to spread and eat away at the person's insides. There are a host of methods available to activate it and that, my good friend, is the real magic behind this. The power lies with those who control the activating agent."

Alan moved toward the President. When he stood next to him, he looped an arm around his friend and flexed. "We go back a long ways, don't we Stephen?"

The President felt a sharp *prick* in the back of his neck. "What! Alan, what did. . . "

"Wait! Wait! Listen, Stephen!"

With his patented Cheshire grin, Alan reached out and took hold of the President's champagne glass. "You and I are about to take a journey—*together*. Let me refill our drinks and then we'll have a seat. I'm about to let you in on a secret—*your future*."

# CHAPTER 1

"We have no more than 60 seconds to get him out of here. We'll drop down, make the snatch and nobody says a word. You guys ready?"

Two guys dressed in green hospital scrubs nodded.

The third man glanced at his watch and whispered, "It should go off any second now."

To remove a patient undetected from a hospital's intensive care unit required split second timing, precise coordination and some old fashioned Lady Luck. Benjamin Hunter lay directly beneath the three men. He had been in a coma for just over a day and was connected to a respirator, heart monitor and pulse oximeter each of which could be read and monitored from the nurses' station in the center of the ICU. The instant those devices were disconnected, an alarm would sound and a swarm of medical personnel would storm the room. Benjamin Hunter was a man of notoriety and a high priority patient—two police officers were stationed outside the room to assure that no one, other than the medical team, would enter the room.

It had been just two days ago when Benjamin had flown to Paris, not only to confront Alex Boudreau about the research she had stolen from his company, but to face the woman who had captured his heart. So much had happened in the past several weeks that led up to Benjamin's lying in a coma at the Beresford Hospital in Paris. From the moment Alex had first entered his life he had been mesmerized by her exotic beauty and he had felt an emotional connection like never before. That day when the two sat nestled together on the jagged and imposing cliffs at Point Reyes and had gazed out over the breaking waves along the miles of shoreline, Alex had unmasked her hidden world and years of anguish poured out of her. Benjamin had known then that they had become one and that the past they had shared, the pain they had known, had bonded them in a way no physical touch ever could.

Alex had mysteriously abandoned Benjamin and had left him alone, swimming upstream trying to escape from his own blind foolishness. Just hours before he had left for Paris, he had a long phone conversation with Alex who had confessed her guilt in stealing the research while at the same time imploring Benjamin to forgive her—she had fallen in love with him.

Standing in the terminal gateway, Benjamin had stared out the window at the aircraft oblivious to the row of boarding passengers. The emotional mayhem that had become his daily routine those past days had again begun to fester. Fear, anxiety and hope had surfaced from the dark corners of his conscience. The woman had made a career of manipulation and deceit. Had he been caught in her web again? Would she be waiting at the other end with open arms and his hellish nightmare would end? Would this be another twisted road littered with his own guts and shattered dreams?

When he had heard the announcement, "Last boarding call for passenger Benjamin Hunter," he had reached down, picked up his travel bag and with a purpose to his stride, he had walked alone down the passageway.

The men in the green scrubs were given strict orders to make sure Benjamin's endotracheal tube was reconnected as soon as possible. Without oxygen, brain cells would begin to die within a single minute and serious brain damage would occur within three minutes. They carried an Ambu bag, a self–inflating resuscitator, and they would be able to reconnect Benjamin's lifeline in seconds.

To distract the nurses and policemen, a fourth team member entered a patient's room at the opposite end of the ICU. He disconnected the patient's respirator and heart monitor and exited as quickly as he had entered. A Code Red alert sounded and the nurses and doctors on the floor rushed into action. The nurses' station emptied and the two policemen stationed outside Benjamin's room joined in the commotion. All attention was diverted to the woman's room at the far end of the hallway.

"Go!"

Two ceiling panels slid back and four ropes, each connected to a pulley system, fell down, stopping inches from the floor. Everything had been measured and precisely calculated. The distance from the bottom of the pulley to the floor was 11 feet 4 inches; the opening to each ceiling panel was 3 feet by 5 feet, the ducting between the 3rd and 4th floor was 4 feet square and ran atop each room with outlets in hallways, linen rooms and storage areas.

All three men repelled down the ropes and landed cat–like on the floor. The only sound in the room was the whooshing of the respirator that served as the lifeline to Benjamin.

Quickly, the men placed a six foot long stretcher under Benjamin and cinched the canvas straps. Securing the ropes to the canvas ties, they unhooked the heart monitor, pulse oximeter and each of the IV bags were removed from the pole and taped to Benjamin's chest. Two of the men pulled on the ropes and lifted Benjamin's unconscious body upward, headfirst, angling it sharply so that it fit through the ceiling opening while the other man slid the curtain across the room's glass window. He grabbed the medical records attached to a clipboard hanging by the door and joined the others. When the hose to the respirator had been stretched to its maximum, one of the men twisted it loose and the plastic joint on the Ambu bag was inserted into the endotracheal tube and Benjamin was given a few rapid pumps of oxygen. The last man climbed back up the ropes and disappeared into the duct way.

They slid the ceiling panels back into place and the pulleys were removed. Small felt covered wheels were secured to the stretcher and Benjamin was silently rolled through the dark passageway.

A fifth team member was waiting with a gurney in a hallway beneath an overhead vent. He gave the all clear sign, the vent opened and Benjamin was lowered to the gurney. A sheet was placed over his face and he was wheeled out of the hospital and into a rent–an–ambulance waiting outside. 52 seconds had elapsed when the ambulance pulled out of the circular drive and headed north on Rue Barbès.

# CHAPTER 2

"**C**ome back in, Alex. The Agency is not like it used to be. You will be given complete autonomy to run this operation any way you want. You have my absolute assurance on that point."

Alex stood on the far side of the room, her back was turned to Director Jean–Claude Bardin and her arms were tightly folded across her chest. She stared out the small bullet–proof window, past the parking lot, and fixed her eyes on the ten foot concrete wall that lined the compound. She remembered back to when she had stood in that exact same spot and she had known then that the wall wasn't meant to keep people out of this high security complex. No, it was meant to keep its own agents on the inside so they couldn't reveal the failed policies and botched jobs she knew so well.

Alex pivoted and slowly walked back toward Director Bardin. She stood behind the Oreille Wingback chair in front of the Director's desk and her hands stroked its plush back velvet. A yellow caution light flashed in her head. Leaning slightly forward, she met the man's intrusive gaze and said, "Director Bardin, when I came here to see you it was not to hear you speak the praises of this Agency. I would not even be here if this Agency had not become involved in Monsieur Hunter's life to begin with. Now his life is threatened."

Alex paused and moved to the side of the chair, closer to the Director. "I will find Monsieur Hunter and when I do I will stop at nothing to bring him back alive and safe. I will ask you once again and you may want to think harder this time before you answer. I will need specific equipment if I am going to free Monsieur Hunter. Can I count on the Agency to supply me with that equipment or should I look elsewhere?"

Director Bardin had been the head of the *Direction Générale de la Sécurité Extérieure,* or DGSE, for the past six years. He had spent his career working his way up the ranks and while he hadn't known Alex personally when she had been with the Agency, he did know of her by reputation. Alex had begun her own career with the Agency and in no time her skill, tenacity and determination had quickly drawn the attention of the Agency brass and she soon ran her own Secret 7 undercover group. Secret 7 had been a DGSE "deep" cover unit that had focused on procuring intellectual property and technology from foreign aerospace and electronic corporations.

Director Bardin knew why Alex had turned in her resignation and he had a profound respect for her. When she had been wrongly accused of wire–transferring money from a mark's account to an offshore bank account for herself, she had beaten the Agency in uncovering the real culprit behind the theft. Even though her name had been cleared and she had been immediately re–instated, she had had enough. She had turned in her resignation and had taken the skills and techniques she had acquired and had ventured into the world of corporate espionage on her own.

Director Bardin rolled his hand across the stub of his left ring half–finger. When he raised his head and spoke, his scratchy voice was muted. "Alex, there is only so much I can do here. If I could do more I would. I do not believe you know Agent Faucher, but she is our best operative and she is doing everything possible to find Monsieur Hunter and to find out who is behind his disappearance. She could be a trusted ally that could help you. She is closely working with the CIA and they have made some serious inroads." He paused and let his words linger.

Alex dropped her hand from the chair and turned away. The Director blurted out, "Alex, wait! Why don't we share information and work together? You know that is the fastest way to find Monsieur Hunter."

Alex completed her about–face and headed for the door. Her voice was blunt, "Not a good idea from my perspective. Thank you for your time, Director."

Director Bardin jumped to his feet and shouted, "Wait, please!"

Alex turned half–way. "I don't know what else you expect me to do, Director." Her mind had already slammed the door to her cooperating with the Agency.

Director Bardin leaned forward. "Alex, we do know that after Monsieur Hunter was ferried out of London, he passed through Madrid. It was a brief stop, maybe a day, and then he departed on a private plane that filed a flight plan for Istanbul. The plane never landed in Istanbul."

"I already knew that, Director, but thank you anyway."

"As soon as I learn anything new I will contact you, Alex. I want to get to the bottom of this just as much as you."

Alex's hand gripped the door handle and she tilted her head toward Director Bardin. "I will not be waiting around for your call, Director. Have a nice day."

Before Director Bardin could answer, the door closed. He reached across his desk, picked up the phone and after a brief pause intoned, "Alison, she is not going to cooperate. Get a tail on her now and keep me posted. I want to know everywhere she goes and we will need complete background checks on anyone she talks to, looks at, passes on the street, thinks about—anyone—*now*!"

# CHAPTER 3

"I see you managed to let yourself in." Alex walked through the foyer of her flat, dropped her purse on the hall table, and threw her coat over the top. One by one she kicked off her shoes and they landed toe–to–toe in the far corner.

At the sound of a deep sarcastic voice, Alex smiled. "You should find a new place to hide the key. Someone in your line of work never knows who may be lurking around."

Alex threw her arms around Phil and gave him a hug. Phil leaned back. "Wait a minute. I've seen that look before. It must not have been a good day for you. Right?"

"Just another day in my life. We have a lot to go over, but first let me put a pot of coffee on," Alex said as she headed toward the kitchen.

"When I walked into your place I half expected to smell the java brewing. I figured you'd know I'd be going through withdrawals after my long flight."

"Yeah. Yeah" Alex had never known anyone who could inhale a pot of coffee faster than Phil. She doubted he had gone the entire flight without a caffeine fix or two or three. "With the amount of coffee you drink I'm surprised you even needed to board a plane to get here. Make yourself comfortable. This will not take long."

"Hey, you've had your share of airline coffee. They serve you two gulps of brown water and expect a smile in return."

Phil Morgan leaned against the kitchen counter and was his easy–going, confident self. He had just flown in from San Francisco and had arrived at Alex's flat moments before she had returned. Phil and Alex hadn't known each other for very long, but they had developed a bond that was based on Alex's grit and moxie and Phil's perseverance and unwavering loyalty to his closest friend, Benjamin Hunter.

It had been only two weeks ago when the two had met for the first time. Phil had discovered Alex in the back yard of Benjamin's house. Her hands had been clenched to the steel meshed fence that had served as the temporary home to an injured eagle Benjamin had brought home from Canada to heal. Phil's initial mistrust and borderline hatred for Alex had not been unfounded. Benjamin Hunter was Phil's best friend and Alex had been the person responsible for his disappearance. She had all but admitted so when they had first met.

Alex's life up to that point had been based on a single minded premise—win. . . at any cost. She had found the one profession that had allowed her to move about freely and unnoticed, living in complete anonymity. Moving from shadow to shadow under an array of aliases and disguises she had been a sought after operative by private individuals and corporations in need of her discreet and professional services. While she had always considered herself a trained agent schooled in the many nuances of corporate espionage, she had known she was really an emissary of greed, serving clients who had desired nothing more than to control and own what was not theirs.

Alex was good. . . very good. She was skilled in martial arts, computer sciences, electronic surveillance, explosives and she had mastered the subtle nuances of seven languages. All of this had allowed her to move around the world as she pleased, unnoticed, and to infiltrate corporate or government targets to steal the technology she had been handsomely paid to deliver to her clients. None of this had been without its risks, but Alex seemed to thrive on finding herself in situations that demanded quick thinking or even creating her own forward looking technology.

Some years back, Alex had been hired by a Russian bank to infiltrate Israeli and Lebanese banks. Her client had their sights on very private information on wealthy bank clients. She had developed a computer virus that targeted a very specific set of financial institutions, but when those companies had discovered the virus, it had already infected more than 2,500 computers.

Most hackers who develop their own attack viruses create innovative and original names for their viruses that punctuate its intrusive effects. Alex had called her newly–created virus *Erdos* after the Hungarian mathematician who had arguably been one of the greatest mathematicians of the 20$^{th}$ century. In order to avoid detection, the *Erdos* virus had featured identical elements of software code with Gurn and Heztrop, two well known state sponsored attack viruses. Each of those viruses had spread very effectively without using the internet through the use of USB sticks. When the news broke that Israeli and Lebanese banks had been attacked and proprietary financial data had been stolen, security analysts, intelligence agencies, pundits and the public had all chanted in unison that a new era of statecraft had hatched.

"You know I look around your place and other than that one picture on the table over there in the corner, there's nothing personal that tells me Alex Boudreau lives here. Not one thing. It's kinda formal, like maybe you had someone you don't know pick everything out for you. I never pictured your set–up to be like this."

"Maybe this isn't really my place. Maybe I borrowed it to throw you off. Maybe I'm not who you think I am?" Alex reached up and pulled her largest mug from the cupboard. "What'd you expect? I suppose you find the hidden cameras?"

"It's just a bit puzzling to me., that's all. You've seen my place, it's littered with my whole life story everywhere you look. I like hanging on to stuff."

"I love your place and hopefully, someday, I can share my life story with others, at least parts of it anyway. But seriously, Phil, you know as much about my past as probably anyone. Would you plaster that all over your walls?"

Phil turned and leaned on his other elbow. "Hey, I'm just noticing things, that's all. Wasn't it you who taught me to always sort out my surroundings?"

"I believe it was and you're a quick study." Alex poured herself a cup of tea and topped off the extra–large mug with freshly brewed coffee. "Here you go, just as you like it."

Phil found a comfortable chair to stretch out his 6 foot 4 inch frame. He took a gulp and puckered. "Whew. . . ahh. . . ooh. . . noow that's hot." He took a sip and swirled it around, savoring the taste. "Ah. . . you remembered. Black, extra strong *and* hot." His large hands completely dwarfed the mug and he felt the steam rising.

Alex leaned against the window that looked out over the street below. Her flat was on the top floor of a row house situated in the Montmarte District of Paris and she had a clear view of the famed white domed La Basilique du Sacre Coeur. Shafts of sunlight filtered through the window and she arched her back and stretched her neck letting the warmth seep in. Alex's father was Moroccan and her mother French and she had inherited the best of their physical traits. Her deep olive brown skin gave her a natural exotic look coveted for centuries by kings and queens alike and her aquamarine eyes were trimmed by jet–black brows as fine as silk.

"Another thing I didn't know about you. I thought all you wore were jeans and sweatshirts. If I didn't know any better I'd say you just got back from a job interview."

Alex held her arms to her side and gave herself the once–over. To blend in with the crowds she had always found a way to dress indiscreetly. A short sleeved scooped neck silk blouse, straight–legged gabardine pants and a single button dark blue blazer had been her uniform of choice for a day at the Agency. She laughed. "Meeting with the Director is like going to a funeral—the dress choices are limited."

Alex took a sip of tea, inhaled deeply and looked over at Phil. "Look, Phil, I really am happy that you have come over here and we will find a way that we can both be useful, but I need to say again this will be very dangerous and I will need to do most everything by myself."

"Alex, this isn't a whole lot different than when we were running all over the Bay Area back home just a few weeks ago. It worked there and it will work here. Ben's my closest friend and I'm not going anywhere or doing anything until I. . . well actually we, have found him. End of discussion. Now, what do you know?"

Alex's fingers brushed through her raven black hair and she nodded slowly, "Okay. Okay. Let me tell you what I know so far and we'll work through this together, but there will be times when I will need to act by myself. Not that you won't be an integral part of things, Phil, but if we are going to go forward with what I think we will need to do, then I need you to promise that if I say no, you will understand. I, too, only care about finding Ben and making sure he's safe." She spread her hands and tilted her head, "Agreed?"

A stubborn nod. "Agreed, but I reserve the right to disagree."

Alex laughed and she felt her limbs relax. She had not allowed her mind to wander or to think about anything other than Benjamin since his disappearance. She was still wrapped in a cloak of guilt and blamed herself for Benjamin's kidnapping. She was stuck in a vortex, spinning endlessly, wondering how all this could have happened. When she had been hired by a long time client of hers to go to the United States and pirate medical research from a company there, it had seemed like just another job. She had retired from the espionage racket and had begun to settle into a quiet life, spending needed time with her frail and aging mother. She had given into the pressure her old friend Andre had put on her to do that one last job for him. He had told her that she had a debt to repay to him, but she had looked at it as emotional blackmail. She was sure she could do that job quickly and return home to continue on with her new–found life. A week, she had thought. I'll be in and out in a week. What she hadn't known was that she would fall in love with the man she had targeted—a man whom she had intended to leave behind looking like a guilt ridden criminal who had high–jacked his own company. Now, that man had been kidnapped by a group of people with enough money and enough political clout to go far underground, beyond the eyes and ears of the government spooks that were now after them.

Phil rose from his chair and walked over to the same window where Alex stood earlier. He looked down and watched the bustling shoppers scurry in and out of the small shops; loaves of baguettes popping out of their bags and fresh cut flowers tucked under their arms. The outdoor tables at the neighborhood cafés were filled with friends enjoying an afternoon espresso and two men were huddled around a round table, their heads leaning over a chess board. At the far corner a street mime clad in a black and white striped shirt, white gloves and a white painted face flipped his suspenders. Adults laughed and clapped while rows of children huddled like a flock of sheep, their mouths forming perfect circles and their eyes gleaming with that 'I just saw Santa Claus' look.

"This is really nice. I know I couldn't live like this with all the crowds and noise, but. . . every time I visit a new place I love to take in the sights. In a way I envy you being able to look out at something like this."

"It is beautiful and in its own way very peaceful. I'm afraid I've never really had the time to appreciate it though."

"Huh. . . yeah I don't picture you as someone with a lot of down time. You oughta try it though. It can grow on you."

Alex rolled her eyes. "This is about as much down time as I usually ever get. Someday. . . maybe. . . I hope."

Phil turned, placed his palms on the window sill and leaned back. "I don't mind telling you, Alex I'm. . . well I'm kinda scared. I'm worried about Ben and I hope we're doing the right thing. Are we?"

The right thing, Alex thought, when have I ever known what was the right thing to do? She took a deep breath and let it slowly escape. "I trust my instincts on this, Phil. I can rely on them better than anything else. Ben's okay—he is, but we need to move fast and be careful. I also have a feeling there will be a few forks in the road that we didn't anticipate. I'm scared too, Phil, but we'll find him. . . and he'll be fine."

"You know everything we went through back home is still pretty much a blur in my mind." Phil tossed up his hands. "Hey, maybe I'll write a book."

He pushed away from the window, walked over to Alex's desk and sat down across from her. He was tired—not the kind of tired that came from lack of sleep, although he hadn't seen a decent night sleep in weeks. No, the luster in his dark brown eyes had faded a shade or two and the parallel creases etched in his cheeks had been recently carved by twin blades of raw emotion and brutal honesty.

"That whole week we spent looking for Ben and the people who were after us was a shit–can experience. I didn't realize how scared I was back then until everything was over. . . well, I thought it was over anyway." Phil raised his head and looked directly at Alex. His eyes narrowed and the luster returned. "I don't know what you do or how you do it, Alex, but you're damn good at it. Whatever plan you've concocted this time you can count on me to be there."

Alex placed her laptop on her desk and booted it up. She reached across and gave Phil's arm a squeeze. "Come here. We have a lot to go over."

# CHAPTER 4

"This is Alex Boudreau. I need to speak with Monsieur Broussard, please."

"Certainly, Mademoiselle Boudreau. I will find Monsieur Broussard and pass you through to him." The receptionist's tone made it clear that she understood Alex's urgency.

As Alex waited for the man she wanted to both thank and curse, she pulled out a piece of paper and began preparing a list of supplies she knew she would need.

"Alex, you are back? Where are you?"

"Hello, Andre. I am at my flat, but I am leaving again in a few hours. I need your help with something while I am away." Her past relationship with Andre had taught her one thing for certain— whenever she had asked Andre for his help she had known it would come with a price. Andre had called them "sacred debts," and he had never failed to collect on those debts.

Alex had a long history with Andre Broussard. As the head of CS Generale, a large French multinational corporation, Andre had first employed Alex as an intern during her years in graduate school and it had been Andre who had urged Alex to pursue a career with the French DGSE. After Alex had left the Agency and had ventured out on her own, Andre had employed her services on numerous occasions and had rewarded her handsomely for her successes. Each assignment had been a success—Alex had never failed to meet Andre's expectations.

"Certainly, Alex. Tell me what I can do for you. Your voice tells me this is important."

Alex knew that Andre was pacing in a wide circle as he spoke. She had seen it too many times. His short, measured steps encircling the tangled web his calculating mind was weaving; a web that would be cast over her once again if she was not careful.

"I will be gone for several days, four at the most and I need you to locate Devon Briggs for me. I am going to need his help."

"I will do my best, Alex. I am leaving town myself this afternoon. I need to be in Geneva for a few days. When I get there I will see what I can do."

"Andre, that's not good enough. I need your assurance that you will do this for me and that you will make this your number one priority. Although I do not blame *you* for what has happened, if you had not involved me in the GEN case to begin with I would be home in Morocco now with my mother instead of preparing for what will certainly be the most perilous venture of my already supposedly ended career."

Andre's voice stiffened, "We have been over all this before, Alex, and I had absolutely nothing to do with the disappearance of Monsieur Hunter. You know that. You, of all people, also know that there are risks involved in any assignment you undertake for me. That's the nature of the game that you have so successfully played over the years. Now, if you are calling me to ask a favor then please do so with a tone of civility. I do not react well to trenchant demands such as the one you have just made."

Alex had been dressed down by Andre before and she knew his tongue lashings could cut deeper than a cracking whip. She had always looked at it as his way of exhibiting the strength that he physically lacked. A short man, Andre surrounded himself with the biggest and finest of everything to project the appearance of self–importance within his world. Alex had never quite understood that about Andre. As head of one of the world's largest multinational companies, he held the absolute power to demand an audience with any world political leader at a moment's notice or to make others kneel in his presence.

Alex knew she had approached Andre the wrong way this time. In spite of his shortcomings and her desire to stay far away from his clutches, he had done some touching and unselfish things for her over the years. "You are right, Andre. I am sorry. This is so important to me on so many levels and I called you because I know you can help me. I will be gone and I will try, but it will be difficult for me to find him while I am away, which is why I need your help, Andre. Can I count on you for this?"

His voice was layered with a smug satisfaction, "I will do my best, Alex. You have my word. This must mean that you are not going to work with the DGSE to find Monsieur Hunter, am I correct?"

"Somehow I think you already know the answer to your own question, Andre."

"Well," Andre laughed, "and somehow I should have known that. As a matter of fact, I did speak with Director Bardin and he is quite upset that you will not cooperate with them."

"Oh, I gave him every chance, but we don't really look at things the same way. So will you help me find Devon, Andre?"

"Yes, of course, I will make that a priority and do what I can."

"Thanks, Andre. I will send you a list shortly of what I need Devon to get and he is to meet me in Accra in four days with the supplies. I need him to help me out in this operation."

"Accra? Tell me what leads you to believe you will find Monsieur Hunter in Ghana?"

"Andre, will you just do as I ask? It is very important—*please.*" Alex had no intention of bringing Andre into the loop on her plan— not yet anyway.

An exaggerated pause, and then, "Yes. Yes, Alex. I will find Devon and get the message to him."

"If you need me you may be able to reach me on my cell until I arrive in Accra. After that I will be unavailable. And Andre—thank you."

"When you. . . "

The line was already dead.

Alex placed a call to her mother in Morocco. She had spoken to her mother only once after returning from California and she knew her mother was worried. She couldn't blame her. Throughout her career Alex had always covered her tracks and had made certain there were no exposed links that would lead to her true identity. Neither her clients nor the few trusted allies she had worked with had known her as Alexandra Boudreau. She had safe deposit boxes scattered across the continents, each storing different passports, credit cards, driver's licenses and other forms of identification and it had not been unusual for her to assume several different identities in any given month.

The one exception was Andre. Andre had entered Alex's life when she had been a graduate student at the University of Paris where she had first set her hopes and dreams on pursuing a career as a university professor. It had been either Andre's unremitting influence or Alex's own smoldering ambitions that had changed that course. She had often thought about the life she might have led if Andre had not redirected her career path, but somehow she knew her life had probably been fated to ride her own personal conveyor belt filled with intrigue, solitude and blind aspirations. Her life as a university professor would have been short lived.

Just weeks ago when Alex had been in the throes of handing over the stolen research to Andre she had been hit with a blunt reality. Her mother's life had been threatened. She had suspected Andre may have been behind the threats and that hers and her mother's lives were in danger. To protect her mother, she had sent her to stay with her uncle Djamel until she knew it would be safe for her mother to return home. Alex now knew that Andre had not been behind those threats, but in her line of work one must always suspect the unexpected.

If Alex's mother knew what her daughter had really been up to all those years and what she was up to now, she felt her mother would again fall ill from all the worry.

A faint accent. "Hello."

"Mother, it is great to hear your voice. Let me guess. You are sitting at the kitchen table looking out at the mountains and sipping your afternoon tea. Am I right?"

A soft voice replied, "Oh, Alexandra, I have missed you. Where are you, dear?"

"I am still in Paris, mother, but I wanted to call to see how you are doing. I probably will not be able to get down to Sidi Lahcen for at least a week. I have some unfinished business I need to clear up and then we can spend more time together." Alex dreaded these calls to her mother. She loved her mother, deeply, but her mother had become reclusive and weak ever since her husband died just over a year ago. Alex had planned to spend more time with her mother once she retired from her life of deceit and she had always enjoyed the peaceful and relaxing days in Sidi Lahcen with her mother. As soon as this is over, she promised herself again, I will spend time again with my mother.

"It seems like this business of yours is always taking up all your time, dear. Maybe someday we will be able to spend time together again."

"We will, mother. I promise. Now, do you have everything you need while I am away?"

"Oh do not worry about me, dear. I am doing just fine. I do miss your father terribly and I wish he was here with me now."

As she always did when she spoke to her mother, Alex cradled in her lap the framed picture of her family that Phil had noticed earlier. Seated on the front porch of their home in Sidi Lahcen, her father stood behind his family with his calloused hands gently clutching his daughters' shoulders. Her mother's eyes caught the afternoon light and sparkled like sapphires and Christina and Alex radiated with joy and happiness—their faces split from ear to ear. Her mother was all she had left now, but she missed her father and sister—terribly.

Alex tried to mask the sorrow and guilt she felt. "He is looking after you still mother. I have to go, but I will call you the second I am ready to fly down there."

"Bye, dear." Her mother's voice trailed off.

"Bye, mother." Alex reached up and caught a tear that squeezed through her lashes. Soon, she thought, she would be able to spend the time she needed with her mother.

Alex had finished packing and slung her familiar dark blue Mammut backpack over her shoulder. She marched into the kitchen, dropped the backpack on the counter and turned to Phil. "Well, what do you think? Are you finished?"

Phil leaned back in his chair and locked his hands behind his neck. His eyes narrowed. "I don't think you've told me everything. There're enough explosives on this list to blow up an entire block, or maybe more. What gives?"

Alex walked over to the table where Phil had been pouring over the list of supplies she needed Devon to secure and bring to Accra. She sat down, picked up the sheets of paper and scanned the list one last time. "I'm planning on taking more than I need. I really don't know yet what I will encounter. What is it you Yanks say? Better safe than sorry?"

Phil glared at Alex. "There's nothing safe about this, Alex, and how the hell does this guy plan on getting all this into the country? He can't just fly in there with this kind of stuff." Phil leaned forward and drilled his elbows into the table, placed his chin in his cupped hands and continued, "Come on Alex. I understand the cameras, the ropes and even the stun grenades, but 30 blocks of C4 plastic explosives is something I don't get. Fill me in."

Alex met Phil's probing eyes. "At this point I've told you everything you need to know, probably more. If something were to happen to you before you arrived in Accra I don't want you to know any more than you already know. I don't want this mission compromised. We are going to succeed Phil—together. This is another one of those circumstances where you will just have to trust that I know what I'm doing."

"Damn you lady!" Phil slumped down in his chair. He shook his head and stared at the ceiling. "Okay. Okay. I'll get things squared away on my end and I'll see you in Accra, *but* from that point forward I'm in the loop." He raised his head and held his hands out in a gesture of compromise. "Okay?"

"Okay, Phil. This will work. . . *I know it.*" At the sound of her own words, Alex felt a lump return to her throat. A recurring reminder that she was about to embark on a mission to find the only man she had truly loved—Benjamin.

Alex finished up the list of supplies, reached under the desk, pulled out a new laptop and booted it up. She knew there was always the likelihood that her own laptop could have been compromised by someone infiltrating it with a keystroker or a Trojan horse that would give them access to her programs. She always kept a separate laptop on hand just in case. She typed up the list and then opened an email account using a new provider. She composed an email to Andre, attached the list and shook her head as she hit the send button. Her past mistakes were pot holes she wanted to sidestep in the future. Once before she had failed to cover her tracks when sending an email and it had almost cost her—dearly. The smallest of details could derail an otherwise perfectly planned assault. She had learned that the hard way.

# CHAPTER 5

The sight of the warm hand–stitched sofa, framed perfectly by floor to ceiling bookshelves each neatly stuffed with leather–bound treasures, beckoned Alex to have a seat. Her travel–worn body was in need of rest, but her mind spun in endless circles as she slowly wandered about the room. One by one, she stared at the framed photographs that lined the paneled wall. Moving from left to right she followed the chronology of this man's life from the time he was a young boy, through his early working years to the decades when he ran a very successful multinational corporation.

There he was standing next to world leaders who probably had the same picture mounted on their own wall of self–importance. Clasping hands with Zimbabwe Prime Minister Robert Mugabe, with the towering Victoria Falls in the background; a somber–looking walk with British Prime Minister Margaret Thatcher in the gardens of Buckingham Palace; and standing in the Oval Office of the White House, he out–smiled the always smiling President Ronald Reagan.

She reached the end of the photographs and her hand rubbed the wood paneled wall. A pang of guilt twisted around her spine. The last picture taken of this man was over 11 years ago and Alex knew why the pictures suddenly ended.

She turned and faced the walnut double doors on the far side of the room. From behind those doors a man would soon emerge and she wondered what she would say to him. It had been almost 11 years since she last saw him and then, only from behind her cloaked disguise. He would not recognize her, she was certain of that, but she needed his help—*now*.

Flashes of memories burst through Alex's mind one after another. Each snippet followed the same destructive pattern. Alex had always found a way to get exactly what she was after, but she had left behind trails of carnage. Lives had often been transformed from success to despair, others' dreams had been shattered like shards of glass and companies had been gutted of their prized proprietary assets.

She shook her head and rubbed her sleep–starved eyes. *That was the past and I have put it all behind me*, she thought. *My life has taken a turn that I never thought imaginable and he will listen—he will help me—I know it.*

Alex had spent two days traveling across two oceans to reach this man. She hadn't slept the entire journey. She had compiled pages of notes detailing what she had learned in the past six days and she had outlined plan after plan, each with detailed steps to accomplish her goal. She was not a person to accept failure and in this case, failure would mean her own life would be void of the one thing she had never experienced or felt—love. No, she would not fail. . . she could not fail.

She heard the sound of the doors brush against the plush carpet and she raised her head. A tall, but frail–looking man stood in the doorway. His prominent chin was raised to show that in spite of his slumping posture and bowed shoulders, he remained proud and confident. His voice was deep and still commanded the respect he had rightfully earned over the years, "G'day I take it yar Ms.

Boudreau? Yar message sounded urgent, so I've set aside some time to see ya. Sorry to have kept ya waiting, but please. . . please come into ma office and grab yarself a seat."

Seated in a high back suede chair, Alex's eyes panned the room. There were no photographs depicting this man's past, no plaques praising his vast accomplishments and no personal keepsakes honoring his many interests. An oil landscape painted on a hardwood panel by the Australian painter Edmund Arthur Harvey hung prominently on the wall to Alex's left. A bookcase filled with classics from Australian writers Rachel Henning, Charles Sturt, Edward John Eyre and scores of others lined the wall to her right. Her eyes had not yet studied the man sitting across from her. Even though she appeared comfortable and at ease, the tension she first felt upon entering this man's house had not waned. She was poised to snap at any minute.

"Well, Ms Boudreau, it's yar shout. What can I do for ya?"

At the sound of the man's voice Alex turned her head and looked at Denis Wilkinson for the first time. He looked tired, yet she heard a strong rumbling in his voice and his eyes reflected the confidence that had made him a corporate icon, not just in Australia, but around the world. She was taken aback by his thick wavy brown hair and the cleft in the middle of his protruding chin. The resemblance was uncanny. The same wavy brown hair that she had remembered brushing her hand through and the same cleft that she had tenderly kissed that moonlit night. It seemed like so long ago when she had shared that magical moment with Benjamin.

"Ms Boudreau?" The man clapped his hands together and the loud snap brought Alex back to the room.

"I'm sorry, Mr. Wilkinson. Yes, it was very nice of you to make time to see me. What I have to say is of the utmost importance and I'm afraid that you will not like most of it." Alex shifted in her seat and reached up to straighten the collar on her blouse. "But I ask you, please, bear with me if you would."

"The floor's yars; give it a burl, Ms Boudreau." Denis raised his hands and gave another quick clap, clap.

Alex got right to the point. "I'm a friend of your grandson, Benjamin—a very close friend. Are you aware that Ben is in some serious trouble, Mr. Wilkinson? Because of the trouble he's in I need your help in finding him."

Denis sat tall, his eyes widened. "Trouble? Find him? Ms Boudreau, I don't mean to frighten ya by this, but I was just released from prison where I served eleven stroppy years for a crime I didn't commit. I've been tryin to get caught up on things and I've been tryin to get a hold of Ben for the past coupla days. It's been bloody hard and I'm not havin any luck. Just what's yar connection to Ben? And what's the trouble he's in? That doesn't sound like him at all."

"Mr. Wilkinson, I'm aware of your incarceration and we can talk about that later, but Ben has been kidnapped and. . . "

Denis barked, "Kidnapped? By who? Do they want money?"

"Please, Mr. Wilkinson, this is a very long story and if you will bear with me I'll tell you everything."

Denis sat back in his chair. Both hands rested on his desk and his fingers tapped softly on the inlaid leather. His eyes laser–beamed in on Alex and his features darkened. Alex began, "I met Ben three weeks ago and I am ashamed to say it was under false pretenses that we fell in love. I was hired by a French corporation to infiltrate a company in the United States and pirate certain medical research. GEN was the name of the company in the States and it is owned by your grandson. They had some research on cystic fibrosis that was close to being approved by the FDA and they stood to make a considerable amount of money. My client wanted that research so it could reap the money for itself. I targeted Ben as the person I would get close to so that I could successfully steal the information. I didn't plan it, but we fell in love. When I returned to France, I phoned Ben and told him everything. I was so sorry for what I had done—for what I had done to him. We had agreed that he would come to Paris and we would sort things out. I wanted to make things right, not just for Ben, but for myself. I was done leading a life where everyone I touched was destroyed."

Alex stood up and walked over to the bookcase and leaned back against it. Her hands gripped the shelf behind her for balance. She had begun the story that she dreaded telling this man, but she knew she must continue. She took a deep breath and let the escaping air ease the tension. "Mr. Wilkinson, when Ben was on his way from the airport to see me in Paris he was picked up by some people who told him I had asked them to bring him to my flat. During that ride Ben must have sensed that something was wrong and a fight ensued. Ben was seriously injured when he jumped from the car and he ended up in the hospital. I did see him in the hospital and even though he was unconscious I know he heard what I had to say. I sat on the side of his bed and I told him everything, again. When I returned to the hospital later that day he was missing and the police were calling the whole mishap an attempted murder and a kidnapping. I soon discovered the research I had taken from GEN also contained additional research on the creation of a lethal virus, a virus of weapons–grade proportion that could be used to kill millions of humans."

Denis no longer tapped his fingers on his desk. The color had drained from his face and for the first time he showed the years that he had carried so well. Alex rushed over behind the desk and placed a hand on his shoulder. "Mr. Wilkinson, are you okay, sir?"

His head remained bowed. "If ya don't mind I could use some water." His hand shook as he lifted it and pointed a finger toward a door just beyond the Harvey oil painting. "Through that door is a small refer. Ya'll find some water thar."

Alex returned with a bottle of water, uncapped it and handed it to Denis. "Here you go, Mr. Wilkinson. I am sorry, this is a great deal to handle all at once, I know. Let's take a few moments before we continue."

"No worries, this is a bloody lot to handle. Yar right about that. I'm just plain knackered. I don't have the strength I used to, but I need to know the rest of what's happened. Is Ben safe, Ms Boudreau? Do ya know where he is?"

Alex knelt down and placed a hand on Denis's shoulder again. She looked into his eyes and said, "He *is* alive and yes, I do know where he is. That is why I've come to see you. I think you can help me bring Benjamin home."

"I'll do anything I can." Denis let out a sigh and continued, "I didn't spend much time with Ben over the years. His mother and I had sorta a fallin out, but I did keep track of him the best I could. His father was always away with the pixies, a real no good son–of–a–bitch he was. It was tragic when his brother William died and after that I tried to track Ben wherever he went. If he ever needed anything, I wanted to be thar to help him. He's been a good lad and he's really all I have left. Tell me, Ms Boudreau, what I can do to help. I will do bloody well anythin within ma power to see that he's safe."

"You look much better now, Mr. Wilkinson. I'm sorry to have to tell you all this. I'm sure it must be very difficult."

"No worries. I need to know what's goin on." He waved a hand, "Go on. . . continue."

Alex stood up, walked back to the chair and sat down. Her hands rubbed the suede on each armrest and she took a moment to collect her thoughts. Finally, she continued, "There is an American company called Sterling Defense Application Corporation. It's a defense contractor with operations throughout the world and I know they are behind Ben's kidnapping. Have you heard of them?

Denis was again sitting tall in his chair and his fingers slowly tapped the top of his desk. "No, can't say that I've heard of 'em, but so many companies started up and changed hands since I was in prison."

"Mr. Wilkinson, I know your company used to have mining operations in Sierra Leone where you mined and processed bauxite. I believe you sold those operations five or six years ago, but it's in your old processing plant in the Koidu District where Ben is now being held. I have detailed satellite images of the surrounding area and the exterior of the plant, but I need to see the original blueprints of that plant. I intend to get Ben out of there, but first I need to see what the inside looks like."

"Ya say we sold the Sierra Leone facilities?" He shrugged his shoulders. "Huh, news to me, but I'm findin out lots of things changed when I was in prison. Wilkinson Mining's operations have been consolidated and much of the overseas operations were sold off. We're focused here in Australia now. I've only been to the Koidu plant once, just before it opened, but I do remember it well. Last I knew the plant never re–opened because of the political problems in that country. If we have the plans somewhere ya can have 'em."

"I will need to scan them and upload them to my laptop while I'm here. That will save a great deal of time. Now, if. . . "

"Ms Boudreau," Denis raised a hand, "why aren't the authorities here askin for these plans? They've gotta be involved in all this?"

"Both the French DGSE and the American CIA are involved. They're working together to find Ben and the people involved with this virus. They will continue to do their job and I will continue to do mine. Believe me, Mr. Wilkinson, I'm the best chance there is to get Ben out alive and unharmed."

Denis rose from his chair. "Excuse me. I need to stretch. I find I can't sit for very long these days without these old joints tightenin up."

Denis walked stiff–legged to the far end of the room and stopped at the window. His back was to Alex and he looked out over the expansive lawn and gardens below. Slowly, he turned around and leaned back against the window sill. His hands steadied him and his head was tilted to one side. His baritone voice was sharper and louder than before. "Yar not with the DGSE. Yar not with the CIA and ya met Ben under some type a scheme, as ya say yarself. Just who are ya, Ms Boudreau? Let's go back to that point."

Sitting sideways in her chair so she could see Denis, Alex's hand reached up and brushed her hair from her eyes. She took a moment to compose her thoughts and then she stood, turned and looked directly at Denis. "When I told you how I met Ben it was in a line of work I had been doing for many years. I was trained as a spy originally. I worked with the DGSE and traveled all over the world stealing technology and financial data for the Agency and French multinationals. It's no secret, Mr. Wilkinson, and the DGSE has openly admitted, that they have operations specifically designed for this. It's how French companies can stay competitive in today's international marketplace. I left the DGSE because they were inept, they were corrupt, and their lack of imagination had left them far behind the other international intelligence agencies. Since I left the DGSE I've been doing the same thing, only on my own. I work best by myself and I'm very good at what I do. I do not want to stand in the way of the DGSE or the CIA. If they can free Ben, I would be the first to offer my congratulations, but I have crossed the finish line first in every instance where I've been up against them. I'm not going to stand on the sidelines and watch. Ben means the world to me, Mr. Wilkinson. I love him and I *will* find him and bring him home. I need your help, Mr. Wilkinson."

Denis had listened intently as Alex spoke. He walked back to his desk and sat down. His eyes never left Alex. His hands were loosely clasped in his lap and he rocked gently back and forth. "I don't know exactly what it is about ya, Ms Boudreau, but whatever it is ya seem like a fair dinkum. I'm inclined to believe everything ya've told me and as a minin man who made a career off a bettin on ma hunches I'm goin to help ya. I'm comin with ya though."

"Thank you, Mr. Wilkinson, thank you, but I don't think it's a good idea for you to get involved in this. With all due respect sir, this is going to be a dangerous operation and as I just told you, I work best by myself."

"Yar gonna need some help. I know some good men in Sierra Leone that could help ya out. Well, if they're still thar. Yar gonna need some connections when ya get thar. I'll call 'em."

"No, don't call them, please. The last thing I need is someone in that country knowing what we're doing. It's a small place, and there's a lot of money passed around in places like that to pay for that kind of information."

Denis stood and walked back to the bookcase. He pulled a leather–bound tome from the top shelf and gently rubbed the time–worn binding. "We have some good Aussie writers here, Ms Boudreau. William Carron, this book," he turned and faced Alex holding the book up with his left hand, "was a book I read several times when I was a young lad. It chronicles the expedition of Edmund Kennedy, one of our great explorers. On one of his earliest expeditions, Mr. Kennedy left with a large party and tried to reach Cape York by land. He got thar alright, but his entire party was killed by the aborigines or they starved. What I learned from this book, Ms Boudreau, was that if ya want to accomplish somethin extraordinary, I mean really extraordinary, the only person ya can rely upon is yarself. On ma early minin explorations it was just me. I wondered off to Woop Woop with a pick and shovel and I didn't return 'til I found an ore vein."

Denis placed the book back in its rightful place and walked over to Alex. "Stand up please, Ms Boudreau."

Alex rose and stood to her full height. Denis was at least a head taller than Alex and he peered down at her. "I understand the need to go this alone. If I was standin in yar shoes I'd ask the same. But, I've one request and one question for ya. Ya'll keep me posted on yar progress, won't ya?"

"You have my word, Mr. Wilkinson."

"Is there anything else I need to know? Ya tellin me the whole story?"

There is so much more, Alex thought. She had wanted to tell Denis the whole story. How it had been she who had set him up for the crime she knew he hadn't committed. She alone had been the one responsible for his years in prison. She reached her hands out and took hold of Denis' arms. The words she spoke came from her soul, "One of the things I've learned over the years is to only reveal enough information to people so that if something were to happen to them my mission would not be compromised. I have not told you everything for that very reason, but everything I've told you is true, especially the part about loving Benjamin. I love him, Mr. Wilkinson, and I will bring him back. *You have my word.*"

# CHAPTER 6

Alison Faucher stood statue–like in the hallway just outside Director Bardin's office. Her feet were spread shoulder width apart, her hands tightly clasped below her waist and her unblinking eyes stared straight ahead.

The office door opened and Director Bardin waved at Alison. "Come in, Alison. Any news?"

"I do not have *good* news, sir. Our agents successfully tracked Boudreau and they remained undetected, but something happened in Australia. When she left Mr. Wilkinson's house she was in a real hurry. She sped out of the driveway and lost our men within minutes. We're trying. . . "

Director Bardin shot up from his chair and his hands flailed. "Damn it, Alison!" He took two steps backwards and leaned against his credenza. His head shook slowly and he loosened his tie. "This can't be. Anyway, go on. Have you found her yet? What are your thoughts?"

Agent Faucher remained at attention. "I have agents posted at the airport and we're checking with the airlines right now. I doubt the airlines will pan out, though. She has more passports than we have stored in this whole building. She only purchased a one–way ticket to Australia and her rental car was under a different name than her plane reservation. That will be a dead–end. If she goes to the airport I am sure we will spot her, but. . . I am afraid there is a good chance we may have lost her for now."

Director Bardin's hands shot up in the air again. "Alison, we cannot lose her. No, we cannot. Has anyone spoken to Wilkinson? If she left there in such a hurry maybe he knows something? Sit down Alison; it looks like we will be here for a while."

Alison marched over to the chair in front of the Director's desk and sat down. Her back was rigid and her feet were pressed firmly into the carpet. Her body molded perfectly into her heavily starched blouse.

"Would you just relax, Alison! It does not help matters to have you sitting there looking like a petrified tree. Loosen up!"

Alison unclasped her hands and stretched her fingers. She leaned back in her chair. There was an uncomfortableness to her voice. "Sorry, sir."

Alison Faucher had been one of the finest agents to rise through the ranks at the DGSE. She had been anything but a bump on a log or a meek intimidated woman. Her frozen facade had been something she had first developed during her training in commercial explosives. Alison had spent two years with the Gendarmerie Nationale before she had joined the Agency. She had been certified by the International Association of Bomb Technicians & Investigators and in no time she had become the Gendarmerie's go–to person in bomb threat situations. After she had successfully defused a bomb that had been planted outside the Rue St Didier headquarters of the Directorate–General of the National Gendarmerie, she had been thrust into an unwanted position of notoriety within the French law enforcement community. The Agency had quickly swooped in and lured her into its fold.

"We do have a couple of credible leads that we are pursuing. Agents Mainard and St. Gelais interviewed Mr. Wilkinson and learned that she may very well be headed to Sierra Leone. He was reluctant to cooperate at first, but the Agents were very persuasive."

The Director tilted his head. "How so?"

"They told him that Ms Boudreau was heavily involved in the kidnapping and attempted murder of his grandson and she was being pursued by several international intelligence agencies. The DGSE was the principal investigating agency in the matter. He soon became very helpful."

"I would imagine. What did you learn?"

Agent Faucher crossed her legs and folded her hands. "She is probably on her way to Sierra Leone to a mining plant that was once owned by Wilkinson Mining. She thinks Monsieur Hunter may be held there. That is what she told Mr. Wilkinson. We have alerted the authorities there to be prepared for her arrival. The moment they locate her coming into their country they will contact us. I already have four top agents en route to the country now and we have an undercover agent already on the ground."

Director Bardin gave a half–smile. "Good. . . good. . . very good. What about the others?"

"Phil Morgan is still here in Paris. He has not made any reservations at this point to leave. There is still the possibility that Boudreau may come back here first. We are prepared for that. Devon Briggs is another matter. We still have not found him and I am not too certain we will. From what I have learned he is very experienced and was originally trained by the British GCHQ."

"Yeah, I know who he is. The Brits did a damn good job training that guy. Somehow Boudreau hooked up with him six or seven years ago and he is a force to be reckoned with. He is no slouch. Keep looking. He is certainly going to be meeting up with Boudreau soon. Anything else?"

"No, sir. That is it for now. I think we will be back on track very shortly."

Agent Faucher rose. "I do have one question though, if you do not mind."

"No, certainly. What is it?"

Agent Faucher had regained her steeled pose. Her feet were evenly spread and her shoulders squared. She took a deep breath and the lone crease in her over–starched blouse vanished. "It seems that the Agency is taking an unusually high interest in this case. Is there something I do not know? Maybe something that would help me in this case?"

Director Bardin leaned back in his chair, tilted his head back and stared at the ceiling. After a few moments he leaned forward, rested his forearms on his desk, and looked right into Agent Faucher eyes. His eyebrows lowered. "Alison, one of the perks, or the nooses, that come with this position, depending how you look at it, is that I have direct contact with President Desjardins. He is monitoring this very carefully. Every morning I give him a briefing and I get calls from him throughout the day. I do not know why this is so important to him. I only know that it is. Keep tracking her and keep me posted. I need to know everything the second you do." He leaned back and heaved a heavy sigh.

# CHAPTER 7

The Villa Monticello had been a luxury boutique hotel located in the central core of Accra near the U.S. embassy, W.E.B. Dubois Center and the University of Ghana. Its restaurant and bar had been the City's most popular eating and watering hole for visiting dignitaries, journalists, businessmen, NGO's and politicians. For that reason Alex had chosen an out of the way hotel located on the other side of town. The Samartine Hotel, comfortable and off the beaten track, had often been frequented by budget–minded tourists.

Alex had landed at Kotoka International Airport and had worked her way through the customs area using a passport with one of her many assumed names. She had been visiting the country as a tourist and had expected to stay for 10 days to see the country's sights and experience its culture. Once outside, she had hailed a cab and had proceeded to the Samartine.

Alex had been to Accra on two previous occasions, both when her services had been retained by Andre at CS Generale. On each of those visits she had checked into the Villa Monticello. Ghana had served as the gateway to sub–Saharan Western Africa and its 250 million people. When Andre had first caught wind that the Ghanaian Ministry of Health had finalized its "Wealth Through Health Program," he had activated his forces and had pounced.

At that time the pharmaceutical market in Ghana had been a mere $300 million per year business, but with the Ministry's new national health insurance plan, Andre had known the market had been poised to at least triple in size. He had identified a foreign owned pharmaceutical company, Phyco Drugs Ltd, which had been on the cutting edge of Artemisinin Combination Treatment, known simply as ACT. ACT had been recommended by the World Health Organization as the first line for treatment of uncomplicated malaria caused by the parasite, Plasmodium falciparum. It had been proven to be effective both in sub–Saharan Africa and in areas with multi–drug resistant P. falciparum in Southeast Asia. If Andre could acquire Phyco, for the right price, he would have the edge in the ACT treatment market and have the ability to produce low cost generic drugs which had then been dominated by Indian and Chinese companies located in the region.

Andre had retained the services of a politically connected Ghanaian firm to begin the introduction of CS Generale to the local powers to be. Andre had been to Accra on several occasions to meet with the country's President and the wheels had successfully been greased to invite CS Generale to participate in the upcoming pharmaceutical boom.

Alex had wasted no time when she had arrived in Accra for that first assignment. Within a few days she had identified the key Phyco officials that dealt with the government agencies and she had learned what she had needed to know abut the company's computer network. From a safe remote location she had accessed Phyco's computer network and had altered the results of the sampling and testing studies for its malaria drugs. The company's deficient manufacturing standards were to blame. She had created a string of internal memos from the plant's head of manufacturing and others, discussing the deficient standards and a separate memo from the plant manager recommending a cover–up. When that information had been leaked to the government, Phyco had been faced with having its licenses revoked, plant shutdowns and legal ramifications for submitting false information to the government. The timing couldn't have been any better for Andre and the Phyco manufacturing facilities; rights to the ACT and all its distribution channels had ended up in his clutches.

Alex entered her hotel room. She stopped in mid–step and her instincts sharpened. She scanned the room. There were no signs that anyone had entered, but she heard water running in the bathroom. She edged over to the wall next to the bathroom door and waited. When the door opened she saw the shadow. She lifted her right leg, cocked it and spun around landing a roundhouse kick in the man's right thigh. Her right hand was about to strike the man in his shoulder blade when she abruptly stopped. "Devon!" She screamed and bent down to grab his arms.

"I had no idea that was you. How did you get in here? Here, let me help you up." Alex put Devon's arm over her shoulder and helped him limp over to the sofa. She walked back, picked up his glasses and handed them to him.

Devon grimaced, but the corners of his mouth rose slightly. "Jeez, Alex. A bit testy I would say. You could've seriously hurt me. As it is I'm sure I have a femoral shaft fracture and I'll need intramedullary nailing, at the very least. Are you proud of yourself?"

"Okay, okay Devon. Sorry, but you shouldn't be sneaking around my room—or any room for that matter. You know better."

Devon rubbed his thigh and winced. "Well you invited me here and I thought I was your guest. Do you always treat your guests with such brutality or were you actually threatened by my menacing presence?"

Alex sat down next to Devon, gave him a hug and patted his leg. "Lucky for you I'm out of practice. You could have just asked someone at the front desk for a key, you know, and come in like a normal guest."

"I learned from the best, so there's no reason for me to sign in and get a key after you taught me how to pick a lock. I thought I'd try it out. It worked."

With her thumb and forefinger, Alex rubbed Devon's chin. "This is a new addition since I saw you last." She cocked her head. "It's sort of like. . . let me think. . . " She craned her head all the way to one side. "You look like the Greek god Pan. He wore a goatee too, you know? Or maybe Van Dyke or Spock, yeah, Dr. Spock."

Devon's scowl morphed into a lopsided grin. "Verrrry funny. I grew this just for you, you know? I didn't think you'd recognize me with this disguise. I'm kind of evil looking." Devon gave his chin a quick stroke. "You know when it grew in I had white streaks on each side so I dyed it. Pretty sharp though, don't you think?"

"Pretty sharp is one way to describe it. You could inflict some serious punishment on whoever it is you're dating these days."

Alex looked around the room again. "Where's your stuff? Hidden somewhere safe I hope?"

"That it is. I picked up everything you asked for and it's stashed away in a couple of lockers in the train station. It should be safe there, but we oughta bring it here soon. You never know who's skulking around."

Devon Briggs had worked with Alex before and the two had a mutual respect for the other's talents. Alex had been a real pro when it came to understanding computers and being able to manipulate programs, but Devon had been in a world of his own.

Devon had been trained by the British intelligence agency, GCHQ, and in no time he had become their elder daemon of tech support. He had never followed the lateral ways of thinking that had been thrust upon him during his parochial schooling in Cape Town, South Africa, where he had grown up. He had never been considered to be a nonconformist or even one to test his boundaries. No, Devon had been different than most in so many ways. To the kids in his school he had been looked upon as the low hanging fruit. He had been the only black student in an all–white school and his frail wiry frame, asthma and klutzy all–thumbs coordination had kept him out of athletic events, further isolating him from the main student population. He had spent his free time in the computer lab, the library or reading whatever he could get his hands on about algorithms and how to find a possible solution to $P = NP$, an open problem in the theory of computation.

When Devon had finally landed at GCHQ, he had been confident he had found a place where he could use his forward ways of thinking to help create new and advanced computer identification and screening systems. The GCHQ, or Government Communication Headquarters, had been formed by the British after World War I as a peacetime code breaking agency and to study the methods of cipher communications used by foreign powers. Its authority had expanded over the years to monitoring diplomatic ciphers and providing the British with signals intelligence. Like so many clandestine intelligence agencies, it had received its share of public outcry over some of its operations. In 2003, GCHQ agents were outed and accused of wire–tapping UN delegates in the run–up to the 2003 Iraq war and in 2009, the GCHQ had been accused of monitoring computers and phone calls of foreign leaders and officials participating in the G20

Summit Meetings in London. More recently, the GCHQ had been accused of obtaining secret information about people living in the UK from the United States' National Security Agency and its Prism program.

After the 9/11 attacks in New York, the FBI had collected over 30,000 computer hard–drives from the World Trade Center site and due to the need to recover information as rapidly as possible they had enlisted other intelligence agencies to help in resurrecting those hard–drives. Devon had led the effort on behalf of GCHQ.

Working in a small dust–free "clean room," Devon had been able to remove and re–engineer the magnetic platters from the damaged hard drives and coax data back to life on 32 hard–drives and mainframes. All of those had contained a disturbing pattern of dirty doomsday dealings. In the days preceding the 9/11 attack a large amount of put options had been purchased on United and American Airlines as well as several major tenants of the World Trade Center. Additionally, large sums of money, possibly up to $100 million had been run through some of those hard–drives just minutes before the attack. Devon had taken that information to mid–level management, but had been told in no uncertain terms to "leave it alone." He had pushed higher up the bureaucratic levels until finally, his computer had been confiscated and he had been forced to take a polygraph test to verify the allegations he had made. Finding himself again boxed in with no ability to use his skills to explore new fields or to create new solutions, he had turned in his resignation and had started a search to find a new home.

The loud drum roll startled Devon, but Alex turned toward the door and smiled. She knew exactly who was there. She walked to the door and placed her hand on the knob. "What's the password?" she asked.

"How 'bout just open the damn door. I'm hot, sweaty and tired. Let me in!"

Alex opened the door. "Nice to see you, too."

Phil stumbled in, dropped his backpack on the floor and leaped onto the bed. His chiseled frame was sprawled diagonally across the bed and his feet dangled over the edge. He kicked off his sneakers. "God it's hot here. I've been walking around for the past half hour trying to figure out where to go and this heat is freaking killing me."

Alex walked over to a small table in the corner of the room and spread out some papers. She booted up her laptop and looked over at her two teammates. "Well, I have one guy who can't walk and another who is stuck to the bed with heat exhaustion. Shall I call in some reinforcements or are you two still up to the task?"

Phil lifted his head off the pillow. "That figures, I guess there's no rest for the weary here."

Devon placed his hands on the edge of the couch and pushed himself up. "Alright. . . alright. I'm coming, but no brute force attack this time, I'm still crippled."

Alex introduced the two men to each other and she began laying out the details of her plan. Between her flights to Australia and back to Accra she had penned meticulous notes making sure every detail had been covered. There would be one chance and only one chance to find Benjamin and free him from his captors. There was no room for mistakes—there never was.

Phil was the first to interrupt, "How do you even know that Ben's in Sierra Leone and once inside the plant how are we going to locate him?"

Alex put her pen down on the table, tented her hands and her forefingers touched her lower lip. "I'm not a hundred percent positive that he *is* inside the plant at this time, but I've traced his path directly there. I know the DGSE knows part of the story, but I don't know if they know it all. I identified the plane he flew out of London on from the air traffic control records. It had filed a flight plan to Madrid and the next day it filed a flight plan to Istanbul, but the plane never landed there. It took me close to a half day to run scans through flight records in locations where I thought the plane may be headed. A Lear 60 has a range of around 2,760 miles before refueling so it covers a lot of ground. Anyway, a Lear 60 landed in Freetown at 3:44 in the afternoon which is just under 5 hours after a Lear left Madrid. The Lear has a cruising speed of around 510 mph so the math all works out."

Alex rose from the table and walked over to the window. She pulled the curtain partially shut and turned around. Her thumbs were locked in the front pockets of her jeans. "Guys. . . Ben *is* in Sierra Leone, I know that. Whether he is at the Koidu plant or not I'm not sure, but after looking through the ownership records of the mine I can't imagine him being held at any other place in that country."

Devon peered over the top of his glasses. "Umm, Alex, why are we here in Accra if they've stashed the guy in Sierra Leone? Shouldn't we be there?"

"I made a seat–of–my–pants decision when I was talking to Andre and asking him to help me find you. I knew he had spoken to Director Bardin and there was always the chance that he'd pass on any information he learned from me about what we're up to. He always plays both sides. I want to have a good look around before we leave to see if we're being tailed. Also, there was no getting around telling Mr. Wilkinson where we were going, so if he's already been questioned by anybody then hopefully that will raise some confusion and they'll have to split up some of their operatives."

Alex walked back to her laptop. "Accra's just a diversion, guys, and we're leaving here first thing in the morning. We'll be at the Koidu plant late afternoon tomorrow." She spread her hands. "That means we still have plenty of details to go through and we only have the rest of today." She sat down and lifted a stack of papers and tapped them against the table several times and then placed them neatly back down. "So, let's go through this again. Phil we'll start with you. I want to make sure that you fully understand your role and what you'll be doing. You wanted to be an integral part of this. Well, that you are so, any more questions before we continue?"

# CHAPTER 8

The Koidu Plant was located on the eastern edge of Sierra Leone in an area of dense jungles and murky rivers. To the north, the Loma Mountains rose abruptly from the granite plateau and savanna grasslands. Alex, Phil and Devon were hidden in a thick grove of trees high above the plant where they had a protected view of the area. They were drenched in sweat from the sweltering overhead sun and crippling subtropical humidity.

Phil was nestled against the mottled grey bark of an aging Khaya tree and looked over at Alex. "What do you think? Maybe another two hours until dark?"

Alex lowered her Swarovski EL binoculars, but her eyes remained locked on the landscape below. "At least that long. Other than those two armed guards patrolling the east side, I don't see much activity going on. But whoever those guys are they mean business. They're each carrying an HK G36 with a Beta Mag. Those are some serious weapons. They're German made—similar to the M16—and expensive. I can't say that I've run into those before."

The trip from Accra to the Koidu plant had been anything but luxurious. Alex had arranged for a private helicopter transport from Accra to Panguma, just sixty miles from the plant. The ride on the Sikorsky S–75 chopper had been smooth and uneventful, but they had needed to make two re–fueling stops along the way. The last stop had been in Monrovia, Liberia and they had just enough fuel to make it directly back to Monrovia.

Entrance into Sierra Leone's capitol city, Freetown, could often be time consuming and burdensome. Passports were always fully examined by government personnel who tirelessly asked endless questions with the precision of a robo–caller. Certificates of vaccinations were needed for both yellow fever and cholera. Although Alex had all those documents meticulously prepared for each of them ahead of time, Panguma had been chosen as the place of entry to sidestep those monotonous delays.

From Panguma to their current hideout, they had rented motorcycles, the preferred mode of travel in that region. Two of the bikes had been equipped with hospital side cars to carry supplies and equipment and to serve as a means to transport Benjamin out, if needed. The red tracks of dirt that served as a road had been dotted with pot holes, rocks and fallen debris and several times they had needed to stop and push their bikes through deep ruts or around fallen trees. The only signs of human life for most of the ride had been a handful of mud–brick homes and patches of litter scattered about the roadside. They had walked the final four miles using machetes to clear the way through the thick brush and vines.

Devon sat at his own private command area lined with limbs and brush he had cut with his machete. His laptop rested on a plank of wood he had smoothed out and set firmly in the dirt. He was ready.

Alex had wanted Devon along because his skill sets were second to none. Watching him command his computer at warp speed, even on a makeshift platform in the middle of the jungle, she knew she had been right.

Alex had first met Devon in London where she had been hired by a client to pirate information from a competitor. Devon had been working as a consultant for Alex's client and that had been the start of a mutual admiration for the other's talents. Several years later Alex had approached Devon about a particular assignment that would be beyond anything Devon had ever undertaken. He hadn't balked at the risks after Alex had offered him a high six figure payout at the end. Devon had jumped aboard.

Alex's client had been Mahindra Aeronautics, India's largest aircraft manufacturer and she had been hired to obtain the plans and specs for the Chinese built Chengdu J–20 stealth fighter jet. It had been speculated within the industry that the Chinese had reverse engineered that aircraft from the parts of a US F–117 Nighthawk stealth fighter shot down over Serbia. Mahindra had wanted to manufacture that aircraft for its own country's air force and it had refused to recognize China's stolen parts as being proprietary.

After Alex and Devon had successfully hacked into the Chinese computers' source code repositories and downloaded the plans and specs, Devon had taken the mission one step further. To avoid a trail back to them he had created what looked like an advanced persistent threat, a cyber threat launched by a foreign government or a sophisticated group of espionage hackers to persistently and effectively target a specific entity. Devon had generated a series of attacks against the Chinese government's computers and the trails had all led back to other aerospace and government entities that seemingly had a similar interest in the aircraft. The interlocking web had been too intricate to unravel. Those endless nights and the sophisticated methods had convinced Alex that Devon had not only become a valuable resource, but a trusted one.

Alex turned to Devon. "Everything on the outside looks exactly like the blueprints we have."

"Except it looks like this plant's been in operation for a while." Devon's fingers scrolled across the keyboard and he lifted his head. "I thought you said it wasn't in use."

Alex shrugged. "It was only used by Wilkinson Mining for a few years. When the civil war broke out in this region in '91 everything around here was shut down and confiscated by the rebels. After the civil war things slowly crawled back to normal, but I didn't think anything was ever done with this facility. Two years ago, I'm pretty sure Sterling Defense purchased it under a bogus entity and I haven't been able to find out what they have been using it for."

Alex peered out through her binoculars. "We'll find out pretty soon though." An older MIL Mi–171 E helicopter sat on a make–shift landing pad 100 feet north of the building. Steel barrels, stacked two high, lined the wall on the west side of the plant and other than the two armed guards there was no other visible security; no security cameras or motion sensors anywhere. Alex felt her heart skip a beat and at that moment she knew her intuition had been correct. Ben was inside there, somewhere, and she would do whatever was necessary to find him and bring him home alive and safe.

Shadows carpeted the sizzling grasslands and crept toward the canopied forest as the scorching sun sought refuge behind the mountains to the west. They continued rehearsing their roles and pouring over the details of their attack. Alex made certain that both Phil and Devon knew their assigned tasks and she paid particular attention to Phil.

She handed a pair of night vision goggles to Phil, but pulled them back as he grabbed for them. "You need to promise me again, Phil; you will stick exactly to the plan. No ad–libbing here on your part."

Phil's face was painted with grit and mettle. His eyes mirrored the steeled determination wrapped around his backbone. Phil was focused. "Come on Alex. I have the same goal as you. We'll get him out."

Alex continued to lock eyes with Phil. "Any sign of trouble or anything unusual that we have not planned for, you will let me know—*right*?"

"That's the plan." Phil scoured the grounds below through his own set of binoculars.

Alex had planned every detail of this mission down to the last item. She knew she had brought more equipment than would be necessary, but she didn't want to take any chances.

Phil's night vision goggles were equipped with earphones and a microphone so the three would be in constant communication. He carried a small first aid kit and six blocks of explosives. When Alex signaled the go–ahead, he was to follow behind her into the facility making sure that he moved from one pre–arranged position to the next. His sole purpose was to help carry Ben to safety if he was injured or unable to walk on his own.

Alex was equipped with 12 cameras, 100 feet of nylon rope and fourteen packs of C4 plastic explosives. Four XM84 stun grenades were secured in pouches tied to her waist belt. All three wore desert digital camouflaged fatigues.

Dusk brought an eerie stillness and the red and orange hued sky filled with a cumulus fleece. The temperature dropped from its midday pressure cooker to a mere simmer and the jungle erupted into an opus of nighttime rhythms—it sounded like an aviary seconds before an earthquake. Anticipatory anxiety settled in and the three waited—their minds in sync and their muscles taut. Benjamin was within their reach.

# CHAPTER 9

"Susan, call Jaspar and tell him to fuel up the plane. I'll be there in a couple hours."

"Yes sir. Where are you off to?"

"I'll tell Jaspar when I get there. Just tell him to bring warm clothes; plenty of warm clothes."

Alan Price hung up the phone and walked over to the wet bar in the corner of his office. He pulled a tulip shaped crystal glass down from the top–shelf and poured two fingers of 19–year–old Saint Magdalene scotch whiskey. He swirled the glass and let the scotch coat the sides. He buried his nose in the glass and inhaled the heady aromas of smoky apples, heather and a hint of toffee. As he always did, he savored that first sip and let the temporary anesthesia numb his taste buds and fire pleasing signals to his brain. He turned, took a few steps toward the mirror and stopped to admire the reflection. Alan was a man of mixed dimensions. His legs were out of proportion with his torso, his waist several sizes larger than his chest and one arm seemed to hang down further than the other. He never focused on any of those anomalies; instead he smiled as he patted down a few misplaced strands of his bone–white hair. It was neatly combed straight back and glistened in the soft overhead lighting.

He straightened his tie and thought how close he was to pulling off his last hurrah. He would soon be sailing off into the sunset without a care in the world—the same world that was about to hand him unfathomable riches.

A voice pierced the invisible shield that surrounded his thoughts. "Mr. Price, President Desjardins is on the line."

"Ah, yes, President Desjardins himself. Thank you Susan, I'll take it."

Alan walked back to his desk, leaned forward and stared at the blinking orange light. He didn't expect this call quite so soon, but he was happy his old friend was being so cooperative. Politicians are so predictable, he thought. It doesn't matter if they are French, American, British, Martians or whatever, they all responded to the color of money. He had certainly sent plenty of that to President Desjardins.

Alan Price was a self–made man who had started Sterling Defense Application Corporation years ago soon after he had been discharged from his brief stint as an enlisted man with the U.S. Army. Sterling had originally made small munitions it supplied to a handful of gun manufacturing companies, but now, its primary focus had been to provide armed security to government installations around the world. It had developed an economic model where governments could save considerable sums of money by contracting with Sterling to provide private armed forces, not only for diplomatic security, but also to train and supplement government armed forces. While perceived as mercenaries by many, Sterling had referred to their company personnel as security contractors. Private military companies like Sterling had proliferated in the past fifteen years to become a $100 billion a year industry. In the past twelve years Sterling had risen from an obscure member stuck in the lower echelon of the pack to the top of the field. Its sheer numbers of security contractors had exceeded the size of most countries' total armed forces.

Sterling had managed to hide beneath the radar of the worldwide media, but its connections to high government officials and politicians alike had run deep. It knew how to line the pockets of political decision makers with money and extravagant perks. It threw lavish parties, plied clients with the use of private yachts and jets and even arranged golf outings in Scotland with Hollywood celebrities.

Alan punched the speaker button. "Mr. President. What an unexpected surprise. I trust everything is going well with you? No ill effects at this point?"

"Under the circumstances, yes things are well, but I did not make this call to discuss my well–being. I want you to know that I spoke with Director Bardin earlier this morning and he assures me he has things well in hand. We are doing everything required on our part."

"Excellent. Good to hear. So you're certain our friend is contained and won't get in the way of our plan then?"

"Like I said, Alan, things are on schedule here. I just hope you have things under control and we can end this little charade soon— *very soon*."

Alan was pacing around his office. He rolled up his shirt sleeves to just below the elbows and stopped to stare at a photograph hanging on the wall. "Stephen, do you remember several years back when you invited me to the Versailles Palace and what you said to me then?"

A long pause and then a soft voice, "That was a while back Alan, and things change."

"That they do Stephen, but I'm looking at a photograph of the two of us that was taken on that very special day. It hangs prominently on my wall here as a constant reminder. Let's see Stephen, what was it you said to me? Oh yeah, now I remember. I think it was, "Alan, I will be forever in your debt. If there is anything I can ever do for you I hope you will ask." You remember that, don't you Stephen?"

"To be very honest with you Alan, I . . . "

"Whoa. . . whoa, Stephen," Alan cut off the President mid–way through his sentence and the corners of his lips turned down, "aren't you *always* honest with me?"

"As I was saying, things have changed. I will do as we agreed and I expect the same from you. When this is over so is our relationship. That is all I have to say for now. Au revoir."

Alan leaned back against his desk, his hands gripped the edge. Yes, Mr. President, he thought, soon our relationship will be over— *as we know it*.

# CHAPTER 10

A Gulfstream G650 is the aircraft of choice for elite corporate executives who spend more time in far away meetings than they do in their offices. Alan had traded in Sterling's G450 just over two years ago when he had known he was going to need a private jet that could fly long distances without the need for refueling stops. The Gulfstream G650 could fly up to 7,000 miles before re–fueling, much further than any of its competitors.

"Just a few more minutes, Mr. Price and we'll be wheels up. Do you need anything?

"Nope, I'm fine, Jaspar. Just fine."

Alan leaned back and the cushy leather molded to his head. He reached down and pressed the mute button on his armrest. The soft hum of the jet engines played in the background as he placed his next call.

Within minutes, Alan had punched in his identification code and password and was connected to Mr. James Dreyfous, the lead trader for Currillion Bank. "Good morning Jim. How's everything this morning?"

"Another excellent market day, that's for sure. How are you, Mr. Stiffleman?"

"I'm about to take off on a short trip and I'll probably be out of phone contact for a few days, but I wanted to double check and make sure my accounts were all in order and working properly."

"Let me punch them up. Just a sec."

Jim Dreyfous had been the lead trader for Currillion Bank for the past six years. Located in the Caymans, Currillion followed the country's very strict privacy laws and was often unaware of the true identity of its clients. He knew that Mr. Stiffleman was an assumed name, most likely, but it didn't matter to him. No, the bank paid him very well to run its trading operations and he could care less whom he was trading for. Just follow the protocol; that was the rules. "Here they are. No activity today and none scheduled in the near future. Your last transaction was when you set the trading accounts up a little over two months ago."

"Okay, I'm going to run some trial transactions on the Stiffleman Account. I'd like to place a market order for today to purchase 1,000 shares of Deutsche Telekom on a U.S. exchange for the Stiffleman Account and use J.P. Morgan as the clearinghouse. I want all shares to be sold tomorrow and make sure you use a different clearinghouse. When the proceeds are available have them wired to First Caribbean Bank, Routing Number 676221121, and Account Number 0891153461."

Mr. Dreyfous repeated the instructions and then asked for confirmation. Alan again punched in his identification code and password.

"Transaction confirmed. The purchase order is being filled at this moment. You'll be able to securely access your account online at any time to see this order and to make any further trades."

"Thanks, Jim. That should do it for now. Have a nice day."

Alan placed his cell down on the seat next to him and reclined back. He closed his eyes and a white grin filled the lower half of his face. It had been only a few weeks ago when he thought his plans had been ruined. When that Boudreau woman had unraveled his scheme to acquire the G–16 virus and the DGSE and FBI swarmed in and had apprehended everyone involved with the creation of that virus, he had counted himself lucky to have eluded their clutches. He had called in an old political marker and within days an entire cover had been created to explain his sudden disappearance. He had found himself in the DGSE headquarters where he had purportedly been for several days briefing the French government on security issues covering its Mideast operations.

Traveling at a cruising altitude of 32,000 feet, he looked out the window at the sapphire blue sky that completely enveloped the puffy sea of grey far below. He pulled a large brown folder from his briefcase and placed it on his lap. "Thank god for political connections," he muttered aloud.

# CHAPTER 11

The Pythagoreans believed that as the stars moved through the universe they made sounds that produced a musical harmony. Humans have never been able to hear this omnipresent concert because it has always been a constant background sound that filled their ears since birth. Alex and her two companions were secluded in their camouflaged bunker in the hills above the Koidu plant and while the stars were silent that night, their minds ticked away in perfect accord as they rehearsed their roles and awaited the moment.

Alex looked over at Phil and he showed no outward signs of being nervous or apprehensive. He lay prone in the grass; his hands gripped his night–vision goggles as he slowly panned the landscape below. His face was flaked with grit from the winds and sweltering humidity, and Alex knew that if their success could be determined by the strength of that man's heart and moxie they would have no problems.

She turned to Devon. His left cheek twitched sporadically as he sat staring at his monitor. His small stature, at least a foot shorter than Phil, and the sweat beading on his narrow brows, gave him the appearance of a man fraught with terror. Alex gave a slight grin. The twitch had been a trademark of his since birth and the root of endless teasing through his adolescent years. No, Alex knew he may not look the part, but he was tough as nails and not someone who could be easily riled. He was streetwise—the hard–boiled type.

"Okay, Devon. Let's get going. Let's plant some plastics."

Devon's smirk was replaced with a cool look of determination. "Roger that. Here goes."

Devon would be the command center keeping track of where Alex and Phil were and he would use the remote eyes that Alex would plant to keep tabs on what was happening both inside and outside of the facility. In a small clearing to his left sat two miniature remote controlled heli–drones. Although they looked like a hi–tech flying toy anyone could buy in a local hobby shop, no hobbyist had ever seen anything like these. Built with lightweight titanium, a battery driven carbon brush insulated motor and light weight foam blades, these birds could travel up to one mile emitting a sound of 20 decibels; no louder than rustling leaves.

Not long ago unmanned drones were only known to the U.S. military and used for wartime operations, but today they were being deployed in everything from monitoring endangered species to filmmaking, and of course, private espionage operations. They were silent night stalkers. Equipped with a gyro–stabilized night vision camera, Devon would be able to maneuver these birds as low to the ground as he wanted and have the vision to bring them down with a pinpoint landing.

Each drone was loaded with one stick of military issued M112 C4 block, a blasting cap and remote initiator. One stick of that explosive weighed only one and a quarter pounds and carried enough punch to easily take out its intended target.

Devon activated the control panel and the first drone lifted into the night air. He controlled the flight with his cursor and within minutes he had landed the first bird on the fuselage of the MIL Mi–171 E helicopter, inches from the rotor drive shaft. The second drone was airborne and Devon silently landed it below the loading dock near the armored cargo vehicles.

Devon nodded. "Drones in place." The night cameras where switched to rotate and Devon was able to have a clear 360 degree view from each bird. "No activity. Go."

Alex nodded and started down the hillside. Phil followed in her wake. Slowly, the two crouched and moved with fluid efficiency, each step landing like a ghost.

At the bottom of the slope there was a fifty yard clearing between themselves and the door they would use to enter the facility. Alex went first. Her night vision goggles gave her a clear line of sight for the whole fifty yards, but they were bulky and her peripheral vision was limited. Every ten to fifteen steps she slowed up, turned her head to each side and then sprinted forward again.

When she reached the building she whispered into her microphone, "All clear, I'm your side vision. She took a quick look in both directions and then, "*Go!*"

Phil exploded out of the brush and across the open clearing making sure his footfalls were soft. He reached Alex in a matter of seconds.

"Stay here and keep me covered. I'll check the magazine."

Alex edged along the side of the building until she reached a small shed–like building separated from the main facility. Mining plants generally had explosives they used as part of the extraction process and they were stored in a separate spot, or a magazine.

From her right pants pocket, she pulled out a Double Ball Pick and in less than 30 seconds she had picked the lock and was staring inside. "Damn," she muttered to herself. She knew this magazine needed to be checked out just in case any explosives were stored inside. Through her night vision goggles she panned the inside and shook her head in disbelief. The place was filled with enough ANFO, or Ammonium Nitrate Fuel Oil, to blow up Kingdom Come.

The fact that ANFO was stored inside was an added safety measure to Alex's plan. She was not interested in killing anyone on this mission, but she was mentally prepared to do so if needed. She took a stick of C4 from her belt pouch, looped the detonating cord through and attached a blasting cap with a remote firing device. She placed it under a block of ANFO. "Okay, Devon, C4 is in place in the magazine. If we need to blow this, let's make sure we are long gone. There must be forty 50–pound ANFO cartridges in here."

"Jesus, maybe I'll leave now." Devon had a remote detonator he would use when, or if, it was time to ignite the blasting cap. His remote could handle ten different explosives and if Alex was going to set more than ten, then he had a second remote on standby.

Alex fell back to her position along side Phil and gave him a pat on his arm. "Now for the easy part."

With her back against the building she moved to her left until she reached a single entry door. Reaching down, she grabbed the door handle. "Figures." It was locked.

She pulled out the same lock pick and within seconds she was inside the hallway corridor. Phil remained outside. Alex had committed to memory the blueprints that Denis Wilkinson had given her and she knew exactly where she was. She would proceed to the end of the hallway, turn right and in another 30 feet that hallway would "T." If she turned left at the T it would lead her past several small rooms and into a large open area at the north end of the building where the loading docks were located. To the right of the T, the hallway led to the mechanical rooms. She planned on taking the route to the left.

Alex carried 12 mini wireless 4.8 GHz color mini–cameras with her. Less than one square inch, each camera could be easily concealed out of sight, controlled and monitored by Devon from his command post. She stuck one camera on the end of a three foot aluminum extension pole, reached up and placed it on the ceiling near the wall. She used double–sided duct tape and the camera stuck to the ceiling like a barnacle. "Camera 1 in place."

Seconds later she heard Devon's voice, "Camera 1 activated."

Alex moved to the end of the corridor. She used a small, flexible extension camera to peer around the corner and everything looked clear. She placed the second mini camera on the ceiling covering the area behind her. Leaning around the corner she placed the third mini camera on the ceiling so Devon would have a view of where she needed to go next.

"2 and 3 are activated. Everything's clear."

Alex pushed forward down the hallway. Steps from the end and before she reached the T she stopped—*voices*. It sounded like two, maybe three people, moving in her direction from the large room down the hallway. "Devon! I hear voices coming at me from the left. Where's the quickest place to dart for cover?"

Devon's screen was broken into quadrants. He had a view of the interior from the cameras Alex had placed inside and he could pinpoint her location from her GPS transponder. All of this was superimposed over the blueprints. "Take four or five steps backwards and see if the door to your right is open. It's a small room. I doubt anyone would be in there."

Alex stepped back, opened the door and entered the dark, windowless room. Her night vision goggles were in her backpack, but she pulled a small LCD penlight from her utility belt. She was in an empty storage room. She reached down and placed a small microchip on the outside of the door and closed it. She changed the channel on her earpiece and she was immediately tuned in to the sounds from the hallway outside.

She controlled her breathing and listened closely. She could make out the voices of two men grumbling about the stifling humidity. When the voices faded she took a deep breath, close she thought, they must have gone to the mechanical rooms. "Did you see anything Devon?

"Two guys walked straight ahead. I don't think they're armed. Everything's clear now."

"Devon. . . Phil. I'll place a camera in the next hallway and then we'll have a good view in both directions. I'm going to go to the left toward the large room and I'll check each room as I move forward. Phil? Once I have the next camera in place start moving. Devon, lead him to the room where I am now. This is as good a place as any to wait."

Alex opened the door and crept back into the hallway. She used her extension camera to look around the corner—*all clear*. She secured camera 4 on the ceiling and stepped back. "You are my eyes right now, Devon. What do you see?"

Camera 4 had several lenses and Devon could manipulate the lenses to see what he wanted. The fisheye lens allowed him a complete 180 degree view or he could pinpoint things precisely by using the fixed 50mm lens. Seconds later, "All clear, Alex."

Quickly, Alex moved into the hallway, turned left and took a few short steps. Everything from here forward would be on her own reconnaissance. She needed to check out each room off this hallway. Each door had a glass panel and she'd be able to look inside first, but her time was limited. If someone would enter the hallway at either end, or come out of one of the rooms, she would be spotted instantly.

Reaching the first door on her left she grabbed for the handle.

"Alex! Behind you! Alex!"

Devon's warning was too late. When Alex spun around she was looking down the barrel of a Walther P38 pistol.

# CHAPTER 12

"Well. . . well, if it isn't Miss Renegade herself. I've always hoped this day would come. You and I, we have some unfinished business and this is a perfect place to wrap things up."

Alex tried to shake her head, but the twine looped around her neck and tied to the wall behind her was drawn taut. Her wrists were tightly bound behind her with the same narrow gauge twine and her hands were beginning to have that tingly feeling from lack of blood. Her eyes circled her surroundings for any clue that may help her. The room was empty except for the wooden chair that held her captive and a metal table across from her. A silver aluminum case rested next to the table.

The man with the handgun pushed his bulky frame away from the table, puffed his chest out and began his scorpion dance in front of Alex. His rubber souls skidding across the concrete floor echoed off the walls. He turned, and in three exaggerated strides stood inches in front of Alex. He bore the muzzle into Alex's temple and bent down. His dark hollow eyes reflected the anger and contempt that had plagued him for years. "Finally! You're going to get what has been owed to you since you first crossed my path." His raucous laugh ricocheted off the barren walls.

"You bastard!" Alex countered his piercing stare and spat in his face.

A clenched fist struck Alex in her left jaw and for a split second her sight was blurred. The pain spiraled down her neck.

"Let me be the first person to welcome you to hell, Alex. For the next few hours my friend here," he eyed the man next to him who stood in the same identical military pose, "and I will personally be in charge of your stay. We'll be testing your tolerance to pain and what you feel now," the man took two steps back and stretched his arms, "well. . . that little bit of blood dribbling down your pretty face, hah, you'll beg me to hit you again."

Alex knew Arnaud Bertrand was not throwing around idle threats. "What happened to you, Arnaud? You used to be one of the good guys. How'd you end up as hell's gatekeeper? Not that I doubt any of your qualifications."

A crisp blow hit Alex on the other side of her jaw and a knifelike pain bolted through her head. "Same old Alex I see; as cocky as ever. I've been waiting years for this day, my friend, years."

She wasn't sure if her jaw was broken, but she felt a warm steady stream of blood drip from her mouth. Her eyelids were half shut. Alex knew that behind Arnaud's swagger and his persona of a murderous mechanical toy lurked the same coward that she had confronted so many years ago.

When Alex had first started her training with the DGSE she had been assigned to the Division des Operations based in Quelend, France. Similar to the U.S. Navy Seals, that division had been deployed on clandestine missions knowing that their cover was unprotected by their homeland. Failure most certainly meant sure torture, isolation or the loss of one's life. It was there that she had met Arnaud, a brash, crude, yet highly skilled agent who had been in charge of training the new recruits. Arnaud had taken an immediate disliking to Alex, the only female in the group of wide–eyed trainees.

Those nine months of training had been both physically and mentally grueling. Aside from learning the necessary skills, the value of teamwork and the need to follow orders had been drilled into them with precision. At the end of five months the recruits had entered the vaunted Hell Week phase. There they had trained for five days and five nights solid with a maximum total of four hours of sleep. Timed exercises, runs, two mile ocean swims, cold water conditioning and crawling through mud flats had been interspersed throughout the five–and–a–half days. In spite of Arnaud Bertrand throwing extra obstacles at Alex and denying her food along the way, at the end of Hell Week, Alex had been one of only four recruits left in the program and the only one who had showed consistent improvement throughout the hazing.

On the last day of Hell Week the recruits had participated in rounds of hand–to–hand combat using Jiu–Jitsu and other forms of martial arts. To make a point, Arnaud had stepped into the ring with Alex and had used his brute strength rather than martial arts' skills. Alex had ended up with a dislocated shoulder. She had pulled herself off the mat and had found the strength and guts to persevere. Moments later Arnaud had lain motionless and unconscious on the training mat. One perfectly placed hand strike to his larynx and his voice sounded like a 60–a–day smoker.

Either because of his pure hatred for Alex or the embarrassment she had caused him, Arnaud had tried to get Alex dismissed by falsifying her training records. When the higher–ups uncovered this, it had been Arnaud who had ended up with a dishonorable discharge from the Agency. When he had been physically escorted from the training facilities he had made his intentions known to everyone— Alex would someday get her just due.

Alex could see the hatred that had swelled up in Arnaud over all those years. His teeth clenched and ground sharply each time his eyes shot poisonous arrows at her. Arnaud's satisfaction would be to watch Alex teeter on the edge of death and scream out for mercy.

The wet twine that bound Alex's wrists, ankles and squeezed her neck was drying. As the moisture fell away, the twine tightened and Alex felt it slice through her skin. Her ankles were numb and a burning feeling cut deep into her neck. Her breathing had been reduced to mere half–gulps and she knew her time was limited.

Hidden inside Alex's left shirtsleeve was a small razor–like blade. Tools like those were standard issue for reconnaissance missions and could be used as a small weapon or as a knife to cut scraps of food. Her fingers stretched and scratched as she tried to reach the blade. She needed time before Arnaud assaulted her with his next round of torture.

"Arnaud, you know you will not get away with this. If I don't get out of here in the next ten minutes, there's an army of heavily armed men outside that will storm in here taking out everyone in their sight. I came here for one thing. Help me and I will make sure you are unharmed when this is over."

"Help you? Oh, that's a good one." Arnaud grabbed Alex's chin with his fingers and tightened his vise–like grip. Letting out a menacing laugh, he continued, "I know you're here for that Hunter guy, but I don't really give a shit. No one that comes here is allowed to leave and I volunteered to make sure that I would have the first go–around with you."

Arnaud placed the metal case on the table and flipped open the latches. Alex knew her fate immediately. When her hands became completely numb and her fingers stiffened, metal clips would be placed on her finger tips and the treatment would begin. The electric shock waves would start off small penetrating only her fingers. Slowly, Arnaud would dial up the voltage and watch her body jolt as electric bolts shot intermittently through her. He would be in no rush to end the torture. No, he would revel in watching Alex writhe in pain and scream out in agony.

Alex's fingers pried at her shirt sleeve and she removed the box cutter from its magnetic clip. Holding the cutters between two fingers she deftly sliced away at the ever–tightening twine. She knew she would have one and only one shot. She needed to make it count.

"Arnaud, when I get out of here and you know I will, the first thing I will do is wash away the stench from your breath and then I'll come back to find you."

Arnaud was bent forward and his hands rested on his thighs. He looked at his comrade. "Brock, step outside for a minute. There're a few things I would like to settle with my old friend here first and I'd like to do that in private."

"But, I think I should. . . "

"No! I want her all to myself for a few minutes." Brock turned and walked toward the door.

"Oh Alex. . . Alex. . . Alex." Arnaud's sinister laugh roared and then he turned and shot a combative stare at Alex. "You're making it even easier than I thought it would be to watch you suffer. There was a time when I thought maybe I couldn't do this, maybe I couldn't watch as cold blood oozed from your veins. No more, bitch. When I look at you now, I'm reminded of the piece of shit that you've always been."

The twine dug deeper into Alex's neck. "Come closer so I can spit in your face again."

Arnaud bent at the waist and thrust his face into Alex, teeth flashing. She winced from his foul breath.

Alex's left hand swung around from behind the chair and her open–palm struck below his chin. The force jolted him upright. Alex re–cocked her arm, released it and connected a hard–hitting fist blow to Arnaud's lower diaphragm. Air gushed from his lungs and he collapsed to the floor.

Alex reached behind her and yanked the box–cutter from the chair's wooden leg where she had stuck it after she sliced through the twine. She cut the rope from her other wrist, ankles and her neck and in seconds she was peering down at Arnaud. She planted one swift kick to his rib cage. I owe you more than that, she thought, but I'm short of time right now.

Brock was reaching for the door handle when he heard Arnaud crash to floor. He turned and rushed at Alex only to have a roundhouse kick land squarely in his chest. His feet left the ground and he crashed spread–eagled against the wall behind him. A well placed knee to the groin and he buckled forward, landing headfirst on the floor.

The hallway door burst open and Alex spun around ready to deliver the next set of blows. "Jesus!" Phil stood in the doorway, owl–eyed.

"Phil! Hurry! Close the door." Alex opened her backpack, pulled out a roll of duct tape and tossed it to Phil. "Let's wrap them up. I'm sure we don't have much time."

Phil reached out and snatched the tape. "Did you find out anything about Ben? Is he here?"

Alex shook her head and grabbed her headset off the floor. "He *is* here. . . definitely."

She adjusted her headset. "Devon. What's going on out there?"

"The hallway's all clear. You guys alright?"

"I was waylaid a bit, but every thing's fine now. I'm going to continue down the hall and Phil, you stay here. I think Ben's in one of these hallway rooms."

Phil turned and looked at Alex. "No! I'm going to be right along side you from here on out. There is no. . . "

Alex's hand covered Phil's mouth. "This is one of those times I told you about, Phil. You stay here and make sure these riffraff stay put. The moment I find Ben I'll let you know."

Phil straightened his arm and gripped Alex's shoulder. He looked down at Arnaud and then back to Alex. "And this is one of those times where I'm going to do exactly what I think is best. These assholes aren't going anywhere." Phil lodged a sharp heel–kick of his own to Arnaud's ribs. "Now, let's go get Ben and get the hell out of here."

Alex bit her lower lip and mockingly raised her arms karate style and Phil's arm reeled in a circle. She grabbed his wrist. "Okay. . . okay. Let's finish tying these guys up and then we are out of here."

Arnaud laid face down and spread–eagled on the table with each limb tightly taped to a table leg. They stuffed his mouth with his sock and taped it shut. He was unconscious and his brick wall persona had crumbled, but Alex took one more swipe at him. The butt of his own pistol hit him squarely in the back of his head. "One more for good measure."

When they finished tying Brock to the legs of the table, Alex took a deep breath. "Now, let's go."

Out in the hallway, Alex and Phil split up. Phil took the right side and Alex the left and one by one they opened the hallway doors. Nothing. Each room was empty.

They reached the large room at the end of the hall and they saw four men outside huddled around the loading dock. They crouched down, sidled over and crouched down behind a row of metal drums.

Keeping a close watch on the men outside, Alex panned the room. A chill ran through her spine. The wall to her right was blanketed with posters, plaques, journals, clothing, and pamphlets: all painstakingly preserved Nazi propaganda and artifacts used during World War II. The first and last place she had seen that much Nazi memorabilia had been in Austria at the Heeresgeschichtliches Museum in Vienna. That had made a huge impact on her at the time on how she viewed the Nazi invasion throughout Europe. The collection in this room was comparable to what she had seen in Austria. Nothing like this was thought to exist outside of museums and many of those collections were highly controversial.

Phil stage whispered, "Jesus, this looks like some kind of war museum."

Alex squinted in disbelief when she saw an airtight glass case hanging on the near end of the wall. *A Portrait of a Young Man,* by Raphael was one of the more well–known works of art that had been plundered by the Nazis and it had by most accounts been destroyed. The oil painting on panel had been stolen from the Czartoryski Muzeum in Krakow and had been one of over 13,000 works of art and cultural artifacts ransacked from Poland alone. Recent rumors had surfaced that the famous painting had been securely sealed away in a bank vault in Singapore; however no pictures had ever been produced to authenticate those rumors.

Alex spoke quietly, "That painting is priceless. Almost everyone believes it was destroyed. What the hell is it doing here?"

It was not just in Austria and Poland where mass looting had taken place, but also in many European countries conquered by the Nazis. Over subsequent years, Holland, Luxembourg, Belgium, France and Italy, among others, had been occupied by enemy forces and stripped of cultural artifacts. Many had been recovered, but most were still missing. Hitler during that timeframe had a personal collection of over 5,000 pieces of art and because *A Portrait of a Young*

*Man* had not been part of his collection, scholars had concluded it had been destroyed.

Alex felt a knot tighten in her stomach. Her skin crawled with anticipation. She looked around the room and nudged Phil with her elbow. She cocked her head in the direction of a small office at the far corner and whispered, "I'm guessing that's where we'll find Ben. Let's get rid of these guys first."

Phil nodded.

"Devon, ignite the C4 by the chopper. As soon as it blows, Phil and I are going into the small office in the corner and if I'm right, we'll be running out of there with Ben in a matter of minutes. If you see anyone come back in here, then blow the loading dock area and that should give us enough time."

"Ohhh yeah—hang tight guys."

"Stay down Phil. We're going to feel this one."

Seconds later, the force from the blast knocked the four men down and the row of metal containers near the loading dock rolled through the room. The men picked themselves up, jumped from the dock and headed in the direction of the chopper. "Let's go!" Alex commanded.

They ran straight toward the office and burst through the door. Conscious and semi–awake, Ben sat in a chair with his legs tightly bound and his shoulders bowed from the weight of his misery. When he saw Alex cutting the rope he lifted his head slightly and rolled his eyes. Alex pulled a small vile of smelling salts from her pocket, snapped it open and held it under Ben's nose. One whiff and he straightened up. "Phil!. . . "

"Shhh." Alex's hand covered Ben's mouth. "Don't say anything. Nod if you're okay and you can walk."

Ben nodded once and started to stand. His legs wobbled and Phil grabbed him from behind and helped him up. He had lost a great deal of weight and his chiseled features looked gaunt and tired. His thick shoulders sagged and his arms dangled listlessly at his sides.

"Let's put this on you and then you go with Phil and you two will follow me."

"What's going on?" Benjamin's eyes were glazed and hollow. He looked at Alex and raised an eyebrow. "Who are you?" He took a step toward Phil and held his palms up. "Phil, how'd you get here? What the hell's happening?" His voice sounded like a strangled whisper.

Alex shot a bewildered look at Phil and he held up a hand. "Ben, are you okay? You don't remember Alex?"

Benjamin shook his head and said, "There's a lot I don't remember, Phil. I know I don't like what's going on here, but I'm not really sure how I got here. How did you get here? How'd you find me?"

Alex stood aside and watched. A cold shiver stung her as she realized the man she loved looked right through her without a flicker of recognition. She had rehearsed this very scene in her mind, over and over. The moment when she would first find Benjamin and know that he was unharmed. Oh no—*oh god, no.*

She tried to speak, but the knot in her throat left her close–mouthed.

Phil saw the naked pain on Alex's face and took charge. "We don't have much time, Ben. We're going to get you the hell out of here. You'll remember Alex, I'm sure of it. In the meantime, I'll stick with you and we'll follow her." Phil nodded in Alex's direction and continued, "Once we get out of the building we'll get you far away from here." He gripped Benjamin's shoulders and gave him a crisp shake. "Trust me buddy. You're going home."

They put a flack jacket on Ben and zipped up the front. He was still wobbly, but standing on his own now. His bewildered look had been replaced by awe and a pinch of optimism.

Alex looked at Benjamin and her heart skipped a beat. She squeezed her hands together and willed the strength in her core to return. Stay focused, she thought, he will be fine. I just need to get him out of here.

Feeling her resolve return she peered outside the office. "What do you see Devon?"

"Six men are out by where the chopper used to be. Smithereens, that's what the chopper is. I don't see anyone else."

"That's probably the four men who were in here and the two security guys we saw outside. There are at least four others; the two guys I saw earlier and Arnaud and the guy with him. We're going to make a run for it now the same way we came in. Keep me posted."

Alex turned and grabbed Phil's arm. "He's all yours now. Just follow close behind me."

She looked at Ben and smiled. "You're going to be okay. It will take us about fifteen minutes to reach the point where we will be safe. Can you make it that far?"

"I'm sore and feel dizzy, but yeah, I can make it."

Her eyes and thoughts lingered on Benjamin. "You will be all right. Nothing can go wrong now."

Alex removed another C4 from her belt pouch, looped the detonating cord and attached a remote detonator. She slid the cartridge into the corner and alerted Devon that she had planted another explosive.

"Let's go!" She was out the door with Phil and Ben trailing behind.

"Both of you stay here and keep an eye out. I'll be right back." Minutes later, Alex returned with the Raphael painting neatly rolled up and tucked under her arm.

Edging through the hallway they reached the "T" when a door opened behind them. Alex spun around and froze in mid–step. She was staring down the barrels of three P38 pistols. Behind the men, still grimacing in pain, stood a hunched over Brock.

"Don't go making any sudden movements. I think you know that nothing would give me more pleasure than pulling this trigger."

Alex felt the dark beads of Arnaud's eyes laser into her skin. She raised her hands above her shoulders. Arnaud aimed his pistol at Alex's forehead and the other two men pushed Phil and Ben back against the wall. "You are about to make another big mistake, Arnaud, and it may very well be your last one. Just let us go and none of you will be hurt."

"Shut up!" His blunt, gravelly voice was laced with hatred. "I think it's you who's made the last mistake this time. Now, keep your hands up and let's go back into this room so I can finish what I had in store for you. Your friends here will get to watch the once great Alexandra Boudreau *squeeeeeal* like a pig." Arnaud waved his pistol at the door. As Alex walked, she felt the man's eyes, sharp as daggers, against her back.

Inside the room Arnaud watched as his two cohorts prodded and pushed their captives to the far wall where they were ordered to sit, or else.

"There's no reason for any of this. I know you guys aren't responsible for anything that's gone on here so why don't you just forget that we were here and let us go."

Arnaud cocked a leg and his left foot struck Benjamin in his jaw. "Shut up! Now that you guys are involved with this bitch you won't be going anywhere either. As soon as I'm done with her I'll take care of you two."

Brock moved forward. "Let me have a shot at her, Arnaud. I owe her big–time."

Arnaud ignored Brock and looked over at Alex. He screamed, "Now get up and walk over to that table! I've wasted enough time with all this!" His words were delivered in increasing decibels climaxing with a loud, "*Now!*"

Alex knew she probably stood a better chance of surviving the shock treatment than battling Arnaud one–on–one. He was built like a bulldozer and his vise–like hands could crush her skull as easily as an over–ripe melon. She glanced at Phil and Benjamin. She couldn't tell if they were up for this, but she hoped they would respond with just the right moves when needed. Alex put on her best smirk. "Let's get on with it, Arnaud. You're not losing that boneless spine of yours again, are you?" Alex pushed herself up from the floor.

Arnaud's haunting laughter morphed into a treacherous glare. He stepped forward and jabbed his gun barrel in Alex's temple. "Maybe I should just blow that bloated head of yours off your pretty shoulders."

"And deny yourself the pleasure of watching me suffer? I have never taken you for one to be so kind hearted."

Arnaud grimaced and leaned forward. Alex's head snapped back from his rancid morning breath and he continued, "I think you're right." He spat in Alex's face and retreated a couple steps. "Move it!" He brandished his pistol in the direction of the table.

"With pleasure." Alex moved to the table and turned around. Facing Arnaud, she held out her hands and said, "Hook me up. Let's see what you have."

Arnaud's feet pounded the floor and in no time he was holding the side of the table. "Lie down."

Alex lay prone on the table and placed her hands over her chest.

Arnaud gave Alex a half–wink and then reached across her and grabbed the leather strap on the side. Alex reacted. With her knuckles half folded, her left hand shot up and caught Arnaud square in the larynx just as her right fingertips struck him in his right eye. Arnaud reeled back and Alex vaulted off the table. She grabbed his pistol from his left hand, fell to her knees and fired two shots, hitting each man in his right wrist. "Grab their guns!"

Phil and Ben were stunned and visibly shaken, but they leaned over and picked up the two guns.

"Hit the floor, Brock—now!" Brock fell to the floor.

"They'll be okay. It's just a flesh wound, but let's get moving. I don't know if anyone heard the shots, but I'm going to assume they did." Alex put on her headset and adjusted the microphone. "Devon, what's going on out there?"

"Jesus, Alex, you're giving me a heart attack. Were those gun shots I heard? Can you guys hurry up?"

"We're on our way. Where are the other six guys?"

"Three of them just headed back inside. They probably heard the shots. Move it."

"Ignite the C4 in the office. We're headed your way."

Alex looked at Arnaud and knew he wasn't going anywhere soon. They bound all four with the remaining duct tape and quickly wound their way through the corridors and emerged outside within minutes.

Fifty more yards and they'd be safe.

# CHAPTER 13

J aspar's voice cackled over the intercom, "We'll be landing in about 30 minutes Mr. Price. Is there anything further you need before we start our landing preparations?"

Alan closed his brown folder and tapped it several times on the table. "Thanks, Jaspar." He looked down at his watch. "I didn't know we've been in the air so long. No. I'm fine. How long will we be on the ground?"

"30 minutes to refuel and to load a few more supplies. We can stay longer if you want though."

"Nope the sooner we're off the better."

A corner office at any company was a sure sign that the executive who occupied that office had paid his dues and had been recognized by the higher–ups. Jim Dreyfous had earned his plush surroundings at the bank and the floor to ceiling glass panels allowed him to keep a close watch on his tight–knit trading posse.

He had completed his morning ritual of staff meetings with his traders and had reviewed last quarter's trading margins. Casual Friday's were a tradition at Currillion Bank, but not for Jim. He was attired in a Brooks Brothers Seersucker suit, white button down oxford shirt and a red tie with narrow white stripes. He looked every bit like a bank executive in this island financial hideaway.

"Anything else, Megan?"

"I didn't want to bring this up in the staff meeting, but I think you should take a look at this." Megan slid a bright blue folder across the desk. "These look like some pretty aggressive trades to me and there's no way they'll be executed unless the market plummets—and I mean plummets like we've never seen before."

Jim reached for the folder, opened it and thumbed through the pages. He shook his head. "I've wondered about this account. The guy has had a lot of money parked here for a few years and he's only made one small trade in all that time." He placed the folder down in the center of his desk. "What's your take here, Megan?"

Megan Holman was Jim's Chief Trader and she was credentialed and very good. Summa Cum Laude at Bucknell University, Yale MBA and she had worked her way to the top of Merrill Lynch's equity trading department. The two had worked well together since Megan came on board two years ago. "There are 32 trades listed here and each one has a good–until–cancelled limit order at a specific price and the very next day they all have sell orders at the market price. $1.368 billion is being traded for a single day. I've never seen anything like this before."

Megan pointed to a page. "Here's SAP AG ADS, a German company and this account has an order to purchase 500,000 shares at $18." She looked at Jim. "That's around one–third of the stock's average daily trading volume and the stock closed yesterday at $71. Jim, each of these transactions follows the same pattern, buy at a ridiculously low price and sell it the next day. What do you think is behind this? It can't be real."

Jim pinched his tie knot and raised a brow. "Very strange. . . to say the least. I'll tell you though, I've seen some trades we've made over the years that make no sense from an investment point of view, but one of the reasons investors have their money with us is to protect their privacy. Unless we believe they are laundering money, then we go ahead and make the trades the client requests."

"What do you know about the Stiffleman account? Do you have any reason to believe the account is being used to launder money in any way?"

"It doesn't fit the pattern of a laundered account. We've had the funds for nearly two years with no activity. Oh, there has been some money wired–out, but very little for an account this size. Most of the money laundering accounts acquire their funds from a number of different sources, they park the money somewhere for a brief period of time and then it's gone. All of the money in the Stiffleman account came from one source so I don't see the need to raise any flags here." Jim leaned forward and planted his elbows on his desk. "We're a bank that protects peoples' privacy, so as long as we have no reason to suspect any illegal activity, we do as we're instructed. Feel free to look closer at this if you want, but I think we're okay."

Megan closed the file and stood up. "Okay. . . okay, I'll make the trades if by some miracle we can execute them at these prices." She walked to the door and turned back to Jim. "You know if we actually do execute any of these orders at these prices, it means my own portfolio has just gone into the toilet. I hope this guy is wrong for my own sake."

"Me too, Megan, and thanks for bringing this to my attention."

# CHAPTER 14

Alex opened her eyes as the sun woke the sleeping night and a melodic chorus began to stir outside. The symphonic caws of the Emerald Cuckoos eclipsed the soft warbles of the Brown Eared Bulbuls. High–pitched hacking sounds from the troops of Diana Monkeys filtered through the canopy of rustling Raffia palms and she heard the ocean waves lap against the powdery white sands. She jumped out of bed and threw on her two–day old clothes. She had to get to Benjamin.

Last night when the Sikorsky chopper had taken off and they had all looked back and had seen the mass of flames in the distance a sense of relief had fallen over everyone. Alex had noticed for the first time that Phil had been relaxed and his dripping sarcasm had returned. Benjamin had given Alex a half–smile just before his head had leaned back and his eyes had closed. There had been no need for words at that point. They had all been exhausted and exhilarated from a long, long ordeal. The only sound during the three hour flight to Monrovia had been the whirling hum of chopper blades. After a one–hour car ride south of Monrovia, they each crawled into down feather beds in secluded and inviting bungalows along Liberia's North Atlantic coast.

When the three had exited the plant, Phil had Benjamin's arm draped over his shoulder after dragging his wobbling friend down the last section of hallway. With the chopper destroyed they had lost the only camera that Devon had been able to use to scan the north area outside the plant. Crossing that last open stretch would have taken too much time and left them all vulnerable to rapid firing assault rifles. Alex had sent Phil and Ben ahead and she had stayed back to provide their cover. Phil had struggled with the size and weight of Benjamin and his pace had slowed to a half–step shuffle. As the two neared the end of the clearing Alex had seen three men round the corner. Before they had raised their rifles, she had yanked a stun grenade from its pouch, pulled the pin and hurled it. It had landed ten feet in front of the men, rolled in a small quarter circle and exploded—the loud "bang" and blinding flash of more than one million candela had hit the three men with immediate flash blindness, deafness, tinnitus, and inner ear disturbances. For extra measure, she had tossed another stun grenade behind them and then she had bolted across the clearing.

Benjamin opened the door, stood to the side and nodded. He had obviously risen before Alex as he stood clean shaven, his wavy brown hair still damp, but neatly combed back. Alex didn't notice that he was also wearing the same clothes; her eyes and thoughts were transfixed on Benjamin. "Good morning. May I come in?"

He waved a hand. "Certainly."

Alex walked into the room and was instantly flooded with memories of Benjamin; wrapped in his arms and sobbing uncontrollably at Point Reyes, swimming stroke for stroke in the icy bay waters, that night he had introduced her to the eagle and had shared his soul and that moonlit night in his room when she had given her soul to him. She reached the middle of the room and turned, facing Benjamin.

"Wait, please." Benjamin closed the door and walked over to Alex. "I still don't know who you are, but whoever you are you risked your life to get me out of that place. I was beginning to think I might not ever get out of there. For that I thank you, very. . . very much."

Alex smiled. A warm tropical breeze wafted through the open windows and filled the room with smells of ripe cocoa plants and African mangos. She stood an arm's length away from the man she loved, but it felt like they were standing on opposite shores of the Atlantic Ocean. She wanted to throw her arms around him and embrace his warmth, his strength and soak in his compassion. Somehow, standing there admiring this man, she knew he would be okay. He had to be. "There is no need to thank me, Ben. I have so much to say to you that I hardly know where to start. Maybe the best place is to find out what has happened to you. You remember Phil, so your memory is not all blocked. What do you remember, exactly?"

Benjamin shrugged his shoulders and pointed to the seating area near the open shutters. "Let's sit down over there and I'll tell you what I do remember, which I'm afraid isn't very much."

Seated on wicker chairs, Benjamin stretched his legs. "There's a gap in my memory and I've tried everything to piece things together with no luck. I remember arriving in Paris and getting into a limousine and the next thing I remember I'm on a private jet being told I'm on my way to Africa. Everything in between is a blur—more like a blank really."

"You were on your way to Paris to meet me. We had spoken earlier that morning. Do you remember that?"

"No. I'm afraid not. I remember the flight to Paris, but I don't remember why I was going there. I've tried to figure that out, but like I said, it's a blank."

Alex placed one hand over the other on the edge of the table and leaned forward. "We fell in love, Ben." She let the words hang and watched a quizzical look spread across Benjamin's face. "Neither one of us expected to fall in love, but it happened. You've been missing for 12 days and I've thought about you every moment of every one of those days. There are so many. . . "

Their heads turned at the sound of the loud drum roll wrapping on the door.

Alex laughed. "Guess who?"

Benjamin smiled. "Yep. . . I definitely remember that." He sat up and his sleep strained voice cackled, "Just a sec, Phil. Be right there."

Benjamin opened the door and was greeted with a bear hug and Phil's contagious smile. "Good to see ya! God, I can't believe you're finally safe!" He pointed to Alex, "You have her to thank, you know?"

"I know. She's just started to fill me in on things." He threw his hands up. "Part of my memory's totally shot. It's pretty strange."

Phil darted over to the opened white wood shutters that framed the picturesque view of the Atlantic Ocean just steps from the room. "Boy, you sure rate, Ben. I have an unobstructed view of the trash dumpster."

Alex chuckled. "Well next time you make the travel arrangements and you can have your pick of the rooms."

Phil turned around. "Hey, you guys won't believe this. "Your TV's not on, but BBC just reported that there was an explosion in the Koidu region of Sierra Leone. They had some overhead camera shots taken this morning and the whole place was leveled. Nothing left but ashes."

Alex knew there would be nothing left of the Koidu plant. Just after they were safely away, she had taken the remote detonator from Devon and hit the button that activated the detonator cap to the

C4 explosive she had placed in the ANFO magazine. The explosion had lit up the sky for miles and she had been certain it would receive the attention she had wanted it to receive. To those at Sterling, or whoever was behind all this, her message had been clear—*we know who you are and we're coming after you*!

Alex tilted her head. "Did they say anything about what happened or what the facility was used for?"

"Nah, just that it wasn't known who owned the plant or what it was used for. Anyway, the whole thing was blown to bits, so what do you say we do a little celebrating?"

Benjamin's smile faded. He walked over to the writing desk in the corner and bent forward. His arms steadied him, his back arched.

"What is it?" Alex placed her hand on his shoulder. "I'm sorry, Ben. Maybe I'm being a bit forward. I know we have so much to discuss. So much has happened. I am sorry. What would you like to do?"

Phil stood with his hands tucked in his front pockets. "I'll leave you guys alone." He turned and walked toward the door.

"Wait! I want you to stay. You've risked your life helping me and I want you to hear what I have to stay."

Alex cringed.

Benjamin stood and faced the two people who had saved him and risked their own lives along the way.

Benjamin raised his arms and locked his fingers below his chin. His head was cradled on his thumbs. "Those guys had developed some sort of a virus and they were using the facility in Sierra Leone to test and develop it. I don't know much about the details of the virus, but I do know that it's deadly. There are no cures, no way to fight it and they have the means to spread the virus within specific populations."

He lifted his head and spread his fingers. "I have the virus. They injected me. I don't think I can really go anywhere."

Phil gasped, "Jesus! Those sons–of–bitches!"

Alex looked shell–shocked. Her eyes narrowed. "Does the virus have a name? Is it G–16?"

"Yeah. How do you know that?"

"Oh, Ben, please believe me when I say I never thought you would be harmed in all of this—never. This is my fault." Alex looked at Benjamin and saw his confused look. "Please, Ben let me say a few things about what has happened. It may clear up some of the confusion for you, but it will surely anger you as well."

"Wait!" Phil walked over and placed an arm around Benjamin. "Alex and you have a real bond, Ben. You're not going to like what she is about to say, but I know that she can fix things. She can help you, so hear her out, please."

Benjamin leaned back against the table, clasped his hands and took a deep breath. His grief was so close to the surface that Alex felt she could reach out and touch it.

Alex's thoughts darted about and she was uncertain where to begin. She needed to tell Ben everything, but had thought it would be best to do it gradually, over time, when he could absorb what had happened. Now that they had injected the virus into him she needed to act quickly. He was in more danger now than before and time was not on their side. Once again, she found herself needing to tell Benjamin the truth, the painful truth; even though she knew it may end any chance of a future with this man.

Alex faced Benjamin and swallowed hard. "When I came to America and I met you it was with the specific purpose of stealing certain research files from GEN's data base. The research files I stole from GEN also had other files attached that were encrypted. I had someone decrypt those files and they contained all of the research data on the development of the G–16 virus. That virus is deadly, you are right about that. But, the virus they have implanted in you is most likely dormant. I am fairly certain of that. They need to activate it with an activating agent or a promoter switch. Phil and I found out who was behind the creation of that virus and everyone was arrested and is still being held in custody. I don't see how this could have happened to you."

Benjamin's arms dropped to the table and steadied him. His legs shook and his face was drawn. "What's happened to GEN?" What research did you steal?" He looked at Phil. "You know about all this?"

"Ben, there's no way we're going to be explain all this to you in a way that will make sense. Not now, anyway. Hell, we expected to get you out of that place and all head back to Marin. You've thrown us as real curve with this virus." Phil narrowed his eyes and continued, "One thing I'm certain of without a doubt is that Alex is the one person who can help with this. She's damn smart and if anyone can figure out how to help you now, it's her. Listen to her."

The only sound in the room was the whirring of the overhead palm thatched fan. Finally, Phil asked, "Ben, tell us what happened at the Koidu plant. Is that where you were injected with this thing?"

Benjamin's head remained bowed and his tone was barely audible, "They had a complete lab set up in the place where they held me. I think they were making the virus there, but I don't know for sure. That's where they injected me and they said if I tried to escape all they had to do was hit a switch and within days I would be dead. They showed me a video clip where they injected the same virus in monkeys and it was horrible. The monkeys melted—*they really melted*—all within a matter of days." His voice tailed off.

Phil made eye contact with Alex. "Alex, who was the guy that had disappeared? You told me that someone was missing."

Alex's arms were folded tightly across her chest. She pivoted and walked back to the bed; pivoted again and returned to Ben. "Sterling Defense Application Systems handled all the security for a containment lab in Brazil where this virus was first developed. They were never linked directly to the group doing the research, if I remember correctly. They did, or maybe still do, own the plant that we blew up yesterday though, so I guess they are involved—very involved. I could see where they would have an interest in owning something like this. They could sell it to the highest bidder and I imagine they would get a fortune for it."

"I think it best that you two spend some time together. I'm going to order us some coffee and breakfast; we have a lot to do here." The door closed behind Alex.

Benjamin's hands were tucked in his back pockets and his chin pointed skyward. His brown wavy hair fluttered in the warm tropical breeze. "I don't know, Phil. . . I . . . I just don't know. I'm married for Christ's sake. I remember bits and pieces of my conversion with Constance, but I don't remember anything about a divorce. Are you sure?"

"Yep."

"I thought she was going to come out to. . . " He stopped and turned toward Phil and shook his head. "This is absolute craziness, buddy. None of this makes sense, no sense at all. I have a hard time believing I asked Constance for a divorce. You know my beliefs about marriage. I don't think I would've just ended it like that."

Phil sat in the sand and leaned back against a palm tree. He picked at a loose strand from his cut–off jeans. "Oh I know exactly how you feel about marriage we've talked about it more times than I wanted to. Look I didn't know you when you married Constance, but I'm certain you loved her then and I'm certain you still love her. But it's a whole different kind of love now. The times you talked to me about Alex and even after you knew what she had done to you, you had this gleam in your eyes—there was a giddy– up in your step. I never saw you like that with Constance—never."

"I don't know about the giddy– up part. . . I don't remember." He stood on one foot and etched half–circles in the sand with the other. "I think Constance and I drifted apart pretty early on. She didn't want kids and I did. She wanted a powerful career and I wanted a big happy family living happily ever after on the ranch. It's worked itself out though, somehow. I'm happy with my life; I've carved out a good situation." He looked at Phil. "Look how much time we get to spend with each other!"

"Bullshit, you're not all that happy. Yeah, you have a great life, but you're the kind of guy that wants to share it with someone— someone special. That just ain't ahappnin' the way I see it."

Benjamin rubbed his forehead and waded knee deep into the surf. "Damn I hate it when you make so much sense. You know that?" He cupped his hands, reached down and scooped a handful of water into the air. "We don't have anything in common really. I thought we did, but we never spent enough time together to find out that we both want different things. I do love Constance, but it's. . . you know, maybe more like a sister, a friend from college, maybe. Hell I don't know, but divorce? My mom stayed with my dad and never divorced him even though she'd have been better off. I have her stubbornness I guess."

Phil grabbed a handful of sand and watched it sift through his fingers. "You know what this reminds me of? You and Constance, I mean. Marriage in most cultures is different than we know it. Look at the ancient Kombai Tribe in Western New Guinea. In that tribe, when a man and woman married there was never any talk about passion, love, honor, nurturing or any of that stuff that always finds its way into today's wedding vows. Passion back then was nothing more than a primal sexual instinct. The Tribal Council was all men and they made laws directed at women. Men didn't have any laws—they weren't restricted. Marriages were arranged by the Tribal Council, but the men were still free to act on their instincts with any woman in the tribe. Marriage was nothing more than a division of work with the women ordered to carry out the bulk of it. It was rare, but there were cases where a couple that were thrown together did develop a relationship more akin to today's marriages. They took care of each other, respected each other and worked together. I don't know if they were any happier, but I suspect they were."

Phil looked up at Benjamin and wagged a finger. "And that my friend is you. You're the type of guy who wants one woman and a relationship where you both operate on the same plane."

Benjamin listened soulfully to Phil's words, as he always did. Phil was one of the foremost authorities on ancient tribal cultures in New Guinea and he had published stacks of journal articles addressing the development of tribal customs in that region. Phil had never been married. When he had been a professor at UC Berkeley, he had buried himself in his work, oftentimes spending months by himself in the isolated areas of that island country. Benjamin had always been fascinated by Phil's endless stories of tribal cultures, cannibalism and tribal punishment and on many occasions the two had stayed up until the early morning hours debating the virtues of the ancient ways of life compared to today's fast–paced grab it while you can mentality. To some, Phil's isolated lifestyle and his eccentric approach to societal mores had been a reflection of his own sexist convictions. Benjamin knew better. To him, Phil's heart and mind were a union of equality, adoration and reverence for all women—all mankind.

Benjamin waded out of the water and back to his friend. His thumbs were looped around his belt and he peered down at Phil. "Well said, Professor Morgan. . . well said."

Phil looked up. "I can go on."

"No doubt."

The two friends looked at each other, fumbling for the right words to make sense of Benjamin's quandary— Constance. . . Alex. . . memory loss. . . virus. . . GEN.

"I really boarded a plane and flew off to Paris to see Alex? I was in love with her? It doesn't make any sense. . . it doesn't sound like me."

"It's all one hundred percent true—every bit of it. I tried to stop you from flying off to Paris. At first, it seemed like a harebrained idea to me, but you were all set to take the plunge. There was nothing I could do, but support you."

Phil dug one foot in the sand and kicked a load at Benjamin. "It's like the time you decided you were going to swim the length of Lake Tahoe. Remember that? I thought it was cool. I really did, but noooo you have to do it at night. . . by yourself. . . pulling some stupid board behind you with all your fuel and stuff. I told you I thought you were crazy. Hell, everybody thought you were nuts, but you went ahead and did it anyway. It was no different when you said you were off to Paris. You're mind was made up—not a thing I could've done about it."

"Oh, that was different. Well, maybe not, but. . . " Benjamin turned, his tone weakened, "How could I have been such an idiot, Phil? She's really destroyed GEN? And I let her?"

"You know, I don't think Alex is the one to blame about GEN." Phil jumped up and walked over to Benjamin. He stood a few inches taller than Benjamin and his sun bleached curly blond hair was in need of a solid trim. Phil was not the type to dwell on his appearance, he never had been. In fact he had always gone a step or two out of his way to confront what he perceived to be modern society's archaic rules that defined the socioeconomic classes by some ill–conceived dress code. On one occasion he had met Benjamin for an early dinner at a tony and pricey Mill Valley restaurant wearing his standard attire of ratty tennis shoes, no socks, stained khaki pants and one of the two or three faded sweatshirts he had owned. When he had arrived, Benjamin shook his head, but sported a half–moon grin. He had ordered two dinners to go from the Maître'd and the two friends had dined al fresco at a nearby community park. Benjamin had nothing but respect for Phil and the one thing he had always counted on was Phil pulling no punches when it came to the telling it like it really was.

"My dad had a saying when I was a kid. He had lots of saying, but I remember this one for some reason. He said the only way to find out if you can trust somebody is to trust them. Seems simple enough, but I don't think it really did him much good. Anyway, when I first met Alex, I never turned my back on her after what she had done to you. But I'll tell ya, after watching what she did to find you, well, that all changed pretty damn quickly. I trust her now. . . completely. You need to do the same, my friend."

Benjamin sucked in his lower lip and bit down. One eyelid was half shut and the other brow was raised. "Hmm. . . "

Phil swung an arm around Benjamin and pointed in the direction of a path that led toward a mango grove. "Let's walk." After several minutes, Phil slid his arm around Benjamin's neck and tightened his grip. "You look like shit. Didn't they feed you anything back there?

What are you down? Maybe ten, fifteen pounds? We gotta fatten you up, bud."

"I could still take you on, anytime." His clinched fist stopped inches from Phil's stomach. "See—you're as slow as ever."

# CHAPTER 15

They sat under a thatched–roof veranda near the beach and shared a meal of collard greens over rice, fried plantains and the Liberian national dish, goat soup. The air was ripe with a rich tapestry of fragrances—the smell of papaya and mango trees wafted through the manicured grounds.

Benjamin was off somewhere in another world. He picked at his food and stared out at the ocean. Phil had spent several hours with him re–telling the horrors of the past few weeks. Benjamin had been totally and completely devastated by what he had heard. He had devoted his time, money and resources to his company, Genetic Engineering Nexus, and for him to hear that the ground–breaking research that had led to a cure for cystic fibrosis had been stolen was numbing. His mentor and friend, and GEN's CEO, Murray Paulson, had been arrested and had been part of the core group that had developed the G–16 virus. Benjamin had thought of Murray like a father and the crushing news of his involvement had shattered him. Embedded in the cystic fibrosis research that Alex had stolen were the complete research files and the roadmap to create the G–16 virus. Benjamin had no recollection of any of those events and now he had to put his life, at least what remained of it, in the hands of the woman who had devastated his company and his life. He had been in love with her? She had deceived him and used him to steal GEN's research? How could he have been so naïve? He had told Phil he would go along with his pleas that he should trust Alex, but he was leery of her and he would proceed, very cautiously.

The working lunch was wrapping up and Phil pushed his chair back. He downed the last of his coffee. "I still think there's no issue here. The entire plant was blown up. Anything that was there is gone—kaput." He looked over at Alex. "That includes the so called promoter switch that you talk about."

"I probably agree with you, Phil, but somehow I don't feel comfortable walking around with a time bomb planted inside of me."

Devon leaned back and clasped his hands behind his head. "Give me a shot at Sterling's computer system. I can get in and search around. There's gotta be something there."

"Anybody know where they're located?" Phil asked.

"I looked that up. They're headquartered in Reston, Virginia, but they have offices all over the world. It doesn't matter though; I can be anywhere and hack into their system. No problem. Let me at 'em."

Phil turned to Alex. "This is the longest you've gone without saying a word. What gives?"

Alex's thoughts were far away. She was piecing together snippets of information that she had learned about the virus and who might be behind all of this now. When Alex had first suspected she had the research data on the virus she sought the help of an old classmate from her grad school days at the University of Paris. Dr. Charles Diderot had worked tirelessly to decrypt the files and decipher the research. The results he had presented to her had stopped her in her tracks. She had never before run across anything so hideous, so vile.

The master mind behind the creation of this synthetic virus had been Dr. Paul Brewster, the rogue director of the Defense Advanced Research Projects Agency, known as DARPA. DARPA served as the research arm for the U.S. Department of Defense and it had a project to design and develop a method to insert electronic circuit probes into insects to create insect cyborgs that could demonstrate controlled flight. The insects could be used in a variety of military and homeland security applications. The contrived perception of that program had been artfully created by Dr. Brewster and he had cleverly pushed through a grant to fund that project and he made sure it had been awarded to a long time friend who ran a company called MIS Holdings.

The reality of that project had been quite different. MIS Holdings had been awarded a $52.5 million grant to manage the project and monitor the results. What MIS Holdings had covertly developed was the creation of a new, synthetic virus containing selected genes that could be turned on and off at will. Insects were to be used as the vector for delivering that virus. The insect would be implanted with a circuit board that was just 8 x 7 mm, with a total weight of 500mg and a battery capacity of 16mAh. Once inserted into the human system by a mosquito, the new synthetic viral genes would make it possible to create tamper–proof cells. This would remove the randomness of evolutionary advancement and give birth to genetically engineered, living, breathing human beings.

The virus could search out an exact DNA pattern which made up a specific race of people. The virus could be altered by its manufacturer to seek out *any* specified race. All other humans would be immune from this virus. The virus, aptly named the G–16 Virus, because there are 16 separate genes which determine one's race, could literally wipe out whole populations within a matter of a few weeks.

Once the virus was activated, the victim's capillaries would clog with dead blood cells, the skin would begin to bruise, blister and then dissolve much like wet paper. The blood would flow freely from the eyes, ears and nose and the victim would begin to vomit the black sludge of his internal tissues. Death would usually occur within five days, at the most.

This was the same virus that had been injected into Benjamin. If that virus were somehow activated, Benjamin would suffer the same excruciating death that the three human test subjects experienced when the virus had first been tested.

"Alex. . . Alex? Are you okay?" Phil reached over and placed a protective hand on her shoulder. "What are you thinking about?"

The far–away bewildered look vanished and Alex rocked back in her chair. "I was just going through a few things in my mind. Nothing. . . really."

Her fingers were tented and covered her mouth. She looked at Phil. "Phil, I think you're correct. Everything was blown up and there should be no evidence of the virus left at the plant. From what I saw I'm guessing the virus was stored in sealed canisters and it would not have survived the heat from the fire. That doesn't end the problem though. They can make the virus again, somewhere, and the virus that is implanted in Ben can still be activated in one of two ways. They can easily re–create the genetically coded promoter switch that they originally made. They can do that anywhere as long as they have the genetic sequence information to that specific gene. I think we have to assume they do. It's not worth assuming otherwise. Also they have an activating agent somewhere that will turn the dormant virus into a live virus the moment Ben comes in contact with it. We don't know what that activating agent is at this point, but it could be placed in almost anything; water, food, a lotion. There are lots of options."

Phil raised an eyebrow. "What do you mean by a promoter switch? It's not a TV remote or light switch that they can turn on anywhere, is it?"

"No, not like that. The synthetic gene they created has a promoter switch built into it. That switch turns the gene off and on." Alex closed her eyes and continued, "Maybe the best way to describe it is. . . you know there are certain cells that when they aren't activated cancer can raise its ugly head and begin to spread. If those cells are activated, turned on, then the cancer could go into remission. It's the same with the G–16."

Alex brushed the hair away from her face and dropped her hands to her lap. Her mind was locked on the monstrous virus and its gruesome effects. She remembered how she had felt when Charles had first told her that it had been tested on live human subjects. A shiver touched her spine. She looked at Ben. How could he be so calm? What kind of inner strength does this man have? "We can't stop and assume nothing will happen. That's just not an option here."

Phil broke the silence. "What are you suggesting? You obviously have something in mind?"

"I have some ideas, but I think we need more information before we decide to do anything."

Alex looked at Devon. "I want you to see what you can find out about a guy named Alan Price. He is the head of Sterling and when all of this broke the first time, he completely vanished. No one knew his whereabouts. He wasn't tied to anything directly, but his disappearance is sure suspicious. Find out whatever you can; his background, his habits, personal life, anything that may give us an idea of his possible involvement in this."

She looked at Ben and was about to speak when she sensed his apprehension and detachment. He looked straight at her, but the warmth and kindness that she admired was gone. His face was flush and his lips pressed tightly together. She knew at that point she had a long way to go before he would trust her or, if that time would ever come. She spoke directly, but softly, "Ben, I would like you to reconstruct everything that has happened to you. Write it all down. From the time you can first remember anything, who you spoke with, what have you observed, where have you been, what was your mode of transport, do you remember any call letters, what have you heard, do you know any names, everything. . . absolutely everything you can remember. Do not assume it isn't important—everything is important—*everything*."

"And Phil," Alex sat forward in her chair and spread her hands evenly on the table, "you should try and reconstruct everything you've been through. It would be great if we could compare notes on what happened back in Marin. There's a good chance I have forgotten some things. Think about the conversations we had after the times I spoke with Charles, the times we met with Constance and. . . "

Benjamin interrupted, "Constance!" He shook his head, "I forgot all about her. Did you talk with Constance, Alex?"

"Yes, both Phil and I did and she ended up being very helpful. We can talk about that later. It's not important right now." Senator Constance Hunter was Benjamin's wife and even though Alex was aware he had asked her for a divorce, she was certain now was not the right time to go into all that.

She re–focused on Phil. "Also, Phil, make a note of what you noticed when we were at the Koidu plant. I know you scoured the place with your binoculars and you were inside the facility, too. Think about it. Write it down."

The three men sat in silence, their eyes focused on Alex. Finally, Phil pushed his chair back and stood. "Well, I guess we know who's in charge here, and I'm good with that." He turned and walked back toward his room.

Alex held her hands out, palms up and laughed. "Well, you heard the man. I guess I'm in charge. Anyone have a problem with that?

"I've got my orders. I'm out of here." Devon closed his laptop and shuffled off.

Alex and Ben sat at opposite ends of the table and each appeared to be fumbling around for just the right words—any words. Finally, Alex leaned forward and looked tenderly at Benjamin. "I can't imagine what you must be thinking about, nor can I imagine what it must be like to not remember the events that led to where you are now. There have been so many things happen in the past few weeks and much of it is blurred to me. I want you to know, Ben, that I am going to do everything possible to make sure the virus in you *never* harms you. I know we can do this and I swear to you we will."

Alex paused and stretched her hands half way across the table and continued, "I know you don't remember any of this, but I've fallen in love with you, Ben. The kind of love that I never knew existed. You have given me the strength to rise above the demons that tormented me for so many years. I will always love you no matter what happens and I know that you felt the same way. I know it Ben. I only hope that we can find that again."

Benjamin's head was cradled on his thumbs and his fingers rubbed the bridge of his nose. His feelings were still raw. He raised his eyelids and looked at Alex. "I trust Phil. I always have from the first time I met him. He tells me that you are the one person, maybe the only person, who can help me now. I don't mind telling you that the thought of that virus being somewhere inside me scares the living hell out of me. Maybe we can focus on that for now and see where things go after that. Is that okay with you?"

Alex smiled and halfway clenched her fists. "Absolutely. . . I know we'll find a way to get rid of that virus. . . I know we will."

# CHAPTER 16

Alan paced up and down the aisle, pausing only long enough to gasp for air and punch the back of a seat. He was rarely one to show his emotions to others or to give the slightest hint of what he was really thinking. The art of persuasion and his learned ability to mask his feelings had been a trademark of his since his political and business stature had grown through the years. When he found himself alone, however, he unleashed his rage and frustration like a mile–wide tornado. Broken chairs, overturned tables, shredded papers, broken glasses and tossed books were all part of the carnage he would leave behind when he had finished his venting. He would then straighten his tie, brush the remnants from his jacket and regain his Cheshire–like smile within seconds.

He punched in the numbers on his iPhone. "This is Alan Price calling. I need to speak with President Desjardins please. I'm sure he is expecting my call."

He sat back down, threw his feet up on the seat across from him and slowly tapped his fingers, one at a time, on his armrest. He counted out loud, "A thousand one, a thousand two. . . " he had methodically counted past two hundred when he heard the President's garbled, "Hello." He calmly asked, "Stephen, I just heard the news about our Koidu plant. Do you mind telling me exactly what happened and why I didn't hear about this from you?"

"I was just briefed on it myself by Director Bardin. We had agents en route, but they arrived several hours too late. The explosion leveled everything and two people were killed. There really wasn't much we could do."

"No, I guess there wasn't since your inept agents can't seem to keep pace with their target. Was this the work of that Boudreau woman again?" The name Boudreau rolled off his tongue with a venomous hiss.

"According to the survivors there and the description they gave, it was probably her. They also told us that Monsieur Hunter was being held there and that he may have left with Mademoiselle Boudreau and two other men. They are not sure about that though. Alan, Monsieur Hunter is the subject of a worldwide manhunt by practically every international intelligence agency. What is going on? I had no idea you were involved with his kidnapping."

Alan shrugged. "Huh. Hunter. I don't really need him anymore so maybe that doesn't matter, but what I do need is for you to find Boudreau and stop her, Stephen. Why can't you do that?"

"It does not help when you keep information from me, Alan. When word gets out that Monsieur Hunter was held at the Koidu plant, a plant we now believe may be owned by you, those agencies will be asking lots of questions and you are the one they will want to talk to. I will be in no position to cover for you any longer."

Alan threw his feet to the ground and tightened his grip on the phone. His knuckles whitened. Thunderbolts of anger raged within, but his voice was steady and calm, "Stephen, you're in no position to tell me what I should be doing about *anything* and I hope I'm not hearing that you may not cooperate any longer. Big mistake, my friend. And no one will be able to trace the ownership records of that plant to Sterling. That detail has been well covered up. My first guinea pig with the virus was Hunter. The same virus has been implanted in him and I can destroy him, like you, at a moments notice. He, like you, wouldn't see anything coming."

For the first time, Alan thought maybe he had made a mistake by involving President Desjardins in his scheme. For his plan to succeed he needed to have the support and cover of one of the European Heads of State and he had believed France was his safest bet. After all, it had been France and the DGSE who had originally laid out the plan to expose those behind the creation of the G–16 virus. Alan had no idea that the DGSE had been pursuing that course of action, but when he had found out, he had parried with his own thrust. By arranging for the kidnapping of Hunter, he had been certain that the authorities would divert their attention to finding Hunter. The media exposure that would be given to someone with the wealth and notoriety of Benjamin Hunter would force them to divert their resources to find him. What Alan had not planned on though was that Boudreau woman. How could she be everywhere, and nowhere, at the same time? His own men had failed to stop her when she was about to expose the virus to the world several weeks ago and now, the DGSE couldn't seem to keep pace with her doggedness.

"Stephen, I'm within days of bringing all of this to a conclusion. Soon, I will have everything I have set out to acquire. When I get it, Stephen, I want to set you free. I want you to go back to your mundane everyday life of glad–handing and pandering. You can once again think of yourself as a leader. Do you understand?"

Alan waited for an answer. When there was no reply, he made certain his demand had been heard. There was no mistaking the peril in his menacing tone, "Mr. President! And I use that term very facetiously, do. . . I make. . . myself. . . perfectly. . . clear?!"

President Desjardins' words were not garbled this time, "We will stop Boudreau, Alan. I know very well why that must be done."

# CHAPTER 17

The eight by ten foot windowless room was furnished with a single table and four government issued metal chairs. The walls were painted a dull white and a single overhead light with two bare low watt bulbs cast shadows over the faded and scuffed linoleum flooring. Just several weeks ago, Paul Brewster had dined at the most exclusive dining room in Washington, D.C.—the Senate Dining Room. He had moved with ease and confidence as he mingled with U.S. Senators, foreign dignitaries, White House staffers and well–heeled power brokers. That same night he had taken a leisurely stroll along the banks of the Potomac River—the night lit Washington Monument towering in the distance. Now he waited patiently in a small room where inmates could meet privately with their attorneys. The District of Columbia Central Detention Facility, or more simply the DC Jail, was used as the interim holding cell for anyone charged with federal crimes awaiting trial.

A guard opened the door and entered the room. "Dr. Brewster, we received a call that your visitor will be delayed, but should be here within fifteen minutes. You're free to wait here if you want."

"Yeah, I'll just wait here. . . thank you."

Paul Brewster had already been arraigned in the U.S. District Court for the District of Columbia and had pled not guilty to each of the twenty–one charges levied against him. The charge of possession of weapons of mass destruction carried an automatic life sentence upon conviction. He faced the possibility of spending six lifetimes in prison if he were convicted on all the charges. His co–conspirators were also being held at the DC Jail and had been charged with similar crimes. The media attention surrounding Paul Brewster and the others had reached O.J. proportions with news cameras and reporters camped around the clock outside the courthouse and the jail.

Paul Brewster had spent most of his career in the nation's capitol and he had made it a point to circulate with Washington's power elite. He had been the Director of the Defense Advanced Research Projects Agency, or DARPA as it had been known in the political ranks. DARPA had been known by many in Washington, but understood by few. It had been the research arm of the United States Department of Defense and while it had budgetary oversight it had little, if any, project oversight. To the cynics of DARPA, and there had been many, DARPA had been the Defense's Department's private intellectual sandbox.

The door opened and Constance Hunter entered the room. Seated on one of the gray metal chairs, Paul looked up and spoke softly, "I wouldn't have recognized you myself if I didn't know you were coming."

Constance draped her trench coat on the table and removed her Nationals baseball cap. Her black hair fell to just below her shoulders. She was normally a woman who was meticulously dressed in designer clothing and adorned with eye catching jewelry. That day she wore blue jeans with a yellow and white striped Rugby pullover, but her shoes were Gucci loafers. She gave Paul a hug, sat down and said, "This is the price I have to pay for having such a famous father.

Sorry I'm late, but I had to find another way to get in here with all the reporters hovering about. They're even camped in front of my house."

"I'm so glad you came, Connie. This is the first time we've been able to talk alone and there's so much I want to tell you. I don't know how much time we'll have, but first, tell me; how are you? This has to be so hard on you."

Constance sat upright, her back pressed against the chair and her legs crossed. Her foot snaked in tight circles and her hands clutched her thighs. She took a deep breath. "I'm not doing so well, dad, but I'm coping with things the best I can." She blinked several times and her black steely eyes remained focused across the table at her father. She continued, "I need some answers from you, dad. They still don't know where Ben is or even of he's okay. I know you've publicly stated you don't know anything about his disappearance, but please, tell me something. I can't help but believe that you know something."

Incarceration had not set well with Paul Brewster and it showed. In just a few days his normally tan coloring had faded, his eyelids sagged and his jowls drooped. He met his daughter's gaze, but his eyes were clouded with moisture. He shook his head. "I wish I knew something that could help, I really do, but I don't know anything about Ben. None of us do. He was never a part of any of this. He never knew what was going on. You have to believe that. If I knew anything I would tell you."

"It doesn't matter what I believe right now. I really can't believe any of this. My own father. . . you've always been the rock in my life and someone I have looked up to. Right now, you're sitting here and Ben is missing, maybe even dead." Constance pushed her chair back and stood up. Her voice raised several octaves, "I don't know what to think anymore, dad! How could you have done this?!"

Brewster jumped up, but Constance held her hands out. "Don't touch me!" She fell back into her chair, folded her arms on the table and buried her head. "What happened, dad? Tell me what happened so I can try to understand."

Brewster slouched back in his chair and his arms dangled at his sides. "I lost my focus somewhere along the way, Connie. I'd worked hard all my life to get where I was and I think people really respected me. They respected what I had accomplished and who I was. Then, I was given the opportunity to make more money than I ever dreamed of and it clouded my judgment. Greed took over. It's as simple as that, really."

"Greed?" Constance shifted in her seat, but her head still rested on her arms. "Ever since I was a little girl, dad, you had drilled into me the importance of honesty. You always said the most important thing you could ever leave me was your integrity. That was more important to you than anything. Did you really mean that all those years?"

Brewster leaned forward and pushed his hands across the table. He laid his fingers gently on Constance's arms. "I can't leave you with that now, but yes, a father's integrity is the most important thing he can leave his child. I believed it then and I do now. I've failed you in so many ways."

Constance looked up. "Why'd you do this dad? Why?"

Brewster's head sank forward and his fingernails dug into the back of his neck. "$25 million split four ways—that's the only reason. Somehow, Alan Price found out about one of our new projects early on. I've known Alan for a while; he's a likable enough guy and a self–made guy. He built Sterling himself and I was probably envious of him in a way. Anyway, when we finished perfecting the virus we were going to deliver it to him and he'd pay us the money. We never got there though. That's when everything fell apart and the FBI swooped in and I ended up here."

"You know the worst thing about all this, Connie?" Brewster looked up. "The virus that we all created is. . . is. . . well, it's unstoppable, there are no cures, no antidotes—none whatsoever. Once it's activated it can't be repressed or stopped. If this were to ever get into the wrong hands it could destroy millions. I would have to live with that."

"And you never thought about the consequences? About what you were creating?"

"At the time, no, not really. I only thought about the money at the end of the road. I think about it a lot now, though, that's pretty much what I do with my time here."

Constance leaned back in the chair and brushed her hair back from her face. She rubbed her eyes and dropped her hands back in her lap. "The last time I spoke to Ben he told me he wanted a divorce. He's met someone else."

Brewster's expression softened. "What? Oh Connie, I'm so sorry. I had no idea anything was wrong with you two."

"Hah, me neither, but I can't blame him. I haven't been much of a wife to him over the years. I've been too wrapped up in my own career to be the woman he deserves." She looked down and continued, "I still love him, dad, but I can't stand in his way. I'm not very good with relationships as you know. I thought everything was just fine with Richard too, but it didn't take him long to figure me out and move on. I think Ben would have moved on a long time ago, but he always believed that marriage was a lifetime commitment. It's all for the best I think."

"Oh, Connie, I'm sorry. I guess I'm sorry for a lot of things right now, but your happiness means so much to me. Are you going to be okay?"

Constance glanced at her watch and stroked her finely tapered chin. "I'll make do. I had better go now, but I love you, dad. I'll do whatever I can for you as your daughter, but I can't get involved in any other way. I think you understand that, don't you?"

Brewster nodded and stood up. "Whatever happens with me is my own doing, nobody else's. You, my dear, take care of yourself and thanks for coming today. It means everything to me."

Constance reached out and gave her father a hug. "Thanks, dad. I'll come again in a day or two."

# CHAPTER 18

I t was 4 o'clock in the afternoon and anvil–shaped cumulonimbus clouds unleashed torrents of rain and a smell of thunder hung in the air. Ocean waves pounded the beach. The sound of the crashing waves and dime–sized pellets hammering the thatched roof, drowned out the voices inside the room, but Alex hadn't noticed. She was again wandering back in time sifting through bits of information and systematically filing the clues and leads in her correct mental folders. She had done this countless times over the years and had known exactly how to stitch and sew the fragmented pieces together.

She heard the sound of hands clapping and she looked over at Benjamin. He clapped his hands again, only louder. "Hel–low, you're gone again." Two more loud clap. . . claps.

Benjamin looked at Phil. "Does she always do this?"

Phil shrugged his shoulders. "Yep, get used to it."

Alex pictured herself sitting in Ben's grandfather's office, just a week earlier. She thought then that it had been part of his folksy style, but now seeing Benjamin do the same, two loud claps of the hands, she was shaken. She has to tell Ben about his grandfather and that it had been her who had set him up and cost him those precious years. She has to tell him, but not now. No, she needed to stay focused on right now. There would be others nows—later.

"Alex!" Ben reached over and clasped her shoulder. He shook her gently. "What is it?"

"I'm sorry. I was off in the past somewhere thinking about. . . things. I'm here now." She rubbed her cheeks. "So, Devon, are you okay with that?" She reached up and massaged the side of her neck with both hands and stretched her chin.

Devon looked anything but okay. His normally boyish grin was replaced with a somber scowl. He finished cleaning his glasses and held them out to get a good look. "Much better." He turned to Alex. "I'm not saying that I could do this any better than you by any means, but if I can do the hacking it would free up your time. It sounds to me like time is important here."

"Initially I need to do it, Devon. We don't know yet if Sterling is the real party behind all this and if they were to discover that their system was hacked and traced it back to you somehow, well, you would be facing some serious criminal charges and I imagine they would press that all the way. I've been involved in this from the very beginning and if anyone is going to take the rap for anything here, well, it's going to be me.

"Thanks, Alex, but I can be useful. I know I can. I'll use my fly–on–the–wall technique—works every time. Come on, I'm in pretty deep so far, so what's the diff?"

"The difference is big and you know it. If we find out that Sterling is heavily involved in this, then you are back on your keyboard—definitely."

Devon saluted. "Yeah. . . okay. . . yeah—I hear you."

Benjamin placed his hands on the table and leaned back. For a man who was carrying around one of the most lethal viruses ever developed and who could disintegrate in a moments notice, he appeared to be remarkably calm. How can he sit there and look like that? Alex thought. Benjamin let out a heavy sigh and said, "We're going to need to go somewhere where we have the resources to do what we need to do. We're pretty isolated here. Let's fly back to my place and we can use that as our base."

Phil perked up. "Works for me. I could even sleep in my own bed."

"I don't think so." Everyone stared at Alex and she continued, "Every intelligence agency and law enforcement group in the world has its eyes out for Ben right now. For all Sterling knows, he went up in flames in Koidu with the others. We don't want the word out yet that Ben is still alive. Maybe later, but not now. In the meantime, Devon rounded up extra passports, credit cards and other identifications for each of us to use when we leave here. So we'll leave separately and meet up at an agreed destination."

Phil's "I'm going home" smile faded. "With your background I didn't think you'd need a passport."

"You don't know how *almost* right you are." Alex replied with a tongue–in–cheek laugh.

Phil smiled. "Well, Ben's right, we need to get out of here. What do you suggest? Where are you going to drag us to this time?"

Devon interjected, "Let's fly back to the States and we'll figure things out there."

The three men looked at Alex expectantly, awaiting a revelation.

Alex rose from the table and looked out at the crashing surf. "I'm going to take a walk for a few minutes. I have to sort through some more things on my own. I'll be back." She was out of the room before anyone could answer.

The wet sand squishing between her toes, the spitting rain and the smell of the salt air soothed Alex's overtaxed mind and weary body. She took herself back to that day not so long ago when she had been with Benjamin at the Point Reyes Lighthouse. She remembered the guttural sounds of the foghorn on the cliff that had made her feel protected and safe. She imagined the feeling of the wind swirling around her.

She was at one of those crossroads where she had been so many times before, where she had been called upon to make a life–altering choice. Yet each of those times involved only herself—her own life. The lives of others had not been hanging in the balance, like now. She had created this mess and she had to find a way to help Ben. That she would do. But would it ever be possible to find happiness in her world when she had caused such misery to others? Would Benjamin be forever cursed if she were to make a life with him? Would he even want to be with her after all she had done? Would she ever know the answers to any of these questions if she did not at least try?

She looked parched, as if all the moisture that made her skin glow and her hair shine had been sucked out of her. She tossed her head back, closed her eyes and took several long, deep breaths. She looked out at the angry sea and it beckoned. She stripped her clothes off down to her underwear, waded into the surf and plunged in—headfirst. Alex had been used to long swims and had often used them to clear her cluttered mind or to sort through pressing problems. She swam out beyond the waves and circled around a cluster of wash rocks far off the beach. With each stroke and with each breath she searched for that mental guiding light that would lead her through her own decision matrix. The gap between her intuition and conscious thought began to disappear. Swimming back toward the beach, her train of thought suddenly jumped the tracks and new ideas began to blossom in her mind. She knew it wouldn't be easy, but it would be simple.

"Gentlemen." Alex swung open the door and marched in. She gripped her wet hair and pulled it back. "Pack your bags; we're off to the States. I'll fill you all in on the way to the airport."

# CHAPTER 19

Reston, Virginia, located in the Washington, D.C. metropolitan area, had been an early leader in planned development when American suburbia had first begun its outward sprawl. Sterling had built its corporate headquarters on the outskirts of the town twelve years ago so it would have quick access to the nation's political decision makers and a first class international airport. The fourteen acre, tree covered campus, served a work force of over 6,000 employees. Its period architecture and state–of–the–art security projected the dignified image of a modern day Monticello.

When Devon and the others had left Liberia they split up and took separate flights to reach their appointed destinations. Devon had met Alex in Frankfurt and had flown with her on a direct flight to Dulles International. They had spent the eight hour flight sifting through the ins–and–outs of the ominous events that Alex was sure loomed ahead. When they had landed at Dulles, Alex had boarded a flight to Sacramento while Devon had woven his way through customs and security and had checked himself into the Hyatt Regency Reston on Presidents Street.

Devon sat at his make–shift work station in the corner of his room and as usual it was meticulously organized. Papers were neatly stacked on the right side, his laptop sat in the exact middle of the desk and his cell phone and electronic toys neatly lined the left side. Looking every bit like he was stuck in an Eighties time–warp, he was dressed in an orange and white freebie t–shirt, tattered white laceless sneakers and homemade denim cut–off shorts. He looked more like a skinny version of "Bluto" Blutarsky in the outrageous spoof, *Animal House*, than the crack computer techno–nerd who had been raised wearing finely pressed school uniforms.

He punched in Alex's number on his iPhone and waited. Before Alex could complete her hello, he launched ahead, "Bah–hoey! I've got access. I'm into the mainframe and past the firewalls. It's Surf City from here."

"That was quick. There were no problems with bugging the shuttle?"

"Piece of cake. I followed the shuttle at 6:30 yesterday morning and the driver stopped at his usual morning hangout, Lake Anne Coffee House. Within 10 minutes max I had fastened a promiscuous network monitor I built from a jailbroken iPhone under his rear bumper. I left his shuttle a block from the coffee shop and I was back in my own van. You should've seen the driver, Alex. When he came out of the coffee shop and couldn't find his shuttle he launched into a frenzied chicken dance. I've got it on video. You gotta watch it."

Back in Monrovia, Alex and Devon had spent hours searching for ways to penetrate the mainframe at Sterling. As they had suspected, the system had been locked tight with a series of Virtual Private Networks and a separate login and password had been needed for each VPN. They could penetrate the VPNs, but it would take time and the longer one spent attempting to penetrate a system like Sterling's the greater one's chance of detection. They had needed to find a much quicker way in.

Their probing had uncovered the fact that Sterling's executives were issued Samsung Galaxy S4 cell phones and that was to be their first point of entry. A big problem still facing cell phone users with Bluetooth had been the lack of intrusion detection. Banks, investment firms, hospitals, law offices and other organizations that housed sensitive information usually had a corporate policy prohibiting BYOD—bringing your own device. They didn't want wireless LAN's or cell phones accessing sensitive company data. Alex knew first–hand that the "no use" policy had been impossible to enforce and a skilled hacker had an unlimited arsenal of attack weapons to drive a truck through the most sophisticated Bluetooth or wireless–intrusion detection system. Once bypassed, the intruder had full access to anyone within 300 feet of the cell phone.

The days when hackers needed to wardrive neighborhoods or business districts probing for low–hanging fruit had become a thing of the past. Through the use of a BlueBug Attack, Red Fang, Bluestumbler, BT Audit or a host of other weapons, attackers could gain full access to a device's AT command set to control the modem and even install a keylogger.

Sterling had a low frequency WiFi network that supported three non–overlapping channels. Anyone inside the Sterling compound using a portable computing device would connect to the wireless system and the amount of data would be staggering. Alex had estimated that by capturing all the data running through three separate networks they would amass one Gigabyte of data per minute and by the end of just one work day that would jump to 1.5 Terabytes.

To keep the cell phone data and the computer data from each network channel separate and to handle the sheer volume, Devon had rented a commercial windowless van that he had set up as his mobile command center. He had equipped his van with four metal racks on each side and had loaded them with one hundred twenty, 5–inch square PC boards, each running a version of Centos Linux, working as a large parallel processor. From his mobile command center he had been able to receive the intercepted network data, or packets, and had run it all through an encryption decoder to decipher the data.

To intercept the data packets, Alex and Devon had decided upon a double barreled shotgun approach. They would attack corporate executives' cell phones with a BlueBug attack *and* penetrate the wireless network within the headquarters building. Once a cell phone's MAC address had been discovered they could swoop in and retrieve all the data stored on that cell phone. They doubted that sensitive passwords would be stored on the cell phones, but the attack was quick and they would retrieve a massive amount of data in no time. It was all low risk with the looming possibility of high rewards.

The primary attack employed by Devon had been monitoring and retrieving the data flowing through the Wi–Fi channels. Once the promiscuous iPhone had captured the data it had been relayed to Devon's van and immediately stored in his mobile disk farm. The data for each channel had been segregated from other channels, and the cell phone data had been stored separately from the wireless data. They had known the cell phone data would not be encrypted so Devon had analyzed those data with a simple pattern recognition program that had isolated key phrases and displayed the context around those phrases looking for anything useful.

As they expected, the Sterling IT department had paid little attention to router upgrades with the older networks, and thanks to the voluminous amount of data that Devon had collected, the WEP security methods used by the out–of–date routers had allowed Devon to crack the different passwords using a BackTrack Linux application. Once Devon had deciphered certain passwords, he had used another Linux app, Wireshark, and had decrypted the individual packets that had been stored over the first twelve hours of gathering network traffic.

"A piece of cake might be an overstatement, but the whole idea really worked? You're able to get access?"

"Hey, it better than worked. I had a nerdgasm it was so damn good. You hit it smack on the nose, Alex, we ended up with just over 1.6 Terabytes of data and the Wireshark blasted through everything."

"So fill me in, Devon. What do you have that we can use?"

"Well, first off I ended up with twelve different login and password matches. I logged onto their network early this morning around two. I figured no one would be working at that hour and I could move around totally free. Most of the matches are low level guys without much access to the highly secure stuff. I didn't catch anything that looks like Price himself, but I did snare a real bonanza of a hotshot, a guy named Arne Branham—heard of him?"

"No. . . no, I don't think I know who he is."

"Well I didn't either, but the guy's the CFO for the whole company. As near as I can tell so far he has access to everything. I haven't hit any roadblocks, yet."

"Wait a minute, Devon you're not logged in as Branham now, are you?"

"Ah, I knew that would get to you. I already checked his calendar and at this very minute he's flying to Los Angeles so there's no way he can try to access anything. I'm going to stay in until he lands and then I'll shut down. And yes, I did check his flight. He's on it and it left on time and is scheduled to arrive on time."

"Okay, it sounds like you have everything covered. You'll call me the minute you know anything useful?"

Yep, you'll be my first call. Listen, Alex I know you'll say no, but this is a perfect time to try out my Back To The Future program—it really is! I can install it right now in Branham's computer and monitor everything from my van. We could hit pay dirt with it. I could have him eating out of my hand."

"No! Absolutely not, Devon! We've already been through that and we've agreed not to use it. It's an amazing idea and you're probably on the cutting–edge of something, but no, we'll stick with what we know works. You can test it yourself another day."

Devon had been intrigued by a cyber attack several years ago in which the attackers had installed harmless looking titles on a national website that had been used by people with epilepsy to access current research on their disease. Once the user clicked the title they had been exposed to a series of rapidly flashing images and there had been cases of people having seizures and migraine headaches. At that time, he had known that flickering images had been used to develop a multi–colored LED flashlight that when flashed with a certain sequence of colors would make its victim nauseous, disoriented, or vomit. Devon had taken that concept and tailored it to a completely different use.

Once Devon had begun looking seriously into the theory of flashing images and mind control he had discovered that the whole idea had been in use by advertisers and marketing engineers for years. With the introduction of digital television sets and monitors, advertisers had learned how to lull viewers into a mildly hypnotic state. Once hypnotized by the screen flicker, various forms of Neuro–linguistic Programming cues were introduced to steer the viewer's thoughts, making them either calm and accepting of the product being sold, or openly hostile and uncomfortable with the competitor's product.

Devon had dubbed his new program Back To The Future and while he had run beta tests to determine its effectiveness, he still had bugs to work out. He had achieved, with limited success, the ability to plant pseudo–memories in a subject to make them believe they had actually experienced an event or had known the facts of an event, even if it had never actually happened. He had known the possibilities of such a program in the cyber–espionage world would be unlimited.

Devon was itching to give it a shot under real life circumstances and he was frustrated with Alex's admonition, but he knew she was correct. "Alright, I hear you. . . again, I won't use it. But the next time we do this together I'll have it one–hundred percent tricked out and you'll be begging me to use it."

"God I hope there is no next time. Not for me anyway. So you'll call the second you find out anything?"

"That I will and, if you change your mind you'll call me the second you do?"

"Don't hold your breath and Devon—great job!"

# CHAPTER 20

The 8,180 acre campus of Stanford University was in the quaint, but mobily upscale community of Palo Alto, California. Its sprawling medical complex sat amidst the Eucalyptus and Costal Live Oaks at the northerly edge of campus. Alex and Ben waited in the office of Dr. Jessica Wasserman, an Associate Professor of Medicine who specialized in pediatric AIDS. Her expertise was a far cry from what Benjamin needed, but she was highly respected and well connected within the medical community. Alex, along with the persistent prodding of Phil, had convinced Ben that he should have a complete medical check up before he embarked on what would surely amount to a treacherous and dangerous venture. Dr. Wasserman sat on the Board of Directors for GEN and Ben had nothing but respect for her. Alex had gone to great lengths to give Ben a new identity to travel undetected through customs and crowded airports. As far as Dr. Wasserman knew, Ben had hired Alex to help him get to the bottom of things.

Dr. Wasserman was a round woman with flame red hair. She had always been blunt, forceful and her pragmatic mind kept her focused on the task at hand. Alex had given her a rundown of Benjamin's attempted murder in Paris and the fact that he had been kidnapped from the hospital while still in a coma. Jessica was sympathetic to

Benjamin's plight, but she was not satisfied with the explanation of the events that led up to his being hospitalized. She needed more answers.

"There are still so many unanswered questions, Ben, about what happened at GEN. How could Murray have been involved in creating that virus? It doesn't make any sense to me or to any of the other Board members. I've been interviewed by the police on two separate occasions and while they didn't admit as much, I think they're looking for evidence linking you to the stolen research. GEN has been devastated."

When talking about GEN and the events he could recall, Benjamin was focused and all business. The more he had learned about GEN and what had happened the more his resolve strengthened and his determination hardened. "Jessica, I know my memory's shot and I can't answer all your questions, but I know without a doubt that I had absolutely nothing to do with stealing the research, helping Murray or anyone else connected to GEN's downfall. You know how important all of that has been to me. It still is."

He stood and walked over to the window and looked out at the parking lot below. "My coming here to see you and to ask for your help probably puts you in some jeopardy with the police. If you don't want to help, I understand. If you honestly think I had a part in any of this then I don't want you to help." He turned around and his eyes met Jessica's. "It's up to you. Alex and my closest friend thought I should be seen by a doctor and I'm here because of their insistence. As far as I'm concerned, I'm going to get to the bottom of things one way or another."

Jessica had been tapping her fingers on her desk while Benjamin spoke. She lifted her hands, entwined her fingers and shook her pressed–together index fingers at Benjamin. "First, you're not leaving here without a complete medical check–up. I've already made arrangements with Dr. Jeremy Riggle to see you. You won't find a better neurologist anywhere." She glanced at her watch and continued, "And he's expecting you in a few minutes. Second, I have no reason to doubt anything you've told me. I've always admired everything about you and what you have done with GEN. I'm confident you'll figure things out. You always have."

Ben nodded. "Thanks, Jessica. . . "

"But first," Jessica jumped in, "let's talk about your medical condition. Dr. Riggle will run you through all the tests and procedures, but I want to monitor things and make sure you get what you need. It's not everyday we see a patient who comes in and says they need a complete check–up and oh, by the way, I have to be out of here in an hour." She leaned back in her chair and smiled, obviously relaxed and feeling more at ease.

Benjamin drove and Alex navigated the back roads, even though he had driven those same twists and turns dozens and dozens of times. They had just left Petaluma where they had bought enough supplies for the two or three days they had expected to stay in a rented house north of the town of Gualala. Heading north on the Bodega Highway, Benjamin set the cruise control and leaned his head back against the headrest. "Two hours, maybe two–fifteen at the most and we'll be there."

Time had sped quickly by that day and each time Alex thought she had been getting closer to fitting pieces together that would give them a way to free Benjamin of the virus, her mind had boomeranged back to intimate thoughts about the man sitting beside her. She had

met Benjamin at the airport in Sacramento earlier that morning and
they had driven straight to Dr. Wasserman's office. It had been the first
time the two had been alone together since Alex had told Benjamin
that she was the person who had stolen the research from GEN and
that she had entered his life with far less than honest intentions. They
had shared a laugh or two when talking about Devon's oddities or Phil's
sarcastic wit, but each time she had steered the conversation to "them,"
Benjamin had become withdrawn and had changed the subject.

Her mind raced. What if the cracks in Benjamin's memory
remain open? There is no way he could forgive me, be with me, or
love me. Love had always been a foreign emotion to Alex and she had
never allowed herself the opportunity to feel her heart pound in her
throat, to feel her skin tingle at the mere sight of another or to give
herself so freely and passionately to another—until now. She had
lived with the belief that love was only temporary, at best, and like
a high from a drug, it's great when you have it, but once it ends you
come down feeling worse than you did before you inhaled.

Alex's cell rang and she recognized the number. "Hello, Jessica,
this is Alex. Let me put you on speaker." She placed her phone on the
center console and hit the speaker button. "Can you hear me now?"

"That's perfect. Very clear. Ben, I wish you could stay for a
couple of days. Some interesting things came back from your DNA
sequencing."

"Can't stay, Jessica. What do you have?"

"Let me address your amnesia first. The MRI is normal so
there are no tumors or inflammatory processes affecting your brain's
storage, processing or recall functions. What you have is retrograde
amnesia, meaning you can recall events that occurred after your
trauma, but you cannot remember previously familiar information
or the events preceding your trauma. As I mentioned to you earlier,

without the benefit of your hospital records we can't make this a definitive diagnosis, but based upon what you've told us it's fairly certain this is the case."

"I remember certain events before I was hospitalized, but not others. As I told you, I remember flying to Paris, but I don't remember why."

"That's exactly what happens with retrograde amnesia. You don't have a full cognitive recognition of everything that transpired. Your recognition is partial."

"Is there any reason why I remember some things and can't remember others?"

"None whatsoever, Ben. There is some research that indicates there may be a pattern to the things you can't remember. Like things related to a particular place, maybe certain sounds trigger the loss or even smells. But, this research isn't conclusive so my answer would be no, there's no known reason why you can remember some things and not others. "

"Okay, so that's your diagnosis. What happens next? Is this going to be permanent or can you treat it in some way? Please tell me you can treat this."

"There's no treatment, Ben. No magic medicine or procedure that's the cure–all. Only time will tell. The brain is amazingly regenerative and the fact that your injuries were apparently not too severe, Dr. Riggle thinks that given enough time, you'll be fine."

Alex instinctively reached over and put her hand on Benjamin's thigh and gave a tender squeeze. Just as quickly, she pulled her hand back and covered her mouth. Benjamin looked over, held his hand up and whispered, "It's okay. Don't worry about it.'

Alex shook her head, gave a half–smile and whispered back, "I'm sorry."

"Ben, are you still there?"

"Yeah. So, I just wait it out? Is that what you're telling me?"

"That's all you can do for now. More importantly, Ben, Dr. Riggle ran a DNA sequencing on you and something very unusual came up. I don't know if. . . "

Benjamin interrupted, "What exactly do you mean by DNA sequencing? Are you talking about my genetic make–up?"

"Essentially, yes. DNA is comprised of a series of ladder–like units called DNA nucleotides. The purpose is to find out how the sequence of those nucleotides leads to whether you have blonde or red hair, whether you have light or dark skin and every other detail from your bone marrow to the tips of your hair. DNA sequencing is nothing more than a looking glass into the origins of what makes every part of you, large and small. Does that make sense?"

"Yeah, for the most part it does. So what did he come up with? What am I made of?"

"It's puzzling, Ben. Scientists have used DNA sequencing of the human genome to develop a virtual blueprint of the human being. It will take a few more days to have definite results on your test, but it looks like you have a gene which hasn't yet been identified and doesn't seem to fit into any identifiable group. It's a first."

Benjamin pulled the car to the side of the road, looked down at the cell and cocked his head. "Does this have something to do with my amnesia? It must."

"No it has nothing to do with that, we're certain. We don't know what it is and that's why I'd like you to come back in for some more tests. You should really consider that."

Alex scribbled on a piece of paper and held it up for Benjamin to see. He nodded his approval. "I can't Jessica. You know why. One question though. Is it possible I could have been injected with something that would maybe, you know, create this extra gene you're talking about?"

"I'd need to check with Dr. Riggle on that, but. . . what are you talking about? *Were* you injected with something? Is that something you remember?"

"No, of course not. I'm just throwing a "what if" at you. I'm just curious."

"I would suspect not, but I'll ask just to satisfy your curiosity, and mine. Ben, I need to ask you one more time to reconsider things. A couple of extra days here may answer a lot of unknowns and give us a better understanding of your condition. It shouldn't interfere with what you two are doing. Please?"

"Sorry, Jessica. No can do on that one. If I feel any ill effects or there's any change in my memory I'll call you. I promise. And, thanks, Jessica, you've stepped forward and been a big help. I appreciate everything you've done."

"Good luck, Ben, and keep me posted."

# CHAPTER 21

lex sat with her arms tightly coiled around her legs and gazed out the window at the Pacific Ocean. Off in the distance the ominous fog bank amassed its forces awaiting the afternoon wind shift when it would creep in and drape the shoreline. Below, the knotted kelp beds bobbed in the waves and squadrons of pelicans dove for their morning feast.

It had taken two days for Alex and the others to make all the needed connections to get them from Monrovia to a rental house buttressed on the cliffs near the bucolic town of Gualala. After she had left Devon in Virginia, she had sat in the first class window seat where she had appeared to be daydreaming as she stared at the miniature landscape below, but she had been mentally sifting through the events of the past few weeks and stitching the fragments together. She had been looking for a pattern, a reason or a motivation to justify this twisted reality. She knew they were on the right track, but they needed more information. There were still too many gaps. . . too many unanswered questions.

Overlooking the vastness of the Pacific Ocean, Alex wondered why she had been tailed when she went to Australia to meet with Ben's grandfather. It had taken little effort on her part to shake them, but she knew that whoever it was they were involved—somehow.

She knew very little about Alan Price, but she was starting to see the seeds of Sterling Defense Application Corporation sprout from the cracks of her mounting evidence puzzle.

Sterling had received billions of dollars worth of contracts from the U.S. Government over the years, but it had never done any work for DARPA, until now. From the inception of the development of the G–16 virus at the National Emerging Infectious Diseases Laboratory in Boston to its culmination at the Health Containment Laboratory located in the isolated rainforests of Brazil, Sterling had been onsite. They had been awarded a contract to provide onsite security—the first time DARPA had ever used an outside security firm. Alex had found no ties between Alan Price, Paul Brewster or any of the others involved in Brewster's scheme, but somehow she knew that connection was more than the long arm of coincidence.

Alex heard a sing–song ring and spun on her bare heels. She grabbed the phone from the couch. "Devon?"

There was no mistaking his excitement. "Are you sitting in front of your computer? You gotta see this."

"Just a sec." Alex sat down at the desk, activated her TeamViewer and quickly connected into Devon's computer. "Okay, I'm with you."

Devon scrolled through the pages of files until he landed on a master file called 'Black Swan.' "This is the pay dirt file and there's dozens of sub–files in here. Look at these." He highlighted the subfiles named BS Koidu, BS Flight Logs, BS Currillion, BS Research. . .

"What's in the Koidu file? Open it up."

"Nah, I haven't been able to get in that one—*yet.* My big fish, Branham, the CFO, only has access to the flight log file, but it's pretty interesting. Watch. . . "

Devon opened the file and a list of logs for each of Sterling's six corporate jets unfolded. "This one here, the G–650, looks like it's the plane that our man Price uses. It's flown him to some pretty ordinary haunts; Paris, Los Angeles, Tokyo, but these here," Devon highlighted two flight destinations, "Manaus, Brazil, two flights, they have to mean something. Isn't that near that research place in Brazil you told me about where they developed that virus?"

"Yes, the Health Containment Laboratory is south of there and Sterling had the security contract down there. Those flights must have been him checking in and. . . look at the date for the last flight." Alex highlighted the flight dated September 14. "That was just a few weeks before all the news broke out about the virus. . . interesting. What are the Hobart, Australia, flights about? It looks like the same plane is on its way there right now."

"Yea, those are puzzling. Each of the eight flights left Hobart and headed south, but there's nothing to the south, except Antarctica."

Alex rubbed her temple and cradled her head in her fingers. "Maybe they have some contracts with some of the research stations down there, but I can't imagine that Price would be the one making all those flights."

"He's the only passenger listed on each of those flights. They might have omitted names of other passengers for some reason, but on the other flight logs they list the passengers by name."

"I have an idea, let's try this." Alex rubbed her hands. "Here's how we'll find out where those flights went."

Phil walked out of the kitchen with a steaming cup of coffee in one hand and rubbing his sleep encrusted eyes with the other. "What's up?"

Alex shot Phil a tongue–in–cheek look. "Coffee? So late in the day?"

"Just because you don't sleep doesn't mean I can't get a little extra shut–eye." Phil sat down on the couch and stretched his legs on the burl wood coffee table. "As usual, you look like you've been up to something."

"That I have. I just got off the phone with Devon. I think Ben will be back anytime now and then we can go over some new information."

"Where'd he go?" Phil asked.

"He drove into town to the store to pick up some things, food and the like. He should've been back by now."

Phil's eyes widened. "I don't think that was such a bright idea, Alex. Ben knows a lot of people in this town. He's practically a local. Someone will recognize him. Bet on it."

Alex shook her head. "There wasn't much I could do. He grabbed the keys and bolted out of here. Anyway, it looks like we won't be staying here very long. I think we're off to Antarctica."

Phil looked over at Alex. "And the reason for that would be?"

"Devon couldn't find anything specific in Sterling's data base about what was going on with the G–16 virus, but they have gone to great pains to cover up whatever they've been planning. The data base is pretty extensive and all the files, except a few, are protected by separate passwords. Access has been limited to just a handful of people. The files we have been able to get into talk about eight separate flights to Antarctica and one is on its way right now."

"Sounds like a fishing expedition to me. Are you sure? Are you holding out on me? Come on, Alex, we're not off to Antarctica just because Sterling happened to have flown there a few times."

"No, there's more and Devon is still looking into a couple of other areas, but I'm pretty certain something is going on down there. Price is on the plane flying there right now, but I'll give you all the details as soon as Ben gets back."

"Okay, I'll wait." Phil took another gulp of coffee. "Oooh, that's good stuff—a perfect brew to kick–start my day. What are you doing now?"

"I just finished up with Devon and I'm going to make myself some tea. It looks like you're already set."

"You can put another pot on, it's fine by me. Hey," Phil sat up and looked at Alex, "you and Ben spent most of the whole day together yesterday, anything new on that front?"

Alex had spent the entire morning racing in overdrive, grabbing at snippets of information and trying to place things in some orderly pattern. She hadn't thought about Benjamin, about them, until now. She finished filling the tea kettle and set it on the counter. Her shoulders dropped and she heaved a sigh. "By new, I suppose you mean about Ben and me?"

"That's as good a place to start as any. Care to share?"

Alex closed her eyes. "He doesn't. . . " she leaned her head back, "remember anything about me, or us. I tried to bring it up a few times, but it was pretty clear that he didn't want to talk about it. I don't know, Phil, I just don't know. The only thing he knows about me at this point is what I have told him, which. . . well, everything that has happened to him has been my fault. I can't deny that. Even if he regains his memory I think there may just be too much damage done for us to. . . to. . . hope for any kind of a relationship. I can honestly say that this is the first time in my life that my heart has been broken. I wish with all my strength that things will work out between us, but I'm afraid that. . . "

The front door swung open. "Ah good, you two are both awake. I've got everything we need to make a real breakfast. Eggs, bacon, sourdough bread, no more rice and fruit. The real stuff." Ben placed the sacks on the counter and stared slack–jawed. "Good morning to you too, or maybe thanks, Ben, I'm starved. Huh?"

Alex shook her head and smiled. "You're right. Sorry. Good morning and thanks! How about I do the cooking and you two can talk about whatever guys talk about. This *is* your neck of the woods you know."

Phil pushed himself off the couch and headed to the kitchen. "No way, I'm the chef this morning and Alex you can tell Ben where we're off to next. I'm sure he's going to love to hear that one."

Ben spread his hands. "Phil, since when could you make anything other than cereal and yogurt for breakfast?"

"Since now, so step aside." Phil grabbed a grocery bag from the counter and watched as the bottom gave out leaving a dozen eggs scrambled on the floor and a puddle of orange juice on the tile. "Shit! I guess I'll whip up my specialty—cereal and yogurt."

They all laughed and Alex and Ben watched as Phil ripped a handful of paper towels from the roll and tried his best to clean up. Ben turned to Alex. "So where are we booked to this time? I was just about to settle in here for a while."

Alex tugged Ben's arm. "Let's sit down. I know you are going to have a lot of questions."

While Phil masqueraded as a short order cook, Alex ran Ben through the pieces that she had spliced together that pointed her in the direction of Antarctica. It was a stretch, but no matter how hard Ben tried to poke holes in her theory, she countered with the logic of a mathematician. There were lots of reasons why Sterling would consolidate the G–16 development in such a remote and hostile environment. The region was devoid of a permanent population and the seventy–one research stations operated by the thirty countries that were signatories to the Antarctic Treaty would balloon to only four or five thousand personnel during the peak summer months. Privacy was almost certainly guaranteed in such an intimidating and sparsely populated environment. What had puzzled Alex the most had been the fact that Sterling's computer files on Antarctica where hidden deep in the system with limited, but highly secure access.

Devon and Alex had been successful in cracking several of the secure files, but the others were hidden behind multiple VPN layers and they would need more time to get into those. They had learned that Sterling had set up a German corporation that employed three German citizens who all worked with its new Antarctic project. The project was called Black Swan and in the past year alone over $16 million dollars was funneled into Grinhaus & Co. KG, a German domestic company, but for what? The answer, she believed, was hidden deep within Sterling's files.

Finally, Benjamin stood up and slowly rolled his shoulders. He walked over to a brass telescope in the corner of the room, bent down and peered through the eyepiece. Alex knew he was troubled by something. He stood still with one hand holding the tripod and the other clasped to the top of the telescope. Finally, he stood, arched his back and turned around to face Alex. "This is getting too complicated. I appreciate everything you have done. Both you and Phil have risked so much, but now, well. . . I think the best thing is to wind things down. I can live with the belief that everything was destroyed at Koidu. I really think I can. So what do you say we all go on with our lives?" He spread his hands and a glimmer of a smile appeared.

"Oh, Ben." Alex walked over to Benjamin, looked into his eyes and shook her head. "No, I am going to find out how we can put a stop to anyone ever activating that damn virus." Her fist tapped against his chest. "I want to go on with my life too. . . " She paused and thought to herself—*our life*, she continued, "but I have to do this first, one way or another. Maybe it's best that I go by myself from here."

Ben straightened his arms and put his hands on Alex's shoulders. He caught her soft gaze and whispered, "It's not necessary, Alex—*really*. We'll be just fine. Let's call it quits and forget about all this."

Alex tilted her head back. Her eyes were glassed over and her heart spoke, "I need to say one thing, Ben. Please hear me out. You have taught me so much in such a short time. I am not trying to thank you or to try and pay you back for all you have done. No, I need to do this for myself; to complete the cycle of the journey you have sent me on. Because of you I'm now able to think about my sister, Christina, and cherish the time I had with her before she died. I'm no longer afraid to talk about her and the pain has been replaced with love, a love I went without for too many years. I have not done many things in my life that I am proud of, I think you know that. Before I can bring closure to that part of my life and start a new chapter full of hopes, dreams and love, I need to make sure you are safe. Every ounce of reason I have tells me this is something I must complete. I know this probably doesn't make sense to you and you don't remember what we had together, but please, Ben, I'm asking you to understand. I will see this through."

Benjamin held the back of his neck. "I'm not blaming anyone for this, but myself. From what you and Phil have told me I had plenty of warning signs about what was happening and I ignored them—every damn one of them. Even if it's true that I was falling in love with you that doesn't justify my putting GEN in jeopardy and ruining what I had worked so hard to build. You're not to blame for any of this—any of it. I don't want to take a chance on putting you or Phil in any more danger. You two have done enough. Let's just let it pass and move on." He flashed his best convincing smile.

"I wish it were that easy. That we could sail off together and live happily ever after, Ben. I wish that with all my heart. But, if I am to rid myself of my past sins and to live that fairytale life, the one I had imagined with you, then I need to do this one last thing. I know I can find a way to get rid of this damn thing." She spread her fingers over Benjamin's heart and pressed. "I know I can."

"Okay. Okay. You're in that take control mode again aren't you? Well, I'm coming with you and my guess is that Phil will come along for the adventure too. Antarctica's not the easiest place to get to, but I have an idea. I'll make a call and see what I can find out."

"I haven't even thought of the logistics behind that yet. What do you have in mind?"

Benjamin walked toward the entryway. "Where's my phone? I haven't talked to him in a long time, but if I can get through to him I know he'll help us.

Alex asked the question and braced herself for the answer, "Who are you going to call?"

"It's a long story and I'll tell you about it later. But I think my grandfather can help us."

Alex cringed.

# CHAPTER 22

The mid–morning sky was a crime scene. Off in the distance loomed dark, menacing clouds punctuated by blinding flashes of lightning and crashing, house–rattling thunder. The expected cold front had made its entrance and Benjamin zipped his coat tight and stuffed his hands in its side pockets. He shuffled his feet through the sand and looked out beyond the rolling waves. The ocean's cleansing process was in full swing. The ebb tide was clearing the broken kelp and driftwood that had washed in from the crested tide. "What the hell did I get myself into?" he yelled out. His voice was muted by the cawing gulls, but he was yelling at himself.

Back at the house, Alex had told him that she was the one responsible for his grandfather's incarceration. She was the one who had cost his only living relative 11 years in the prime of his life and had destroyed the reputation he had spent a lifetime cultivating. Benjamin could only stare at Alex in disbelief before he had stormed out and walked along the beach. Distaste filled his mind. "How could I have been so stupid, so naïve?"

From what he'd been told everything had turned upside down since Alex had entered his life. The company he owned had been gutted and its research to cure cystic fibrosis was now in the hands of another company—maybe many companies. He had devoted precious years to finding a cure for the dreaded disease that took his twin brother from him at the tender age of ten. It had taken Benjamin years to recover from the loss of his brother and the cure that GEN had developed had all been done as a tribute to his brother, William. Alex had singlehandedly destroyed that—all of it. Because of her, and his own stupidity, his life had been threatened, he had been kidnapped and now he had a lethal virus implanted in him that could end his life at any second. He had been played the ultimate dupe by a woman he probably had loved, a woman who probably had made his heart come to life and someone he probably had wanted to spend the rest of his life with.

With two quick toeholds, he scaled up a rock and sat on the edge staring out toward the ominous horizon. The sooner I get out of here the better. I need to get as far away from that woman as possible. He closed his eyes, pounded a fist on his thigh and searched for the words to scream out, but there were no words to unleash his anger.

Below, he heard the accent that had mesmerized him not long ago, "Ben." The lines around his eyes narrowed, his insides simmered.

Alex broke the lingering silence. "I know you are angry with me. You probably hate me for all the grief and anguish I have brought to your life, but I would like to say a few things first. May I sit down? Please?"

Benjamin arched his back and motioned beside him.

Alex sat beside Benjamin, pulled her legs to her chest, wrapped her arms around them and—*squeezed*. With her chin on her knees she looked at Benjamin. "You have every right to blame me for everything that has happened to your life since you met me. I can't blame you for now wanting to close the door and keep me as far away from you as possible. Before you do so, there are a few things I would like to say."

Alex squeezed her legs tighter and took a deep breath. "When I went to your house to check on the eagle I went into your den. I knew you kept the key to the cage there. When I opened the drawer I saw a faded news clipping and I picked it up. I had no idea that Denis Wilkinson was your grandfather—*no idea*. I made another promise to you that day. One of so many promises I have had to make because of what I have done to you. I promised you that day that I would clear his name no matter what it took."

Her fingertips brushed his thigh and his jaw clamped—*tighter*. She drew back. "Your grandfather is out of jail now, Ben. I did clear his name and all of the charges that he was convicted on have been overturned. When I met with him I wanted so much to tell him everything, how it was me who was responsible for the missing plutonium, not him. That it was me who cost him those prized years and the disgrace it brought him. I just couldn't though. He agreed to help me find you and I knew he would have thrown me out if I told him what I had done. I couldn't take that risk. I needed to find you and time was precious. He told me that day that he always kept track of where you were and what you were doing. He is so proud of you, Ben. I will tell him everything about me as soon as I am through with ridding you of this virus. I need to do it for me and he should know. He should know who I really am."

Benjamin dropped his hands to the rock, kicked his legs out and pushed off, landing in the sand below. His arms shot up in the air, fists clenched. "Jesus, Alex! Grandfather Wilkinson is the only family I have left and now I feel like I'm responsible for his troubles. How the hell could you?" He looked at Alex through the slits of his eyes, his face hardened. "What other things have you done that I don't know about? Is there another wrecking ball out there that's going to slam into me? Is there?!"

"*No!* I have told you everything, Ben." Alex stepped on the outcropping below and jumped down onto the sand. She reached out and grabbed both of Benjamin's hands and held them tightly. A single tear hung from the corner of her eye and she looked soulfully at Benjamin and whispered, "I love you. . . I *love* you. It seems like every time I turn around I am apologizing to you for something. . . for something I have done. I know that you love me—or that you *did* love me. I have shattered so many of your own dreams by what I have done, but I hope you can understand that I have never meant to hurt you. When I called you from Paris and told you what I had done to you I didn't expect you to understand any of it. My pleading to you then was from my heart just as it is now. I know I have so much still to prove to you and I am asking that you give me that chance. There is nothing left from my past that you do not know. I'm sickened by it all as I know you are."

She looked down at the sand and her voice softened, "I have never given a thought to the fact that I've been hurting people all these years. It really never occurred to me. . . until I met you. You've made me see the person I have been and I don't like that person. I am so sorry for all of that, I really am."

She let go of Benjamin's hands and clutched his shoulders. "This is the last time I will have to tell you I am sorry. I will never let you down again. I am *sooo* sorry for everything, Benjamin."

Benjamin reached up and pushed one of Alex's hands aside. "Let's walk." He stuffed his hands in his pockets, turned and slid his bare feet through the sand.

Alex wanted to yell. She was gripped with a frightening fear. The fear of losing this man was terrifying and she was walking alongside him in unfamiliar territory. Before she had met Benjamin her life had been void of any meaningful relationships. Since the death of her sister, Christina, Alex had isolated herself in her own small world. The cause of Christina's death was never known and inspite of her parents support and love she had blamed herself for her sister's death. Alex had done everything she could have done to help her sister, but the gap between the mind and the heart of a small child is wide. She should have done more, she should have saved her—she had failed. Unable to cope with her sister's death, Alex had turned her pain into an all–consuming obsession. She had withdrawn from her normal sociable and effervescent self and had thrown herself headlong into a life of driving ambition. Her only goal had been to push her mind beyond her known boundaries and to win. That had been her plan— to escape the flood of guilt that had surrounded the burning question she could never answer "why her and not me?"

Alex had loved and hated her line of work, but those years of intrigue and living in a world of aliases and undercover operations had laid a solid wall of bricks and mortar that held her anger and guilt captive. Alone and isolated, her emotional and physical abandonment had been buried deep within the chambers of her mind never to be examined, never to be confronted and never to be released—until Benjamin entered her life.

They walked in the chilled mist and shuffled their feet in the sand. The circling gulls, the waves crashing on the rocks and the barking seals were drowned out by inner screams ricocheting in their minds.

When they reached the end of the beach, Benjamin stopped and turned toward Alex. He rolled his shoulders and looked up at the fleeting clouds. "I'm going to call my grandfather and we're going to go see him. You're going to tell him everything and then I'm going to Antarctica with you. I know he'll help with the arrangements to get us there."

Alex mirrored Benjamin's frozen expression. "We'll leave right away. And, thanks, Ben. Thank you."

Benjamin let out a deep sigh, pulled his left hand from his pocket and held it out, his fingers spread. "As for us. . . it's all unchartered waters for me. . . We'll see." He turned and walked toward the steps to the house.

Alex watched as the only man she had ever loved, the man who defined everything she had ever hoped for, the man who had freed her from her inner demons of guilt and anger, climbed the wooden steps two at a time. Her lips parted and she bolted after him.

# CHAPTER 23

Benjamin and Alex walked up the steps and stood in front of the massive front door. Benjamin rang the doorbell and took a step back. "I never thought I'd be nervous to see Grandfather Wilkinson."

The door opened. "Mr. Hunter. It's such a pleasure to see ya. Please. . . please come in." The woman stood aside and waved a hand.

Stepping inside the foyer, Benjamin was immediately flooded with memories. He had not been inside that house since he was 7 years old, but it seemed like only yesterday. The circular stairway leading upstairs was rimmed with a polished oak railing. His grandfather had been the first person to autograph his shiny white plaster cast that he had received just moments after he had been admonished to be careful as he started his long slide down the banister. He knelt down on one knee and rubbed a small square of abalone tile set conspicuously in the beige tiled entryway. It was at a beach at the north end of his grandfather's property that he dove for abalone for the very first time. It had taken him several hours, but he had finally popped a shell set deep under a rock ledge and camouflaged under thick strands of eel grass. He had gasped for air when he had surfaced and had proudly held the shell with both hands over his head. Benjamin smiled as he remembered that day and how his grandfather had stood on the beach cheering and finally waved him in and greeted him with a champion's ceremony.

"Memories. . . So many memories here."

"Holy dooly! Mr. Hunter! I'm sure ya don't remember me, but I'm Lisa Gordon. Ma father worked for Mr. Wilkinson for nearly forty years and when ya were very young we played sillybuggers together outside in the woods. I've taken over ma father's duties and when Mr. Wilkinson told me ya were comin I was so surprised. Pleasantly, I may add." Lisa reached out. "Here, let me take yar coats."

Benjamin and Alex handed their coats to Lisa. "This all takes me by surprise, but I do vaguely remember playing in the woods the last time I was here. In fact you taught me a marbles game. . . what was that called. . . ? Oh yeah, bounce eye—that was it. Lisa, wow, this is great. So you're working with my grandfather now?"

"Aye, have been for mosta ma life. He's a fine man. The best thar is. Come now, though, he wasn't expectin ya 'till this arvo. He'll be gobsmacked that yar here now."

Ben laughed. "I knew I should've brushed up on ma Aussie. I'm goin' to be laggin' behind a bit in figurin' out what yar all sayin'."

"Aye, no worries mate. What is it the Yanks say? It's like ridin a bike, somethin like that."

Lisa led Benjamin and Alex into Denis' office. "Ya two make yarself at home. I'll go find Mr. Wilkinson and tell him yar both here."

Benjamin walked over to Denis' desk and placed his hands on the inlaid leather. "This is the exact desk he gave to me. I didn't know he had another one." He stroked his chin. "I can't tell you how many times I thought about him when I sat at my desk. Sometimes I thought he was right there with me." He slid his hands across the desk and rubbed the nicks on the rounded corners. He picked up a small abalone shell placed prominently on one side of the desk. A tarnished brass plate was affixed to the shell that read "Ben's First Abalone." Tears welled up in his eyes. "All these years. . . he kept this here on his desk all these years."

The office door swung open. "Ben! Ma God Ben it is ya!" Denis moved at the speed of a man half his age and wrapped his arms around Benjamin. "Damn boy look at ya! Yar as strong as a saltwater croc and half agin as good lookin."

Benjamin gripped Denis' shoulders and gave him a shake. "And you! You look like you could still maneuver your way through the Outback with a 50 pound backpack and carrying a pick in each hand. You look great!"

"Have a seat, botha ya. What can I get ya? I know we got a lot of talkin to do, but how 'bout we pop a tinnie and celebrate some?"

Denis pointed a finger at Alex. "You remember where ma refer is, don't ya? Grab three tinnies and we'll get caught up on things."

Alex smiled. "Yes sir. Three tinnies coming up."

Alex sat and watched as Denis and Ben spent the next hour talking about everything from Ben's first dive to the times they camped together in the Outback and about the wooden ship they carved and whittled together in the backyard. They laughed, shared tears and toasted to memories. She marveled at their mannerisms and thought how odd that two people from different eras who had spent so little time together could be so much alike. They laughed together in perfect pitch and she shook her head each time they'd emphasize something with two sharp hand claps—clap. . . clap.

"Okay ya two; let's find out what's happenin here. Since ya called me I've been makin yar arrangements to get to Antarctica and yar set to go whenever yar ready. Just give me the word. When do ya want to go and what do ya need why yar here?"

Benjamin looked directly at Alex. "I think Alex here is the best person to fill you in on things. Alex?"

Alex had been sitting on the side of the room while the two men reminisced. She stood and walked over to the same high back upholstered chair she sat in not long ago. "Mr. Wilkinson, there are a. . ."

Denis interrupted, "Hell, call me Denis. Or grandfather. We're practically family the way I see it."

Alex sat down and pressed her shoulders into the chair. "Well, thank you. I am somewhat uncomfortable with that right now, but I do hope that someday it would feel natural for me to call you. . . grandfather. I would love that." Two fingers whisked her hair from her eyes and she continued, "Now, there are a couple of things I want to tell you about first and then we can talk about our Antarctica trip."

Alex recounted the details surrounding Benjamin's escape from the Koidu plant, about the virus and Benjamin's memory loss. Denis asked countless questions and Alex answered with complete candor. He had his reservations about their Antarctica venture and he felt they would be better off enlisting the help of the authorities. In the end he relented and pledged his full support to their efforts.

Alex stood up and walked over to the Harvey oil painting on the side of the room. She turned around and bowed her head slightly. "Mr. Wilkinson, there is something I need to tell you. Something you will not like and when I finish I am sure you will feel quite differently about me than you do now. This is not something I am proud of or something that comes easily for me to talk about, but I would like to ask you to allow me to finish before you say anything." Alex raised her head and looked at Denis.

Denis met Alex's gaze. His hands lay comfortably in his lap, his jaw jutted forward and he raised his two thumbs. "Go ahead. Ya got ma 'tention."

Alex drew a deep breath—then another. "When I was here before, you asked me if I was telling you the whole story and I said I had not told you everything because I didn't want my mission compromised. That was true. I came to see you because I knew you could help me and I loved Ben. I loved him then and I love him. . . now. . . more than anyone will ever know. I was afraid if I told you certain things that you would not believe me and you would not help me." Alex walked back toward the chair and continued, "It is important that you believe that, Mr. Wilkinson."

Denis' jaw twitched back and forth.

She stood behind the chair and looked over at Benjamin, then back to Denis. "Twelve years ago I was in Australia working for a client, a competitor of yours at the time, and I was responsible for 200 pounds of Uranium 235 disappearing from one of your storage facilities. I altered the Bill of Ladings so that it looked like the uranium was shipped to an approved facility when in fact it was shipped to my client in a country that was not a signatory to various international non–proliferation agreements. I covered my tracks by making it look like your company was intentionally at fault. It was because of me, and no one else, that you spent those years in prison. There is nothing that. . . "

"Belt up, Ms. Boudreau, just belt up."

Denis slouched down in his chair and his breathing slowed. Benjamin jumped up and ran over to Denis. "Grandfather! Are you okay?" He knelt down on the floor and put his hands on Denis' legs. "Should I call someone?"

Denis shook his head slowly. "I'll be okay. I need a minute."

"I'll get some water." Alex ran through the side door and returned with an opened bottle of water and handed it to Denis.

Denis was still shaking his head and muttered slowly, "I. . . knew. . . it. . . I. . . knew. . . it. How. . . could. . . that. . . have. . . happened!"

Alex stood to Denis' side. She reached down and grasped the armrest, but before she could speak Benjamin grabbed her hand and pulled it away. "Don't! Just stand back."

Before Alex could retreat, Denis reached over; his hand completely encircled her forearm. He was regaining his strength and he slowly sat up in his chair. He looked up at Alex and then over to Benjamin. "Ben, thar's no need to be angry with Ms Boudreau."

Denis pointed to his desk. "Could ya hand me the water?"

He took a few swallows, cleared his throat and looked over at Alex. "When ya were here I knew thar was somethin about ya. I thought a lot about ya after ya left. A couple French agents stopped by and asked all sorts of questions about ya and wanted to know what ya was up to. I told 'em everythin that ya told me because I thought at the time the more people that were out lookin for Ben the better."

Denis took another sip of water and straightened up in his chair. "I still don't know what it is. Yar good at what ya do, that's for sure. I knew thar was someone who set me up and I sure tried everythin to find out who it coulda been." He paused and took a few slow, deep breaths. "I knew someday I'd find out who did this to me and I knew exactly what I'd do to that person when I found out. If this had turned out any differently ya wouldn't be standing about now. That was ma plan."

Denis looked over at Ben and motioned for him to come over. He reached out and took hold of Ben's hand. "This is some woman ya found for yarself. When she left here the last time thar was no doubt in ma mind that she loved ya and thar was no doubt that she'd find ya. She's damn good at what she does and I'm damn glad she's on ma side now. She whooped me once and I don't wanta have to go up against her agin."

Denis waved at Alex with his other hand. "Come here." Alex walked over and reached for Denis' hand. "Ya two are two special people that are a lot alike in some ways, maybe a lot a ways. I couldn't be any happier for ya. Now put some smiles back on and let's have us all another tinnie!"

# CHAPTER 24

Four walls, no windows, an eight foot ceiling and vinyl flooring gave the room the appearance of a cheap motel that was rented by the hour. But it was furnished with tens of thousand of dollars in state–of–the art computer and electronic equipment. One wall was covered with memorabilia of past Antarctic explorations; a photograph of the German ship MS Schwabenland with its two Dornier aircraft on board hung prominently in the middle. The arctic veteran and geology professor, Erich von Drygalsk, who had led an expedition to the region in 1901and Alfred Ritscher standing at the helm of the Kriegsmarine in 1938 adorned the two sides of the Schwabenland photo.

"Take me on a little tour, Lukas. I'm wagering you've exceeded all my expectations down here. You've been a great asset to me and when this is all over I think a bonus is in order for you."

"I'm just doing my job the best I can, Mr. Price, but a bonus? Now that'd be very generous of you."

"Well, you've earned it. Say, Leon told me he's been having some troubles with the PistenBully the past few weeks. Have you taken a look at it yourself?"

"We worked on it this morning right after Jaspar called. The runway needed some more packing. It's pretty temperamental, but there's nothing wrong with her we can't fix on our own. Leon gave Jaspar a list of some spare parts we could use. No hurry, though."

The PistenBully 600 Polar was an all purpose utility vehicle that served a myriad of purposes in each of the research stations on the continent. With a band of modular steel plates wrapped around each of the two continuous tracks, the vehicles were used to plow or pack new–fallen snow. Jaspar always called Lukas just before leaving Hobart to get a "hands on the ground" weather forecast and to remind him to pack down the runway.

Alan rose from his chair, put an arm around Lukas and drew him tight. "Show me all the great things you're doing here. I want to check it all out for myself. This could be my last trip down here and I would like one final tour of the place."

Lukas opened the door and led Alan down a narrow hallway to an octagonal shaped room that at first sight appeared to be nothing more than an abandoned lab. Tables were cluttered with equipment used in the facility: a High–Order Genetic Assembly System used for oligonucleotide stitching; a $CO_2$ incubator; two thermal cyclers; and three fluorescent microscopes. At the far end of the room a glass panel revealed a storage room filled with neatly shelved shiny stainless steel cylinders.

"Well, it's all done. You're looking at 32 canisters, each packed with the G–16 virus and enough liquid nitrogen to keep them at a steady temperature of –270 degrees Fahrenheit. At that temperature the viruses should last indefinitely. Well past our lifetimes, that's for sure."

Lukas Müller had worked exclusively for Alan since Grinhaus had been first formed. It had been no accident that Alan had met Lukas, brought him into his fold and made him the President of Grinhaus. Lukas had felt a true sense of pride and accomplishment that such a title had been bestowed upon him even though he had been acutely aware that Alan made all the important decisions himself.

Alan had met Lukas seven years ago in Berlin. He had been in the throes of finalizing his plan to rehab the Black Swan Bunker, which would serve as the focal point for his whole scheme. Lukas had been a civil engineer with middle–of–the–road credentials that had lodged him permanently in the middle of the pack. What had distinguished him to Alan had been his lack of family ties and the fact that he had recently gone through a divorce. Alan had hired Lukas as a consultant to Sterling and had sent him off to physically inspect a number of facilities Sterling had used as staging centers for its operations. Lukas believed he had been hired by Sterling when in fact his paycheck had been electronically deposited in his checking account using a string of untraceable offshore accounts. Alan had made sure Lukas had been paid a sum considerably beyond his real worth in an effort to gain his loyalty and to assure that he would be around when he was finally needed.

Alan had grown fond of Lukas during that time and had enjoyed his company when they had been together. Lukas himself had been a history buff with unique knowledge of the myths and lore that had surrounded the days before and after the collapse of the Third Reich. Alan had learned of this early on and they had spent hours bantering about what they each had believed to be true or just some fanciful story. Alan actually enjoyed Lukas' company and trusted him, although trust was an unfamiliar concept to him.

Alan placed his hands on the glass, leaned forward and grinned. "Well done. Well done, Lukas. When I leave here shortly I'd like to take a couple of those canisters with me. Why don't you have someone bring two of them to the front office?"

"Certainly, Mr. Price."

"Tell me Lukas; since you've been here you've had a chance to go through everything down here. Is there any reason to believe that any of this would collapse? The walls aren't going to come tumbling down are they?"

Lukas shook his head. "I'll tell you, Mr. Price, the only way I could even imagine that could happen would be if this whole continent melts. I don't know how they built this, but it's a real engineering masterpiece. I've been through every square inch of these tunnels and they're all reinforced with steel beams that have been anchored right into the ice. That's a pretty solid footing in my book. I can't even fathom the equipment and manpower it must have taken to bore the tunnels and set those beams."

Alan put his arm around Lukas and led him to the door. "Yeah, it was some feat alright. Come on, let's head back to the office and see what we can so about getting you out of here. You're probably itching to get back home."

# CHAPTER 25

"We should be at our destination in about an hour. Any of you mates gonna need anythin before we get there?" The Naval Lieutenant stood at a crisp attention outside the galley.

Alex spoke first. "Thank you Lieutenant. We should be fine until then."

The Lieutenant nodded, made a sharp about–face and closed the door to the cabin.

Devon was slouched back in his seat twirling a pencil between his fingers. "Well, in a little over an hour you two are going to be giving up your warm confines for some god–forsaken ice box. You guys ready for that?"

Benjamin laughed. "It won't be so bad, Devon. When I was here years ago we didn't have Gore–Tex and the quilted freezer suits that they use now. Wool jackets and leather boots were it, but it didn't seem that cold." He laughed again. "But we did have warm showers and hot drinks at the end of each day waiting for us on the boat."

Denis had made the arrangements for the three to be transported from Hobart to Casey Station in Antarctica. He knew the government owed him a favor; in fact the way he had looked at it they had owed him a lifetime of favors. He had personally called the Prime Minister to plead his case. Even though the Prime Minister had pushed and cajoled Denis to find out the reason for his urgency, ultimately he had acceded to Denis' request without knowing the reasons behind it. Denis had agreed with Alex that secrecy was mandatory if they were to succeed. The fewer people that knew what they were up to the better. The Australian Navy had agreed to fly them to Casey Station, one of Australia's three permanent research stations on the continent and the only one with a runway capable of handling intercontinental jets.

They sat around a table with naval charts of the region spread about. Devon had spent the past few days learning everything he could about Antarctica and it had been apparent he had been a fast learner. He had drawn his own log detailing the flight information he had for each of Sterling's flights to the Antarctic region. The last registered landing point for each of Sterling's eight flights and the one that had landed just four days ago had been Hobart. Using the dates and times for those logs, he had accessed real time satellite images and had traced each of those flights. After a re–fueling stop in Hobart each flight had followed the 142 degree East Longitude and had landed at an unknown destination approximately 38 degrees West Longitude and 87 degrees South Latitude. The area had been devoid of any international research station and there had been no apparent reason to land an aircraft there.

Alex pointed to a small cove, Vincennes Bay, in East Antarctica. "This is Australia's Casey Station where we'll be landing, and we'll use it as our base of operations. When we leave there we'll take a ski–equipped LC–130 Hercules that'll take us right to. . . here." She stuck the pen point near the Sterling landing spot. "The biggest problem we're going to have is to find a place to land that is close enough to this point without being seen. Even though it will be two or three in the morning, the sun is up and we could be spotted."

Ben leaned back in his chair with his hands clutched behind his neck. "So what's Plan B? What if we do get spotted and it's not the good guys?"

Alex gave a half–smile. "Then I guess we will end up in the bad guys' lair sooner than later. That's not necessarily a bad thing either. The satellite images do not show any structures in this area, so once we land we really won't know which direction to go. If we're spotted well. . . we will make the best of it."

Devon piped in, "Kind of like having the ice shelf in front of you break off and hoping you can walk on thin air, if you ask me. Better yet, it's like placing a bet on a horse named Tripod. Come on, Alex, you need something better than that. You can't put your lives into a bunch of guys' hands who could give a shit whether you're alive or not. If you happen to see someone first, how 'bout *you* shoot first and forget about the questions? That's my Plan B."

"No shooting! We are going to have a hard enough time finding. . . " Alex stopped in mid–sentence, jumped up and dashed over to Devon. She spun his laptop around. "This is a long shot, but it just hit me."

Alex's fingers danced across the keyboard. For the next few minutes no one spoke. They had been around Alex long enough to know that when an idea popped into her head there was no interrupting her. Finally, "Devon! Remember the other day when we were talking about the Polar Hole theory? We both dismissed it as just another good–for–nothing myth, but maybe there's something to it."

She whirled around and rose from her chair. She placed her hands on the table, leaned forward and saw the expectant look in her companions' eyes, as if they were awaiting a revelation. "This is a very strange idea, but one that we should really think about."

Devon winced. "Oh–oh, here it comes."

She stood tall and began to move about; her steps were slow and deliberate. "There's a group out there that have proposed a theory that the North and South Pole each have a polar opening and those openings were formed when the earth was first created and they've evolved over time. The earth's centrifugal force threw matter away from the axis of rotation which left hollow openings at the two axis points."

Ben raised his head. "A good theory Alex, but I would imagine that these Polar Holes would have been discovered by now. What about satellite images? Or past explorations to the area?"

"That may just be the clincher. Let me show you something."

Alex sat back down and scrolled through the files on Devon's laptop. "Devon and I logged into NORAD's computers looking for that answer and here it is." They all huddled around Alex peering over her shoulder at the image on her screen. "Look at this. This shows the flight paths of all the polar orbiting satellites at the North Pole. The interesting part of this satellite image is that on the Russian side of the pole there are no orbiting satellites between about 115 degrees and 155 degrees East Longitude. Some of the first satellites put up over the North Pole vanished. The proposed theory is that this may have happened because they flew over the polar opening without realizing it. That's one explanation, anyway, and it makes some sense to me. But, after that, polar orbiting satellites have all been placed in orbit so that they don't pass over the polar opening. That may be why we see the void here where there are no current satellites."

"Were any of those early satellites ever found?" Ben asked

"Not that we could discover, but if you believe in the Polar Hole theory there is no gravity inside the hole. For this to happen the two polar holes would need to extend all the way through the earth so there would be no matter over the polar openings to exert equal gravitational acceleration towards the center of the Earth. If anything were to fly over one of these openings, depending upon its altitude, it would vanish into space or follow the curvature of the opening into the earth and crash inside the hole."

An air of cynicism rang in Ben's voice, "Come on, Alex. This Polar Hole theory seems logical enough and would be a good case study for the classroom, but better minds than ours and with far more sophisticated equipment have looked into this and they've come up blank—right?" He raised a brow and continued, "Why are we suddenly going to find this rabbit hole?"

"Absence of evidence is not evidence of absence. Do you have any better ideas?" Alex countered.

Ben placed his hands on the table and looked around. "I feel like we're flying off into an unknown mathematical equation, more like a black hole, or to someplace where hundreds of others have been but no one really knows what's there. . . like the Bermuda Triangle maybe. All I can suggest is that when we get there we'll see something that will give us some type of clue. I can't imagine that Sterling has landed a plane nine times in the same place and nothing's there."

"I'm not trying to talk anyone into this idea, Ben, not at all. I agree with you it is pretty far–fetched and the weight of scientific evidence would support that. But, the location where they landed those flights also supports this whole idea."

Ben cocked his head. "How so?"

Alex continued, "The original polar holes when the earth was created would have had to have been located at the north and south axis points. Over geological time we know the earth has tilted a few degrees. Large, planet sized comets have struck the earth during this timeframe and that has had an impact. One really interesting fact Devon and I found was when the Pyramid of Giza was constructed over 4500 years ago its orientation was perfectly aligned at the time with the earth's original axis of rotation and it pointed toward what was then called the North Polar Star. When archaeologists discovered the passageway they determined it had actually shifted 2.3 degrees. The earth's axis may have tilted since the construction of that pyramid."

"So if there were polar holes at the earth's creation you're saying those holes have now shifted. Wouldn't new holes appear over time at the axis points?

"Yes, you would think so, but remember with the time span we're talking about it would take millions of years for an effect like that to occur."

"I would assume that the size and configuration of the holes would change if they have shifted. They probably wouldn't have closed up, though, in such a short time span."

"No, probably not." Alex paused and looked at Ben. "Now, stay with me. Here's why I think this just might work."

Alex pulled out a chart of the North Polar Region and stuck her pen very close to the North Pole. "Right here is where the center of the hole in the Arctic is; at 87.7 degrees North Latitude and 142.2 East Longitude."

"How so again?" Ben asked.

"The Pyramid of Giza gave us the 2.3 degrees and that would be from 90 degrees, so that's your 87.7 degrees. There's not much to go on for the Longitude location, but here is how I get there. We know that each of the Sterling flights followed the 142 degree longitude coordinate south after it left Hobart, crossed over the South Pole and landed at 87.4 degrees West Longitude. There was a small Russian passenger plane that went down somewhere near the 145 degree longitude line in the Arctic region in 1937. A large scale search effort failed to find that plane. The instrumentation they had back then wasn't as accurate as today and it could have skewed the location. Severe weather would have also affected their position. The plane simply disappeared. It may have disappeared into the Arctic polar hole. I think all this makes sense."

Ben sat still and rubbed his chin. "Maybe you're on to something. The 87 whatever latitude makes sense as a starting point, but the longitude could be off by quite a bit. Still, I like the idea. Well done."

"Keep in mind though, if this theory is correct the hole itself won't be exactly small in diameter. We could be talking twenty or thirty miles wide so even if the longitude is off some we still could be pretty close." Alex leaned back against the table and dropped her hands to her thighs. She had convinced herself that this was all worth a try.

# CHAPTER 26

"We're above all the turbulence now, Mr. Price. It's safe to walk around—and let me know if you should need anything."

Alan sat in a reclined seat in the middle of the plane. When he heard Jaspar's voice through the overhead speakers he brought his seat upright and stood up. He walked across the aisle where Lukas sat shuffling through some papers. Placing his hand on the back of Lukas' neck, he smiled. "I'm going to retire to my room for some privacy. Make yourself comfortable and if you need anything just buzz Jaspar. He can get you anything you may desire." Alan nodded and covered his smirk with his hand. He retreated to his aft stateroom.

Lukas rubbed the back of his neck, turned and shot Alan a puzzled look as the door closed behind him.

Inside his private stateroom Alan sat down, threw his feet on his desk and let out a loud sigh. Leaning back he closed his eyes and rubbed his thickset white brows. He could see tape stretched across the finish line and within a matter of days he would crash through that tape and raise his arms in triumph. Nothing could stop him now. Soon he would enjoy the spoils of his riches and use his new–found bounty to acquire even more. It was as limitless as his own imagination.

Alan picked up his phone and dialed.

"Ah, Mr. President! As always it's a pleasure to hear your voice. How are things today?"

"Quite hectic actually. I left a rather important meeting to take this call. What can I do for you?"

"Far be it from me to belittle anything you do, but I can't think of anything more important than taking a call from me. Wouldn't you agree?"

When Alan's goading failed to draw a response he quickly erupted, "Stephen! When I ask you a question I expect a reply. For one thing, it's common courtesy and even more importantly it's what I demand out of you. *Am. . . I. . . making. . . myself. . . clear. . . here?*"

"You have always made yourself perfectly clear to me, Alan. Now, what can I do for you?"

"I expect to be in Paris within the week. When I know the precise day I will let you know. Make sure you're around. I have your speech all written out and we can go through the details when I arrive. I'm sure you will be pleased with what I have prepared for you."

"Speech? I am afraid I do not quite understand, Alan. You never said anything about a speech. . . or anything else for that matter. What is it you have planned and just when is all this going to end?"

"Don't get too far ahead of yourself, my friend. The end is near, but let me just say that very soon you will be headline news in every newspaper and wire service throughout the world. Isn't that something all you politicians dream about?"

"Listen, Alan I have been. . . "

"Talk with you shortly, Stephen." Alan hung up the phone and punched the intercom button. "Jaspar! Bring me my scotch. It's time to celebrate. This is out last trip down to this god–forsaken hell hole."

# CHAPTER 27

Before they had left Gualala, it had been decided that Phil would stay behind. Despite Phil's outcries, someone needed to dig deeper into the dealings of Sterling and its CEO, Alan Price.

Alex had stopped in Santa Rosa, purchased a prepaid cell phone and had it delivered to Phil. She had reminded him to keep it on him at all times and to only use that phone when he needed to talk about anything that had to do with their plans. Just in case the house phone ended up being bugged it would be a good idea to use it periodically for other calls. Phil's protests had each been rebuffed by Alex, but he had relented and agreed to stay behind. His parting words, "It takes 42 muscles to frown and only four to extend my middle finger," had been just the kick in the pants that Alex had needed to lift her spirits.

Alex had a strong feeling that Price was the mastermind behind whatever it was they were looking for. She didn't buy his alibi that had first been put forward by the DGSE. When the news had first aired about the G–16 virus and the organizations and people behind its development, governments from around the world had been screaming for information and they had been screaming at the DGSE, the intelligence agency that had broken the news. No, the DGSE knew what had been happening or they wouldn't have kept

Price's disappearing act under wraps for two days. They must have known what Price was up to and how deep his involvement in all this went.

They had known very little about Alan Price at this point. His success with Sterling had been well chronicled on the web. His name had shown up on almost every major politician's political contributions filings. That had no doubt been a part of his strategy to obtain lucrative government contracts. Last year alone, Sterling had been awarded over $5 billion in new contracts by different U.S. government agencies, on top of the billions he had been awarded in previous years. While other countries didn't have the stringent political campaign finance reporting requirements that the U.S. had, Alex had been certain that the same strategy of greasing politicians' palms had been used with foreign heads of state and high–ranking officials. Sterling had contracts with each of the major European countries, South Korea, Russia, Brazil and scores of others. It had recently broken into the Middle East in a big way when the House of Saud, Saudi Arabia's royal family, had retained Sterling to put together an 800 member battalion of foreign troops. That new armed force would conduct special–ops missions inside and outside the country, defend oil pipelines and skyscrapers from terrorist attacks and quash internal revolts. For the Royal Family to rely on a force largely created by Americans, they had introduced a volatile element in an already combustible region where the United States had been widely viewed with suspicion.

Alan Price, on the other hand, didn't seem to have the background one would expect for the leader of such a powerful and politically connected company. His only consistent trait was that he had been a perpetual middle–of–the–packer. He had been adopted by a couple from Wales and the family had soon immigrated to the

United States. Settling in St. Louis, he had attended public schools and had received his Bachelor's Degree from American University, in Washington, D.C. He had spent his spare time reading obscure books about military tactics and engineering designs from World War II. He had been a mediocre student at best and had seemed destined to lead a mundane, uneventful life. It had come as a surprise to everyone that knew him when they had learned he had been accepted into the German Studies doctoral program at UC Berkeley.

He never completed his studies and he had dropped out of Berkeley after two and a half years. He had been a junior author on three publications all dealing with myths attributable to the Nazis both before and after the war. The Third Reich had visions of lasting for thousands of years and although it had lasted only twelve, that brief period had spawned magical myths that had been adhered to by most party officials. The Thule Society, The Ark of the Covenant, the New World Order had all been believed by the Nazis to be true.

Alan Price had spent much of his graduate school time researching the myth of the Hollow Earth. The Nazis had derived their beliefs from ancient underworld myths, that various things might be buried deep within the earth;—kingdoms, planets, phantom universes, super humans, even aliens. Hitler had been a fervent believer that the earth was hollow and the German military had launched several expeditions in an attempt to confirm that notion. The Germans had made annual expeditions to Tibet between 1926 and 1943 seeking to make contact with their Aryan forefathers in Shambala and Agharti—cities they had believed existed beneath the Himalayas.

Phil had started his search for clues about Alan Price by downloading from the University archives papers that Price had co–authored. Phil, himself, had spent his entire academic career at Berkeley. Well before he had left academia he had become one of the leading authorities in the ancient cultures of New Guinea. He had resigned his tenured faculty position and had left on no uncertain terms that he had been upset at the University's demands that he limit his radical voice and active participation in anti–war protests. He had not been one to compromise his beliefs under any circumstances; not then and not now.

Phil had called around and had searched the web for any information on the primary authors for each of Alan's co–authored papers, but he had reached a dead end. All except Dr. Maiman were deceased or had health issues which affected their reliability. When Phil had spoken to him he did recollect working with Price, but he couldn't remember anything unusual or striking about the man. He had recalled that he seemed to prefer a life of solitude rather than collaborate with others, but that had been the extent of it.

"Dr. Morgan? I'm sorry I've kept you waiting, but my whole afternoon is now free. Please. . . please sit down." Dr. Spence Maiman moved around the side of his desk and motioned to Phil to take a seat.

"Hey, no problem, Dr. Maiman, and please call me Phil. The Doctor tag never really felt like it was me, even when I was a professor."

"Okay then, Phil it is, and if you're more comfortable calling me Spence, please do so; it's all the same to me." Dr. Maiman put a thumb behind his tie and pushed it out. "Your Greenpeace sweatshirt gives away your Berkeley roots. Down here on the Farm our outfits are much more formal. We don't even observe casual Fridays around here. Maybe in another ten years things will change, who knows?"

Phil laughed. "I haven't been back on the Berkeley campus in oh, maybe five years. I'll bet things have tightened up some by now. Maybe you should lead the charge down here, you know, free–the–neck or casual–for–a–day."

Dr. Maiman smiled. "I've settled into the mold of being a good company man. I was never inclined to go up against the system or buck the flow. Kind of hard to imagine that I spent six years at Berkeley and came out as an establishment kind of guy, don't you think?"

"Nah, there's all kinds of people everywhere. That was probably one of the things I enjoyed the most about academia was rubbing shoulders and swapping ideas with so many different types of thinkers." Phil crossed a leg and leaned down to re–tie the laces to his sneakers. "So, Alan Price, a real enigma. Shall we get started? I don't want to take up too much of your time."

Dr. Maiman leaned comfortably back in his chair. "Okay, hopefully I can be of some help to you. After we spoke yesterday I tried to search through my memory logs to remember things about him. Oh, I know who he is today, who wouldn't? He's in the news now and then with his company, Sterling Defense, but I'm not so sure I can recall anything special or unusual when we were at Berkeley together."

"Well, let's give it a shot anyway." Phil opened a notebook and pulled out a pen and scribbled down a few notes. Looking back up at Dr. Maiman, he continued, "As I mentioned to you, I'm writing a biography on Mr. Price. I'm not sure exactly why, it's not anything I've ever done before, but there's something about him that intrigues me. I'm still trying to wrap my thoughts around it, but I'm enjoying the process. He doesn't seem like the type of guy who could have created a mega–company like Sterling, but he sure did. Anyway, I know you two were at Berkeley together for a few years and you authored a couple of publications together. Your doctorate degree was in Germanic Studies and even though Mr. Price didn't complete his degree he seemed pretty focused on the Third Reich. Is that a pretty fair statement so far?"

Dr. Maiman rubbed his chin and shot Phil an approving nod. "You know, now I remember a few conversations I had with Alan. He quizzed me more than once about my father. My father was in charge of the concentration camps in Norway and he was stationed at the Akershus Fortress in Oslo for the last year of the war. Before that, he was in Berlin with the Third Reich. I had already come to grips with who my father was and his political beliefs. It was something I blocked out when I was a kid, but eventually I came to terms with it and I didn't let it eat at me. Alan had a real infatuation with everything and anything about the Nazis. He knew more about them than I, but he was fascinated by the stories I remembered about my father and his connections within the rank and file. My father was a Colonel and as a physicist. He was involved in some of the party's early weapons research well before the war broke out."

"Maiman?" Phil cocked his head. "That's a Jewish name, isn't it? Seems at odds with a Colonel in the German army back then."

"Odd would be an understatement. No, my name back then was Von Schröder, but when I moved to the States I changed it. I was starting a new life and I wasn't overly proud of my heritage as you can imagine. Anyway, I knew a Maiman when I was in Berlin so I borrowed his name. It seems to fit."

"Makes perfect sense to me. You mentioned your father was involved in some research. What kind of research?"

Dr. Maiman let out a laugh. "Ask Alan that one. He seemed to know more about the early research than me. I don't really know what my father worked on. I was very young and he never talked to me about his work. I only learned about some of the things as I got older and looked into it myself. I don't know what research he was involved with specifically, though."

"Do you now anything about Alan's personal life back then that may be useful?"

"Hmm. . . " Dr. Maiman looked up and his thumb stroked the underside of his chin. "We never did much together outside of our studies and I'm not really sure he had much of a personal life, anyway. He was always at his desk when I arrived and he was there when I left. That's where he lived as far as I knew."

"When was the last time you saw Mr. Price? Do you two still keep in touch?"

Dr. Maiman shrugged his shoulders and shook his head. "Oh, we haven't seen one another or spoken in a lot of years. When he left Berkeley I know he traveled for a few years. He spent some time in Germany, if I recall correctly. . . oh yeah, South America, he traveled down there, too. He called me a few times and wanted to get together, but I had started a family by then and whatever free time I had was precious. We talked on the phone off and on, but we never did find the time to meet up. The next thing I knew he was a corporate hotshot. I never saw that one coming. So, what's all this I hear in the news about his disappearance, then his reappearance and the G–16 virus? Pretty heady stuff. Have you talked to Alan about any of that?"

"No, Mr. Price has pretty much shut me out of the loop as far as allowing me to interview him. When I finish my manuscript though, I plan to run it by him first to see if I can get some comments at that time. Until then I'm flying solo trying to learn what I can."

Dr. Maiman glanced over at this computer screen. "Give me a minute here. I need to take a look at this." He opened up his email and read a short note. "Well, so much for a free afternoon. Dean Henderson wants to see me, and that usually means he's going to need something right away. I'm sorry, but we can continue this another time if you'd like?"

Phil rose from his chair and extended a hand. "You've been very helpful, Spence. You've given me some very useful information and if I have any more questions, I know how to find you. How's that?"

"Excellent and I'm interested in taking a look at your manuscript, as well, when you've wrapped it up. Come on, I'll walk out with you."

# CHAPTER 28

E arlier in the day Phil had placed a call to Senator Constance
Hunter in Washington, D.C. She had been unavailable until
later that day, but Phil had been certain the receptionist had
understood the urgency of his call. He had needed to talk with her–
*now*.

While he generally liked Constance, Phil suspected she had
gone through her own soul revival in the past weeks. He hadn't
seen or talked to her since he and Alex had confronted her several
weeks ago about Ben's disappearance. It had been Phil's harsh words
that had finally caused her to break down and confess to knowing
more than even they had suspected. The news that Paul Brewster,
the Director of DARPA and the man behind the creation of the
G–16 virus, had been her father had stunned Phil. That revelation,
coupled with Brewster's long relationship with the other culprits in
the G–16 scandal, led to their eventual arrest, but Ben's whereabouts
had remained a mystery.

Constance had married Ben seven years ago, and almost
immediately they had fashioned their own paths. Ben had poured
his energies into the work of his foundation, The William Hunter
Foundation that he had established to help fund research to develop
a cure for cystic fibrosis. Ben's twin brother, William, had been

stricken by the disease and died from it when the two were only 10 years old. For years Ben had blamed himself for his brother's death and it had sent him spiraling downhill. He had pushed himself to the brink of death on a handful of occasions. As a young adult, he had the financial means to travel all over the world and living on the outer edge had become his everyday coping mechanism for his deep–rooted guilt. He had mountain climbed in the Himalayas, ice climbed in the Canadian Rockies, run with the bulls in Tamil Nadu, India, gone free diving with Whale Sharks in Sorsogon, the Philippines and raced on the Grand Prix circuit. He had become withdrawn and isolated and had taken on whatever physical challenge he could find that had death as a potential outcome.

A few years before he had met Constance, he had finally pulled himself up from the depths and rid himself of the demons that had haunted him. He had unshackled the chains that imprisoned his mind and he had freed himself from the guilt and shame he had harbored over not being able to save his brother's life.

When he had married Constance, he had looked forward to raising a family on the ranch he had purchased in Montana. That vision had been short–lived as Constance had quickly set a plan in motion that she had had since she had been a child. In no time she had become a United States Senator and Benjamin's dreams had been shelved.

Constance had connections to just about everyone in Washington's political and social circles and they could use her help to dig into those power structures for information about Price. Constance knew that Phil was Benjamin's best friend and she would suspect that he was aware that Benjamin had asked for a divorce. Her wounds would be raw and he would need to tread lightly and play things close to his vest.

Phil heard a knock on the door and a puzzled look shot across his face. He walked to the door and slowly opened it. A young man in his late twenties, at best, stood on the porch with his hands tucked inside his pants' pockets. "Yes?"

The young man reached up and swung his hat around so the brim faced frontward. "Hey man, I'm glad someone's home. I'm like way behind schedule and my girlfriend gets all over my ass when I'm late," he threw his hands up and laughed. "Which, my friend, is most of the time. So, since you're home, do you mind letting me use your phone to give her a call?" He waived his cell phone. "This thing doesn't work around here. You'd save my sorry ass, man."

Phil stepped aside. "Come on in. The phone's over there on the kitchen counter. Can't miss it."

Phil kept an eye on the young man and listened in from a safe distance to his short conversation. Boy, he thought, why would a guy get stuck with a woman like that? Better yet, why would a guy put up with a tongue–lashing like that?

The young man hung up the phone, turned toward Phil and muttered out loud, "Bitch."

Phil's arm swung around and pointed to the front door. "Okay, glad I could help. I hope things work out for you."

The young man tipped his baseball cap and murmured his thanks.

Phil watched through the window as the young man slammed the car door and sped off. His hand covered his mouth and his fingers massaged his stubbled chin. Nah, he thought, couldn't be. I'm just being paranoid.

Phil grabbed the phone on the first ring and after a few minutes he finally said, "Yes, Constance, he's fine, but he's not out of danger yet by any means."

"What do you mean? Where is he?" Constance's voice was rattled and on edge.

"Look, Constance, Ben's fine and that's about all I can tell you right now. He's not out of the woods yet, and it's best that no one knows that he's safe. We need to keep this on the Q T until we figure out a few more things. Understand? We need your help, but that's all I can tell you right now. Okay?"

Phil imagined Constance sitting in her office with the phone crammed in one ear and her fingers nervously tapping away on her desk. He had seen it many times. Her fingers tapping to a sharp beat while her mind moved with the same cadence. Finally, "Okay Phil, I understand, but I need to know more about what's going on. Is he really okay? And what do you mean by *we*? Who else knows what is going on? I suppose that Boudreau woman is at the heart of this somewhere."

Constance's tone when she slurred the name "Boudreau" told Phil that she may not have come to grips with the fact that her life with Ben, as she had known it or maybe had imagined it, was over. She and Ben had not had the time to talk further about a divorce since he first told her he was in love with Alex. Ben's disappearance and the intervening events had put their breakup on hold.

"Ben told me that he talked to you about a divorce and I know you guys haven't had a chance to talk about it any further. Right now Ben's fine, he's safe and that should be all that matters. You guys will have a chance to talk things through later, so I hope you can put that aside for now and help us out. We need your help Constance."

"Phil! I've been worried to death. Since Ben disappeared and then I found out my father was involved with that virus I've been beside myself with guilt. I don't know what to think. My father assures me that he had nothing to do with Ben's disappearance, but still I have so much guilt with all of this. Right now I just want to know that Ben is okay. Where is he? Is he really okay? What's going on, Phil?"

"Look Constance, I can't tell you where Ben is, not yet anyway. I've been with him and......"

Constance cut Phil off in mid–sentence. "Phil, I have a right to know. I'm still his wife and I want to know what's going on. I know our marriage is probably over, but that's the least of my concerns right now. I want to help in any way I can, but you need to give me more information about all this. You can't keep me in the dark."

Phil leaned against the kitchen counter with the phone jammed between his shoulder and ear and his free hand dug into the back of his neck. "Ben's fine, Constance, but. . . " Phil drew a quick breath. "He's been infected with that virus and there's a risk that it could be activated at anytime and. . . well. . . we're trying to make sure that'll never happen."

"Oh God no! I was told that the virus had been contained and there was no way anyone could get a hold of it. No, Phil, that can't be right. . . It just can't."

"It's true. . . unfortunately. The virus can be activated by something called an activating agent and we don't know if anyone actually has this and if they do have it where it is or who has it. Until we can find out more we need to keep all this quiet."

"I understand, but I still can't believe something like this has happened. When I talked to my father he told me there is no antidote for this virus. Once it's activated there is no known cure. No. . . what can I do to help?"

Phil brought Constance up to date with what they knew about Alan Price and how they suspected he was the mastermind behind all this. Constance had met Price on several occasions, but didn't know him well. He had appeared before her committee, the Senate Armed Services Committee, a number of times and she had met him socially at fundraisers and other political events, but she wasn't able to provide any information about him that could help. She agreed, though, to ask around and see if she could learn anything.

"One more thing, Phil. It sounds like Ms Boudreau is still involved with this. Is that true?"

"Yes, she is, Constance. It was Alex who found Ben and rescued him from where he was being held hostage."

"And she is with him now?"

"Constance. . . one thing I've learned about Alex is that you definitely want her on your side. If there's anyone who can find a way to finally put an end to all this and to repress the virus, it's her. The thought of that may hurt you, I know, but right now the important thing is that we find a way to make sure that Ben is finally safe. You and Ben will have your time together to sort through things."

"Thanks, Phil. I'll see what I can find out and you *will* call the minute you learn anything new—*please?*"

# CHAPTER 29

T he howling downdrafts penetrated Alex's quilted freezer suit. "We had better tether up here. This is close to a whiteout right now and if it gets any worse we could get separated."

Ben held his hand over his mouthpiece to block the wind. "Well, at least no one's going to spot us in this stuff."

When the LC–130 Hercules had begun the 1,422 mile flight the weather prediction had been cloudy with only a slight chance of snow. By the time they had landed it was snowing heavily with winds gusting to 35 miles per hour. They had been prepared for the –36 degree temperature, but with the strong possibility of whiteout conditions in front of them extra precautions were mandatory.

Alex and Ben watched as the LC–130 lifted off and disappeared into the blanket of white that completely surrounded them. The roar of the engines faded and was replaced by the sounds of the whirling winds. Their headsets were the only connection to the outside world. Devon had remained back at Casey Station where he could track their location by the GPS tracking device they had tightly secured to the inside of their freezer suits.

Their plan called for the LC–130 to fly to the Amundsen–Scott South Pole Station to re–fuel and wait there until Alex signaled they were ready to return. The Amundsen–Scott Station was operated by the United States and it was the closest station to the geographic South Pole. The station's name honored Roald Amundsen and Robert F. Scott, who had led expeditions to the South Pole in 1911 and 1912.

Ben was the first to throw his backpack on and the other two heard his sarcasm cackle through their headsets, "What do you say we head due south?"

Devon chimed in, "Hey, we went through that yesterday. You do have directions there, everything's not south you know."

Alex shot a smile at Ben and jumped to his defense. "Ben's just being Ben, Devon. Don't worry about him. He won't fall off the earth."

They had already rehearsed the different ways they could address their location and give directions to each other. Near the South Pole, Grid directions were used rather than compass directions. In the Grid system, North was along the Prime Meridian or 0° Longitude, pointing toward Greenwich, England. South would be 180° Longitude, East was 90° and West was 270°. They carried plastic coated maps with them they could refer to if needed.

"Okay, let's get moving. Devon, we're off. I'll wait for your instructions." Alex waved at Ben and the two began their journey.

For the next 30 minutes, Devon plotted their course using the coordinates he received from their GPS transmitter and he relayed instructions back to them to turn right or left until they were eventually headed toward their agreed upon destination—87.7 degrees South Latitude, 37.8 degrees West Longitude—the Polar Hole.

Devon was holed up in a communications room where he constantly switched back and forth between his two laptops. He tracked their movements on one, and he had logged on to the

NORAD system on the other keeping a constant eye on any satellite surveillance that might indicate something was afoot. With the heavy snowfall and the cloud cover he seriously doubted he would see anything.

The South Pole was covered by a moving sheet of ice more than two miles thick that drifted thirty feet per year in the direction of the Weddell Sea. On January 1, 2013, the area had been re–surveyed and a new marker had been placed at the South Pole coordinate—90 degrees South Latitude. Seven brass planets displayed on a copper inlay showed the position of the planets as viewed from the South Pole on Jan 1, 2013. In the very center was a small copper star that marked the South Pole.

The elevation at the South Pole was just over 9,300 feet above sea level and as Alex and Benjamin trudged toward their destination, Benjamin was the first to feel the effects of the high altitude. "I'm breathing way too hard for what we're doing here. I need to slow up a bit." He tugged on the rope just to make sure Alex heard him.

Alex stopped, turned and after a few steps backwards she saw Benjamin. "Let's take a few minutes here and regroup. I can imagine that after what you've been through you're feeling the effects of the altitude. We need to keep moving, though, just to stay warm, but we will slow up."

"Devon? At our current pace how long do you think it will take to get there?"

"You're maybe a third of the way there, so another two hours I'd say."

"Alright then, let's do it in three."

For the next three hours they trudged forward into a frozen plain of endless white in the middle of the highest, windiest, coldest, driest and loneliest continent on Earth. The snow had stopped falling, but the wind continued to gust and swirl. The diffuse lighting from the overhead clouds put them in a thick sea of fog and with the smooth surface of the fresh snow they couldn't judge the steepness of the slopes around them. They were completely surrounded by white in a one–dimensional world. Each step had to be carefully placed in front to make sure the surface was flat or to see if the terrain was changing. They threw snowballs in front of them to break the snow's surface and to try and see if there was any definition to give them any hint of where to place their next step.

Devon remained in constant communication. He used topographical maps to determine the slope of the terrain and to plot their progress. "I think you may be exactly where you want to be, assuming that Hole theory of yours has any merit. Can you see any better, Alex?"

"No, not really. Everything is still white and the light is so flat we still can't get a perspective on what's in front of us. Ben, let's start moving ahead in a parallel formation. We have twenty feet of rope between us so we'll be able to cover a wider path that way."

With Ben twenty feet to Alex's left they inched step by step forward.

"Stop!" Ben screamed through his headset and Alex halted in mid–step.

Alex and Devon shouted in unison, "What is it?!"

"I'm not sure, but it's not white. I'm going to get on my hands and knees and inch forward and check it out. Hold on."

Ben moved forward doing a slow crab walk in the snow. Suddenly the snow broke loose from under him. "Oh shit!'

"Ben!"

"Ben!"

The rope tightened. Alex dug her heels in and held tight.

# CHAPTER 30

The two sat huddled together in a vortex of the whistling windstorm. They were each tired in their own way, but the adrenaline rush after Benjamin had slipped had re–heightened their awareness and renewed their strength.

"It's a good thing there wasn't more rope between us. My feet hung over something. Maybe a few more feet and it would have been my whole body." Benjamin looked over at Alex, their faces inches away from each other and gave her a nudge. "I would've really tested your strength then."

Alex gave a lips–pressed–together smile. "I had your back."

Their headsets chattered with high pitched static and Devon's voice was barely audible. "I have your position right at 87.7, give or take. Can you see anything yet?"

"No, but I was pulling Ben upward so we've reached some kind of downward slope. How far down does it go, Devon?"

"The topo shows it should be flat for quite a ways, maybe fifteen miles it looks like. The elevation change should be minimal."

Ben countered, "Well that was pretty steep. The snow broke and I slid down something that was too steep to walk down."

Alex slid her pack from her shoulders and untied two bands of rope that were attached to the sides. Benjamin shot her an inquisitive look. "More safety precautions?"

"We may be on the edge of a crevasse." Alex continued to uncoil the rope. "We're going to need some longer ties. I'll tie one end to my harness and you can lower me down. I'll take the first look and then we can decide upon our next step."

Benjamin grabbed the rope and pulled it toward him. "I'm probably the only one here with any climbing experience. I guess this is one of those times where we get to learn a little about each other." He leaned into Alex. "You've done some ice climbing?"

Alex leaned closer. "None. That's why I should do this and you should stay here. You have the experience and we will probably need you later."

"Nice try." Benjamin smiled. "Overruled. I'll make the first attempt." He reached down and grabbed the end of the rope.

After cinching up and giving a few last minute instructions to Alex about the ins– and–outs of belaying, Benjamin turned on his stomach and began to slowly slide down the slope. The rope was marked in ten foot increments so Alex could keep track of his descent. At the twenty foot mark she heard Benjamin yell out, "I'm at the ledge. Hold on now and let the line out slowly. Keep it tight."

Inch by inch she released more line. She held her breath, but the altitude quickly reminded her to breathe. She felt her lungs expand as the icy air warmed and she gave a quick exhale. With each sound of Benjamin's voice over the headset she winced. "I can't believe what I'm feeling. Let out all the line you have."

Alex held the rope tight, "What's going on?"

"I'm not sure, but give me some more slack, lots of it, and I'll let you know."

"Alright, but that's it until I get an answer."

She let out the rest of the rope, knotted the end to another coil of rope and held tight.

Ben screamed out, "You're about to be in the science books, Alex! I'm practically floating in air! This is unbelievable! This place is huge. Let out everything, I'm going exploring."

For the next fifteen minutes, Alex uncoiled the rest of the rope, but she kept a tight rein on Ben.

The feeling of near–weightlessness was unlike anything Ben had ever experienced and Alex could hear his screams of joy and amazement echo across the vast cavern below her. She was trying to relay all this to Devon, but she only heard an intermittent voice drowned out by the static.

"Devon, I don't know if you can hear me or not, but I am only getting bits and pieces from you. We must be losing our connection so I'm going to turn off my headset. I'll try to check in periodically and see if the connection is any better."

"Ben, I am going turn my headset off, but first you should come back up."

"I hear something Alex. A soft humming, maybe a hundred feet above me. I'm going to check it out first."

"Okay, but maybe just a few minutes more. You need to come back up."

"Roger that! Off I go!"

Alex continued to try and get though to Devon, but the static became constant. She was certain their connection had been lost. I wonder what he heard, she thought. I know he knows our coordinates, but that may be it. She shook her head in disbelief. All of this was beyond anything she could imagine.

"Alex! I'm holding on to some kind of vent and I think there's a fan or something on the other side. The vent's attached from the other side, but I may be able to pry the cover off with something. What do you have that I might be able to use?"

"I have a Leatherman. Let me see if I can find something that I can use to attach it to the rope and slide it down. Just a minute."

"No, come on down and bring it with you. Grab my pack too. You're going to love this."

Alex shook her head. "I don't think so, Ben. That doesn't sound like the safest plan."

"Hammer a piton into the ice and tie the rope to it. Slide a carabiner through the rope and your harness and when you get to the edge, give yourself a push. In seconds you'll see what I'm talking about. Come on, you'll love this. Come on Alex, this vent has to lead us somewhere and I know you can't resist a good challenge."

Alex grabbed Ben's pack and slowly slid down the same path he used. She dug her hands into the ice and held on. A vast gray silhouette was just beyond her reach, but the diffused light still prevented her from seeing any dimensions below. It felt like she was about to slide onto an endless gray tarp that she knew covered a bottomless pit below. She took a deep breath, not really knowing if it would be her last and she hurled herself off the edge.

# CHAPTER 31

Ben dropped down to the floor; Alex followed. They had either passed through a time–warp or were standing in a hidden repository of Nazi artifacts. Alex's eyes panned the far wall and her jaw dropped at the sight of the MS Schwabenland photograph. The cogs in her memory banks spun into overdrive. "I don't believe this." She held her breath and then heaved a sigh.

Alex knew that before the Second World War, the Nazis had built weapons research labs and had moved munitions facilities and high–value industrial plants underground. Some of those facilities had been vast, encompassing miles of underground tunnels and they had housed both the industrial means of war production and the workers themselves. The underground complexes of the Jonas Valley south of Nordhausen in Thuringia had served as a center of government and most notably a research center for advanced weaponry. The Nazi's far–reaching network of underground facilities for weapons production had been discovered throughout Germany, Austria, Czechoslovakia and Poland.

A shiver crept up Alex's spine. "Devon said Price was a war buff, but this is beyond anyone's wildest imagination. I've heard. . . "

"Alex. . . I'm. . . " Benjamin stopped in mid–sentence. His lips formed a circle, but he couldn't speak. Blood drained from his face.

"Ben, what is it?!" Alex rushed to him and grabbed his shoulder. "What is it, Ben? Are you okay? What's going on?"

Benjamin reached out with both hands. "Alex. . . Alex m. . . my memory. . . I remember things. I remember you! I remember. . . *my memory's back*!"

Alex tightened her grip. She wanted to grab him, embrace him with all her strength, yet she was drowning in uncertainty. Those past days since she had first found Benjamin and had learned that he no recollection of her had left a part of her hanging over an abyss. She had been fighting a battle within her being. That had been an unfamiliar battle for Alex, the only one she had never fully prepared for. Struggle had always been second nature to her, and she was used to being the victor. This time was different. This was not the battle she had perfected—the one within her mind. She even knew how to struggle within her heart. That narrow intersection—where the mind crossed paths with the heart, where reason conflicted with emotion, where the intellect clashed with passion—was somewhere Alex had never been.

There was no way she deserved someone like Benjamin. She knew that. She had deceived the first and only man in her life who had lovingly opened himself up to her and shared his innermost thoughts and dreams. Her past had been littered with countless lives she had destroyed. She had come into his world and had destroyed it. Her whole time with him had been based on a lie, a ruthless deception. There was no way she was worthy of this decent, kind and pure man. A stark, cold reality had taken root within her—her aimless wandering would continue—without Benjamin.

Was she dreaming? Was his memory really back? She stood still. "Alex!"

Benjamin threw his arms around her and pulled her close. His chin rested on her head and his eyes were closed. "God what happened?! I remember things now—everything. Alex. I remember you, going to Paris to meet you, jumping from the car. I think I remember everything. This is all so sudden." His hands reached up and his fingers cradled her face. He looked tenderly into Alex's eyes and his voice quivered. "What's going on? This must've been so hard on you. I'm so sorry that. . . "

Alex pressed her hand across Benjamin's lips. "Quiet. This isn't a time to be sorry. No. . . no. . . " At that moment all the emptiness she felt became a distant memory.

Alex closed her eyes, stood on her toes and pressed her lips against Benjamin's. They stood locked in an embrace, their lips tasting the other's passion and their hands caressing and exploring for what each had longed for. Alex's legs trembled, her heart pounded. She was lost in the moment, the moment she was afraid had disappeared.

Benjamin slid his hands down Alex's sides and pressed his thumbs into her hip bones and cupped his hands around her buttocks. He gently rubbed her nose with his. "You've stuck with me through all this. I remember everything you've told me since you helped me escape from Koidu. I didn't know what to think about it at the time, but I want you to know now, I love you. This has been such a strange ordeal, Alex. We'll get through this together and then we can start to really get to know each other—the right way this time."

Alex met Benjamin's longing gaze and returned one of her own. Her eyes dampened and her heart opened. "I've been so afraid you wouldn't remember anything. In so many ways it might have been better for you not to remember all the horrible things I have done— *done to you*. In so many ways I've turned your life upside down. . . "

"No, Alex," Benjamin cut her off, "in so many ways you've given my life meaning. A lot of things were missing in my life before I met you. Things I didn't even know were missing. Oh yeah," he tilted his head back and chuckled, "a lot has happened, that's for sure. But, all that's part of life and here we are now, stuck in some tunnel in the South Pole looking for something that probably doesn't exist. I wouldn't trade this experience for anything."

Alex smiled and pressed a finger into Benjamin's lower lip. "Can I say one more thing?"

Benjamin mumbled, "mmm. . . mmm."

"When I returned to the hospital and you were gone no one knew where you were or what had happened. I sat on your empty bed and made two promises to you. I promised that I would take care of your eagle and release him to the wild when he was ready. I have done that, Ben. Your eagle has returned to his mountain and he is with his mate again. I also promised you that I would find you no matter what and bring you home safely. I have found you, but you're not safe yet. I will find some way to get the antidote for this virus or to repress it so you will be safe. When that's done I want more than anything to have a calm and peaceful life. Does that make any sense?"

Benjamin cupped his hands under Alex's chin and lifted it toward him. He looked into her eyes and saw the tears she was holding back. "I want to know the name of your first grade teacher, scrambled or over easy, your birthday, the name of your first boyfriend, the first dream you ever had and. . . I want to know what side of the bed you want to wake up on in the morning." He pulled her tight and pressed her head against his chest. "We have a lot to teach each other."

"I don't want to let you go. I could hold you forever, but the sooner we get started down here the sooner we'll get out of here. You're not going to believe what we've stumbled onto."

The two scouted around the room and Alex filled Benjamin in on what she believed was an underground facility possibly built by the Nazis around the time of the Second World War. She pointed to the photographs on the wall, the swastika flag in the corner and the shelves of medallions, badges, coins and munitions.

Alex pulled a leather bound book from a shelf and opened the pages. "*Mein Kampf.*" She shook her head in disbelief. "This is an original. It's the first volume of Hitler's autobiography and it details his early political ideology. He actually wrote it when he was imprisoned after his failed attempt to seize control of Munich; 1923, I think."

Benjamin stood next to Alex and rubbed a finger along the open page. "It makes my hair stand up to even think about this." He looked up and his eyes swept the room, "Let's finish looking through the rest of the drawers and get out of here—the sooner the better."

Alex placed the book back on the shelf and nodded. "You're right. This whole place is eerie. We'll finish looking around and find another way out of here."

The two rifled through the drawers and cabinets, searching files and boxes. "Look at this. If this thing works we can get some help. Whatever this place is I'm almost certain it's been kept a secret." Alex picked up an Iridium Satellite Telephone. "There's no power to this. It's dead. If I can find a way to charge this maybe I can get a call through to Devon and tell him what's going on."

While Alex searched for a replacement battery, Ben pulled rolled–up sheets of paper from a circular bin and unfolded the set on a table. The writing was in German, but he could tell by the diagrams what he was looking at. "Come here, Alex. This is written in German, but I think this is a set of plans for the whole inside of this tunnel."

Alex pressed her hands on the edges of the diagram and held it flat. "You're right. These are the schematics for the Schwarzen Schwan Bunker built in hmm. . . 1942. The Legend down here tells us what each of these markings mean."

"You speak German? What's that mean?" He pointed to the bold name on the bottom corner.

"I do. Schwarzen Schwan Bunker means Black Swan Bunker. This looks like a copy of the original schematics and the markings all represent items that were added in 2011 and 2012."

They thumbed through the pages one at a time. The drawings showed the layout of the underground bunker with its mechanical systems for heat and ventilation; structural details for the walls, ceiling and flooring; electrical plans for self generation and even plumbing details for an odorless waste removal system. "It looks like a set of 'as–builts' that we can use to explore this place. Look, Alex, this has to be the main entrance right here." Ben placed his forefinger on a spot located down a hallway. "Let's check it out. I knew there had to be a better way to get into here than the way we came."

Ben rolled up the set of plans and tucked them under his arm. He looked over at Alex and smiled as they walked toward the door leading to the hallway. "Maybe we shouldn't be in such a hurry to get out of here. I saw some sleeping quarters in one of the hallways that we just might want to check out first." He gave her a half–wink.

Alex completed the wink. "And when did you learn how to read minds? Or am I just that obvious?"

Ben reached over and put an arm around Alex's waist and pulled her close. His fingers brushed her cheek and then cradled the nape of her neck. He leaned into her and parted his lips. Finally, Alex pulled back and looked at Ben, her aquamarine eyes were crazed with excitement. "We can look for that exit route later." Ben reached down and grabbed the door handle.

When the door flung open Alex turned, took one step and froze. They both stood in the doorway looking into the barrels of twin Sig Saur P–6 9mm's. "Congratulations, you two are the first unannounced visitors we've had down here. Now explain yourselves."

Ben etched a smile on his face and took a step forward.

"Stop!" One look at these men and they both knew they were trouble. One was stocky, grubby and hairless and his cold eyes bored into them like a shark's circling its prey. The other man was half a head taller with an oval face and a scar below his left eye. They stood like mechanical robots programmed to shoot first and ask questions later. The man with the scar raised his gun and pointed it directly at Ben's face. "We have our orders and we have no problem carrying 'em out. There are a dozen ways for us to dispose of your bodies and no one will ever know what happened to you. So I suggest you tell us who you are and what you're doin' here."

Ben raised both arms in a gesture of surrender. "I don't imagine Mr. Price would approve of this type of hospitality. Don't you think?"

Raising his hands slightly higher his smile turncd to a solemn grimace and Ben continued, "We are both investors with Mr. Price in this enterprise down here. We were supposed to meet him here a few days ago, but we were delayed by the weather. That happens around here, as you guys must know. Now, I would appreciate it if you'd lower those guns and tell us exactly who you are. And, where's Mr. Price?"

Each man lowered his gun, but kept them aimed at the two intruders. The man with the cold eyes took one step forward. "Two things wrong with your story as I see it. Mr. Price didn't say nothin' about nobody droppin' by and I doubt that he would have had you come through the back door. His manners are much better than that. Now, if you two would follow me, we'll take you some place very comfortable." They each moved aside and stood opposite each other with their backs to the wall. Beads of perspiration rolled down the side of each man's face and their cloths were soaked with sweat. "And keep your hands up where we can see em." His cold eyes darkened and he motioned with his gun.

"I have a feeling you'll regret this." Ben kept his hands high and walked past the two men with Alex at his side. Just before they reached the end of the hallway one of the men yelled out, "Hold it right there! Now open the door on your left and go in—one at a time—and very slowly."

Alex pushed the door open. She thought about slamming the door shut just as Benjamin entered the room, but quickly discarded the idea. The door wouldn't stop their bullets and she couldn't see any escape route from the room.

"Okay, take off your vests and empty your pockets. Pull them out so we know they're empty."

Ben slowly started to remove his vest, but Alex hesitated. She saw what was behind the window and she would rather take her chances against these two than be stuck in that room. "So tell me, have you two been left behind here to rot along with us? My guess is yes and since we have a plane and people waiting for us outside you're probably better off siding with us at this point. Loyalty was never something that Mr. Price has rewarded in the past, just in case you didn't know that. Why do you guys think you're so special?"

The taller of the two glanced at his partner and let out a throaty laugh. "Don't worry about us, we'll be fine. Now, I'm not goin' to tell you again, empty your pockets!" He brushed the sweat from his forehead.

Alex huffed her displeasure, but slowly followed orders. "Okay, I'll do as you say, but this is the last time I'll offer either of you a way out of here. Once you lock us inside of there," she motioned with her hand, looked briefly at the window and continued, "all bets are off. You'll need to find your own way home. Although pretty soon, when our friends up above decide we're missing, they'll storm in here with more firepower than you have down here. I wish you both luck."

A single shot was fired and landed between Alex's legs. The bullet hit the floor, ricocheted up and lodged in the wall behind her. Benjamin reacted on instinct, but before his first step landed he felt a bullet graze his calf. "That's just a flesh wound. The next one won't be. Now both of you! Get on with it!"

When they entered the locked room a chill swept over them. It wasn't from the freezing room temperature that had already penetrated their clothing or from their knowing there was no escape. They each looked at the rows of shiny stainless steel canisters marked with a bright red warning label and they knew exactly where they were.

# CHAPTER 32

"Save your strength, Ben. That won't do any good."

Benjamin cocked his leg and kicked the door. Nothing. He had been kicking the door and the window for the past few minutes, but there were no vibrations, no cracking or no jarring of the hardware. Everything was locked solid. "This has to break at some point. I'll keep trying."

Alex stepped forward and wrapped her arms around Benjamin's shoulders. "We need to come up with another way to get out of here. That keyless deadbolt lock connects to a steel door jamb. You're not going to kick that thing open. This room was designed to keep people out, so we're stuck here unless we can come up with some other way to get out."

Ben slumped to the floor and Alex sat down beside him. "Damn, I can't believe this! We should have taken our chances against those guys when we had the chance."

"You're probably right, but here we are. I don't see any ventilation in here either so I'm assuming the room is air–tight. We need to control our breathing the best we can until we figure something out." Alex reached around Benjamin's legs and leaned into him. "Maybe thirty minutes of oxygen and that's it."

"I knew we should have just left things alone. We never should've come here." Benjamin panned the room and then his head sunk to his knees. "Thirty minutes—that's it, huh?"

"Maybe more, I don't know."

"Have you ever been in this situation before? Tell me you have a way to get us out of here."

Alex leaned her head back against the wall. "I think my whole life has been like this, moving around inside four walls trying to find a way to get out. Eventually, I learned how to live inside the box and I never knew what was on the outside until I met you." She turned her head and looked at Benjamin, "I love what I found once I got on the outside. I don't want to lose that."

Benjamin lifted his head, turned toward Alex and brushed the hair from her eyes. "Just so you know, Alex I wouldn't have traded the short time I've had with you for anything." He glanced quickly around the room and then back at Alex. "This isn't the way I expected things to turn out though, stuck somewhere like this. It's odd, don't you think, I've got some damned awful virus stuck in me and looking around I'm surrounded by the very same thing that we were trying to get rid of? Do you think that's what they have stored in all these canisters?"

Alex's eyes flickered with a hint of excitement. "You know. . . " she murmured, biting her lower lip. She stood up and pulled one of the canisters from the shelf. "Do you think you have a few more kicks left in you?"

"What do you mean?"

Alex cradled the canister in her hands. "This is our get out of jail card—liquid nitrogen. I should have thought of this earlier." She placed the canister on the ground and dropped to her knees. "We can pour some liquid nitrogen on that metal door handle and it'll shatter like broken glass. All of the particles in metal are organized in an orderly and repeated pattern, but once it's exposed to the extreme cold of the liquid nitrogen those same particles will be rearranged in a random pattern, the same as glass. So the door handle will shatter and all you'll have to do is give it a good solid kick. That will break the handle off and the deadbolt will be exposed and we'll do the same with it."

"How do you know these things are filled with liquid nitrogen?"

"See that insignia on the side of the shelf that looks like a snow flake? That's the international cryogen warning symbol. I'm guessing that each of these canisters is filled with the G–16 virus and liquid nitrogen is used to preserve the virus. Anyway, we won't know until we try."

Alex loosened the toggles and removed the lid. She snapped off one of the toggles and dropped it in the canister. It shattered instantly. "There's our answer. Let's bust out of here. We'll have to do this quickly. I'm sure the noise will bring those two guys running back here in no time. "

Alex carefully lifted the canister and poured a small amount of liquid nitrogen on the door handle and within seconds it had visibly splintered. "A sharp kick should break this off."

Benjamin cocked his leg and kicked the door handle from the side. "One more, Ben. Give it one more kick."

With the second kick the handle completely shattered and Alex pulled the final broken pieces from the hole. She saw the deadbolt through the cut–out and doused it with more liquid nitrogen. With two more sharp kicks the door flew open and they quickly gathered their belongings.

They waited a few minutes hidden behind the door and then Alex whispered to Benjamin, "No sign of them. Let's take our chances."

Alex opened the door and the two moved silently down the hallway back toward the room where they had entered the bunker. They reached the closed door and Alex peered in through the small window. "They're both on the floor. Something's happened to them. Take a look."

Benjamin stared through the window and his face turned white. He looked like he had just been exposed to gangrene. "Those guys have the virus. It's just like the video they showed me at Koidu. God, I can't believe this."

They glared through the window and watched saucer–eyed as the two men, balled up in a fetal position, squirmed on the floor. The virus was eating away at their internal organs and they writhed in pain, helpless and unaware that a lethal virus was destroying their cells at a rate that would bring an end to their agony within days.

Benjamin turned away and leaned against the side wall. "Let's just get the hell out of here." He pointed down the hall. "The shaft to the main entrance is down the hall. Let's go."

"Wait here." Alex turned the door handle and looked at Ben. "I'm going to get the hard drives. There may be something on them that will be useful later."

# CHAPTER 33

"Alex!? Alex, can you hear me?"

Alex's eyes half–opened, but there was a blankness in her a stare, a disconnect to her surroundings. Benjamin brushed her hair from her eyes and felt her forehead.

Benjamin was the first to come to and sit up. All he knew at that point was he was in a small room with two cots, a table and a single window set high on the wall. He had no idea how they had gotten there or where they were. He leaned down and kissed Alex on the cheek. "You're okay. Just rest. I'll be right here."

Benjamin rose from Alex's cot and walked to the door. He looked out through the small window to a barren hallway. The door was locked from the outside so whoever had brought them there wanted to make sure they controlled their movements.

He had no idea what had happened. The last thing he had remembered was feeling lost. They had left the Black Swan Bunker and had regained communication with Devon and a plane was on its way. Their GPS transponders had been working and Devon was leading them back to the location where the plane had landed earlier that day. Benjamin hoped that maybe they were at Casey Station and they were being kept in isolation to make sure they were alright. A comforting thought, but somehow he didn't believe it.

"Oh, I feel like I just awoke from a week's sleep." Alex was sitting up on her cot with her hands stretched high above her. She craned her neck. "I can feel every muscle in my body. I feel like one big knot."

Benjamin took three quick steps and was back beside Alex. "I know what you mean." He put his arms around Alex and held her tight. "Give yourself a few minutes and you'll be just fine."

"I have no idea what happened, do you? Where are we?"

Benjamin relaxed his embrace and looked at Alex. "Nope. No idea. All I know is that door is locked and we're stuck in here." Benjamin leaned into Alex and nudged her shoulder with his. "It look's like another fine mess you've gotten me into."

Alex smiled and punched Benjamin's shoulder sparingly. "Very funny, Mr. Hunter. . . very funny."

The two paced round the room partly to get their blood flowing and their joints loosened and partly to ease their nerves. They searched their collective memories for anything that would help them remember what had happened. They heard voices in the hallway and then the door opened.

A tall stick figure of a man stood in the doorway with a vacant stare. "Monsieur Hunter and Ms Boudreau, I am Clément Sauve. You must be hungry beyond belief. If you would follow me, we have a meal already prepared for you." The man stepped back into the hallway and motioned for them to follow.

Alex looked at Benjamin and shrugged, "We're famished."

In no time they had each inhaled scrambled eggs, sausage, toast and a bowl of rehydrated fruit. Sitting back and sipping her second cup of coffee, Alex looked over at Mr. Sauve sitting at the far end of the table. "Well, thank you. Excuse our manners, but that was some meal. Maybe you can fill us in on some things?" She held her hands out in a classic "what's up?" "You could start by telling us where we are and how we got here."

Mr. Sauve's hands moved in sync with his words as he spoke, "In due course, Ms Boudreau, you will be told everything. I expect Agent Faucher will be in here any moment and she can tell you everything. Until then, if you need anything else, please let me know."

Alex remembered her brief meeting with Director Bardin in Paris—Agent Faucher. . . DGSE. How could they have found them down here? What are they looking for?

Benjamin shot Mr. Sauve a puzzled look. "Who is Agent Faucher? Is this some type of police facility? Just tell us where we are, come on."

Both hands waved. "Like I said, Monsieur Hunter, you will know everything in due course. I am sorry, but that is all I can tell you at this point."

Benjamin pushed his chair back and shot up. "I'll just have to get some answers for myself then. Alex, let's go and see what we can find out."

"Wait!" Mr. Sauve held his arms out just as the door opened. Alex and Benjamin turned around and saw a woman march into the room.

Alex recognized the traits that branded her DGSE. The hair was squarely trimmed to just above her chin, the tan blouse, although overly starched, was a sign of a high ranking agent and the navy blue pants and black shoes completed her undercover uniform. Even the black thick–rimmed glasses that magnified her fierce blue eyes were standard issue. Agents were trained to blend in with the masses, to breathe anonymity and to portray an unassuming profile. The Agency had a saying, "If you want to hide a needle don't hide it in a haystack, hide it with other needles." This particular agent had obviously never mastered that technique. She stood at attention; back straight, shoulders squared, arms tightly pressed to her side and she looked straight ahead. She had a block–wall persona that repelled any thought that she would in any way be approachable.

Alex remained seated, but brought herself to her full upright position. "Agent Faucher, I assume."

Her lips parted ever so slightly. "Mademoiselle Boudreau." A sharp nod.

"Monsieur Hunter." Another nod.

"You two must have been exhausted. But now that you have caught up on your sleep and have eaten, we should talk about how you can help us." She motioned with her chin. "Please sit down, Monsieur Hunter."

"I'll do that, but there's some explaining to do on your part, like what the hell is going on?"

Seated around the table all eyes darted about trying to get a read on each other. Agent Faucher had her hands spread shoulder width apart and gripped to the edge of the table. "Mademoiselle Boudreau, I have read your file from the Agency so there is a great deal I know about your background. I presume you know very little about me so let me explain some. I have been running an operation looking for Monsieur Hunter since his mysterious disappearance from the Beresford Hospital. My orders are to make sure he is safe and to bring him back to Paris. You have made this more difficult than it should have been, but now that we have Monsieur Hunter we can put all that behind us."

Alex and Agent Faucher locked stares. Agent Faucher blinked first. "We will be leaving tomorrow, so until then, Monsieur Sauve will make sure you two are comfortable and have everything you need."

Alex bit her lower lip and then said, "We can discuss where we go and when in a moment, but first tell us where we are and how we got here?"

"Very well." Agent Faucher pulled her hands apart and re–clasped her fingers. "We have been following you since you left Paris for Sierra Leone. We arrived several hours after you blew up the Koidu plant and we arrived in Gualala just after you left there. We were able to locate you again and track your position here thanks to the GPS transponders you were wearing. When we picked you up you were conscious and alert, but it was clear the cold was having an ill effect on you. So we gave you a shot of Rohypnol and brought you here to the French Concordia Research Station. The closest human contact, other than us, is at the Vostok Station, 560 kilometers from here. So quite simply—*we* are all you have."

"Why did you have to drug us? And with Rohypnol of all drugs?"

"It's a sedative, as I am sure you are aware, and knowing your background the way I do, Mademoiselle Boudreau, I did not want to risk the chance that you would go rogue on us. I'm sure you know what I mean by that."

"There was a plane on its way to pick us up. If they're not here by now I'm sure they will be shortly. Why don't you just give us our things and we'll be on our way. No hard feelings on our part."

"I am sorry to disappoint you, Mademoiselle Boudreau, but no plane is on its way here. Your transponders were *accidently* thrown from our plane fifty miles or so from where we found you. If someone was looking for you they won't find you here. And don't worry about your belongings; we are taking very good care of your things."

Alex sensed that Agent Faucher was enjoying this more than she was letting on. She had had enough. "You have drugged us, kept us locked in a room without our consent and now you're taking us back to Paris while we still have some unfinished business down here." Alex stood up and leaned forward looking down at Agent Faucher, "I don't think so. We'd like to place a call to a few people. Could you please show us where we can find a phone?"

"There will be no phone calls by either of you and as to Paris; Monsieur Hunter is the only one I will be taking there. If you wish to stay here and take care of your unfinished business I may be able to arrange that for you."

"Just one moment." Benjamin pounded a fist on the table and continued, his tone trumpeted his irritation, "I'm an American citizen, as you obviously know, and you have no more right to hold me here against my will than you do to take me to Paris against my will."

Benjamin pushed his chair back with such force that it toppled over and came to rest against the far wall. "If you're not going to help us find a phone then I'll find one on my own." Benjamin turned and started for the door.

"Stop! You're not going anywhere yet!"

The moment Agent Faucher shouted out at Benjamin, two armed agents appeared in the doorway. Their hands rested on the handle of their holstered weapons.

"Wait, Ben!" Alex shot up and grabbed Benjamin's arm. "We'll find another way to handle this."

# CHAPTER 34

Alan Price was back in Reston sitting comfortably with both feet on his desk and holding a glass of Scotch in his lap. A single finger circled the rim of his crystal glass and it whistled a high pitched tone. Alan was tired, but his eyes were as wide open as his future. Soon, very soon, he would amass a fortune far greater than most of the clients he protected and most of those had acquired their staggering wealth from looting the coffers of the countries they had ruled.

His intercom buzzed. "Sir, President Desjardins is on the line and he says it is urgent. Would you like me to patch him through?"

President. . . Stephen. . . Des. . . jardins. Alan took a sip of scotch and swirled it around his tongue. What a weak excuse for a leader, he thought. President Desjardins enjoyed unprecedented popularity in his country, far beyond what most politicians could only dream of achieving. Yet to Alan, President Desjardins was nothing more than a political glad–hander that could be bought and sold like the rest of them.

"Yes. Put him on, Paula. Thank you."

"Mr. President. A delightful, if unexpected surprise. I trust everything is well with you?""Alan, I have some information that I think will please you. I spoke with. . . "

"Stephen!" Alan's voice had a scolding tone, "Aren't you even going to ask how I am? Where are your manners?" Alan silently chuckled to himself as he continued, "Sometimes I wonder if you even like me. Do you Stephen? Do you like me?"

Alan knew that President Desjardins was searching for the right words, the right approach to avoid a verbal confrontation. The man was spineless and would say whatever he needed to steer clear of a war of words. Finally, President Desjardins continued, "Alan, we have a long relationship, the two of us. I've always considered that relationship to have a solid foundation and because of that I have always felt we could dispense with certain platitudes. There will be time to talk about other things, but first, I thought you would want to know that we have Alex Boudreau in custody along with Benjamin Hunter."

"Well, that is good news. Where are they?"

We have them detained at our Concordia Research Station in Antarctica. I spoke to Director Bardin just moments ago and he assures me they are both under our control."

"I don't trust that woman, Stephen. What the hell was she doing in Antarctica anyway? Where'd you find her?"

"It is the damnedest thing, Alan. She and Hunter were wandering around very close to the South Pole waiting for an Australian plane to arrive when we picked up their location from their GPS transponders. We are interrogating each of them right now, but from what Director Bardin tells me there is no way in hell we will get any information out of Boudreau. I do not think we can legally keep her detained for too long since she has not committed a crime, so what would you like us to do with her?"

Alan's mind clicked into overdrive. What the hell was she doing? She couldn't have found the Black Swan Bunker. Impossible.

"Stephen that bitch could ruin everything—I mean *everything*. Just get rid of her. I don't care how you do it, but do it—*now!*"

"Alan you do not know what you are asking. Those two are the target of a worldwide search. Every intelligence agency in the world has them on their radar. If something were to happen to Hunter there would be endless questions and investigations. His wife is a U.S. Senator. We can not kill them, Alan. We just cannot, it is too risky."

"You don't have to worry about Hunter, Stephen. I'll take care of him myself, and when Boudreau sees what happens to him, well it's better for all of us that she doesn't live to tell about it. Just get rid of her, Stephen!"

"I will talk to Director Bardin. I do not like this one bit, Alan. I cannot make any guarantees, but I will see what we can do."

Alan's voice dropped two octaves as he issued his final command. "You will kill Boudreau *now!* If you don't," his voice returned to his pompous tone, "then you'll end up suffering the same fate as Hunter. It's an excruciating death, Mr. President. Remember?"

Alan slammed the phone down and stared at it; his fingers tented and pressed against his lips. Minutes clicked by before he pushed the intercom button.

"Yes sir."

"Paula, call Jaspar and have him go out to the G650. In my stateroom there's a metal attaché case. Have him bring it to me at my house—*now!*"

# CHAPTER 35

"I see you can't sleep either." Benjamin looked at his watch. "God, it's only 2:20 in the morning. How do people get any sleep around here when it's never dark?"

Alex sat on the side of her cot fully dressed. "Do you know how to fly a plane?"

Benjamin threw his legs out and sat up. "No, I've never done that. Why? What are you thinking?"

"We're going to fly out of here." Alex snapped her fingers. "That's our best bet."

Benjamin cocked his head to the side. "I like your thinking, but how are we going to do that? I suppose you're a pilot?"

"Never flown in my life, but how hard can it be?" Alex stood up and slowly paced around the small room in tight circles. Her nervous energy was reflected in her voice, "From what I can tell this is a small facility. It looks like there only two buildings, the one we're in here and the other one looks like a maintenance building that just may house an airplane or two if the wind sock is any indicator."

"Do you even know where we are, exactly?"

"I remember seeing the different research stations in Antarctica when we were looking at the map on our way to Casey Station. We're probably 1100 kilometers inland from Casey and that's about the same distance from here to the other French station, Dumont D'Urville. I assume they get their supplies flown here from Dumont D'Urville, so whatever plane they have outside must have the fuel capacity to make that flight."

Benjamin leaned against the wall and stretched his sore muscles. "I still don't know how we'll fly out of here since neither of us knows how to fly, but. . . well, go on."

"There aren't many people here and I'm not worried about the scientists. They probably don't even know who we are or why we're here. Sauve is a non–threat, we can handle him easily. Faucher and her two henchmen are another story. They're trained and armed, so we'll need an element of surprise."

Alex stopped in front of Benjamin and reached for his hands. Holding them tightly, she looked up into his eyes and paused just long enough for the corner of Benjamin's lips to rise. "You're not flying to Paris without me, but when you do it will be because we're finished with this whole mess. We can walk the banks of the Seine, sit in my favorite café and watch couples lost in their own imaginary worlds stroll by arm–in–arm. We have a few things to get out of the way before we can share that dream, but I know we can do this. I'll need your help and you'll have to trust me. I know what I'm doing, Ben."

Benjamin pressed his lips together and tightened his grip. "I do trust you, Alex, but. . . " he shrugged his shoulders, "who's going to fly the plane?"

Alex moved in closer and whispered, "We'll learn together."

Alex knelt beside Benjamin's cot and she turned the instant the door opened. "Please we need some help. He's not breathing."

Mr. Sauve took two steps and he felt a hand grab his shoulder. He spun around and caught Benjamin's fist with his nose. Alex heard the sound of splintering cartilage and raced over to him, bent down and snatched his keys and radio.

Benjamin rubbed his knuckles.

"Nice shot. Let's go."

They locked the door behind them and left Sauve stretched out on the floor. They each had a role to play if they were going to fly out of there. When they reached the door that led to the other building, Benjamin put his hand on the handle and looked back at Alex. "If you're not there in five minutes I'm coming back."

Alex pushed on the door. "Go, I'll be fine."

Benjamin ran across the ice–covered ground and disappeared into the building. Alex turned and with cat–like steps ran down the hallway. She needed to retrieve their backpacks and the hard drives she had taken from the Black Swan Bunker. She was certain they had already rummaged through their belongings, found the hard drives and dumped them. Hopefully, she could find them and retrieve something useful.

She had no idea where their backpacks were stashed, but she had an idea where the hard drives might be.

The place was like a morgue with its eerie silence and dull smell of nothingness. She crept slowly forward parting the stale air with her anticipation, her senses on high alert. She turned right at the end of the hallway and stiffened.

"Hold it right there!"

Walking toward her was one of the agents pointing a Beretta M9 at her chest. His grimacing expression hardened the creases across his forehead and he held the Beretta firmly, but with trained familiarity. "We had a feeling we'd be running into you tonight. Where's your friend?"

Alex stood with her arms at her side and her fingers clenched. "Asleep. I'm just taking a walk. I need the exercise."

"Well turn around and you can walk right back to where you came from. Exercise time is over."

A muffled sound came from behind the agent and he flinched. Alex grabbed the man's gun, pressed her thumb into the back of his hand and twisted—hard. His arm folded up, she pulled the gun from his hand and her knee landed a blow to the man's ribcage—he crumbled.

Alex pointed the gun at the other agent just before he drew his gun from his holster. "Take it out. . . slowly. . . and put it on the floor. Then take three slow steps backwards."

Alex kicked the gun behind her. "You boys are making this way too easy for me. Now, if you'll show me where our backpacks are I'll be on my way."

The agents glanced at one another with the foolish expression of two little boys who had just been caught playing with matches. Neither spoke.

"Okay, the more I have to work at this the more you two will suffer when I finally get what I want. You!" She pointed the gun at the second agent. "Turn around and the two of us will follow you back to the room where you came from at the end of the hall."

Alex stayed far enough behind the two agents so she was beyond their reach and they led her into a room that was identical to the one that she had been locked up in with Benjamin. Two sleeping cots lined the walls and a small table sat in the corner. To her right, two backpacks leaned upright against each other. She shook her head. "Yeah, you two are making this really easy. Now back up against the wall and keep your hands up above your head."

Alex kept the gun pointed at the agents as she rummaged through her backpack. Everything was there, even the hard drives. All of her effects were out of place so they had obviously uploaded or erased the hard drives, but hopefully it wasn't all lost. She glanced at her watch; she'd have to wait until later. She needed to get to the plane.

Pulling a rope from her backpack, she bound each agent to a cot, placed a strip of duct tape over their mouths and beelined it for the airplane.

Benjamin was sitting in the cockpit when Alex burst through the door. He gave her the thumbs up and she slid the hangar door open. In the minutes that Benjamin had sat and waited for Alex he had tried to familiarize himself with the control panel and learn what each gauge, knob and handle controlled. He had raced Formula One cars in Europe years back, but that gave him little confidence when he looked around at the sheer number of gauges and controls that lined the cockpit. Nonetheless, when he signaled the thumbs up to Alex it meant he was ready to start the engines and get out of there.

Benjamin started the left engine and the propeller cranked up. The right engine sputtered, and then kicked into action. One by one, he began a final check of the gauges.

They knew they were going to have to give the twin engines enough time to warm up before they could taxi out and give the plane full throttle. What they didn't know was how much time would be needed to warm up both engines.

Alex ran to the right side of the plane and as one foot landed on the wing–step a hand grabbed her shoulder and yanked her to the ground. She covered her head with her arms and curled up into a defensive ball—a barrage of kicks came from every direction.

Her attacker dropped down, pressed a knee into Alex's chest and pelted her with a series of sharp elbow strikes to the head. A quick palm strike to her attacker's face sent her assailant reeling backwards. Winded and groaning in pain, Alex kicked her legs in the air, pushed off the floor with her hands and sprung to her feet.

She wiped the blood from her mouth and faced her attacker— Agent Faucher. She moved forward. "Agent Faucher, I should have known I'd run into you at some point. Let us get out of here. This really isn't your fight."

Agent Faucher drew her gun from her holster and Alex reacted. She cocked her leg, snapped her knee and a front kick landed in the Agent's chest. She crashed against a storage case, shattering its glass front.

Their eyes locked on the gun lying on the concrete floor— they jumped. Agent Faucher's fingers clutched the handle *and* Alex grabbed her wrist and twisted. The gun fell from Faucher's hand and slid across the floor underneath the storage case.

Alex pushed herself to her knees just as a boot hit her in the chest. . . then another. . . then another. Agent Faucher grabbed a metal bar and swung it downward at Alex's head. Alex folded her arms across her face and upper body in an X and rolled to one side. The metal bar grazed her hip. Alex spun around and a scissor sweep with her legs caught Faucher in the shin and behind her knee. Faucher buckled and hit the floor—hard.

Alex stood and planted her feet, a sharp pain shot through her chest and her head pounded. Faucher rolled over, vaulted to her feet and spun—a roundhouse kick flew inches from Alex's face.

The two stood facing each other. They moved in a small circle waiting for the right moment to launch an attack or to parry the next assault. "Your file is very accurate and I see you have kept up your skills. But give it up, Boudreau, there is no way you are getting away from here." Faucher nodded at the plane. "Especially that easily."

Alex was poised for an assault and the two continued their hypnotic dance, slowly circling, arms flinching. Their cobra stares traced one another's every move. "There's no reason for this Allison. You're out of your jurisdiction here and we haven't done anything to warrant all this. . . attention. Back off. . . let us go."

Agent Faucher's hand swept across a table and she grabbed a handful of nails. She placed the two–inch nails between her fingers and clenched her fist. Her impromptu Wolverine claws sliced through the air. "My orders have changed since I first talked to you. I *am* bringing both of you back to Paris. Only with you. . . it does not matter if you are dead or alive."

"This doesn't need to be personal, Allison. Come on, back off. I'm going to ease myself back to the plane and you can stand right here."

Alex took one step backwards and Faucher lurched forward and threw a series of figure one strikes at Alex. Her armed fists thrashed from all directions. One swipe grazed her face leaving striped talon cuts. The last one caught her on the shoulder, shredded her jacket and she felt blood dripping down her arm.

Alex retreated. Each step kept her just out of reach of the lashing spikes. She felt the crunch of broken glass beneath her feet. She looked down and without thought she dove, hit the floor on her bruised ribs and grunted in pain. Her hand reached out and grabbed the sharpest piece of glass within her reach. She turned just in time and saw Faucher standing over her. Her spiked fist cocked and then released for the fatal blow.

Alex twisted to her side, brought her arm up and jammed the glass spike so deeply into Faucher's leg she hit bone. . . just behind and below the knee.

Faucher crumbled, but her nail–armed hands flailed. Alex rolled to her side and jerked the glass down with all her strength, separating tendon from bone—blood spurted.

Alex, weak and dazed, pushed herself up. She bent over Faucher and gave her two sharp kicks to the head. No, Alex thought, Faucher would not be going any where on foot for quite some time.

She spun around and ran to the plane.

Alex missed the wing–step altogether as she jumped straight up to the wing, flung open the door and crashed on the co–pilot seat. She was out of breath and all she could yell was, "*Go!*"

Benjamin froze when he saw Alex. "You're bleeding. Jesus those cuts look serious. Let me look. . . "

Alex pushed Benjamin's hand away. "Later. . . Just go. . . just go. . . I am fine."

Benjamin eased the throttles forward and the plane lurched ahead. Once out of the hangar he was able to throttle up and throttle down the two engines to maneuver the plane onto the runway.

"Here, press this against your cuts." Benjamin handed Alex a cloth he had found tucked in the side pocket of his door. He shot her a quick smile, pushed both throttles all the way forward and looked down the runway. "I think I can get us off the ground, but I'm not too sure how to land this thing, yet."

Agent Faucher staggered out of the hangar and leaned against the door. Using both hands to steady her aim she fired off the entire clip, but she was too late. The nose lifted and the plane left the ground. It was out of reach.

Alex rested her head against the headrest and pressed the cloth firmly against her cuts. Her ribs were sore, her jaw pulsated and her spine felt like it had played musical chairs with a sledge hammer.

Benjamin put a hand on her thigh and gave a squeeze. "I have no idea how you did what you just did. Are you okay?"

"I'm not sure yet, but I think so. Anyway we made it." She looked at Benjamin and with her one good eye gave him a wink. "How does it feel to be a pilot?"

Benjamin looked out the window toward the horizon where the edge of the earth met the pale blue sky. "It's a lot of responsibility. I haven't even asked my only passenger where she'd like to go."

Alex tilted her head to the left and smiled. "North."

They both laughed. It felt good to be together and to be surrounded by nothing, but each other.

# CHAPTER 36

J ust 40 miles from the halls of Congress, the narrow streets of Middleburg, Virginia were lined with historic 18<sup>th</sup> century red brick buildings. Like most old–money retreats, Middleburg was a guarded, private place protecting the country squires, high–powered political brokers and equestrian champions that resided behind the whitewashed wood fences in the surrounding green hills. Middleburg had long been a retreat from the limelight for public figures. John F. Kennedy spent weekends there during his presidency, and Jackie rode in the local fox hunts. Elizabeth Taylor and Senator John Warner had their low–key wedding at his Middleburg estate.

Alan Price had never donned a pair of jodpurs or wore a riding helmet, but his home, Y Knot Farms nestled at the end of Ramblewood Lane, was a fully equipped 128 acre equestrian estate complete with a 12 stall barn and paddocks. The circa 1850 colonial home had been completely renovated by the previous owner and Alan had it furnished in period antiques. No less or no more elegant than the other estates in the community, Greener Pasture Farms assured Alan the privacy he had so often craved.

His home office had been his throne when he was in residence. He had what he needed to connect to everything that was going on at Sterling Defense and he had spent his most productive hours at his computer pouring over the company's financial projections, political issues, balance sheets and other mundane issues that he detested, but knew were part of the territory; a territory he alone had created.

That evening he sat in front of the fireplace and watched the roaring flames dance with their kaleidoscope of colors; the bright orange flames flickered with edges of red, green and blue hues and the heat bellowed off the firebrick. This was the one room, no the only place on earth, where Alan totally let go of his inhibitions and he didn't care about what others thought. He could relax knowing that at that very moment nothing else mattered.

He was rehearsing the events that were about to unfold and making sure that the slightest of details had not been overlooked. He was certain that nothing now stood in his way. Yes, he thought, this would be the final payback he had waited all these years for and in return, he would be rewarded with billions. The word billions reverberated over and over in his mind.

He heard his cell phone, but he couldn't remember when it started to ring. Very few people had his cell number so anytime it rang it was important. He strained to push himself from his chair and grabbed his phone from the edge of his desk. He recognized the number. "Hello Stephen. More good news? Don't tell me—Boudreau is history."

"Hello, Alan. I am sorry to inform you that Mademoiselle Boudreau has escaped. Just hours ago she stole a plane from our research facility in Antarctica. We are trying to track her location right now, but the satellite coverage in the area is poor."

"Damn you, Stephen." His crystal glass shattered against the stone fireplace. "You imbecile! How could that have happened?"

"I do not have all the details at this point, but I am sure we will be able to track both of them down. There are a limited numbers of places that they can land that plane."

Alan tore through the room, frantic with rage. Broken lamps, toppled chairs and punched picture frames trailed behind his flailing arms and kicking feet. How could this keep happening? That woman is the only person standing in my way. . . If I need to. . . Alan stopped in his tracks, held his cell phone out and stared.

Yes, he thought to himself. He pressed his phone against his ear. His arrogance had retreated and he calmly, but forcefully said, "Stephen, thank you for the call. You continue to do what you can and I am certain you will find Boudreau and do the right thing. In the meantime, I have a few ideas of my own."

# CHAPTER 37

"**B**en, you need to get back here now. Whatever that gene is in you it's not like anything that has been seen before. Dr. Riggle has consulted with some of the best geneticists around and no one has a clue what it is. It may possibly be something dangerous. Please, Ben, listen to me."

"I hear what you're saying, Jessica. Let me call you back. Give me a few minutes."

Benjamin hung up the phone and turned to Alex. "Jessica has talked with some specialists and they're all concerned about the gene they found in me. For good reason obviously, if they only knew. Maybe we should level with her about what I have. Maybe she can find a way to get rid of this thing. What do you think?"

"I've been operating under the assumption that the fewer people that know about this the better, but this might be an exception. Do you trust her, Ben?"

"I think I do. I don't think she's talked with anyone yet so, yeah, I trust her."

Alex nibbled on her lower lip and stared out the car window. "It probably wouldn't hurt. Maybe we could have the research data on the G–16 sent to her and she could find someone to take a look at it.

Without that data it would take them weeks, maybe longer to come up with anything."

"How are you going to do that?"

"I know Dr. Diderot destroyed everything he had. He was too scared to keep it any longer after everything broke out. I'll have to call Andre and have him forward it on. He's the only person I know that has it. God, I dread having to make that call, but I will."

Benjamin called Dr. Wasserman back and gave her the complete run down. She had read about the G–16 virus in the papers and had followed everything about it because of its connection to GEN and Benjamin's disappearance. She was horrified. She had always been a woman who expressed her opinions when called upon and in this particular case she had let Benjamin know in no uncertain words that he was playing Russian Roulette with his life by not coming in and getting immediate medical attention. He agreed to stop by and provide an additional blood sample, but that was it—he was not going to take the time to have any additional tests run. Dr. Wasserman acceded to Benjamin's demands that absolutely nothing could be said about any of this to anyone. She would wait for the research data and Ben would call if anything new arose.

The past few days had been hectic with little time to sleep. They had landed safely at Casey Station, but not without a series of hair–raising moments. Benjamin had brought the plane to a skid halfway down the runway and to cut his speed he had tried to zig zag the plane. On the second zag the plane had slid off the runway and the right side landing gear had collapsed. When they had come to a grinding halt they had been surrounded by technicians and firefighters who had grabbed them from the cockpit and pulled them just out of reach before the plane had burst into flames. They had flown back to Hobart on the same Australian Navy aircraft and eventually had caught a flight to Sydney and then on to San Francisco.

When they had landed in San Francisco, Alex had called Phil and it had been decided they would all meet at another house along the coast that Phil had surreptitiously managed to occupy without anyone, including the owner, knowing his whereabouts. "Tell Ben it's the old Hanneman house. He'll know the one I mean and he'll agree it's as safe a place as we'll find. Joel's gone for at least a week so the place is all ours."

Benjamin laughed uncontrollably when Alex told him of Phil's plan. He knew the place well. It belonged to a good friend of theirs, a friend they had met ab diving and ever since that day they would meet up anytime they were in the area for a dive. Both Phil and Benjamin had been frequent visitors to the Gualala coastline over the years. They shared the same passion for diving in the twisted kelp beds and underneath ledges in search of the gnarled and crusted Red Abalone. To both, it was more than a sport and more than just the pursuit of a delicacy that had been savored by gourmands' worldwide. There had been days when the surf pounded and the winds howled and even the best divers would remain ashore. The waters could be deathly treacherous at times. But those rare days, when the ocean was as flat as a lake and the air crisp and still, were the ones that all ab divers held in their memories, within easy reach.

On those rare, but memorable days, lying on the sea floor amongst the starfish, urchins and schools of Cabezon and Rockfish, a diver was presented with a a palette of colors as the sun's rays poured from above and flickered through the prism–like waters. When Phil and Benjamin had met Joel it had taken a single dive for the three to realize that they were kindred souls that shared not just the thrill of the competition, but the serenity and solitude that came with entering the oftentimes unforgiving, but also tranquil underwater world.

Benjamin knew Phil had located the ideal spot. The house was in Sea Ranch, a planned community just south of Gualala and it was as secluded and private as they came. A perfect hideaway to hole up and plan their next move.

The original design concept for Sea Ranch had been patterned after the Pomo Indians who first settled the area. The Pomo philosophy had been simple—live lightly on the land. They had adhered to their own philosophy by living in simple houses made from sticks and bark and only taking from the sea and surrounding forest the amount of wildlife or resources they would consume. Nothing had been wasted. To Ben, Phil, Joel and others who frequented or lived in the Sea Ranch community, it had become a modern day testament to the Pomo philosophy. Well over half of the 5200 acre ranch had been preserved as forest reserve and dedicated common open space. It had become a community where one could live in harmony with nature, without fences, and stroll unobtrusively through quiet redwoods or comb the undisturbed sandy beaches in search of washed up treasures.

Alex, Ben and Devon had stopped in Santa Rosa to load up on a few necessities before their planned rendezvous with Phil. Alex had purchased a new laptop while Ben had scurried through the grocery store aisles loading a cart with everything he thought they would need for the next few days. He had found a bottle of '08 Dunah in the wine section and tucked it away. He knew the uncorking of that bottle would bring a smile to Alex's face.

Driving up the switchbacked road just north of Russian Gulch, Alex asked, "Have you noticed the white Taurus that's behind us?"

Benjamin glanced at his rearview mirror. "I do now, why?"

"It's been following us since we got onto 101 in Santa Rosa. What are the odds they're going to the same place as us?"

"Don't know. When we get to the top of this hill we'll turn off at Meyers Grade and see if they follow. Most everyone heading north stays on Highway 1."

Minutes later, Ben turned onto Meyers Grade and they watched the Taurus follow in their path.

"Well, let's assume we're being followed. Do you know a place around here we may be able to lose them?"

Benjamin smiled. "That I do. I'll wait until we get up by the school, there's a perfect cut–out place there. In the meantime I'll drive slowly and see how far behind they lag. How does that sound?"

"You're in charge."

"That'd be a first." They broke out in laughter.

They reached the top of the grade and Ben tapped Alex's shoulder. "Look behind you. See that peninsula off in the far distance? Do you know what that is?"

Alex turned and looked out the rear window. Off in the distance a long peninsula jutted far out from the fog covered land. She shook her head. "No. Should I?"

"That's Point Reyes Peninsula. It's too far to see the lighthouse, but that's where it is." He reached over and squeezed Alex thigh. "If I could've remembered that particular day when I was held at Koidu it sure would've helped. That day's pretty high up the list of my all–time perfect days."

Alex placed her hand over Benjamin's and her eyes glowed. "For me too, Ben. I can't tell you how many times I've thought about that very day. I think that's where it all began for me." She leaned her head back and remembered the guttural sound of the foghorn on the cliff that had made her feel protected and safe. She imagined the feeling of the wind swirling around her. That had been the day when she had taken the difficult journey to heal her wounds, her suffering, her loneliness. She had freed herself from her guilt–ridden years of blame and sorrow for the death of her sister and on that day she and Benjamin had become one—the past they shared, the pain they knew had bonded them in a way no physical touch ever could. "I finally broke down that day and let everything come pouring out. That was. . . "

"Hey you two," Devon was stretched out in the rear seat feeling like a third wheel at the prom, "you can continue this love fest later, but right now we have some business to attend to, like. . . uh, we're being tailed. Does that mean anything to you guys?"

Alex turned around and waved a hand. "Okay, okay you win." She noticed the Taurus was keeping its distance. It was in no hurry to pass. "How far are we from where you think we can lose them?"

Benjamin looked straight ahead. "Um. . . maybe five minutes."

They drove in silence through the redwoods and open green pastures and the Taurus kept a measured distance. They were now convinced it was a tail.

"Hold on, here we go."

Benjamin sped up and after the second bend in the road he made a hard right into the entrance of the Horicon School and screeched to a halt behind a fence and grove of redwoods. Seconds later the Taurus sped by, obviously in a hurry to catch up.

Benjamin swung the car around. "It looks like we called that one. Let's wait a few more minutes and then we'll take off."

Alex had regained her focus. She had been euphoric ever since Benjamin had regained his memory and they had rekindled what she had feared might have been lost. She silently scolded herself for letting her emotions get in the way of her instincts. Focus, she repeated. . . focus. . . focus. "Is there another way to go? It wouldn't be smart to follow along the same road."

"I'm guessing they turned left on Timber Cove Road. That's the quickest way back to Highway 1 and the normal route. I can keep on this road a bit longer and there are some back roads that will get us close to where we're going without having to follow Highway 1. That's our best bet."

Alex sighed in relief. She had regained her focus. "That sounds perfect. I'll keep my eyes out for them or anyone else for that matter. That was too close for comfort."

# CHAPTER 38

The cool and calm demeanor that usually followed Alan Price throughout the day had been left by the side of the road—he was restless. Small beads of sweat hovered on his puffy cheeks and his breathing was exaggerated. He sucked in an occasional gasp to keep his composure. He sat in his high–backed leather chair, his shirt sleeves irregularly rolled–up and his tie dangled from both ends of the collar on his buttoned downed Oxford.

Arnaud Bertrand had met with Mr. Price personally on a number of occasions and it was not unusual for those meetings to be held late at night. Alan worked around the clock and he demanded the same commitment from his legionnaires. "You've been with me for sometime now, Arnaud, and I value your loyalty. I've called on you in the past to step forward and you always have. Are we treating you okay? Things are going well for you?"

"Yes sir, Mr. Price. Things couldn't be any better. I'm still reeling from what happened at Koidu, though. We made some tactical errors there and failed our mission. If there's ever anything I can do to make that up to you I hope you will let me know."

"Let's not play the blame game, Arnaud. Those things happen in our business, but we try our best to keep them all to a minimum.

Our client understands that as well. I do have something for you to follow up on for me, though."

"Name it, Mr. Price, and I'm on it."

After Arnaud had been discharged from DGSE, he had gone to work for KKR International Risk, one the pioneers in the mercenary security contractors business. Six months after the Twin Towers attack in New York City, Arnaud had been lured away from KKR by Sterling and he had risen through the corporate ranks in dramatic fashion. He had served as a training commander for new recruits, an operational leader on numerous field assignments and he had eventually been brought into the inner fold at corporate headquarters where he had been in charge of special reconnaissance missions that had been known to only a handful of Sterling executives. It had been in that position where he had caught the eye of Alan Price and he had soon found himself working directly with Mr. Price on selected missions.

Alan leaned back in his chair and gripped the armrests. "That Boudreau woman is causing us all sorts of headaches and I'm tired of taking aspirin to make her go away." He chuckled at himself, but his frown remained. "I want to hit her hard and make sure that she never crosses our paths again."

Arnaud's eyebrows peaked. "Nothing would give me more pleasure than to run into her again. Just tell me what you want."

Alan rose from his chair. "Can I get you a drink, Arnaud?"

Arnaud's eyes followed Alan as he walked to the wet bar. "No thanks, sir. I never drink on the job and I'm biting at the bit to get back to the assignment you're talking about."

Alan poured a double scotch for himself and took a long sip. "Ah. . . the drink of kings and noblemen. Let's get started."

For the next hour the two huddled around a small conference table at the far end of Alan's home office and discussed Alex Boudreau. Alan filled Arnaud in on the importance of why Alex needed to be stopped, but he cut short from revealing the whole truth. He detailed the botched attempts of the DGSE to stop Alex and Arnaud gave a noticeable wince each time Alan flew off into a tirade at the mere mention of the name—*Boudreau.*

Alan stood and walked back to his desk. Arnaud followed. He neatly placed some papers on the corner and turned to face Arnaud. "You're the perfect guy to handle this, Arnaud. You gather together whoever you need to help you and *every* resource we have at our disposal is available to you. If there's any paper work you need to expedite just bring it to me and I'll move things along. I don't want anything to stand in your way. You're to report directly to me."

"I already have some ideas on a team to put together and I'll have a list of gear and supplies first thing in the morning."

Alan placed his hand on Arnaud's shoulder and looked him in the eyes. "I'll remember this." He shook his head and leaned into Arnaud. "Remember, I never want to have to hear her name again."

Arnaud returned the glare. "You never will, sir. I promise."

# CHAPTER 39

Benjamin and Phil were outside cleaning a couple of abalone that Phil had caught earlier that day. Those two had a long–standing tradition of diving together and seeing who ended up with the biggest abalone at the end of the day. Alex was unfamiliar with the sport of free diving for abalone, but she chuckled as she heard the two bantering about who was ahead in their spirited competition. She listened to them laugh, argue and poke fun at the other. She was struck by the closeness of their bond and for the first time realized that there was no one in her life to share the same camaraderie that those two openly shared. They had a deep mutual respect for the other and there was nothing one wouldn't do to help their friend. Phil, she knew, had risked his own life to save Ben's and she was certain Ben would so the same. If she needed help, who could she turn to? Who would be there?

"A penny for your thoughts."

"A penny? You can't buy anything today for a penny. . . Or a dime. . . or even a quarter. You'll have to raise your offer."

"Well, a penny's all I have right now." Devon took the chef's knife from Alex and nudged her aside. "Those tomatoes aren't going to dice themselves. I'll take over. What's up, anyway? You're in another of your out of this world trances again."

Alex reached across the sink and pulled a framed photograph from the wall. "When you look at this picture what do you see?"

Devon's finger pushed his glasses back up to the bridge of his nose. "Three guys doing some kind of a tribal dance maybe. I don't know, what's the big deal? What am I supposed to see?"

Alex shook her head. "You're hopeless. I see three friends happy to be in the moment with each other. Look at the size of that mallet Ben is using to pound the abalone. It's got to be the size of one of those shells hanging on the wall in the living room over there. And I can tell by the expression on Phil's face and his arms waiving in circles that he's making some sarcastic remark to Ben and loving every minute of it. The other guy, I guess, is Joel and he's a part of that same bond."

Alex hung the picture back on its nail and leaned back against the kitchen counter, a far away look was etched on her face. "Let me ask you something, Devon. Who would you turn to if you were in trouble and needed some help?"

Devon kept dicing the tomatoes and twisted his head from side to side as he spoke. "Hmm. Does this have to do with you? I'll bet it does."

"Yes and no, but really, are you close enough to anyone who would step forward and help you out if you needed it?"

"Probably my brother. I haven't seen him in three, maybe four years. He's still in South Africa and we do stay in touch by email. I'm sure he'd help if he could. Yeah, he'd help out. The problem though is he's sort of a ne'er–do–well, never really amounted to much so I'm not sure he could help me anyway." Devon put the knife down and looked at Alex. "If I really got in trouble I'd want to track you down. Yup, you're the one I'd call."

"Well thanks, Devon; I'd be there for you."

Devon pushed the diced tomatoes into a bowl, his head still bobbing from side to side as he spoke, "How about you? Is this what you've been lost in thought over?"

A glimmer of a smile broke through her rigid façade and she relaxed her hunched shoulders. "I was listening to those two outside and I was struck by the realization that there is no one in my life, other than my mother, that I am really close to." She pulled a glass from the upper shelf and filled it with water. Taking a sip, she continued, "My sister and I shared a bond together that was special, very special, but she died when I was only ten. If she were around today I'm sure we would be close like sisters are supposed to be. Ever since she died I've spent my life blaming myself for her death and avoiding anyone who got close to me. It was Ben who brought me to the final realization about my sister and I can now look back and think about those precious times we shared together. Did I ever tell you how that happened? How Ben helped me with all that?"

Devon waved the knife. "Oh, only a dozen times or so, but whose counting?"

"Okay, I get it. I won't bore you with it again. You know I look back on things now and it's been a really lonely existence. Just me against the world. Kind of sad when you think about it, huh?"

"You're asking me? I could count my friends on the fingers of Capt. Hook's right hand. I can talk to people online, no problem, but put me in front of someone. . . you know face to face, and my mouth puckers and I can't even get a stutter out. I'm all dressed up with no one to see. So I think I win the sad–sack category, hands down."

Alex took another sip of water and gave Devon a sharp smack on the back. "You're not even close, but I guess we are a lot alike when it comes to our relationships."

"One big difference that I see." Devon put the knife down and turned toward Alex. "I've heard and seen enough to know that you and Ben seem to have something pretty good going on. He strikes me as the type of person that once he decides to make something work he doesn't stop until it does work. Kinda like you. I'll bet you could count on him in a New York second."

"Yes, I could. It's really all because of Ben that I've even thought about any of this. I know how much he means to me now and I don't want anything to change that—nothing. I don't know if I'm capable of sustaining this feeling or if I could even live up to his expectations. My past seems to have a way of leaping in front of me and I trip all over it. How long could he, or anyone really, put up with that? Not very long I'm afraid."

Devon laughed. "Jeez, Alex are you kidding me? Let me see if I have all of this right. Clue me in if I miss anything. You pranced into his life and stole research from him, devastated his company, threw his grandfather in jail, he's been hospitalized, kidnapped, fallen into a coma, injected with probably the most lethal virus known to man and when he finally remembered you he was doing cartwheels in a tunnel underneath the South Pole. Does that sound about right? Most guys would've run away from you at the first sign of trouble. But this guy? What does he do? Everything you'd ever want. That's what he does. Right now I'd say you've got it made in the shade. No worries as they say."

Alex burst into laughter. "That's just what Ben's grandfather would say—no worries. Only he would have called me mate—no worries, mate. Come here." Alex threw her arms around Devon and gave him a big hug.

Ben and Phil burst through the front door beaming with pride and overflowing with good spirits. They each held out a plate of freshly cut and pounded abalone. "Okay you guys have to choose." Benjamin put his plate on the counter and continued, "I make the best abalone around, hands down. It'll be tender and flavored just right. Phil, on the other hand, will end up over–cooking his and it'll be tough as nails. It's up to you who you want to be the chef tonight." Benjamin threw his arms to the side, his fingers pointing to himself.

"Not so fast there, my friend. The culinary talents when it comes to cooking this delicacy are all mine." Phil pounded his chest. "Tonight I offer you the choice of abalone relleno, abalone Thai or the traditional abalone sautéed in butter with minced cloves of garlic. Now, if you're really adventurous, I'll even create my one–of–a–kind abalone kickasserole." Phil kissed his fingertips and then waved a disappointing hand at Ben. "This guy has one way to cook this delicacy—charred and tough."

"Hold on," Benjamin wrapped his arms around Phil and pulled him back, "my abalone has become world renowned and my recipes are used by the finest chefs. There's no. . . "

Phil and Benjamin continued their self–praise and mockery of the other and soon all four where laughing and poking fun at one another. Finally, Alex held both hands out and with a parting motion pushed the two away. "I'm starved so let me suggest a compromise. The kitchen's plenty big for both of you and it looks like there's enough abalone here to feed us for several days." She slowly brushed her hair aside. "Sooo, what I propose is you each cook some any way you want and Devon and I will be the judge. We'll have an official cook–off."

Benjamin shot Phil an I–got–you–now look. "Prepare to taste the most mouth–watering gastropod ever served."

Phil bent at the waist and bowed to Alex and Devon. "It's my honor to prepare and serve for you the ideal combination of fresh abalone with the subtlest of spices. A mouth–watering delight, if I may be so modest."

The double serving of abalone that night was served on a candlelit table with all the accoutrements of the finest five star restaurants. Wild Porcinis and watercress were picked from the nearby meadows and a fresh fruit salad with homemade lime dressing was all complimented by the bottle of Dunah that Benjamin placed in front of Alex. Of course she recognized the wine from their meeting at the Olympic Club and when Phil learned the details he cried foul. "No fair," he said, "you're bribing one of the judges. I can't believe that even you would stoop so low."

The next two hours were spent eating what would be by anyone's standard a gourmet meal beyond gourmet, sipping wine, laughing and listening to Ben and Phil recall their many experiences together along this part of the California coast. To Alex, this had been one of the best moments she could remember in a long time. She beamed with an equal mixture of pride and amusement as she watched Benjamin in his element recite one tale after another with Phil topping each story with one of his own.

Finally, Alex rose from the table, gathered some plates and headed to the kitchen. "And where would you be going?" Benjamin asked as he pushed his chair back.

"Let me clean up some and you two can keep going. I'm sure we're only part way through your adventures and I can hear everything from the kitchen."

The four divided the clean–up chores and in no time the kitchen was spotless and they were lounging in front of the fire. Phil and Benjamin prodded Alex and Devon for the final results of the great abalone cook–off, but Alex deftly put off any announcement. She had been trying to conjure up a way to make it a tie, yet each would think they came out the winner.

"I think we should get an early start tomorrow. We all needed tonight to relax and unwind, but we have a lot to go over. It's still not perfectly clear to me what we need to do so we should lay everything out and maybe some pieces will fall together."

Reality clouded the room. That night had been filled with fun and laughter, but the danger facing Benjamin was still real—nothing had changed.

The four sat by the fire and went over what they hoped to accomplish tomorrow and at least preliminarily they had a rough sketch of a plan. Tomorrow would be a big day. Phil rose, walked over to where Benjamin was sitting and gripped his friend's shoulders. He gave a couple of squeezes and said, "It's good to have you back, buddy. Tonight was great, like old times, only better." He looked over at Alex. "Thanks, Alex. Thanks for everything."

Phil and Devon each retired to their own room and Alex sat on the couch nestled in Benjamin's arms. No words were spoken. Each was lost in their own world walking hand in hand with the other somewhere between the fantasy of tomorrow and the reality of the moment. To Alex, her life had been nothing more than a long string of yesterdays all tugging, pulling and preventing her from any tomorrows. She ran her fingers across Benjamin's leg, then sat up and stared at him with a wide–eyed smile. She softly cooed, "Remember when you said you wanted to know which side of the bed I like to wake up on in the morning?"

He nodded with approval.

"Well, I don't know the answer myself, but we will by tomorrow morning."

Gently, Benjamin put one arm under Alex's legs and scooped her off the couch. At the foot of the stairs he whispered, "You can tell me now. My abalone was the best, right?"

She lifted her head and gave Benjamin a kiss on the cheek. "I think the wine tipped the scales in your favor."

# CHAPTER 40

The Pacific Ocean that morning was gently lapping on the sands of Walk On Beach, one of the more picturesque beaches along the Sea Ranch coastline. The beach was bordered on each side by time–worn rock outcroppings and Benjamin stood on the cliff above and looked down on the stretch of sand. Behind him the morning light edged over the mountain and off in the distance he saw a silhouette walking toward him. Charging down the cliff trail he leaped over rows of driftwood logs and soon stood before Alex.

"You snuck out early this morning."

A wool scarf was tucked inside her dark blue parka to repel the chilly morning mist. "Good morning." She leaned forward and gave Benjamin a kiss. "I couldn't control my thoughts. There are so many unanswered questions and we have so much left to do. I thought a walk would help me make some sense of things."

"Well, fill me in. What are your ideas?"

Alex put her arm around Benjamin. "Walk with me."

They walked arm in arm down the beach stopping occasionally to pick up a shell or admire a piece of driftwood. First thing that morning Alex had put in a call to her mother. That call had been brief, but she had wanted to check in and see how she was doing.

When Alex had told her she was uncertain when she would return, she had felt her mother's sadness, her loneliness; it had been the same, each time Alex had called over the years and had told her she still had work to finish up. Alex had often wondered when she had been away how her mother was doing and she had always looked forward to returning to Sidi Lahcen. Those brief times she had been able to spend with her mother in between assignments had been the only times Alex could remember when she had been able to relax and rid her mind of the treacherous trails she had carved. When she had said goodbye she had promised herself, again—very soon, mother— very soon this will all be over.

Next, she had called Andre. She needed him to send the research data on the G–16 virus to Dr. Wasserman. The conversation had been like so many she had had with him over the years. He had been unwilling to part with the research believing that he was most likely the only person to have access to it and it could prove to be a valuable asset to him in time. They had played their typical game of chess, but Alex had been unable to checkmate her opponent. She had known Andre had needed to gain some financial advantage if he would to agree to cooperate.

"He doesn't intend to use the virus himself does he?"

"If there's a way for him to make money with it somehow, he'll find it and end up doing it. He's driven by money and the power that it brings him. It's as simple as that."

Benjamin shook his head and squished his feet in the sand as they walked. "It's always about money isn't it? How much does he want? I'll pay him his ransom if that's what it takes."

"Hold onto your money for now. I ended up making him a proposition and I think he took it. We'll see."

"What'd you offer?"

Alex shoved a shoulder into Benjamin and with a mocking Italian accent she whispered, "I made him an offer he couldn't refuse." The both laughed, and she continued, "I told him I was still looking for you, but in the process I ran across something worth far more than the virus research. I'd pass all the information on to him the moment I learned that Dr. Wasserman received the research and everything was there. He probed me for more information, but in the end he figured I must be on to something and ultimately he agreed to my offer."

Benjamin tugged on Alex's arm. "Come on tell me. What are you talking about?"

"What we found in Antarctica, Ben, it has real value, both scientifically and more importantly as far as Andre is concerned— monetarily. He'll find a way to profit from it. Besides, what are we going to do with it?" She held her hands out, palms up.

That morning the four sat around the dining room table devouring the breakfast that Alex had whipped up. Abalone omelets with fresh strawberries, Canadian bacon and freshly squeezed orange juice. The mood was reflective as they each thought about the perils ahead until Devon insisted that he was casting his vote in favor of Alex's omelets being the best–cooked meal. Ben and Phil quickly started back into defending his own masterful creation until finally, Alex raised both hands in a halting gesture. "How about we all agree that we have just eaten the best meals any of us have had in the past week, probably longer, and then we can get down to business. We have a lot to go over."

Heads nodded in agreement, the barking stopped and they spent the next several hours pouring over the pieces of the puzzle that they somehow needed to fit into an orderly pattern. Phil brought everyone up to date on what he had learned about Alan Price, and

Devon talked about Sterling and its serpentine connections to power structures throughout the world. Alex and Ben relayed their findings in Antarctica and the fact that they were still being tailed by someone.

Phil had some serious doubts about Antarctica. "It defies the laws of physics, as we know it. There's no way a weightless environment can exist here on Earth—impossible."

"Impossible? That's the same response people gave to those that thought the earth was round." Devon stroked his goatee.

"Very funny, but times have changed, Devon. We can measure the earth's density with seismic waves, we have satellite images and the trans–polar voyage of the USS Nautilus is proof enough that no Arctic hole exists near the North Pole. That submarine passed directly over the pole without incident."

Alex leaned forward. "Phil, what you're saying is all correct, but I've seen it; I've felt it and I experienced it. I don't know how to explain it, but both of us," she looked sideways at Benjamin, "experienced very little gravity inside that hole."

Benjamin nodded. "I've already told you what I saw, Phil. It's. . . well, real. It's really real. Sure the light was flat and I didn't have a true perspective of how massive that place really was, but I'll tell you I lost count of how long it took for my screams to bounce back at me. The further down I went, gravity seemed to disappear. Before I pulled myself back up to the vent I think I was suspended in mid–air. The rope just dangled there. So, go ahead, Phil, be the naysayer or like Devon said, keep believing the earth is flat."

Phil chewed on the end of his pen and his head shook. "Sorry, guys, I still say it's impossible."

"Then how about we talk about something we all agree on—Alan Price." Alex wanted to get back on track.

The profile on Alan Price was confusing, but there were certain threads that were consistent throughout his life. Some of those threads had spilled over into other areas. His story was much more than an obsessive history buff collecting Nazi memorabilia. His interest in World War II and the Nazis had been apparent from his early schooling years and had followed him through his studies at Berkeley, and now he had amassed an extraordinarily large collection of Nazi artifacts. There had to be a reason those artifacts had been stored in Koidu and the Black Swan Bunker, and some way that had to be connected to why the virus had been stashed in those two places.

Devon was convinced that because the Koidu and Black Swan Bunker information had been hidden so deeply in the Sterling computer network and because of the complexity of the security walls surrounding it, that Sterling may not have much direct involvement in any of this, if at all. The access had been too limited to be a corporate plot. The creation of Grinhaus & Company and the transferring of money through various offshore accounts to fund its operations supported his assumption. Even Sterling's CFO didn't have access to those accounts. He still had not been able tie anything to Sterling's coincidental connections to the Twin Towers, but his gut told him there had to be something there and he wanted to pursue it further. It was no coincidence that within months after the Twin Towers attack Sterling's business revenues soared.

Alex had harbored a slight suspicion that Benjamin had not actually been injected with the virus at all, but it had been a ploy on Price's part. The discovery by Dr. Wasserman that an unknown gene had been found in Benjamin's DNA makeup dispelled that suspicion and created an even greater urgency in her to connect the pieces. The two men they had left behind in the Black Swan Bunker had been suffering from the initial effects of an active virus eating away at them from their insides out. She had been unable to shake that vision. That could be Ben at any moment and there would be nothing she could do.

Phil sat back down at the table and took a sip of coffee from a freshly filled mug. He had put two and two together and came up with five. "I think it's time to go to the authorities. I know you'll probably be against that, Alex, but we're stuck. We need help."

Alex's voice reflected her resolve, "Absolutely not! That's not a choice. The moment that Price hears the authorities are looking at him as a suspect he'll activate the virus. He doesn't want anyone around who knows anything. I think that's why he killed those two men at the Black Swan. They knew too much."

Benjamin reached into his shirt pocket and pulled out his cell phone. "It looks like it's Jessica. I'll take it. Give me a few minutes." He stood and walked toward the kitchen.

When Benjamin returned the three were huddled around Alex's laptop. He sat back down in his chair and laid both hands on the table. "Dr. Riggle is coming to see me. The latest blood sample I gave them apparently has some interesting results that he doesn't fully understand so he wants to go over some things with me." He glanced at his watch. "He'll be here in a few hours."

# CHAPTER 41

"I want to run a series of DNA sequencing tests on you as soon as you're finished. I'll set up one run in Sydney and another one here when you return. We're not sure if the alteration will be immediate or occur over time, but if we see any changes in those tests we'll know a lot more."

Benjamin stood in front of the picture framed window and stared past the redwoods and out to the Pacific Ocean. His arms were folded and his head cocked to one side. When he turned around, Alex recognized the look on his face and she cringed.

She'd seen it before when he had told her about his brother, William, and how as a young boy Benjamin had spent several years learning all he could about finding a cure for cystic fibrosis. William eventually died from the disease and Benjamin felt he had failed—he alone had been responsible for his brother's death. Years later he had come to realize that wasn't true, but he had learned at a tender age that some diseases had to run their course. Medical minds lagged far behind the cures needed for many diseases.

He tucked both hands in his pants' pockets and leaned back. "Dr. Riggle, I don't understand everything you're saying. In fact, I don't understand much of it at all. What I think though, is that the odds of actually having any effect on this gene by going into a weightless environment are slim, very slim at best. It may turn out to be just a big waste of time and I'm not sure how much time I really have at this point."

Dr. Riggle remained seated on the sofa. In his mid–forties, he gave the appearance of a nervous man uncomfortable in his own skin. One eye twitched when he spoke, his fingers moved from one itch to another, he tugged at an ear, scratched his forehead, rolled his shoulders and crossed and re–crossed his legs in one continuous motion. He tugged at his ear again, and said, "We're well under one percent in finishing up an epigenomic map. In fact, one percent would be a massive overstatement. I'm afraid I can't give you any certainty at this point if that's what you're looking for."

Dr. Riggle had spent the past hour explaining the science of epigenomics and how a layer of biochemical reactions could turn genes on and off. The epigenome can change according to an individual's environment and researchers had already linked certain human cancers with epigenetic changes. In fact they know it's part of the reason why identical twins can be so different, and it's also why not only the children, but the grandchildren of women who had suffered from malnutrition during pregnancy were likely to weigh less at birth. It was known that certain cancers follow from the deactivation of tumor–suppression genes and if those genes could be reactivated the cancer could go into remission.

Alex walked over to Benjamin, put her arm around his waist and leaned into him. "This is a long shot; I agree. But look at the change that occurred in this gene from the one time you went into the Hole. Your two DNA sequencing tests show those changes. Both Dr. Riggle and Dr. Wasserman are convinced that's why your memory returned so suddenly and I think those are reasons enough to give this a try."

"I don't disagree with you Alex, not at all. It's just that. . . well. . . " he let out a long sigh and turned to Dr. Riggle, "there are so many questions in my mind and so few answers."

"I would expect that to be the case, Ben. One of my professors in med school used to tell us that asking questions was priming the pump of understanding. You need to understand the risks with all of this before you can make any decision. I understand that perfectly, so. . . so let's take all the time you need. I'm in no hurry."

For the next several hours Benjamin peppered Dr. Riggle with questions and the two men were locked in debate, not a debate against one another, but a debate as to whether scientists truly knew the effects on the human body from exposure to a weightless environment.

The real scientific interest in human exposure to weightlessness began with NASA when President John F. Kennedy announced his goal of landing a man on the Moon and returning him safely to Earth by the end of the 1960s. NASA had amassed a colony of chimpanzees and they had begun a systematic and rigorous training regimen at Holloman Air Force Base in New Mexico as part of the Mercury Atlas missions. Ham had been the first chimp selected to enter the space program.

Shortly after Ham's historic launch, Enos had been chosen as the first chimpanzee to be launched into Earth's orbit. Because he would be exposed to a weightless environment for a prolonged period of time, Enos was placed in a specific training routine. After exposing him to aircraft stalling techniques and psychomotor training he had been given the green light. On November 29, 1961, Enos boarded *Mercury Atlas 5* where he successfully completed two orbits around the Earth. Enos's flight had been a full dress rehearsal for Lt. Colonel

John Glenn, who became the first American to orbit the Earth just three months later.

The International Space Station had proven to be a Shangri–la to conduct research on the effects of long–term weightless exposure on the human body. First launched in 1988 as a habitable artificial satellite, the International Space Station had been used to conduct a collection of experiments of far reaching impact. Research on the reaction of the cardiovascular system to exposure to microgravity, expression of microbial genes in space and, the effects of the gravity altered environment on behavior and ageing had all led to medical advances that would not have been possible without a weightless laboratory to carry out the research.

Dr. Riggle had a colleague with the Sanford–Burnham Medical Research Institute who had been the principal investigator on a research project studying the effects of weightlessness on the hearts of fruit flies. Although the research had not yet been published, Dr. Riggle had spent hours with his colleague addressing the issues of weightlessness and using Benjamin as a hypothetical. Dr. Riggle had been convinced that there was a very strong likelihood that if Benjamin could be exposed to a weightless environment for several hours or longer, the unknown gene would be repressed and silenced—permanently.

Benjamin sat on the sofa opposite Dr. Riggle. He no longer saw the ceaseless quirks and twitches that he had self–consciously tried to avoid when they had first met. He smiled and remembered back to that day where he had learned that things were not always as they first appeared to be. His grandfather had taken him and William on a camping trip when he was seven years old. They had sat on the banks of a raging river peering out at the rushing water and had been mesmerized by the sound of the water rushing over the boulders.

They had intended to cross the river at that spot, but the current had appeared to be too strong, too deep and too treacherous to forge their way across. After a few minutes his grandfather had asked them to look downstream. "What do ya boys see down thar? Does the river look any differnt to ya?" All that he and William had been able to see was water and more water. They shook their heads. "A river never dwells in the past, boys. What yar lookin at is the precious sound of the now, and that now isn't too invitin. But downstream's the future and I can tell by the widenin of the banks and the flow of the water that that's where ya wanna be—the future."

Benjamin wanted to look to the future. He wanted to put all this behind him. Dr, Riggle had presented him with a path—a windy, twisted and never–before–traveled path—but it was a path—a way to the future. He no longer saw the tugs, scratches or twitches. "I only have one more question for you." Benjamin locked his wrists over his head, leaned back and looked Dr. Riggle in the eyes. "All of this seems to point in one direction; I should give this a try, but. . . how do we know that the opposite won't occur? While I'm down in that hole the gene will end up activating instead of repressing?"

Dr. Riggle leaned forward. "Animal and human cell cultures have been studied at the International Space Station and it has been experimentally proven, over and over, to have the same gene expression effect. Specifically, all of the studies show that exposure to microgravity causes an altered immune function and increased vulnerability to infection. What I'm really saying, Ben, is the overwhelming scientific evidence shows that certain genes are suppressed, not activated, during exposure to microgravity."

Dr. Riggle explained in detail the studies that had been done in this field. Dating back to the original Apollo flights, blood samples had been drawn from the primary and backup crews before launches and post flights. By analyzing the lymphocyte response and gene transcriptions they had been able to isolate the gravity–dependent gene expression patterns. Those patterns had been limited to the specific genes that primarily affect the body's immune and bone forming systems.

"So, I run the risk of having any number of genes suppressed. Is that what you're saying?"

"No. The studies conclude that microgravity affects the immune and bone forming systems, but there is no evidence beyond those two areas."

"I need to do one more thing before I decide what to do." Benjamin put an arm around Alex and led her to the window. "Let's walk down to Shell Beach and take a swim. The cold water, the waves and the salt air will help me make the right decision. You game?"

"Show me where we'll swim and I'll decide how much of a head start to give you."

Within minutes the two were out the door walking hand–in–hand down the trail to the beach with their swim gear slung over their shoulders.

# CHAPTER 42

P hil stood in front of the television and screamed, "Get down here—everybody! Get down here—*now*!"

The three others converged into the room at the same time, their eyes still half asleep. Benjamin spoke first, "What is it, Phil? It's one in the morning what. . ."

"Shh, listen! The President of France is about to speak."

"The news I have today is disturbing and shocking and it stirs emotions in me that I never thought would surface. France has been investigating this now for close to a year and today I am saddened to announce that the German government has sanctioned and has been actively involved in carrying out viral weapons research that was originally started by the Nazis at the end of the Second World War. We have credible and undeniable evidence to support this claim. Toward the end of that war, the Nazis sent two ships to Antarctica, U–530 and U–977. It has always been pure speculation that those ships ferried German research scientists and equipment to establish a laboratory. That may remain speculation, but it is now convincingly clear that there is an underground laboratory in Antarctica that was originally built during that War and today it's operated as a research facility. The laboratory currently has in storage the same G–16 virus that our intelligence agency discovered just three weeks ago.

The G–16 virus is being manufactured and stored there today. We have discovered a complex chain of money wire transfers that have taken place over the past two years where money was transferred from the German Treasury through various offshore accounts and eventually into the account of Grinhaus & Co. KG, a German domestic company. Our intelligence agents have photographs of the laboratory which also serves as a storage area of rare Nazi relics. It is the intention of the French government to. . . "

Devon shot out of his chair. "I knew it! I knew there was a connection! Sterling, Price or someone connected with them is behind this just like the transfer of money before Twin Towers. It's the same!"

Alex ran to her laptop and booted it up. News stories had already flooded the internet. The German government had vehemently denied knowing anything about the allegations and had formally requested the French government to release to the public all documentation supporting its claim. The European financial markets were in a freefall. The Frankfurt Stock Exchange had already dropped 197 points, its biggest drop since March, 2008; the London Exchange was suffering its worst loss since October, 2008, when it fell almost eight percent; the Euro had fallen 3.2 % and crude oil prices had soared. The news had spread with lightening force and financial trading houses and political leaders from around the world were all clamoring for answers.

Alex knew that the answers would come, but not before the financial underpinnings of the European markets were ripped to shreds. Political leaders never acted quickly enough to calm financial traders who were piqued to a frenzy and acted on frayed nerves and jittery instincts. She had seen her share of market havoc and she had created some of her own.

She didn't have to reach too far back in her memory to remember Germany where she had caused a three hour trading outage and untold embarrassment for the Frankfurt Stock Exchange. That Exchange used a Linux–based trading system named CAAC 40. It had been considered the fastest trading system in the world, with trade completion speeds of up to 132 microseconds. Her initial surveillance had uncovered what she had known were DGSE agents looking for the same technology, but Alex had struck first. She had stolen the computer code that had allowed the Exchange to engage in those trades. She had encrypted the files and had transferred them over the internet. She had then deleted the program she used to encrypt the files and had deleted the computer's 'bash history' which recorded the most recent commands executed on the computer.

Less than a year ago, she had infected the computer network of the Tel Aviv Stock Exchange with a Trojan horse; she called "Nightmare," that had shut down the entire network for a three hour period. One week before Alex had intended to shut down the exchange, she had infected several computers within the Exchange's computer systems. The virus had silently spread across the Exchange's computer network, but had remained dormant until thirty minutes before the Exchange had been scheduled to open on the day Alex had programmed the attack. At the exact pre–programmed time, the virus had activated and had overwritten the host computers' "boot block" and then the in–memory operating system. All of the computers had crashed at the scheduled time, trades had been halted and the exchange's IT personnel had scrambled to find the problem. Once the virus had been discovered, they had re–booted the operating system for each computer and within three hours trades had resumed, but not before Alex had uploaded the files she had been after.

"Devon, come here!"

The three crowded around Alex and she showed them what she had pulled up her screen. "We've seen the name Grinhaus & Co. before. Devon, remember the money transfers that ended up in Grinhaus' account? We never located the origin of the funds, but we know from Sterling's records that it had something to do with all that. Can you backtrack those wire transfers to see where they originated? I'm betting the German government is not in the loop at all."

"I'll try. What are you thinking?

She pointed at her monitor. "This should make it clear. These are the corporate records of Grinhaus and its three corporate officers. The one listed here, Leon Schulz, I'm certain is one of the men we left on the floor at the Black Swan Bunker."

"And you know that how?"

"When I went into the room to get the hard drives I searched each man for an ID. They didn't have any, but when I went through the hard drives later Leon Schulz's name was everywhere."

Benjamin asked, "I thought you said the French erased the hard drives?"

"They did, they erased the C drive on each hard drive, but there was a shared drive which was used to keep both computers up to date with each other. They were obviously in a hurry and didn't touch the shared drive, so all the information is in tact."

"So you think there's a connection between Sterling and Grinhaus?

"There has to be. Schulz is an officer of the company and he's dead. Grinhaus shows up in Sterling's computer files and we all know that Price had been to the Bunker at least once, probably more. We have some fast work to do before the European markets close or the financial consequences will be disastrous."

"Wait a minute, Alex." Phil leaned forward and drilled his elbows into the table. "None of this has anything to do with the virus in Ben and what we need to do to find a permanent way to get rid of that thing. It's interesting, that's for sure, but we're getting sidetracked."

"Not really, it has everything to do with the virus and finding a way to help Ben. Price is behind this. I can feel it—I know it. His plan has been set in motion and at this moment he's probably safely hidden far away from everyone. He's sitting back and watching the action."

"So where are you going with this?"

Alex leaned back and looked at each of them, one at a time. "Devon, you'll see what you can find out about the origin of the funds that landed in the Grinhaus account, okay?"

Devon was already pounding his keyboard. He gave a quick nod.

"Phil." Alex paused briefly to assess Phil's demeanor. He was focused. "You have a lot of digging to do. There's a reason behind why Price has set things up the way he has. His whole fascination with the Nazis from the time he was a child up to storing rare Nazi antiques in both Koidu and the Bunker have to play into this somehow. Dig deeper. You told us he was adopted, so see if you can find out anything about his birth parents. Those records could be tough to find, but Devon and I can help you out there. See if you can find out anything about how, where, when and from whom he purchased or stole all those antiques. There are some real collectors' items there. Anything you can find out about his fascination or connection to the whole Nazi thing would be helpful to us."

"Yeah, I'll definitely need some help with the birth records, but I think I'm good to go with the rest."

Out of the corner of her eye, Alex saw a bewildered look painted across Benjamin's face. His shoulders were bowed from the weight of his angst. "What's that look about? Are you okay?"

"I'm still not sure where you're going with this, Alex. Even if Price is connected to all this how does that help us? It doesn't really get us any closer to what we're looking for—to get rid of this damn thing."

Alex nodded and looked at Benjamin. His nerves had to be frazzled and he probably felt he was sitting on the edge of his last moment in time. Any second that damn gene could be activated and he would end up like the two men on the floor of that bunker. "Come here."

She stood and took Benjamin's arm and led him to the living room. "Let's sit down."

"I don't think there's anything for you to worry about right now. Later, well yes, but not right now. I've dealt with too many people like Price over the years and I'm certain that right now he's engrossed in watching the markets and counting the money he's somehow making. It's always about money with people like him. He's not spending any time thinking about you or if he should activate the virus." Alex put a hand over Benjamin's and gave it a squeeze. "I'm certain of this and if I'm right then he may have just given us the time we need."

Benjamin leaned forward and gave Alex a kiss on her forehead. "Is this your instinct talking or do you really believe this."

"Both!"

"Okay then, I'm on board. What do you want me to do?"

"I want to first find some of the things we're looking for and then we'll decide. I think we're going to need some help here in the States and that help might come from Constance. If that's the case you should be the one to call her."

"Constance? I should call her, but. . . what does she know about any of this?

"She doesn't know much. She knows you're alive and that you've been infected with the virus, but that's it. Phil's talked to her a few times in the past week. Are you okay with calling her and asking for her help?"

"I've thought about her and I've thought I should give her a call at some point. Phil mentioned he told you I had talked to her about a divorce. I was surprised about her reaction at the time, but with everything that was happening then, it makes perfect sense to me now. Anyway, that's still what I want and I'll call and ask her to help in any way you want."

# CHAPTER 43

At four in the morning a syrupy fog blanketed the coastline shielding the starlit sky, but inside the Sea Ranch house every light shown brightly and the fire crackled. The past few hours had been a hive of activity as the four searched for answers, motives and clues behind that sudden announcement made by the President of France. They all believed that Price was behind everything and Alex was certain that money was the motive. Over the past few hours the European markets had suffered their worst one day loss in history. Securities, commodities, currencies were all spiraling downward and France had not stepped forward and offered anything other than the accusations made by its President. Because she knew the accusations were false and all the evidence pointed to Price; Price operated the Bunker, the priceless Nazi antiques had been acquired by Price and Price was the one who had been behind developing the G–16 virus, she had focused her attention on Price.

Moments before Devon burst in, Alex had discovered another link to Price. Lukas Müller was the President of Grinhaus & Co. and he had recently met the same fate as Leon Schulz. The Frannziskus–Krannkenhaus Hospital in Berlin had reported the death of Lukas Müller. He died from an unknown virus and the authorities had contacted the CDC in the United States to assist in investigating the virus.

"Alex! Look at this!" Devon burst into Alex's room and set his laptop on her desk. "The money trail here is ooooozing with guilt. Over the past two years Sterling has made twenty–two wire transfers into a Cayman Island bank called Currillion Bank and each transfer was made to the account of David Stiffleman."

"Who is that?"

"I don't know—yet—but I'll find out. It may just be a made–up name, but the interesting fact here is that all of Grinhaus' deposits into its accounts with Bankhaus Lampe in Frankfurt over this same time period came from the Stiffleman account at Currillion. There were some intermediate transfers along the way, but the routing and account numbers throughout the trail all match."

Alex leaned back and looked up at Devon. "Is the amount transferred to Grinhaus the same as Sterling transferred to Currillion?"

Devon shook his head. "Not even close, Alex. Sterling transferred over $2 billion into the Stiffleman account and Grinhaus has received about a quarter of that amount."

"So much for the German government financing them. Can you get back into Currillion's system and do some more digging? We need to find out more about what's gone on with the Stiffleman account."

Phil overheard their conversation and walked into the room and stood between the two. "Did I hear this right? You've just hacked into the computer system of two banks? You've gotta to be kidding me. You've probably broken more laws in the past hour than I ever knew even existed. Are you nuts doing things like that?"

Devon shrugged. "Hey, hacksters do this all the time so don't go getting your knickers in a twist over this. Traveling around inside a bank's computer system is easy weird to me and some good info is coming our way."

"Devon knows what he's doing, Phil. He's in and out before any alarms sound and his digital tracks are covered. I know it's not really the *right* thing to do, but what choice do we have? Really?"

"Yeah. . . yeah, it's just bizarre to me. Nothing's private anymore in this world."

"Amen to that. One more thing, Alex. Currillion has an omnibus account it uses to trade securities with several of the major brokerage houses. Funds from a number of its accounts are placed in the omnibus account and each day after the markets close it reallocates the funds back to their original account. The Stiffleman account is tied to this and over the past two years it has only made one trade and that was less than two weeks ago. It bought and sold one–thousand shares of Deutsche Telekom and when the funds cleared they were wired to another account at First Caribbean Bank, also in the Cayman Islands. What strikes me as odd is a single trade of around $10,000 is pretty small for a $1.5 billion account, yet the entire Stiffleman account is pledged to the omnibus account, like maybe it's planning a larger trade."

Alex leaned back in her chair, her chin rested on her thumbs and her fingers were tented. This information fit perfectly into her suspected motive. Somehow Price had set up a system to make security trades and to have the money wired to a separate account at a different bank.

"Devon, if Price plans to use the Stiffleman account to buy and sell securities he'll have to place a buy order. Can you find out if he has placed any orders or if he has pending orders in place?"

"Nah, I tried that, but I ran into an iron shield. I can get cash balances, deposits and transfers from the Stiffleman account, but the ties to the omnibus account are protected with different passwords and separate firewalls and for some reason I can't crack those—not yet, anyway, but I'll get there."

"Yes, but if the entire account is pledged wouldn't that mean pending orders have been placed? Something is going to happen very, very soon."

Devon nodded. "I suspect you're right. I looked at two other accounts linked to the omnibus account and they didn't pledge their entire account balance as collateral. In fact, the pledged amount was close to the value of their trades."

Alex chuckled. "You're a genius, Devon. Sit down, let's get back into Currillion and do some more snooping."

# CHAPTER 44

"Ben, Devon, you need to get in here!" Before Alex had finished, Benjamin and Devon bolted into her room and stood there as she finished up with Phil.

"It looks like we have everything we need. Phil has just given me the last piece. We need to act quickly." Alex turned to Phil, "Why don't you tell them what you just told me."

Phil was straddling the arm rest of the couch. One leg was tucked under with his knee pressed against the cushion and the other shot out to the side. It had been several days since he last showered and his hair was matted and a thick beard covered his chiseled jaw. His eyes though, were crisp and alert. He had everyone's attention. "It turns out Price's name when he was born was Alan Stiffleman; he became Price when he was adopted at two years old. Alex explained to me the David Stiffleman connection at the bank. Anyway, David Stiffleman, his bio–father, was killed by the Nazis toward the end of the war. British airborne troops were sent by glider to sabotage a heavy–water plant in Norway and they ran into some bad weather and crashed. There were five survivors and they were all taken prisoner and held at Grini concentration camp until January, 1943, and then they were hauled into the woods, blindfolded and shot in the back of the head by the Gestapo. David Stiffleman was one of those men. So Price's fascination with the Nazis is based on pure hatred."

Benjamin broke the silence, "So he's probably spent years planning this or at least dreaming about it. The guy has a real obsession."

"It answers some other questions, too." Alex locked her fingers. "He probably came up with the Grinhaus name by using Grini, and remember Phil telling us about Price's interest with Dr. Maiman's father's connections within the Third Reich? His father was stationed for a period of time at Akershus Fortress which was the primary German concentration camp in Norway. His father oversaw the operations at Grini. Price must have been aware of the tie–in there."

Benjamin asked, "What about Price's mother? What happened to her?"

Phil looked at Benjamin and smiled. "You'll love this. Does the English town St. Margarets at Cliffe ring a bell?"

Benjamin nodded. "Yeah, of course. Why?"

"Price was born there and soon afterwards the whole town was evacuated to make room for military personnel. His father was stationed at the nearby RAF Hawking airfield and Price moved with his mother to Canterbury." Phil's elbow shot into Benjamin's side. "It looks like we'll have some extra sightseeing to do there this summer."

Benjamin sighed, "Something tells me that swim won't be happening next summer."

Alex looked up. "What are you guys talking about? What swim?"

Benjamin twirled a pen in his fingers and Phil put a hand on his shoulder. "Our man here is on the start list to swim the English Channel this coming summer. The swim starts from a beach next to St. Margarets at Cliffe. Kind of ironic, huh?"

Alex shook her head and smiled. "I know about your Catalina crossing, but it looks to me like you have your mind set on swimming's' Triple Crown. If you're signed up for this summer—well, we'll just have to find a way to get you there. You can't pass that up—no way."

Benjamin set the pen on the table and rolled his eyes. "If I get there great, but right now I'm not looking that far ahead. We'll see."

Somehow, Phil knew Benjamin had not given up on his dream to swim the English Channel next summer. His voice was far from convincing. As soon as Benjamin had crawled over the rocks and had planted his feet firmly in the sand at the Palos Verdes shoreline, he had raised his hands and pumped his fists. After completing the grueling 21 mile Catalina Channel crossing he had every right to celebrate. It had been one remarkable swim. He had later told Phil that he hadn't been celebrating the Catalina swim when he had crawled out of the water. No, it had been at that very moment when he had raised his fists and shouted to the heavens that he had set his sights on the English Channel. He had wavered a few times over the past year, but Phil knew that nothing would stand in the way of Benjamin swimming from Dover to the French shores of Calais next summer. This was just another obstacle thrown at him, that's all. Once Benjamin made a decision on anything, it was near impossible to derail his commitment.

Benjamin cleared his throat and continued, "So, what about Price's mother? Do you know what happened to her?"

"Okay, back to business then." Phil nodded. "Yep, I do know she died when Price was around two years old, that's why he was put up for adoption. The adoption records list both parents as deceased, but they don't say anything about the cause of death."

Devon straightened. "Easy enough to find out. I don't know if it matters, but give me her name and I'll search the death certificates around that time. I'll figure it out."

"Okay, check that out, but stay focused on Currillion's records. There's something there, I'm sure of it."

Alex looked at her watch and bit her lower lip. She knew they had to move—and now. "Ben, you should call Constance. In a little over four hours the New York Stock Exchange will open and if I'm right it'll be a bloody day. In the meantime, I'm going to attack this from a different angle."

"I know the CEO and I'll call her as soon as we're finished, but I don't know. . . it seems like there are a lot of "ifs" and I can't imagine she'd close the entire Exchange down on my call alone."

"I've told you everything we know and if we're right, the markets will open in the toilet—you know that. Until everything I've told you is out in the open and the authorities have substantiated things, it's going to be ugly. You know how long all that will take. Constance we can't wait that long. We just can't."

Benjamin had called Constance at her home in Georgetown and had given her a complete rundown on what was going to happen in less than four hours time. Alan Price had painstakingly orchestrated a series of events that had all been designed to not only extract revenge for the death of his father by the Nazis, but to also pad his personal bank account with several billion dollars in a matter of a few short hours. They hadn't been able to determine which securities would be purchased from the Stiffleman account, but they had confirmed that the entire account was going to be invested as soon as the exchanges opened. The European markets had closed with their largest single day losses ever and the Dow average, in pre–open trading was down over 1200 points. The wire services and internet sites were all asking the same questions and no answers had been forthcoming from France.

"When will all this be public, Ben? The markets can't stay closed indefinitely and, even if they are closed, trading will continue between brokerage houses."

"Alex is close to putting together something to send out and. . . "

"Alex? Boudreau, that's her name, right?

"Wait, Constance, let me explain something that. . . "

Constance quickly cut Benjamin off, "No, Ben it's okay. I've met her a couple times, she probably told you and those weren't pleasant encounters for either of us. Actually, I was furious when I first found out about the two of you, even jealous. But, you know, I've had a lot of time to think about things since you first told me you wanted a divorce. In fact, time is about all I've had lately. Since Ms Boudreau appeared, I am losing the only two men I've ever loved. My father. . . well, he'll most likely do some long prison time for what he's done. Ms Boudreau had nothing to do with that, nothing at all. That was all dad's doing and I think he's prepared for the worst there."

"I was shocked when I first learned of Paul's involvement in this, Constance, I. . . I really was. I always admired him. I don't know what to say."

"Thanks, Ben, but there isn't really much more to say at this point about dad. But, when. . . when you first told me you wanted a divorce, well I didn't believe it. When I found out about Alex Boudreau I wanted to scratch her eyes out. I blamed her for everything and I even blamed you for falling for another woman. I've had the time to reflect back on us and it's fairly obvious what has happened. I'm sorry, Ben. What I am sorry for though is that I've let you down over all these years we've been married. I have been selfishly focused on myself and my career. I've put my career above you and our happiness. I can't blame you for calling things off and wanting to start a life that you deserve. Nothing would make me happier than to know you've found a life with someone you can share your dreams with. You've always had big dreams, Ben, and you should follow them. I want you to be happy and I won't stand in your way any longer."

"Thanks, Constance. I knew we had to have this talk sometime and I didn't really know what to say or how you'd react. You know, I never knew how empty my life had become until I met Alex and I think at that point I realized how much damage we had done to one another over the years. I don't mean we were trying to hurt each other. It's nothing like that. We just never gave one another what we each needed. You deserve to be happy too, and as much as I love you—and I do love you—I'm not who or what you need."

"You always have had a way with words, Ben. And, as usual, you're right, I had my chance to be that type of woman for you, but I don't think that's really me. Who knows, maybe some day I can find that kind of love and happiness, too, with a man who can share my life and be content with who I am."

"I'm glad you understand. I wish things could've worked out differently for us and just so you know, there're no hard feelings on my part, none at all. You gotta admit, though, we did have some good years, inspite of how things turned out."

Constance laughed to hide the tears that Benjamin knew she must be holding back. She was not an emotional woman by nature, far from it, but he had seen real tears over the years and he knew that deep down she did love him. "Yes, we did. We've had some wonderful times together and there will always be a part of me that will love you, Ben. I hope you know that?"

"I do, and thanks, Constance."

"But right now, I need to know about that virus, Ben. Has it been removed? Are you really okay now?"

"Well that's the million dollar question and I don't really have an answer for you. I've had some medical tests run and I still have the virus; that much I do know. It appears that the gene carrying the virus has mutated some and we are exploring an idea to have the virus totally repressed through further mutation of the gene. So I guess the answer would be I'm going to be fine, it just might take some more time."

"Ever the optimist—that's you. I worry about that more than anything, Ben. Please keep me posted."

"I will, Constance."

"I'd better run. You've given me plenty to do this morning as if I didn't already have enough on my plate. I'll call the CEO now and do the best I can, but I wouldn't put all your cards on this. Keep doing whatever you can on your part also."

"Thanks, Constance. Thanks for everything. I'll be in touch."

# CHAPTER 45

Alex had been in situations before where she had to assess her prey. Every facet of her target had to be analyzed and any mistake, slight or not, would mean certain failure of her mission and life threatening consequences—prison or even death at the hands of her mark. She had faced men like Alan Price before and she understood what made them tick and what they wanted most out of life. Given enough time and the right information she could scent out any man's weakness.

The Chinese have a saying that a decision made in haste is always a bad one. Alex had weighed everything through her personal decision matrix and she knew they needed to act quickly. A hasty decision had to be made.

Alex measured the mental account of each man seated in his now familiar place around the dining room table. They were like moths around a bright porch light waiting for Alex to speak. They were each tired. Alex nodded her approval as her eyes swept around the table. Phil sat erect and even though his eyelids drooped, they still reflected the mettle and grit that defined his spirit. He was tough, focused and determined to see this through.

Devon's tic was twitching faster than his darting eyes. He looked nervous, tenuous and his mouth was buttoned shut. His face was the color of a man who had just seen a macabre vision of his impending death. Alex smiled. If he had looked any differently she would be worried.

Benjamin's hands were spread on the table and his thumbs traced the rounded edge. He had regained his weight since they had first found him at the Koidu plant. He was again physically fit; defined by muscle and tendons, but he looked as though a wave of emotion threatened to break over him.

Alex held her breath. "Are you okay, Ben?"

With a hint of sarcasm he replied, "Oh yeah. For a guy who any second could enter the food chain of a vulture I'm. . . I'm just peachy."

Phil jumped in. "Come on, Ben, this is all coming together. You'll be back to your old self in no time." He reached across and gave Benjamin a jab to the shoulder. "Hang in there, Bud, we're at the finish line."

Benjamin nodded. "I'm fine. . . just fine. I know things are going to work out, but I can't help having a flashback every once in a while looking at those two guys in the Bunker. That could be me—any minute."

"Well it's not going to be you. Not now or not ever." Phil looked at Alex and dropped a brow. "So? Fill us in. What's our next step?"

"Phil's right, Ben. All this is coming together and will be over soon—very soon." Alex knew too well that the darkest hollows often led to the brightest vistas. They needed to act quickly and this would be all over.

Alex straightened in her chair. "We're going to have to move lightening quick if we're going to pull this off. Before we leave for Antarctica I want to throw a few diversions at Price so that he'll need to pull all his resources back just to cover his own ass." She glanced at her watch and continued, "The markets here will open in less than three hours so that's our time limit."

Phil raised an eyebrow. "And what diversions do you have in mind or is it something I don't want to know?"

"Don't worry, Phil. You and Ben need to make our travel arrangements to Antarctica and Devon and I will take care of the diversions."

Devon's interest piqued. "Ah. . . I can tell by your tone that I'm going to be having some fun—*finally.*"

"This is right up your alley. I want you to close down the New York Stock Exchange and any other exchanges we can here in the States and I'm going to make sure they won't have the power to open on time just in case."

Ben shot a quick glance at Phil. "What are you talking about? Why do we need to do that? Why don't we just get the hell out of here?"

"I don't want Price or anyone else following us to Antarctica. Once we get there I think it best we follow Dr. Riggle's orders and then get out of there. Price is planning on making an absolute fortune from some stock trades he plans to execute today. Once we put a stop to those or at least delay them he'll pull everyone in that's working for him and devote his attention there. We'll have the time we need to get you inside the Polar Hole and out of there before there's anything he can do. That's our best option, Ben."

Ben looked confounded. "How are you going to close down the exchanges, Alex? Why don't we wait until I hear back from Constance?" His neck craned, "Better yet, why don't we just tell the authorities what we know and have them take care of Price?"

"Call Constance again and see if she knows anything yet. I'll prepare a complete synopsis of what we know and I have the perfect way to set it up for the authorities, but I doubt the government will move fast enough and even if they do we could always stop what we're doing. I don't want to wait long enough for the authorities to act. I'll give them everything they need—and more."

Phil stiffened. "This sounds to me like you're about to do one of those things that I don't understand, but I like even less. This isn't going to be legal is it?"

Alex met Phil's gaze. "I doubt you will like it, Phil. But there's a big difference here. . . We'll all be sort of a digital Robin Hood in the end. Price plans on making a killing and that means others will take a financial beating. Even though we're just looking for a diversion we may actually end up saving millions of dollars for some other investors." Alex looked at each one of them. "It's one of those things where you," she paused and pointed a finger, "*all of you*. . . are just gong to have to trust me."

A moment of silence was followed by three heads nodding in unison.

It had been more than a few years since Alex had hacked into computer networks operated by U.S. Government Agencies. She had her string of successes. She had erased critical files and shut down over 300 computers for a 24 hour period—her target had been none other than the United States military. A separate operation involved penetrating the National Institute of Health and pirating government sponsored research dealing with immune cells, called microglia, and their effects on brain development. Neither of those cases appeared anywhere in the media outlets because the agencies had not wanted it known that their systems were penetrable.

Things had changed since then. The proliferation of state–sponsored cyber–terrorism had brought a sense of delayed urgency to the United States government. An independent report by Mandiant had reported that since 2006, a Chinese sponsored hacker house had penetrated 141 Advanced Persistent Threats against 141 U.S. companies spanning 20 separate industries. The more recent barrage of attacks against U.S. banks had been believed to be the work of the Iranian government. State–sponsored attack groups had become nothing more than war rooms poised to launch cyber assaults. In response to what many had called a cyber Pearl Harbor, President Obama had increased the Cyber Command of the Defense Department to 4,000 personnel, up from 900.

Alex and Devon set up their own war room in the den and began preparations for their two–pronged assault. Devon pulled his hands from his keyboard and cracked his knuckles. "Alex, what do you really want to do here? I still don't understand why you want to delay trading activities this morning. What am I missing?"

Alex didn't stop her programming or even look up, but she did answer in earnest. "If we send information to the Justice Department or some other agency how long do you think it will take for Price to get wind that he's a target of an investigation? Weeks and then some— and we don't have that long. I want to get Ben down to Antarctica now—*right now*—and try this whole weightless experiment. After listening to Dr, Riggle, I think it just might work. I don't want to risk being intercepted by Price or anyone else."

"Yeah, but why will closing the exchanges help us out?

"Price has created a way to make a great deal of money in a very short time. We know that the French President's speech was filled with inaccurate facts, right?"

Devon nodded.

"Somehow, Price is controlling the President. How? I don't know, but it probably doesn't matter. The international stock markets have all reacted to that speech and they've plummeted. In most cases, they've suffered their largest losses ever. When the news breaks that there is no basis behind anything the President said, the markets will all recover their losses, quickly. So, this morning when the exchanges open, Price will buy stocks at a very low price and since he controls the news he'll let it be known, some way, that the President had overreacted and there is no truth to his allegations. The stock prices will quickly recover; he'll sell and make an absolute fortune. It's really that simple."

"I think I get it. So, he buys a stock, like for $10 in the morning and sells it later for $30. Is that the idea?"

"That's all there is to it."

Devon shook his head "Brilliant. You know, I wish I had saved up some money. I'd buy some stocks this morning, myself. Damn."

Alex lowered her brows and stared at Devon.

"Just kidding. . . really, but the part about wishing I'd saved up some money is true. So, that makes some sense now, but do you really think we can stop those trades from being made? That seems pretty ambitious."

"We'll just have to give it a try. Whatever we end up closing will only be closed for a few hours before they figure things out and you know what? It's impossible to shut down all trading activities these days. The New York Exchange only handles about 12% of all U.S. securities' trades and they have a separate electronic exchange called Arca that handles another 12%. Throw in NASDAQ and it amounts to about half of all trades."

Alex stopped programming and sat back. "Most trades nowadays are handled by computer market makers that could be located anywhere; they don't have to be sitting on the floor of any exchange.

But if we hit the known exchanges we'll draw the attention of the right people. That's all we need to do."

"So you're not looking at really crippling anything? More like a kidney punch or a blow to the knees?"

Alex nodded. "You remember the Doomsday virus a few years ago? It didn't really do anything, but it caught a lot of attention. People everywhere were worried that at a time certain their computers would crash. When that time came nothing happened. Remember?"

"Yeah, it generated tons of work for me because everyone was paranoid."

"We're going to throw a Doomsday problem out there that will draw the attention of the right people. Hey, we need a name for our virus. . . any ideas?"

Devon pushed his chin up in the air with his thumbs. "Yup, let's use the Creeper name. You know, the first computer virus."

Most any programmer who had created a virus knew the program Creeper. It had first surfaced in 1971 on ARPANET, the scientific/military network that had preceded the modern internet. DEC computers across ARPANET had been infected by Creeper, a self–replicating virus. It had exploited a vulnerability in DEC PDP–10 computers running the TENEX operating system. While the worm hadn't been malicious, once it had accessed a machine and replicated itself, it had broadcasted, "I'm the creeper, catch me if you can!" on the terminal screen. The Creeper spawned the beginning of programmers' attempts to develop virus removal programs and The Reaper, designed to comb through computer systems in search of a virus soon appeared.

"No, we need to raise the bar some. I want everything about this virus to point directly to Price so we'll tie him someway. Maybe something with a Germanic slant?"

"Die Walküre. . . you know Wagner's opera. It sounds eerie and it's as German as you can get."

"Close, but I love Wagner and the whole The Ring of the Nibelung series. I don't want to taint him that way. Maybe Hindenburg, or Aryan. . . Hah! Do you know what Schadenfreude means?"

Devon shook his head and spread his hands. "Uh. . . never heard of it."

"It means deriving pleasure from the misfortune of others. Does that sound like Price?"

Schadenfreude or maybe Schadenfreude Flu, but no one will be able to pronounce it. We need something that will stamp our mark. You know something people will remember. This could be a pretty famous virus once it's uncovered."

For the next few minutes they work–shopped names and ideas and then Alex shouted out, "Got it! *Loki*, the trickster god from Norse Mythology. He appeared in different forms like a salmon, a seal, a fly and even an elderly woman. I like that. . . *Loki*."

Devon's eyes widened and with tongue in cheek he mused, "He died when the gods tied him up using the entrails from one of his sons. Too bad Price doesn't have a son."

Alex laughed. "Oh no, one Price is more than enough." She looked at her watch. "I'm almost done programming this so let's finish up. I'd like to get this off in the next thirty minutes."

Alex knew she would have little problem penetrating the computers of Con Edison, the company that provided electrical power to Manhattan. Power companies had been slow to embrace the digital age. They had continued to operate under the mindset that stability and reliability were more important than anything— just keep the lights on. As a result they had continued to use the same software that had always worked without adding needed security patches. Their systems were a mixture of three different, but interlinked, components: a network of conventional office computers; control software that directly controlled equipment; and a thicket of specialized hardware such as switches and valves.

Alex completed the *Loki* virus and was ready to launch. She attached the virus to emails that she would send to random people in different departments at Con Edison. The benign email requested the recipient go to a link that contained new corporate policies for the use of vacation time. Once the recipient went to the link the virus would enter their computer and begin to spread. The virus contained false control readings that would trigger control systems to automatically react by cutting down power, eventually stopping all power output. This had been the precise strategy used by the Stuxnet worm in 2010 that had shut down Iran's nuclear processing equipment. The power cut back would be instantaneous, yet Con Edison would be able to override the shut down once they determined the control readings were false. Alex hoped the delay would be at least an hour, hopefully two.

Alex sat back and took several deep breaths. She knew that once she launched the *Loki* virus it would infect the Con Edison system and the power shutdown in Manhattan would have far–reaching effects. She was willing to take that risk. Her emails containing the *Loki* virus were batched in a group and once she hit the "Send" button, they would all be routed through Sterling's servers and the Con Edison IT personnel investigating the infected emails would have a digital footprint leading them directly to Sterling.

One tap of her finger and her outbox emptied.

# CHAPTER 46

"That should do it, but let's review it one more time." Alex stood. "Why don't you look it over while I go get something to drink? Do you want anything?"

Devon shook his head and mumbled, "Nope, I'm good."

Alex opened the refrigerator and pulled out bottled water. She gripped the chilled bottle in both hands and pressed it against her cheeks. The night before the glow from the crackling embers had provided all the warmth the four needed to stretch out and relax as they pondered their options. Several hours ago Benjamin had stoked the same fire and filled the fireplace with freshly cut wood. Alex drew a deep breath and the ripe scent of fresh pine soothed her frayed nerves, but the heat from the fireplace had raised the house temperature beyond her comfort zone.

She pulled off her sweatshirt, draped it over a bar stool and walked over to the living room window. She pressed her forehead against the glass and stared out at the pre– dawn wonderment. Morning mist dripped from the tips of the redwood branches, squirrels scurried down the tree trunks to start their morning chores and a family of quail marched in an orderly cadence down the dirt trail that led to the beach. For a brief moment Alex imagined herself sitting in her mother's kitchen, sipping tea, laughing and recounting stories of her early childhood. She smiled at the memory of Christina sitting on her father's foot and holding his leg. Horsey they used to call it and her father would bellow in laughter each time Christina would shout out, "faster daddy. . . faster daddy."

Alex heard a loud thud and her head snapped back. She pivoted and saw Phil standing at the foot of the stairs. "I cleared eight steps on that jump and nailed the landing. Hey, where's Ben? I got some info you'll both want to hear."

Alex turned her palms out and shrugged her shoulders.

"Ben! Ben! Get over here. I've got some damn interesting stuff."

"What is it?" Ben walked out from the den, pushed his hands through his hair and stopped at the kitchen counter. He leaned on one elbow. "Okay, you have my attention. What do you got?"

Phil's eyes darted from Alex to Ben. "Our man Price has a baby brother. Care to take a stab who it might be? You both know the guy."

Alex and Benjamin shared the same bewildered look. Alex shook her head. "Do we really want to know?"

Phil looked right at Benjamin. "Paul Brewster; he's Price's younger brother by two years."

"Impossible!" Benjamin's eyes narrowed and his chin dropped. "Paul was raised in Fresno. That's where Constance was born. I've been to the gravesite where both his parents are buried. I've even seen their gravestones, Phil. What are you talking about?"

"Hear me out, buddy. I figured this would be news to you." Phil plopped down in the wicker chair, crossed his legs and began, "Devon helped me earlier to try and find birth records at St. Margarets at Cliffe, but there aren't any records that old online anywhere. We sort of hit a dead end, but I started making some calls. I got a hold of a lady in the Parish Records Department and I used my best impersonation of an English gentleman and she did the digging for me. She found the birth certificate for Alan Stiffleman, 3.97 kilograms born to David and Gretchen Stiffleman. I then did the same thing in Canterbury only I found a death certificate for Gretchen Stiffleman and she ended up dying during childbirth. It took a few more calls to find out the rest, but Gretchen and David Stiffleman are listed as the parents on the birth certificate of Nicholas Stiffleman."

"Hang on, Phil." Benjamin drew a quick breath. "I'm with you on Price. I know you found the adoption records for Price and all of that makes perfect sense, but Paul Brewster can't be Nicholas Stiffleman. He was born and raised in Fresno—*I know it.*"

"He was raised in Fresno; you're right about that. The same outfit that handled Price's adoption also handled Brewster's and they were each adopted separately right after their mother died. The infant named Nicholas Stiffleman was adopted by an American couple named William and Thelma Brewster. They resided in Fresno, California."

"Bill and Thelma, that's. . . that's his parents' names. . . the same names I saw on the gravestones. I. . . " Benjamin's cheeks puffed, he blew out a gust of air and raised his hands. "Paul never said anything about being adopted. I'm sure Constance doesn't even know this or she would have told me. She knows how much I've always liked her father. She would have told me if she knew. This. . . this is. . . well, it's hard for me to believe, Phil. You're certain of this, huh?"

"Yep. My English lady friend copied the docs and emailed them to me. I can show them to you."

Benjamin bit his lower lip and arched a single brow. "You know I think his middle name might be Nicholas. I'll ask Constance that one and that would be the last piece I'd need to believe all this."

Benjamin clasped his hands behind his neck and looked over at Alex. "This probably doesn't mean anything to us. . . I mean as far as what we're doing anyway. What's your take on this?"

Alex was leaning against the armrest of the sofa with her hands planted on her thighs. "The two have some bad karma to say the least, but it does explain one thing, I think. At some point Price found out that his father was killed by the Nazis and he probably blames them for the death of his mother as well. It was the threat of a Nazi invasion that evacuated St. Margarets at Cliffe and maybe he believes his mother wouldn't have died and life would have turned out much differently if that hadn't happened. It's just conjecture at best, but all this ties up one loose end. Price is planning on making a ton of money and at the same time embarrassing Germany with its alleged current ties to the Nazis. That's his stroke of revenge."

"Show me the copies, Phil and then I'll give Constance a call."

"What was that about?

Alex pulled up a chair and sat down beside Devon. "I'll tell you later. Have you gone through this one last time? We need to get it off now."

"Yeah, but let me show you this first." Devon opened a Google search and for the next few minutes they scrolled through the news about the power outage in Manhattan. Loss of power had completely shut down all operations in Lower Manhattan and Con Edison had reported the problem as a switch malfunction. They were predicting power to be back on within several hours. Rumors were already circulating about the possibility of the New York Stock Exchange not opening for early morning trading.

"So far so good. Right?"

Alex nodded her approval.

"I went through your coded message and you're right again; it'll take the best government spooks at least a couple hours to bust that one."

Alex had created her own cipher, but with enough clues to expose the key and allow skilled code–breakers to decipher the code within a couple of hours—three at the most.

An Enigma coding machine had been invented by the Germans in the 1920s and had been used by the government and military to encrypt and decrypt messages. It had used three electro–mechanical rotors, each containing twenty–six letters. Once a message had been encrypted, it had to be inserted into another Enigma machine to decrypt it. The Polish Cipher Bureau had eventually re–engineered the machine and had learned how to decrypt intercepted messages and today, Enigma codes could be created through mathematical formulas.

By combining an Enigma Code with a simple Monoalphabetic code, Alex had created a cipher which, at first glance, looked unbreakable. She knew, though, that the Monoalphabetic code portion would be easily recognized and would provide the code–breakers with enough information to decipher the balance of the enigma code.

"Hey, wait, let me show you this one, I want to add it in." Devon scrolled down and showed Alex his addition written in the same code. "This is my chance to get my 9/11 theory in front of some people who may actually give a damn. Once they decipher the message then all they have to do is post something on 4chan and I'll forward them everything I have." Devon shot Alex a grin. "I'll bet you didn't know that I kept everything all these years; transaction records, names, dollar amounts—*everything.*"

"No, I didn't know that, but I'm not surprised. You're the best digital pack rat I know." Alex leaned back. "Why 4chan? I'd suggest Outlaw Forum, it has a better following."

Alex had used the Outlaw Forum in the past to help her find information and to find it quickly. She had used it just weeks ago to search for someone who may have information on who was behind the development of the G–16 virus. The Outlaw Forum sprang from an original group called Masters of Deception. Masters of Deception was a New York based hackers' group that originally collaborated to hack the Bell Atlantic phone switches and the various microcomputers and mainframes used to administer its telephone network. The membership in that group had been impossible to track, but through a joint task force, six of the members were eventually indicted and within months each had plead guilty. The Outlaw Forum was believed to be an extension of the Masters of Deception group, but they had remained untraceable through the use of code names and sophisticated trail cover–up techniques.

Devon pushed his glasses back up to the bridge of his nose. "I love the Outlaw Forum, but it's monitored pretty heavily by all the spook agencies. It might be too obvious for this. 4chan, that's the place. I'm on it all the time looking around for things. Hey, here's a good one. Remember when that candidate. . . what's her name. . . you know she ran for Vice President in 2008. . . "

"Sarah Palin."

"Yea, that's her. Someone hacked her Yahoo email account and posted a screenshot of her password on 4chan. That's how it was all made public. Did you know that?"

Alex laughed. "No. . . no I didn't know that one. Look Devon, I have no problem sticking your 9/11 inquiry in, but put it at the end of the message, maybe even a separate paragraph and that way it won't slow down anything on their part by trying to decipher this."

"Right on boss. I'm copying. . . and. . . and. . . it's pasted. There you go." Devon turned to Alex. "Well played, Alex. This will scare the living hell out of them and Price will be a dead man."

"Oh! I almost forgot—one more thing." Devon scrolled through his files and flashed another grin. "At exactly 9:30 every screen connected to the Exchange's network will see this pop up in bright colors. It's brilliant, if I do say so myself."

Devon clicked a happy face icon and in bold red, white and blue colors his screen displayed:

### ALAN PRICE CATCH ME IF YOU CAN.

Alex roared with laughter. "I love it! You're too funny, Devon." She tilted her head. "You know as long as you're adding things in you may as well code this and add it."

Alex typed a few coded words on Devon's laptop. "Huh? Price and Brewster are brothers?"

"That's the part I was going to tell you about later."

# CHAPTER 47

L ower Manhattan was awash with frayed nerves and frightening visions. The power outage that morning had created havoc for bridge, tunnel and subway commuters. The streets were filled with idle workers staring up at the tops of skyscrapers—the horror of 9/11 still hovering in their memories. The Police and National Guard had already lined the sidewalks and building entrances in an effort to provide order and stability to a mounting surge of angst and fear. Cell phone systems had overloaded with panicked callers reaching out for information.

Inside the pillared building at 11 Wall Street, meetings of executives, top IT professionals and security personnel had been underway for the past hour facing a deadline to make an unprecedented decision. The New York Stock Exchange was under cyber attack for the first time in its 221 year old history and faced a forced shutdown of its historic trading floor. Hurricane Sandy had swept through the East Coast in October, 2012 and had forced the first weather–related multi–day shutdown of the U.S. stock market in more than 120 years. The snow and rain wrought by Sandy had come fourteen months after Hurricane Irene had hit the New York region and had prompted exchanges to ready contingency plans, though markets had remained open then. The NYSE, like all U.S.

stock markets, had closed for four business days following the terrorist attacks of September 11, 2001. Each of those episodes had all raised questions about the financial sector's ability to handle the next disaster.

"The power outage has left us short–handed, but we have every available person working on this. I doubt we'll have the information you need before the markets are scheduled to open."

"I need more to go on than what you've given me, Julian. I can't make a decision like that on a hunch. How much time do you need to find out if this virus really has the capability to erase our trading data?"

"An hour. . . two. . . maybe three hours. It's hard to say, but I do know that if it's as effective as we believe, then our data will be irretrievable. We'll lose it all, permanently. I wish I could give you a better answer, Ms Kraemer, but that's as much as I know right now."

The *Loki* virus had been discovered in the early morning by an IT department head when he had turned on his computer. An email had appeared in his inbox titled 'Personnel Department'. When he had opened the email the words *Loki Virus* appeared in bold type followed by a cryptic message. In the middle of the message, written in English, had been the sentence, "Like Con Edison, your system is now infected with the Loki Virus and at precisely 9:30, when the Exchange is activated, all data in your system will be wiped out—permanently." The remaining parts of the message had been written in a code that no one within the department had been able to make any sense of. Following protocol, they had immediately contacted Homeland Security and the FBI believing that the attack had been related to the Con Edison shut down and possibly the work of terrorists.

Arlyn Kraemer stood in front of the conference room window that looked out to the trading floor below. Traders were milling around the trading stations preparing for another day of business–as–

usual, unaware of the perils that could occur when the 9:30 opening bell rang. She had spent twenty–two years at Goldman Sachs before she had become the CEO of NYSE Euronext just nine months ago. Her first order of business had been to prepare a detailed plan to cope with any disaster that could render the company's downtown Manhattan location inoperable or inaccessible. A plan had been prepared and submitted to the Security and Exchange Commission, but it would be months before the SEC would rule on the plan. She knew she could shut down the floor based 100 human traders and move all transactions to its sister exchange, Arca. The shift to Arca would make the all–electronic exchange the "primary market" responsible for setting opening and closing prices for stocks, a critical part in the calculation of indexes and fund valuations.

"I'm inclined to shut down the operations below and have everything transacted through Arca. I can come up with a reason for why we shut down things here and at least we'll be able to open and trade without any interruptions."

"Arca has the same problem, Ms Kraemer. They run on the same operating system and shared network. The Loki virus will erase their data as well. It's the same risk."

Ms Kraemer turned and leaned back against the window. Her hands swept through her hair and pulled it back. She lowered her head, pushed her elbows together and ground her teeth. When she had been with Goldman Sachs she had been one of the outspoken critics who had believed that if the Exchange shut down due to a disaster that there would be very few customers willing to buy stocks and the result would be a market free fall. She still held that belief, but now she was the one who would have to test that theory.

"Call Homeland Security again and see if they know anything further on the virus, or the code, then let me know. I have less that fifteen minutes to make a decision and I really have no idea what I'm going to do."

"I spoke to an FBI agent just before I came in here and they're concerned that this Loki virus may be similar to the virus that shut down trading on the Tel Aviv Stock Exchange last year. The Israeli government bills itself as one of the world's savviest in the field of computer technology, so if hackers were able to shut down an exchange there then the FBI believes there may be reason to believe the same could happen there."

"What are the similarities? They really think it might be one in the same?"

"They don't have any answers, yet and I'm sure they were only telling me enough to make us worry. Those hackers called themselves "Nightmare" and they infected the Tel Aviv Exchange's network and the system was unable to execute any trades for exactly three hours. It was completely shut down."

"Did they lose any data?"

Julian shook his head. "Don't know. I don't think so, but I don't know."

A voice came over the intercom, "Ms Kraemer, Senator Hunter is on the line and says it is very important that she speak with you."

Ms. Kraemer sighed audibly. "I'll take it in my office." She looked at Julian. "Find that out, Julian. I need to know."

The office of the Chief Executive Officer contained all the time–honored trappings one would expect for a company that served as the centerpiece for the world's financial markets. Rich walnut paneled walls, plush Persian carpets, shelves filled with crystal tombstones commemorating historical stock offerings and portraits of Anthony Stockholm, the Exchange's first President elected in 1894 and Winthrop H. Barnes, the patriarch of the only known lineage to have five generations of Exchange members. A framed diploma from Wharton School of Finance was the only visible personal item of Ms Kraemer. Her one–hundred hour work weeks left her no time for personal boasting.

Seated at her double pedestal desk, Ms Kraemer leaned to the side and hit the speaker button. "Tell me you have something new, Constance. I need something quick."

"I'm making one last plea, Arlyn, in hopes that you won't open the Exchange this morning."

"I need more than a plea from you, Constance. After we spoke earlier I was left with the impression that you know more than you're letting on. How did you know that we'd be attacked by a virus? There's no way we're going to know if the virus is in fact perilous in the next few minutes and I really don't want to take the risk that it may destroy our data." Ms Kraemer pushed herself up, drilled her fists into her desk and leaned into the speakerphone. "Help me out here, Constance, what do you really know?"

"The virus is real, Arlyn. The person who developed the virus has done this type of thing before and I have every reason to believe they are serious."

Arlyn Kraemer and Constance were more than professional acquaintances. When Constance had first run for the United States Senate, Ms Kraemer had reached out to her Wall Street colleagues and had bundled several million dollars in political contributions for Constance. They had traveled in the same social circles and the two had often dined privately together whenever one had business to attend to in the other's city. On two occasions, Ms Kraemer had been the guest of Constance and Benjamin at their Montana ranch. Constance had many acquaintances, but very few trusted friends. Arlyn Kraemer was as close to Constance as anyone.

"Constance! If I don't open the Exchange and this thing turns out to be a hoax I can kiss my tenure here goodbye. I'll be laughed right out of here."

"The last piece of information I just found out about concerns Alan Price. He's the one who manipulated the European markets yesterday and he's probably going to make a fortune within hours after the markets open here. If you. . . "

"I already know about Price." Ms. Kraemer sat back down. She shook her hands and dropped them to her lap. "The email that infected our system came from Sterling Defense's server. The FBI is searching their offices in Virginia and they're looking for Price right now. Listen, Constance. I know you're holding something back from me—I feel it, and I know that Price may have had something to do with Ben's disappearance. Is that what this is all about? Does this have something to do with Ben?"

Ms Kraemer looked at her phone and saw she had two calls on hold and her inbox was cluttered with a string of unopened emails, all received in the past few minutes. She looked at her watch and grimaced. "Help me out here, Constance. I don't have any more time to spare."

"Arlyn, I know that Ben is safe. . . for now. I spoke to him minutes ago myself, and all the information I've passed on to you came from him. He told me about the computer virus and about Price. That's more than I should be telling you, but you need to know that."

"My God, Constance. How did Ben get himself involved in all this? You must be beside yourself."

"It's not like that, Arlyn. He's. . . well he's. . . that's all I can tell you at this point. Once you decipher the message that came with the virus you'll know everything and you'll. . . "

"What does the message say, Constance? No one has figured it out yet."

"I don't know—I really don't. But, I'm asking you to keep the markets closed until you find out."

"You know you're going to be the star witness in probably a dozen investigations when all of this comes out. On top of everything with your father, the press will make you into their personal whipping boy."

"I'll deal with that when it comes, but Arlyn, please do what you can. I'm not in anyway using our friendship to influence you. There is more to this than either of us know and you need to decipher the message before you open the market for trading. I really believe that."

"Okay. . . okay, thanks. I've got to go."

Arlyn Kraemer looked over to the portrait of Winthrop H. Barnes. She had become accustomed to the fact that wherever she stood in her office the man's eyes always stared right at her. She could walk from one end of her office to the other and his two deep set brown eyes followed her every step. What would he do? she thought.

She looked at the Exchange clock—four minutes to the opening bell.

# CHAPTER 48

I t was a sharp contrast to the week before when the gusting winds and white–out conditions had amplified their fear that they had been venturing further and further into a vortex of no return.

They stood on the hard–packed crust and marveled at the untamed terrain that surrounded them. While Antarctica could be bone–chilling cold, it was not all ice and snow. About 1,200 square miles of the continent were made up of "dry valleys" where mountains and ridges kept out any precipitation.

Off in the distance a jagged mountain range broke through the crusted surface and the ice capped peaks shimmered in the thin air. The air was crisp and calm and despite the sub–zero temperature their hoods were pushed back and absolute silence surrounded their thoughts. The abyss before them held their hopes that within the next few hours their globetrotting search would come to an end.

"I'll be damned. The earth *is* round." Phil slowly shook his head and stood slack–jawed as he gazed out over the unknown chasm. "I. . . I never would've believed this if I hadn't seen it for myself. . . *never.*"

"And you're standing on the very bottom of that big round ball. Wait until we get inside then you'll really be blown away. It's like skydiving with no sense of movement. Even when you're upside down you don't know it." Benjamin dipped his shoulder into Phil. "Told ya so."

"It's huge!"

"Yeah, when we were here before we had no idea how big this was." Benjamin lifted an arm and pointed. "What do you think? Maybe ten. . . fifteen miles across?"

"Beats me. What do you think, Alex?"

Alex shrugged. "Ten to fifteen is as good a guess as any. This is all so surreal to me. I don't think I've ever stood anywhere before in total silence and been able to see forever."

Phil tucked his hands under his armpits. "I've stood in the opening of caves and there's always a cold wind blowing up from the cavern. The wind makes a hissing sound and you feel it. I don't feel any wind, none whatsoever."

The three stood near the lip of the Polar Hole, their heads bobble–heading in all directions. The lip was steep and appeared to be evenly shaped as far as they could see. Small pyramids of ice jutted through the pure white hard packed surface. Benjamin had earlier described the sides of the Hole as a series of near–vertical ice cliffs and at one point he had seen a narrow crevasse open and extend far beyond his sight. Exposed areas of sandstone and limestone poked through the ice, their surfaces smooth and dry. Even though the diffused light had made it difficult for him to feel his true bearings and to see for long distances, he had been certain that below him extended a vast nothingness leading to nowhere.

Phil reached in his pocket. "I brought this along to prove you two guys wrong, but now, I'm not so sure." He cocked his hand to his head and threw a rock as far as he could toward the middle.

They waited. . . and waited. Finally, "Not a sound." Phil turned and headed toward their pile of supplies.

It had been just two days ago that they had left Grandfather Wilkinson's home. He had made all the arrangements again to have them ferried to Casey Station. Their spirits were buoyed by the prospect that this would soon be over and they would return to their safe havens and resume their lives.

Alex grabbed her backpack and slung in over her shoulder. "Let me go down through the entrance and plant these explosives. You two wait here and I'll be right back and then," she beamed, "we'll do some skydiving as you say."

"Hey, we'll go with you. I'm sure Phil wants to take a look around."

"I'm sure he does, but unless you're used to the stench of dead bodies I don't think it's a good idea."

Phil looked at Benjamin and they both shrugged. "We'll wait here."

Once inside the Bunker, Alex moved about quickly. She had been right about the stench. She stayed out of the main room, but she peered through the window and saw what remained of Leon Schulz and Franz Kruger. Piles of dark, hardened blood surrounded what was left of two decomposed bodies. Her own stomach lurched and she turned her head. That could have been Benjamin, she thought. Please, God, let this be over. She taped two sticks of C4 Plastic Explosives to the door, looped the detonating cord through each and attached blasting caps.

She returned to the storage room where the G–16 virus was safely stored in shiny stainless steel canisters. She knew there was enough deadly weaponry in the room to wipe out an entire civilization, and more. For extra measure she planted six C4 plastics in the room and wrapped the detonating cords together to insure they would all explode at once.

Finally, she planted two C4 explosives at the base of the entrance and started her climb up the steel ladder. Her stomach was nauseous from the putrid smell and she choked from her own gag reflex. She ascended the ladder steps two at a time and when she reached the top she threw open the hatch door and retched. She laid half way out the opening gasping for fresh air.

"Look who the hell it is!"

. The sound of the scratchy voice and the arrogant tone raised the hairs on the back of her neck. She laid still.

A blunt boot kicked her in the side of the neck and she lurched back, pain rifled down her spine. She heard muffled voices of protest. Oh God, no, she thought, there's no way. She pushed herself from the ground and leaped off the final step of the ladder, landed on her feet and quickly spun around.

"Surprise! Your worst nightmare has returned and your time is up."

Alex ignored the man and looked right at Benjamin and Phil. They struggled to loosen the ropes around their arms and their screams were muted by the tape wrapped tightly around their mouths. Two men armed with handguns stood behind them.

She moved her eyes and looked directly at the third man, the one she wished she had finished off earlier. Her face hardened and she lowered her brows. "I thought you had had enough, Arnaud. I can't believe you've come back for more. You know you're not going to get away with any of this."

Arnaud stood with his feet shoulder width apart and firmly planted in the packed snow. He held a Walther P–38 in his right hand and aimed it at Alex. He looked around and then clenched his fist. "I don't see anybody around that looks like they can help you out this time. Those two guys," he waved his gun, "they're not going anywhere, except maybe in that hole and that'll leave just you and me."

"Kill us, Arnaud. Go ahead! You know you won't get very far. It's not worth it."

Arnaud roared with sarcasm. "You think I give a damn? My life is broken into increments, lady. One day at a time—that's it. I won't give a shit about tomorrow until tomorrow. Today is all that matters and I'm going to make the most of it."

Two bullets landed inches from Alex's feet. "Now walk over there and sit down next to your friends. When the show begins, you get a ringside seat."

Arnaud moved to the side and Alex walked slowly toward Benjamin and Phil. "Peter, bind her tightly, but don't gag her. I want to hear her screams. Jason, you keep your gun pointed at her and keep a close eye on her, she can be slippery. If anybody's going to load her up with bullets though, it'll be me."

Arnaud tilted his head upward. "Ah, it seems like we have company coming. Hear that?"

In the distance they heard the roar of an engine and watched the snow part as a snowmobile approached. Minutes later, two men heavily clothed in quilted freezer suits climbed off. One man stayed behind while the other trudged over the packed snow. His steps were labored and he used hiking poles to steady himself on the slippery footing. When he reached the others he stopped and took a long look at each of them. His hood was drawn tight and a protective mask covered his face. He reached out with one of his poles and jabbed it at Alex, lifting her chin. "You, Ms Boudreau, I have been looking for. . . for a long time. You've caused me a lot of trouble, you know that?'

Alex looked at the man as if he were some form of loathsome pond scum, then scanned her surroundings looking for something. . . anything that she could use. She knew she had to free herself somehow, and when she did, what would be her first move? She didn't know if the two recent arrivals were armed, but she knew the other three men were. She'd have to find a way to get those three together. She stretched her fingers, but the rope was tight. She'd need something else.

The man swung his other pole and hit Alex in the jaw. He took the blunted point and jabbed it into her shoulder. "I'm talking to you! When I ask someone a question I expect them to answer."

All eyes were on Alex. She couldn't place the voice or the wide girth of the man, but she felt the cold stare of his dark eyes partially hidden behind the snow mask. The pain in her spine resurfaced and her shoulders twitched. She rolled her eyes. "I don't make it a habit to remember people like you."

The man unlaced his hood and slipped off his mask. "You should change your habits because it's people like me that destroy people like you."

"Mr. Alan Price," her lip curled at the sound of his name. "I, too, have been looking for you. I'm surprised you made it down here now that your face is plastered on wanted posters throughout the world. Did you really think you would get away with everything?"

Alan re–tied the strings on his hood and leaned forward; his hiking poles bowed under his weight. "I've been working on all this for as long as I can remember and I would've succeeded if you hadn't butted in. I should've had Arnaud track you down and kill you months ago. That was my one mistake and I won't make it again."

He continued his downward stare at Alex, but spoke to Arnaud, "Let's end this and get out of here. It's too damn cold and I'm already sick of looking at her."

"If you don't mind sir, I'd like to settle an old score of my own with this bitch. I want to see her suffer before I let her know what I have in store for her."

Alan snickered. "Suffering's good. . . get on with it then."

Arnaud stood tall and glared down at Alex, Benjamin and Phil. He walked over to the edge of the rim and kneeled down on the snow. He pulled a piton from his pocket and pounded it into the ice. "Jason, tie one end of that rope around Hunter and the other end to this piton. I want Alex here to get one more good look at him before we cut him loose."

Arnaud took a small plastic clip from his coat pocket and opened it. He removed a small vial and shoved it inches from Alex's face. "Is this what you're looking for?"

"You bastard! Arnaud don't! This is between you and me. Don't involve anyone else. If you're trying to even the score some way then throw me down there. Don't do this."

Arnaud's eyes were crazed with hatred and he crowed, "Oh don't worry, Alex, you'll get a turn."

Benjamin squirmed and rolled into a tight ball. He moved from side to side trying to keep Jason away. Phil made a feeble attempt to knee Jason, but his legs were too tightly bound. Peter moved in, restrained Benjamin and within minutes the rope was securely tied around his harness and they dragged him to the ledge.

Arnaud held the vial inches from Ben's face and turned to Alex. "Watch!"

He squeezed Benjamin's cheeks and poured liquid into his mouth. He turned to see the horror on Alex's face.

"Ah. . . this feels good. There's nothing you can do now, Alex. Very soon Hunter will end up just like the two guys you found below." He flipped his wrist and the vial disappeared into the depths below.

"Throw him over!"

Terror filled their eyes as they watched the rope uncoil loop by loop until it drew taut. They screamed, pulled at their ropes, corkscrewed in circles, but it was useless. There was nothing they could do.

Arnaud moved over and gave Alex and Phil a swift kick to the ribs. "There's no one to blame but you, bitch."

Alan beamed and threw up his arms. "Perfect! Great job, Arnaud!"

He walked over to Alex and bent down. "And you, may you rot in hell!" He turned toward Arnaud. "I'm going back to the plane. Take your time and let me know when she joins Hunter and is out of my way for good."

Arnaud nodded. "Peter, why don't you go back to the plane with Mr. Price and wait there. Jason and I will be long shortly."

# CHAPTER 49

"Jaspar, bring me a band aid! I cut my finger on this damn piece of paper."

Alan was stretched out on the leather couch in the Gulfstream's rear stateroom. His head was propped against a pillow and his breathing labored. He brushed his forehead with his shirtsleeve and thought it must be the altitude. His felt lightheaded and woozy. The beginnings of a cold, that must be it.

Jaspar knocked and entered the room. "Here you go, sir."

He picked up the empty mug of hot chocolate and looked again at Alan. His brows lowered. "Are you okay? Can I get you anything, Mr. Price?"

"I must be coming down with something. I'm a little light–headed, but I'll be okay. Is Peter okay?"

"He fell asleep the moment his head hit the seat."

Alan stared at the ceiling and small beads of sweat formed on his eyebrows. He wiped his brows once again. "I think I've had enough of this place." He looked at Jaspar. "How about you? Are you as tired of this place as I am?"

"It's not the destination I'd pick if I had my druthers, sir, but it has been an experience."

"That's one way to put it." Alan closed his eyes. "Let's get out here now, Jaspar. Fire up the engines and let's go."

Jaspar cocked his head to the side. "But what about Arnaud and Jason? They should be here shortly I would imagine."

The corners of his lips rose and Alan strained to open his eyes. "I don't need them anymore. Arnaud's resourceful, he'll figure something out."

"Wha. . . " Jaspar's jaw froze. He stood in a tin soldier pose unable to speak or move. His eyes widened from the shock of leaving two men alone, two men he knew, in such an unforgiving environment.

Alan closed his eyes and in a muted voice spoke, "Maybe you could bring me another hot chocolate first? That would be nice."

Finally, Jaspar turned, but before he reached the door Alan added, "Make that an Irish coffee, yeah, that'd be better, an Irish coffee."

Jaspar closed the door behind him.

Devon tapped his fingers on the desk and stared at his screen. He had lost radio communication with Alex several hours ago, but still had contact through their GPS transponders. "They've been in the same place for too long. I can't imagine what they're doing."

"How long did you expect them to be there? Should we send the plane back now?"

Devon looked up at Ian and shrugged his shoulders. "Don't know. The weather satellite isn't showing anything to worry about so we should probably wait a little longer. I don't know why their headsets aren't working though. There shouldn't be any weather interference. Seems strange, that's all."

Devon had made the flight to the Hole with the others and then had returned to Amundsen–Scott Station where the plane would refuel and he would monitor their progress. The plan had called for him to watch the weather and to keep track of their location and progress. The moment anything changed, the plane would return and pick them up. They had wanted to steer clear of the white–out conditions they had encountered earlier and avoid the risk of losing anyone. If they had to make several trips to make sure Benjamin could stay in the hole for the allotted hours, that's what they would do. They were past the point of taking any risks.

Ian Thorpe was a Lieutenant with the Australian Navy and had been designated as the point man to make sure Devon and the others were given everything they needed. He had been unaware of the details of their venture, but whatever they needed he'd make sure they'd have it. "The plane's on standby so just let me know."

"This is strange. Look at this."

Ian looked over Devon's back and peered at his screen. "Where'd that come from? It looks like a plane moving away from where we landed earlier."

"Yeah, it is. We never saw anything in this area earlier. Let's get going—*now.*"

# CHAPTER 50

S urrounded by an eternity of ice, the walls of hopelessness were caving in. Alex's arms and legs were cinched tight and she had been unable to loosen the bind. Her pleas to Arnaud had gone unanswered. He just stood there with his arms crossed and his eyes squinting as he stared off in the distance. Alex's mind played mental ping pong with the guilt, sorrow and anger that plagued her. She knew Arnaud would kill her next, but she didn't care at that point. Benjamin's life had been ripped from her and if he wasn't already dead, he soon would be. Her strength was fading and her hopes dimmed, but she continued her struggle to exorcise her doubts—somehow.

"Jason. Pull him up."

Jason shot Arnaud a defiant look. "What? I don't think he's been down there long enough. Let's leave him."

Arnaud glared back. "Just do it. Pull him up—*now!*"

They all turned when they heard the roar of the jet engines in the distance.

Arnaud muttered, "That bastard."

"Arnaud! You can't do this! We have a plane it's the only way you're going to get out of here. Price just left you for dead. Please! Don't do this."

Arnaud ignored Alex's overtures and yelled at Jason, "Pull him up and hurry!"

Alex continued to press Arnaud, trying to appeal to his senses while Phil stared at Jason reeling in the rope.

When Benjamin's body was pulled over the lip, Arnaud and Jason dragged him over next to Phil. Benjamin was still bound tightly, but he was not at a loss for words. Anger shot through his eyes and he screamed obscenities and threats at Arnaud. He struggled to free himself, but Arnaud turned away. He walked over to Jason and reached out. "Hand me your gun and go untie Alex. I'll keep these guys covered."

"Untie her? Are you kidding? Let's just put a slug in each of these guys and find some way to get out of here. What the hell are we going to do? The damn plane's gone!"

Arnaud's voice was firm, but calm, "Just untie her, Jason. We'll get out of here." Arnaud grabbed Jason's gun and tucked it in his waist.

The second Alex's legs were untied she sprang to her feet. "Wait!" Arnaud yelled. "Untie her hands, Jason."

Alex rubbed her wrists and glowered. "We'll get you out of here, Arnaud, but first we need to help Ben. You activated that damn virus in him, but we may have a way to still save him."

"I wouldn't worry about him. Here. . . " Arnaud tossed Jason's gun to Alex. "Untie your friends."

Jason screamed, "What the hell are you doing, Arnaud!?"

Arnaud turned and pointed his gun at Jason. "Listen, there's more going on here than you know. We're getting out of here, but first I want to make sure Hunter and the others are safe."

Alex brandished her gun at Arnaud. "What's going on, Arnaud? Tell me!"

Arnaud lowered the gun to his side. "I'm on your team, Alex. I have been all along. I know it doesn't look that way, but that was the point. I'm still DGSE. I've been undercover for the past fourteen years. Sort of a counter spy. I infiltrated Sterling twelve years ago because we thought it was involved in money laundering. The French President has been infected with the virus and he's at risk this very moment—the same as Hunter. We've been searching for some way to save him, just like you have been for Hunter. We need to help each other now, Alex. I haven't had any luck finding a way to help the President."

Alex kept her gun pointed at Arnaud and motioned to Jason with her other arm. "You, go over and untie those two."

Arnaud gave Jason a stern nod. "Go ahead, untie them."

"Forgive me Arnaud if I don't believe your whole story, so right now I'm going to keep this gun pointed right at you." She looked at Benjamin through the corner of her eye. "Ben, are you okay?"

Benjamin's eyes were trained on Arnaud. "Yeah, I feel fine, but what the hell is going on?"

Alex turned to Phil. "Let's get Ben back in the Hole—now. He needs at least four hours in there and he needs to go down further and since the virus has been activated, maybe longer. Ben, are you okay with that?"

Ben was already retying the rope to the harness. "Yep, the sooner the better. I want to get out of this place for good."

"Phil, see if you can find our headsets and call Devon. Let's get the plane back here now."

Alex motioned with her gun. "Drop it, Arnaud—slowly. . . *very slowly.*"

Arnaud bent down and dropped his gun on the ground. He stood with his arms wide apart. "Alex, there's nothing to worry about. That was water I poured down Hunter. Nothing's been activated. He's fine. I can explain everything."

"I'll bet you can, but save it. Are you ready, Ben?"

"Alex, listen! The virus has been activated in the asshole that flew out of here and left me to rot here—Hunter's fine."

"Price? Is that who you're talking about?"

"Yes. I injected him with the virus on the flight down here when he was asleep and I poured the activating agent in the plane's water supply. In no time there'll be nothing left of him. His days are numbered."

# CHAPTER 51

"Alex, my dear!"

Alex recognized the soft accent and immediately spun around. A smile filled her face when she saw Margrit standing with her arms tightly folded and her foot slowly tapping away on the cobblestone patio. She rushed over and gave her a hug. Holding Margrit's shoulders in her hands she bent down and looked into her eyes. "It's so good to see you, Margrit."

Margrit's foot continued to tap and she spoke in a soft, but scolding voice, "You ran off so fast when you were here the last time and without even saying goodbye. What's an old lady like me to think? Hmm?"

Alex laughed. "You're right, as usual. That was rude of me, but I had good reason to dart out of here like I did." Alex placed her hand on Margrit's chin and turned it to the side. "I ran out of here to call this man you're looking at, Margrit. This is Benjamin Hunter. Ben, this is Margrit Monier. She's been my mother away from home for many years."

Margrit nodded and with a twinkle in her eye she blushed. "He is rather handsome. Now I can understand why you were in such a hurry." She motioned to them both. "Please, come in. I'll put you at my finest table and wait on you myself."

"I know it's cold out, but we would really like to sit outside on the patio today."

"You will do no such thing. You'll catch your death of cold out here. Now, both of you—come in—dépêchez!—dépêchez!" Her hands twirled in the air.

Seated in the corner looking out at the patio, Alex recounted story after story of Margrit and her restaurant. The Lapin Agile was Alex's favorite restaurant in all of Paris and was located five short, but windy blocks from her flat in the Montmartre District. Whenever she was in Paris she would walk through the narrow streets to sit by herself and enjoy Margrit's home cooked meals. The red and white checkered tablecloths, burning wax candles and simple rustic furniture was always a warm welcome and Margrit made it a point to fill her table with homemade bread, special soups and pastries. "You need to put some meat on those bones of yours young lady," she always told Alex. "You've wasted away to nothing—mangez!—mangez!"

Alex pointed out the window and showed Benjamin where she had sat when she had made up her mind to call him. It had been less than a month ago when her thoughts and feelings had been flooded with despair and grief. When she had left Benjamin's bedroom back then he had looked so peaceful. She had believed that when she had walked out that door she had thrown away her one chance for a life of happiness and dreams.

Now, as she sat across from Benjamin she was reminded of the sound of the foghorn from Point Reyes and how it had made her feel protected and safe. She felt that way once again. She reached across the table and put her hand over Benjamin's and squeezed. "When I ran out of here to call you that day this is what I wanted. I wanted to be with you more than anything and feel like I do right now—safe and in love."

Benjamin smiled and leaned into Alex. "Do you think I'll ever be safe hanging around you? You seem to have a way of bringing excitement into my life in more ways than one."

Alex winked. "I think for a while I'd like nothing better than to have a few dull moments occupy my time."

"Maybe we could start that tomorrow." Benjamin leaned further into Alex and kissed her gently on the lips.

"I can wait if that's what you two would like."

Alex dropped her head and her face flushed. Without looking up she said, "Ben, I'd like you to meet Andre Broussard. Andre, meet Benjamin Hunter."

Benjamin rose from his chair. He knew they would be meeting Andre, but he was still uncertain what to think about this man. Alex had told him about her relationship with him and he was clearly an intriguing person, but Benjamin hadn't warmed to the idea that there was a decent bone in his body. To Benjamin, Andre was the reason his life had turned upside down and he had almost died— twice. He extended his hand, his jaw tightened, "Mr. Broussard."

Andre gripped Benjamin's hand. "Please, call me Andre." He motioned to the empty chair. "May I?"

Benjamin nodded.

Alex broke the silence, "Well Andre, I'm guessing that this is now the end of everything, as we've known it. I am now officially retired, again. Agreed?"

Andre picked up his napkin, snapped it and placed it across his lap. "I've never been here before. What do you recommend?"

Benjamin looked at Andre. "We were just about to order coffee." He looked down at his watch. "We have an appointment shortly."

Andre tilted his head back, his eyelids narrowed and he looked down his nose. "Monsieur Hunter, you have many reasons to dislike me, but you don't really know me. You and I, well, we have many things in common and that is one of the reasons I wanted to meet with both of you today." He continued his unblinking stare and then looked over at Alex. "Did you hear about Monsieur Price?"

Alex met Andre's stare. "No, what did I miss?"

"The autopsy results are in and it is a first. He did die from his own virus although the medical examiner did not identify it as such and they are ruling out any possibility of foul play. Can you believe that?"

"I don't really care. The fact that he is dead is all that really matters to me."

"And to me as well." Andre took a sip of water, brushed a speck of dust from his lapel and continued, "This Alan Price character may have been involved in some other rather nefarious deeds. Director Bardin informed me that they have evidence that Mr. Price may have had some advance warning of the Twin Towers attack that happened in New York years back. They have uncovered wire transfers and stock trades made by his company, Sterling Defense, which occurred just moments before the attack. I can only imagine that you must have had a hand in all this. Am I right?"

Alex kept her deadpan expression and met Andre's unblinking stare. "You don't say. I wonder how all that came about? I guess we'll never really know, will we?"

Andre smiled. "In due time we may. Answers to our questions always seem to present themselves at the most opportune time."

Andre placed his folded hands on the table. "President Desjardins has asked me to convey his sincere gratitude to you for all you have done and if there is ever anything you should need, all you have to do is ask. At this very moment he is on a plane to Antarctica with Arnaud. His medical team has been unable to identify any unrecognizable gene in his system as was done with Monsieur Hunter." He nodded at Benjamin and continued, "But he does not want to take any chances."

"Thanks, Andre, but I don't need anything except to be left alone. Let me ask you about Arnaud, though. Is that really true that you hired him when he was discharged from the Agency? Why did you do that?"

"Arnaud told me he filled you in with all the details since he was discharged and yes, they are most assuredly true. He also told me that you exacted some revenge of your own on him. He still has some bruised ribs that will take some time to heal and he is not certain if his voice will recover."

"We talked about that and he explained he was trying to get me alone so he could explain things when I attacked him the first time. One thing for certain, he plays the part of an undercover agent very well. He wouldn't tell me why you hired him, though. Why did you?"

"I am always on the lookout for people who have unique talents. You of all people should know that. Arnaud had a great many talents of his own, but he was young and brash when he first ran across you. I knew that given time and the right training he would some day be a very valuable asset. When I hired him it was with the blessing of the Agency and they had agreed to reinstate him in due course if he could overcome his slight transgressions as I called them. My instincts were right then and now it has paid off."

Alex snickered. "Paid off? What are you getting out of all this?"

"It is not like you think, Alex." Andre turned to Benjamin. "Monsieur Hunter, what would you think about partnering with CS Generale?"

Benjamin sat with his elbows on the table, his hands tented and his chin resting on his thumbs. "I've always gone about things on my own and I like it that way. Right now I'm looking forward to going home and finding out just what is left of things there." He raised one brow. "You pretty much gutted everything I had at GEN, so I don't expect there will be much left to salvage. But, I'm sure you will be hearing from me later about all that."

"I have gone through your research on gene therapy and your genetic drug. It's very impressive." Andre paused and raised his shoulders. "I think you are the best person to bring both of those to market. I am willing to forget I even have your research and I certainly won't give it to someone else. I am out some money, though and I would need to be reimbursed."

Benjamin threw his chair back and exploded to his feet. He pointed at Andre and shook his finger. "There is no way I will pay you a dime for what you stole. You'll never get approvals through the FDA. I'll guarantee you that and I'll have you tied up in every court in any country where you try and deliver those drugs." Benjamin looked at Alex, "Come on Alex, I've had enough of this guy."

"Monsieur Hunter, please." Andre tossed his hands up. "Please, I understand your anger, but before you leave you should hear what it is I am offering. I think you will reconsider things on your part."

Benjamin placed both hands on the back of his chair and leaned forward. "Let's hear it."

"First, I am very happy for the both of you. I am glad things have worked out. Now, I do expect to be paid for my agreeing not to use your research, but I am only asking to be made even—no profit." Andre looked over at Alex, nodded, and continued, "Alex, I did pay you a rather handsome fee for your services. I would like that back."

Alex waved a hand at Benjamin. "Let him finish. He always ends things on a high note. I want to see what's coming."

Andre laughed. "Very insightful, Alex, Yes, we have worked together a long time and you know me well. Now, that Polar Hole you two discovered has caused quite a stir in certain international circles. Have you read about that?'

Alex spoke, "We haven't read anything. Go on."

"Well it is far from settled yet, but it looks like the French government will be given control over the use of that area. They will be allowed to determine which countries can use the Polar Hole and the brand new research station that will be built by the French and Americans." Andre squinted and looked at Alex. "It does not appear there is anything left of the Black Swan Bunker."

Alex smiled. "Chalk one up for the good guys."

Andre continued, "What the two of you have accomplished down there has sent ripples through the entire epigenome community. Scientists are already lining up with ideas to study there. The possibilities are endless. Now, who do you think the French government will award the contract to for all of this?" He paused and let his smug grin answer his own question.

Benjamin slid his chair back to the table and eased into it. His clenched jaw had relaxed and he waved a hand. "That place has tremendous possibilities. Alex and I talked at length yesterday about the types of research that could take place there. So. . . what are your plans? Just what is it you're proposing?"

"I have no plans. That is why I wanted to meet with you today." Andre pulled the napkin from his lap, folded it along its original creases and draped it over his wrist. "You see, Monsieur Hunter, my company has not focused much on research over the years. Our success has come from acquiring new cutting–edge medicines and then manufacturing and marketing them. We're very good at that and your company has developed a drug that we would be very interesting in putting into our marketing channels. I would like to see Genetic Engineering Nexus lead the research and development activity at the Polar Hole and I am prepared to make a sizable financial commitment to your company if you are interested. Does that appeal to you, Monsieur Hunter?"

Benjamin rubbed his chin and his mind ticked off the possible reasons that Andre could have for proposing such an arrangement. Finally, both hands gripped the edge of the table and he looked at Andre. "First off, I'm not too sure what I'll end up doing with GEN or if it's even worth salvaging at this point. If I can find a way to put it back together I will—that I know. Secondly, whatever you paid Alex to steal our research will be paid back to you." He looked at Alex and she tipped her head. "As for the rest, let's just agree to talk further at some point. Right now, Alex and I have another appointment to keep and my heart is set on making sure we do just that." Benjamin reached over and took Alex's hand in his.

Alex whispered in Benjamin's ear. He nodded.

"Andre, I'm only going to reimburse you for half the fee you paid me. That part you won't like, I am sure, but I am also quite sure you can find some way to make up the difference with this." She reached down next to her purse, picked up a canvas and rolled it across the table to Andre. "You can take all the credit for finding this and seeing that it is returned to its rightful spot."

Andre untied the rolled–up canvas and spread it out on the table. For the first time Alex saw the whites of his eyes. "Oh my. . . oh my." His hands quivered as he stroked the edges of the canvas. "A Portrait of a Young Man, by Raphael. . . I . . . I cannot believe my own eyes."

"It's most likely the original."

Andre continued to caress the canvas and he spoke softly, "I came from a humble background and my father told stories about one of his ancestors, the Italian painter Pietro Perugino. Raphael was an early apprentice of Perugino, his technique of putting the paint on the canvas in smooth layers and the use of sweet gentle faces, he learned this from Perugino. I cannot believe I am holding the original painting that has been lost for so many years. This is priceless. . . absolutely priceless."

"Yes it is—*priceless*, but I am only giving it to you so that you can return it to its rightful owner. If you make something along the way I don't care, but you must return this, Andre."

"Oh, that I will, you have my solemn word on that." Andre finger whisked a tear from his eye, and continued, "You see most art historians believe this painting is actually a self–portrait of Raphael himself, but there are some who believe that is not the case. The other belief is this painting is a portrait of Perugino as Raphael believed he would have looked as a young man, before they met."

Andre took a deep breath and looked at Alex. "I will return this painting to its rightful place, but first I will have several experts examine it for authenticity and to determine if this may in fact be the young Perugino himself. I can't thank you enough, Alex."

Alex shook her head and smiled. "You're most welcome, Andre, and as I said earlier, I am now officially retired, agreed?"

Andre's default facial expression, a frown, had returned. He stood and held his gaze on the two sitting across the table and then his lips turned slightly upward. "I am very glad I got the chance to meet you, Monsieur Hunter. It has certainly been my pleasure and I would like to continue these discussions at a more convenient time for us both. One more point before I leave. You are a very lucky man, Monsieur

Hunter, and not just because you are here today after all you have been through." He looked at Alex, his eyes blinked several times and then his stare returned to Benjamin. "Alexandra is an extraordinary woman, Monsieur Hunter. But, of course, you already know that. She deserves to be happy and to share her life with someone she loves and I wish both of you a lifetime together filled with rich memories."

Andre placed the napkin down neatly beside his plate and brushed his fingers along the creases. He squared his shoulders, tucked the canvas carefully under his arm, turned and walked briskly out of the restaurant.

# CHAPTER 52

The night was still and the full moon cast eerie shadows amongst the snow capped groves of Shore Pine and Nootka Cypress. An occasional hoot from a Barred owl returning from a night's hunt was the only sound in an otherwise quiet, peaceful night.

She was lost in thought as she gazed out to the North at the sheer jagged cliffs. She pulled the zipper up and closed the jacket's collar around her neck and jammed her hands back into its fleece lined pockets. The temperature had dropped in the pre–dawn hour, each icy breath rose like tiny clouds. Soon, the sun would rise and the forest would awaken with a symphony of restless birds and animals preparing for yet another day's harvest.

"It's beautiful here at this time of day." Benjamin walked up behind Alex, wrapped his arms around her waist and pulled her into him. "This was a perfect idea."

Alex leaned her head back and tucked herself into Benjamin's shoulder. She whispered, "When I was here last, this is everything I hoped for."

When Benjamin and Alex had left Paris they had flown directly to Vancouver and made their way to the Queen Charlotte Islands, 80 miles off the rugged Northwest coast of British Columbia. It had seemed like a lifetime ago when Alex had released the eagle that Benjamin had nursed back to life. She had watched, soulfully, as it soared up into the sky and off to find its lost mate.

They had arrived the night before and pitched a tent at the edge of the meadow—the same spot where Alex had released the eagle. They stood silently sharing each others warmth and inner thoughts. Alex was warmed by her own peaceful glow. She felt safe and for the first time she saw a future that would bring her happiness, passion and serenity. Her life had taken on a new meaning and she would no longer be cloaked beneath a veil of secrecy and deceit. She lifted her head and pressed her cheek into his. "I love you. . . I love you, Ben."

The sun peeked over the horizon and a bright glow painted the treetops. At the far end of the meadow a pair of moose waded through the stream, their guttural grunts awakening nests of Lark Sparrows and Western Bluebirds. The piping *wuk, wuk,* warbles of Pileated Woodpeckers announced to all that they had found their prey, burrowed in dead trees or a nearby fallen log.

Alex squirmed in Benjamin's embrace. "This would be the moment when you say something like, 'I love you, too, Alex'." She pinched his thigh.

He piqued. "You're right. . . you're right, I was lost in thought somewhere. I do love you, Alex." He pulled her closer.

"What were you thinking about?"

"I was looking at that stream and it made me think of Grandfather Wilkinson." His chin rested on her head. "He had his own way of explaining the mysteries of life to me whenever we stood on the banks of a river. I think I've told you some of his "lifeisms," that's what Will and I used to call them."

"You have and they're wonderful. Tell me. . . tell me what you're thinking."

"It's about forgetting the past. Let me see if I can put this into my own words."

He pulled her in—tighter. "Entwined within the body of a river is a mind and spirit flowing in present time. The river never looks back—to the past. It harnesses all its energy to reach its full potential—the future. The river has learned that if it looks back it will miss the sounds, smells, the sanctity—its own beautiful music—of the present."

They watched as the eagles soared higher, each circle larger than the last. Two eagles turned and flew toward them, higher and higher they climbed with each flutter of their outstretched wings. As the pair drew near, their shrieks echoed through the valley and then the larger of the two, the male, swooped down. They watched as the majestic bird descended from the heavens and leveled out above the stream, floating effortlessly toward them. The regal creature exposed its talons and glided to a halt atop a nearby tree. It cocked its head to one side and its piercing golden eyes locked onto Benjamin. Benjamin took several steps forward, inching closer to the bird. He tipped his head from side to side and the bird mimicked each movement. Benjamin's breath was still, his heart pounded and he gazed at the grand creature that he had nursed back to health. The eagle lifted its head and shrieked to the heavens above. Its cry echoed through the narrow valley and its mate, circling above, bellowed the same crackling shriek.

Time stood still. Benjamin opened his arms and the eagle spread its wings. Silently, each gave his thanks for teaching the other that we all exist within one another, and that we are all a part of one another's soul.

The eagle spread its wings—wider—and jumped. With a single downward flap it lifted upward. . . and upward, back to its mate. Benjamin whispered, "Goodbye, my friend."

Alex caught a small tear drop that fell from the corner of her eye. Her heart pounded with joy. She turned her head and looked at Benjamin. "Where do we go now? Mill Valley or Paris?"

"I don't know." He shook his head. "It doesn't really matter to me as long as we're going there together. I do have one request though."

"What's that?"

"We won't be going off on any more of those jaunts that seem to somehow find a way of drawing you in. Not soon anyway, right?"

Alex pushed her elbow into Benjamin's side and laughed, "As long as you stay out of trouble. . . . . . "

A musical tone beeped from Alex's coat pocket. Benjamin smirked. "Maybe I spoke too soon. That sounds like another call to action."

"Well, my action time is over—really! It might be my mother though; she's one of the few people who have my cell number."

Alex pulled out her phone and opened the text message. Her eyes furrowed and her lips curled as she read the message.

*The greatest trick the devil ever pulled was convincing the world he didn't exist–prepare to meet your maker.*

"What is it?"

She lifted her head and let out a muted laugh. "I have nooo idea. Something about sleeping with the fishes." She leaned back, nestled her head against Benjamin and closed her eyes. "I think I'd like to stand here with you a little longer and listen to the river's music."

# ACKNOWLEDGMENTS

The cliché "It Takes a Village" has been applied to so many different accomplishments, but it really does describe the immense help I have received to be able to finally type my last period and get this story to my readers.

Nancy Roberts, once again, has put in another Herculean effort as my editor. Without her continued presence in my writing career I am certain I would still be struggling away on my first book. Thank you so much Nancy for your patience, insight, guidance and your unique ways that make me strive harder to become a better writer.

Although this is a complete work of fiction, one thing I endeavor to accomplish is to make the story as real and factual as possible. Since I know so little about so many things I have called upon certain experts I know to lend a guiding hand. Sgt. Daniel Powell of the Davis Police Department was my explosives and firearms pro and was able to help me develop some tricky, yet realistic scenes. My son, David, is a Black Belt in Karate and was enthusiastic and very detailed in helping me develop a fight scene between two trained and skilled fighters. Alan Stiffleman tried his best to keep me in the realm of possibility when it comes to the inner dealings of stock trading and the exchanges. I hope I stayed on the right side of those boundaries, Alan. Bob Upshaw, once again stepped forward and went many, many, many extra miles with me so that I could present some clever and manipulative ways to use computer technology in a not so good way. Dr. Murray Gardner has followed up where he left off in my earlier book and worked tirelessly with me to find a way to suppress the gene that carried the G–16 virus. This is all very technical and confusing to me, but Murray persevered and hung in there with my incessant questions. Robin Walton has again created a cover for this story that I think is nothing short of stunning. She's a real pro.

One thing I find absolutely essential is to have people read portions of what I've written and to provide me with the most brutal, harsh and honest criticisms possible. Each of the people that read drafts fulfilled that requirement to the max. Bill Henderson, Jim Sauve, Therese and Djamel Tiab, Diana Connolly, Lisa Gordon and Jennifer Frances and all of those who read Wings to Redemption and graciously shared their opinions with me. I thank each one of you profusely.

A very special shout out to Moose, who was at my side throughout this entire journey. I couldn't ask for a better companion *and* dog.

My wife Kristen, who was such a big part in writing Wings to Redemption, helped me out this time in an entirely different way. When I write, I absorb myself completely in the story and I spent a considerable time away from home writing Latitude 87.7. Even when I was at home I was away—mentally. Without her understanding, love and support I would not be writing the acknowledgment section right now, I'd probably still be on the first chapter.

I look forward to hearing from my readers in the coming months and years. It takes time and effort for you to compose your thoughts and opinions, but I assure you, I read every comment I receive and take each one to heart. It Takes a Village to pen a story and each of you are a part of the process I have come to love so much.

Thanks You!!

www.PaulHLandes.com

Made in the USA
San Bernardino, CA
27 August 2013